DESTINY'S BRIDE

"I don't believe you!" Isabel almost shouted. "I don't believe any of this. It's . . . absurd."

"It doesn't matter if you believe it or not," Stands Alone answered calmly. "It is true. The pact will be kept. You will be my bride."

"I could never be your wife," Isabel said.

"You cared for me once," Stands Alone said. "You will care again, but this time even more so." He caught her arms and pulled her towards him until their chests almost touched. "We played together, we laughed together. We held hands. . . . We kissed."

"I was just a child! I didn't know any better!"

His dark gaze slid from the top of her head to her toes, and slowly back up, lingering on her breasts. "And now you are a woman. And you do know."

"Yes, I do know better. I could never feel anything for you."

Stands Alone's dark eyes met hers. "Nothing at all?"

"Nothing!"

"We shall see," he murmured. Then, with unexpected swiftness, he embraced her more tightly, and his lips were on hers. Her heart pounded wildly as he ravished the sweetness of her mouth. . . .

BELOVED CAPTIVE

Lauren Wilde

Zebra Books
Kensington Publishing Corp.
http://www.zebrabooks.com

To my grandchildren, with love—

ZEBRA BOOKS are published by

Kensington Publishing Corp.
850 Third Avenue
New York, NY 10022

Zebra and the Z logo Reg. U.S. Pat. & TM Off.

First Printing: October, 1997
10 9 8 7 6 5 4 3 2 1

Printed in the United States of America

Prologue

"Your son is a superb horseman."

The words were spoken in Spanish, but the powerfully-built Comanche chief had no trouble understanding. The Comanche had been equally adept at learning the Spaniards' language and adopting their horse culture—except that in the latter, the Indians excelled. No one, the world over, had ever been as skilled in horsemanship as the Comanche, other than the Mongols who had conquered Asia and terrorized Europe centuries before. Unlike those Oriental cavalrymen, the Comanche had only attained the horse less than a century before, making their advanced skill with the fleet animals a truly remarkable feat. The Comanche had taken to the horse as if they had been created for one another. A mounted Comanche was not simply a man and an animal; the two seemed to blend into one another to form one creature, powerful, swift, yet incredibly graceful and altogether splendid. The Comanches were well aware of the special affinity between them and the "God dogs," therefore Chief Yellow Sky accepted the Spaniard's compliment matter-of-factly, replying in Spanish, "All of the *Nema* ride well, even our women."

Augustine de Espejo's brow creased thoughtfully before he responded by saying, *"Nema.* I don't believe I have ever heard that word before."

"That is what my tribe calls itself. It means, 'The People.' "

"But we have always called you *Komantcia.*"

Yellow Sky scowled. "That is a Ute word which means 'those who are against us,' or enemy. If you wished to know our name, you should have asked us, not them. We are not your enemy."

The last was said with emphasis, a pointed reminder to Don Augustine of the two men's precarious relationship. The entire New Mexican "kingdom," as the province was called in Spain, was suffering terrible Indian depredations, if not from the Comanches, the new lords of the southern plains, then from the Apaches, whom the Comanches had pushed from their native homeland to the south, or the Navajos or Utes. The colonial government offered little or no protection to the Spanish settlements scattered mostly along the Rio Grande River or to the pueblos, whose Indians had become royal wards through the efforts of the Franciscans. There were less than eighty soldiers in the entire New Mexican Providence, scattered in little groups in isolated presidios hundreds of miles apart, and they were poorly armed. Most of the soldiers didn't even own a horse, so they were totally ineffective at chasing down and punishing the raiding Indians, much less rushing to a Spanish village's defense when it was under attack. Therefore the settlements were totally at the mercy of the marauders. When Yellow Sky and his braves had ridden into Rosario three years before and offered a peace treaty, Don Augustine, as spokesman of the village, had gladly accepted, even though he knew these same Indians were probably plundering the rest of the countryside. The horses they brought to trade carried Spanish brands, some from ranchos deep in Mexico, but Augustine voiced no complaint to the Indians trading stolen goods. Why should he, when the Spanish government traded in the same manner, and paid ransom for Spanish captives, only encouraging the Indians to do more raiding. In New Mexico, in 1755, it was every man for himself. The people of Rosario were grateful for the peace treaty, for not only had it opened trading opportunities between the two groups, but the Comanches protected them from the other Indian tribes as well, protected them much better than the Spanish government could. Yes, the last three years had been good for Rosario. Its crops had flourished. The flocks of sheep that grazed the common ground on the hillsides above the village had multiplied threefold. But no one knew how long the peace would last. The Comanches had made it on a whim; they could just as easily break it. No one felt the pressure any more keenly than Don Augustine, as spokesman. Being well-to-do and highly respected could sometimes be a terrible burden.

Becoming aware that Yellow Sky was awaiting an answer, Augustine tore himself from his reflections, pasted a smile on his face, and answered smoothly, "You are correct, my good friend. We are not enemies. I should not call you by that terrible name. From now on, I shall call you by your correct name. *Nema.*"

Yellow Sky nodded his head in silent approval, then turned his attention back to the hillsides overlooking the village. So many sheep grazed there, the rolling land appeared to be gray, instead of green. He watched with pride while his son dismounted his horse, then ran up a hill with two other children, scattering bleating sheep everywhere, while a sheep dog barked furiously at their heels.

His eyes also on the children, Augustine asked the chief, "How old is your son?"

"Spotted Coyote has seen nine winters."

"He is very tall for his age, then," Augustine observed. "I would have thought him much older."

Yellow Sky beamed. He was especially proud of his son's height. It gave the boy a certain dignity that his other, stockier son seemed to lack. "His mother was of the *Par-kee-na-um,* the Water People. It is said they stretch themselves to make themselves tall, but my wife said that was not true. They are great runners and excel at ball games. That is why other tribes will not play ball with them. They always win."

"Why are they called the Water People?"

"Because they always camp near streams or lakes. Every *Nema* band has its own name, usually after something that makes them different from the other bands, but we are all one people. There are many, many bands, but we never fight one another, like the Apaches do," Yellow Sky ended with a scornful sneer.

"I wasn't aware each band had a name," Augustine remarked. "What is your band's name?"

"The Buffalo Slayers."

"But all Indians kill buffalo," Augustine objected. "How does that make you different?"

"We do it better than any of the others," Yellow Sky answered with unabashed arrogance.

The sound of female laughter drew both men's attention back to the three children on the hill. Two figures, their long, black braids flying out behind them, were far ahead of the shepherd boy struggling to keep up with them. For a moment, the two men watched the fleet girl and the bronze-skinned boy in silence, both thinking the children looked wonderfully free and unfettered. Then Yellow Sky commented, "Your daughter is very spirited."

A frown came over Augustine's face. "Yes, she is. A bit too spirited, according to my wife. She thinks it unseemly."

"Why?"

"A daughter should be sweet, docile, well-mannered. She should be seen and not heard. But there are times when Isabel is much too lively. I keep telling my wife that Isabel just has a zest for living, that she'll calm down and mature. After all, she's still a child. She's only six."

Because Yellow Sky had a special softness in his heart for Spotted Coyote, he recognized the wiry little Spaniard's weakness for his daughter and did not scorn him for it. But he could appreciate the wife's concern. His people also felt women should be quiet and subservient, but that didn't change Yellow Sky's admiration for the girl's spirit in the least. He found Isabel's vivaciousness and keen intelligence very appealing. He looked back up at the two children, now running hand-in-hand through the lush, green grass, their mingled laughter tinkling in the clear summer air. It was evident that they were oblivious to everything and everyone else. At that moment, they seemed very much one being, one spirit. A sudden inspiration came to Yellow Sky, an idea so powerful that he could only surmise it had come from Our Sure Enough Father, Himself.

Barely able to contain his excitement, Yellow Sky turned to Augustine and said, "It is my understanding that your people arrange your children's marriages when they are very young, that it is done to unite families and strengthen fortunes."

"That is true."

"Has a marriage for Isabel been arranged?"

Augustine had no idea why Yellow Sky was asking such

a strange question, other than simple curiosity. "There was a marriage contract made between myself and another don when Isabel was a year old, but his son was killed when the Apaches attacked his ranch last year. So far, I have not made another arrangement." And at the present time it didn't appear that one was likely to be made, either, Augustine thought glumly. Almost every wealthy Spaniard's son in the area had been contracted for, and Augustine's fierce pride would not allow him to marry Isabel to anyone lower on the social ladder. His honor demanded more of him, to say nothing of his very class-conscious wife. No, he would wait until another eligible son was born and present his proposal. It wasn't at all unusual for the woman to be older than her husband in these arranged marriages. After all, they were not made for either love or physical attraction.

Yellow Sky broke into Augustine's musings by saying, "The *Nema* sometimes arrange marriages to unite two families, if it is to both's advantage. My band and your village have been at peace for three years now. Both have prospered. Would it not be well if this peace would last forever? And what better way to seal our agreement than by betrothing our children?"

It was all Don Augustine could do to conceal his absolute shock and horror at what Yellow Sky was proposing. To even suggest marrying his beloved Isabel to a barbarian of an inferior race was an utter abomination, and yet he knew Yellow Sky would take offense at a refusal. Then he, and likely the entire village, would be slaughtered on the spot. What should he do? Augustine wondered. What could he possibly say? Damn the sly Comanche! He had trapped him!

"Why do you hesitate?" Yellow Sky asked suspiciously. "You said Isabel was not betrothed to another. Do you not think my son is good enough for her?"

Augustine heard the anger in Yellow Sky's voice. A shiver of pure fear ran through him. "Of course not!" he replied hastily. "It's just that . . . that our ways are so different."

"Different? How?"

Augustine groped wildly for an answer that Yellow Sky might accept, then seizing a possibility said, "For one, your multiple marriages. Forgive me. I do not mean any insult, but my people do not allow more than one wife. Isabel would find this difficult to accept."

Yellow Sky scowled, then said, "There are good reasons for this. A good hunter kills many buffalo, and it is too much work for one woman to tan that many hides. She needs other wives to help her. Then the man can be generous and give to the poor. That is much respected among my people."

"My daughter does not know how to tan a buffalo hide," Augustine pointed out.

"She will learn," Yellow Sky answered calmly. "My wife will teach her. There are many of your people in our camps, captives we have taken. They have learned our way. Your daughter will, too, except she will have other women to help her and it will be much easier for her."

"But still, she would feel dishonored if there are other wives," Augustine countered. "Spanish women do not like to share their husband's affections with another. Marriage guarantees a Spanish woman her husband's fidelity."

Yellow Sky knew Augustine was talking about sexual faithfulness and knew the Spaniard's claim was a bold-faced lie. The Spaniard might have only one wife, but as a rule, he certainly didn't limit his sexual activities to her, not if he could help it. Yellow Sky had observed that Spanish men boasted of their sexual conquests of

other men's wives and daughters, while fiercely protecting the virtue of their own. Seduction of the forbidden
female was almost a game to them. It amazed him, for
adultery was almost unheard of among the *Nema*. But
perhaps the Spanish women did not know of their husbands' infidelity, or approve of it, Yellow Sky mused. In
that case he could see a Spanish woman feeling dishonored, particularly with *Nema* men sharing their sexual
favors so openly with their multiple wives. And Yellow
Sky would not like to see his daughter-in-law dishonored. Honor was one thing the chief understood. But
it was much more complicated than that.

"There are other, even more important reasons why
the *Nema* allow more than one wife," Yellow Sky informed Augustine. "It is my son's duty to assume responsibility for his brother's wives and children in case
of his brother's death. His brother would do the same
for him. That is why brothers share wives in all ways
and—"

"In all ways?" Augustine interjected in shock. "Are
you saying brothers bed one another's wives?"

"Yes."

"That's disgraceful!" Augustine blurted.

"Why?"

Suddenly Augustine realized he was treading on dangerous ground. He couldn't say because it was immoral.
That would sound too condemning. "Well, how do you
know whose child your wife bears, yours or your
brother's?"

"It doesn't matter. You are father to both your own
and your brother's children, and he is father to yours."

"What about inheritance? Don't you want your children to inherit your property?"

"The only property I have is my horses. I will give

them to whomever I want before I die. Everything else is to be destroyed at my death."

"How do your women feel about this wife sharing?"

"It is our custom. They accept it."

"That is what I mean about our ways being different. Isabel would die before giving her body to a man other than her husband. It would be a sin."

Yellow Sky scowled. "A what?"

Realizing the Comanche had no notion of sin or damnation, Augustine replied, "A terrible wrong. It would dishonor her even more than sharing her husband with another wife. She would feel shamed."

Yellow Sky gazed off for a moment, grappling with his decision. But the feeling that the union was meant to be was still so strong, he really didn't think he had any choice. If Our Sure Enough Father wanted him to bend in this case, he would bend. Yellow Sky turned to face Augustine squarely and said in a solemn voice, "I will give my word that Spotted Coyote will take no other wives, and that he and my other son will not practice their brotherly rights. Your daughter will be expected to share no one's pallet but Spotted Coyote's. It will be difficult for him, particularly if he has to wait several years after each child before easing himself again, but he is strong."

Augustine's curiosity got the best of him. "Why do you wait several years?"

"*Nema* couples do not lie together as long as the woman is nursing. For some women, that can be as long as five years."

No wonder they had multiple wives, Augustine thought. Five years was a long time to be celibate, particularly for a married man who was accustomed to having his lust regularly satisfied. Perhaps too long. "Maybe your son will not agree to all this," Augustine suggested hopefully.

"Do Spanish sons not honor their father's marriage agreements with others?"

"Of course they honor them!" Augustine answered indignantly. "To not do so would disgrace the family."

"The same is true for my people." Yellow Sky looked back at the hill, then added, "Besides, I think our children are attracted to one another."

Augustine could see Isabel and Spotted Coyote holding hands. That in itself was bad enough, but his daughter was gazing into the boy's face with adoring eyes. She doesn't know what she's doing, Augustine thought fiercely. She's just a child. She doesn't know he's a savage.

"Well, my friend, what do you say?" Yellow Sky prompted. "Shall we seal our treaty with this betrothal?"

It occurred to Augustine to risk saying he did not agree, that he still felt it was not in the best interest of his daughter, and it was his sacred duty to protect her. Had he done so, and stuck by his decision, Yellow Sky would have dropped the issue, albeit reluctantly. The chief greatly admired one who spoke with courage and conviction. But Augustine didn't have the valor to challenge the Indian chief. Instead he answered weakly, "I agree."

"What? You spoke so low I could not hear you."

"I said, I agree," Augustine muttered a little louder.

"Good! It is settled. Our children shall marry," Yellow Sky answered expansively. "All we need to do is set the time. My people consider a girl a woman when she is fifteen or sixteen. Is that age agreeable to you?"

Augustine was still in a state of shock. Yellow Sky was

moving much too fast for him. "Yes," he answered
numbly.

"Then we shall go sit in the place under the big cottonwood tree," Yellow Sky said, taking Augustine's arm
and leading him away. "After you have gathered your
witnesses, and I have gathered mine, we will smoke my
pipe to seal the bargain. Then our people will be at
peace forever."

Later, at his hacienda a few miles from Rosario,
Augustine sat in his darkened study deep in thought.
Suddenly the heavy door swung open, and his wife
stormed into the room, a furious look on her face.
Shocked by his wife's unprecedented behavior, Don
Augustine shot to his feet and said, "Dona Velia! What
in the world has come over you? You didn't even
knock."

"Knock? When I have just heard the most upsetting
news?" Dona Velia responded in a shrill voice, her
chunky body quivering with anger. "What is this I hear
about you betrothing Isabel to a barbarian?"

"Who told you that?" Augustine demanded.

"Ramon."

Damn his head shepherd, Augustine cursed silently.
He had planned on keeping the news from his wife for
the time being, since she had not been at the village
that day. Velia wouldn't lower herself to mingle with
savages as the others did. He needed time to formulate
a plan. Now she was forcing his hand.

"Well?" Dona Velia asked sharply. "*Did* you do this
terrible thing?"

"Yes, I did," Augustine admitted.

The blood drained from Dona Velia's face, and the
room seemed to spin around her. Then regaining her

composure, she asked furiously, "How could you? Where is your honor? How could you disgrace us in this manner?"

"Yellow Sky tricked me!" Augustine answered defensively. "Before I knew what he was about, he had found out Isabel was not betrothed, and asked for her hand. I was afraid to refuse, for fear he would take insult."

"Insult?" Dona Velia shrieked. "What about *his* insult? Have you forgotten that Montoya blood runs in our daughter's veins, pure Castilian blood?"

Augustine winced. His wife was always throwing her pure Spanish blood in his face. Did she know, or had she only guessed there was a bit of Aztec in his bloodlines? He had never admitted the taint to her or anyone else. Nor would he now, he vowed. He was lord and master of this household. "Silence! I have forgotten nothing. Nor have I forgotten that the blood of conquistadors runs in her veins, *my* legacy to my daughter." When his wife just glared at him, Augustine continued, "There is no reason to be so disturbed. Isabel shall not marry that heathen. I have no intention of keeping that agreement. Yellow Sky tricked me, and I shall trick him in return."

Dona Velia didn't think it at all dishonorable that her husband should break his word. Yellow Sky was an Indian, a nothing, the lowest of the low.

"I have already started putting distance between Isabel and the boy," Augustine continued. "He shall never lay eyes on her again. I told Yellow Sky that it was taboo for a man to see his betrothed before the day of his marriage, that Isabel would no longer be allowed to go to the village, for fear his son might be there. Yellow Sky told me I need not confine her, that he and his son will not return until the day of the marriage. Until then,

Rosario and the surrounding countryside shall remain under his band's protection."

Dona Velia noted that the last was said with a certain smugness. Then she responded bluntly, "Isabel should never have been in the village in the first place, when those barbarians were there. I told you that. If you had listened to me, this would not have happened."

"Nothing has happened, nor will it!" Augustine retorted, irritated at his wife's superior attitude.

"It already has happened. You have insulted your daughter. What will Isabel think when she realizes you pretended to betroth her to a savage?"

"She will never know! Only two people in the village have any knowledge of this, my witnesses, and I have warned them never, never, to repeat it to anyone. Ramon should not even have told you."

"I am your wife, Isabel's mother," Dona Velia answered firmly. "He thought I should know. But I agree with you. Isabel must never know." She paused, scrutinized her husband, then asked, "How do you intend to trick the barbarian?"

"I haven't thought of a way yet," Don Augustine admitted. Then, with fierce determination, he added, "But never fear, my dear. I will think of something."

One

Isabel de Espejo sat on an adobe bench in the shade of the patio veranda and watched as a servant woman removed loaves of bread from the *horno* at the opposite end of the courtyard. Carefully lifting the steaming round bread from the igloo-shaped mud oven with a long wooden paddle, the servant at work seemed such a familiar sight to Isabel, as did the woman kneeling near the oven and cooking corn tortillas on a sheet of metal over a stone-rimmed fire. Had it not been for the gnarled mesquite tree the servants worked beneath, Isabel could have imagined herself sitting in the courtyard of her home in New Mexico, but there were no mesquites in that part of New Mexico, while here in the Chihuahua Desert of northern Mexico that was all that grew: dense thickets of mesquite brush, cactus, creosote, and thick patches of an obnoxious weed called *chamizo*. Isabel longed for the sight of a piñon pine, or a graceful aspen, or even a common cottonwood that grew beside streams in her homeland. The longing brought on yet another pang of homesickness, a soulful malady she had lived with ever since she had been sent to this place five years before.

Isabel's thoughts drifted back to the day her father had informed her that he and her mother had decided to send her to her maternal uncle's home in northern Mexico. His explanation for the unexpected upheaval in her life had been that her uncle would be able to arrange a marriage for her with one of the local rancheros' sons, since Isabel's *novio* had been killed by Apaches and no other marital opportunities had presented themselves in New Mexico. So at the age of fourteen, Isabel had been sent south with the annual livestock drive to the city of Chihuahua in northern Mexico, 600 miles away. In the company of several of her father's sheep-herders and their families, she had spent a month traveling on a bone-jarring, wobbly *carreta* pulled by an ancient ox, following a mule train loaded down with woolen blankets, buffalo hides, dried meats, deer skins, turquoise, and strips of dried green and yellow peppers. They were surrounded by thousands of sheep and goats. The trading goods were to be bartered at the January fair in Chihuahua, while the animals would be sold to the mining districts hungry for meat that surrounded the city. As the train moved farther south, traveling along New Mexico's pitiful El Camino Real, yet more people and animals joined it, until when Isabel left it in San Elizario, twenty miles south of El Paso del Norte, it numbered 2000 people and over 150,000 head of livestock, a procession that left a cloud of dust that could be seen fifty miles away.

At San Elizario, Isabel had been met by her uncle and an army of his vaqueros, who escorted her back to her uncle's ranch. The mounted cowhands were a total shock to Isabel, for they were *Indio* and mestizo—part Indian—and it was Spanish law that no Indian could mount a horse. The Indians who rode horses in New Mexico had stolen them from the Spanish, but here, the Spanish deliberately allowed the Indians to ride, even demanded it of them as a part of their work. It was hard for Isabel to comprehend, for horses were supposed to be possessions of the wealthy and privileged, a gentleman's means of transportation, hence the term *caballero*. In New Mexico, horses were still scarce and owned by the elite. Why, her own father had possessed only one horse, until the chief of the Comanche band that had befriended her village had generously given him several more. Isabel had asked her uncle about his flagrant disregard for Spanish law, something the older man didn't appreciate. The females in his household wouldn't have dared to question his decisions. But he had answered despite his displeasure, explaining that since the missionaries in Texas chose to ignore the law, mounting the Indians on the ranchos they managed, the hidalgos had decided to follow suit.

It was the first of many differences between New Mexico and northern Mexico that Isabel was to experience. Her people raised sheep, goats, a few burros, as well as crops. New Mexico was a part-agriculture and part-ranching society. Here, it was nothing but ranching, and all in raising the tough, black *criollo* cattle. Her father's land grant had been much smaller, which was why he had to graze many of his sheep on the larger common ground, while here the royal land grants were huge, sometimes covering a hundred square miles. Despite the long distances from Mexico's cities, the Spaniards' existence on these cattle ranches was much more lavish than that of those in isolated New Mexico. Back home, except on very special occasions, everyone had worn clothing made of *jerka*, a crude wool and native cotton weave. Here, even the vaqueros wore silk scarfs and embroidered cotton shirts and rode on silver-studded saddles, while the dons wore velveteen, and gold-embroidered suits with pants split up the sides to reveal sparkling-white underwear. Their women wore silk, high-necked blouses, kid slippers, lace scarfs, and tortoise-shell combs.

The homes, too, while still made of adobe and built around a central patio, were more lavish. Much larger *casas* than those in New Mexico, they possessed expensive red tile roofs, instead of flat log ones, and the walls were often covered with calico and the windows decorated with crimson worsted curtains. True, some things were the same. Just as in New Mexico, carved, painted *santos* with fierce facial expressions rested in niches in the two-foot-thick walls, and fireplaces sat in the corners of the rooms. But back home, the furnishings, although elaborately carved and colorfully painted with bold mineral dyes, had been made of soft pine from the mountains, while here they were made of heavy oak, the massive tables topped with white marble. Sharing the walls with the religious statues here were many gilt-framed mirrors. Even the household servants were in excess. Each child had his or her own personal maid, while the dona had two. Four servants did nothing but grind corn; six prepared meals. There were a dozen washerwomen, and as many spinners and seamstresses.

The Mexican rancheros' social life was as extravagant as their homes and clothing, for there was always something going on: a rodeo, a fandango, an outdoor picnic, a fiesta, a horseback contest of some kind. Despite the large distances between the ranches, the people managed to convene, thinking nothing of traveling as much as thirty miles in one day, then often staying weeks at a time. The *casa* was generally a beehive of activity.

But despite all of the luxury and excitement, Isabel missed New Mexico. She missed the simpler life, the slower pace, the friends of her childhood. She missed the bleating of the sheep, the bark of the sheep dogs, and rubbing her face into the soft wool of a young lamb.

She missed seeing the beautiful Jemez Mountains, floating like a blue, misty cloud on the western horizon, missed seeing the tassels on the corn that grew beside the streams shimmering in the sunlight. She missed the cool, crisp air of fall and the golden aspens. She longed to see her father, and yes, even her strict, haughty mother. But most of all she longed to see. . . .

Isabel sighed deeply, then shook her head in self-disgust. How silly of her to long to see *him*. Even if she could, things wouldn't be the same. She and Spotted Coyote were adults now, and the innocent days of their childhood were gone forever. They came from two entirely different worlds, and his was much beneath hers. Even worse, he was Indian, an inferior race. She hadn't known all this then, but she did now. For five years, her aunt and uncle had been sharpening her Spanish class-consciousness. Still, those days in Spotted Coyote's company were deeply etched in her memory, particularly the last day when they had escaped Pedro and were alone for a few moments. She had never felt so free, so happy, so utterly alive. Colors had taken on new vibrancy; the grass had felt softer, the sun warmer; the air had smelled sweeter. It was as if her eyes had been suddenly opened and all of her senses awakened, allowing her to relish the true, astonishing beauty of the world for the first time. Then, she had never seen Spotted Coyote or his father again. Other members of the band had come to trade every now and then, but never them. Thinking it strange, she had asked her father about it, but he had curtly dismissed her question. She still found it puzzling, and deep down within her was this strange, persistent yearning for something she knew could never be.

"Isabel? Did you hear me?"

"What?" Isabel asked, suddenly torn from her musing.

"I asked what you were daydreaming about this time," Magalena answered with undisguised disgust.

Isabel could imagine her cousin's reaction if she told her she was thinking about an Indian boy. Utter shock, no doubt, followed by contempt. "About New Mexico."

"Again?" Magalena snorted. "I can't image why. From what I've heard, it's a barbaric place. You don't have near the comforts we do. You've admitted that yourself."

Isabel looked up at her cousin. Magalena was a replica of her mother, Dona Angelina. Short, stout, pinch-faced, dressed with excruciating care in her dark, high-necked dress, towering comb, lace mantilla, and expensive Chinese fan—which she was constantly fluttering—, Magalena looked so prim, so haughty, it was hard to believe she was five years younger than Isabel. Which was why Isabel thought Magalena's outspokenness so impertinent, only making it easier to dislike her. Struggling to control her feelings, Isabel answered, "Well, nevertheless, I am homesick."

"Well, maybe your prayers will be answered," Magalena informed Isabel with her usual snottiness. "I overheard my father telling my mother he is finished with trying to find you a suitable marriage, that he plans to write your mother and father and tell them he intends to send you back on the first available train. He said you are incorrigible, whatever that means."

Isabel knew what it meant, for despite her cousins' high breeding and rigid training, Isabel was much better educated than Magalena. Isabel's father had taught her how to actually read a little, something almost unheard of for a female. And rather than feel insult at her uncle's disgust with her, Isabel gloried in it. She had worked very hard to bring him to this point, obstinately and boldly refusing every offer made for her hand and once more shocking him with her utter audacity, for females traditionally had no voice in the making of marriage contracts. But Isabel had convinced him the females in New Mexico did have some say so, and if they were against some particular match, their feelings were respected. It hadn't exactly been the truth, but her uncle had known the women in New Mexico were more independent—his own sister actually managed her husband's estate when Augustine was away on business!—and had swallowed Isabel's tale. He'd had no idea Isabel had decided to refuse any and all offers because she had no desire to stay in this country where, despite all of the comforts and luxury, life was so rigid, and the women were treated even more like chattel than in New Mexico. Don Jose had simply become exasperated with trying to please her and given up. Isabel felt a little sorry for her uncle. He had certainly tried hard, and long enough. "I'm sorry your father feels that way," Isabel told her cousin, "but perhaps it's for the best. It wasn't really very fair for my mother to ask him to intercede in my behalf, when he still has your younger sisters to provide arrangements for. His immediate family should come first."

Magalena heartily agreed that immediate family should come first, particularly since that included her, but she didn't like Isabel taking the news so calmly. Her New Mexican cousin was much too pretty, much too much in demand at the picnics and dances. Ever since Isabel had arrived, Magalena had been jealous of her and had gone out of her way to bait her. Magalena had hoped the news that her father had given up on her would upset Isabel. "But what will you do, with no marriage offers?" she asked bluntly. "What will become of you?"

Isabel shrugged her shoulders, then answered, "It's been five years since I left my home. Perhaps things have changed, and there are more opportunities."

"You had better hope so! You are nineteen, practically a spinster," Magalena told Isabel. "If you don't watch out, you will end up like *her.*"

Isabel glanced at the duenna Magalena had motioned towards. As usual when they were outside, the older woman sat on a bench across the courtyard from them and fingered her rosary beads. Magalena's spinster aunt accompanied them everywhere they went, from morning prayers until they retired to their rooms each night, watching them like a hawk. Despite the fact that Isabel hated being guarded, hated that every movement she made was being monitored to make sure she behaved like a proper Spanish lady, she felt sorry for the woman. Maria existed on the fringes of the family, not actually belonging, taking orders like a servant and being treated with contempt, although she had been brought up in gentility. Her only crime had been that no marriage contract had been placed on her. There were only two places for a single woman in hidalgo society, to become a duenna or enter the convent. Isabel fervently vowed that neither would happen to her, that she would marry beneath her station first. Of course, that, too, would be disgraceful, but at least she would belong someplace, would have people who genuinely cared for her. Then seeing the smug expression on Magalena's face, she coldly informed her cousin, "Young ladies do not have chaperones in New Mexico."

"No chaperones?" Magalena asked in shock. "Then who protected your virtue?"

"I did. I know right from wrong."

"That's disgraceful! No wonder no contract was made for you."

Isabel could have pointed out that her virtue had had nothing to do with it, that her *novio* had been killed, but Magalena's righteous attitude irked her so badly she didn't even bother. Instead she answered, "I would rather have no contract than be forced to marry an old man, like you."

"My betrothed is *not* old!" Magalena responded hotly.

"You told me he's fifty. That's old enough to be your grandfather."

"Age has nothing to do with it!"

"It does, if what Beatrice told me is true."

"Your servant?" Magalena scoffed. "What does she know about it?"

"She's married. She knows what happens in bed. You do know you will have to go to bed with him, don't you?"

Magalena paled, then nodded, telling Isabel the girl hadn't known. It was probably something she wouldn't be told until the day of her marriage, Isabel realized, then felt a twinge of pity for the girl, but not enough to make her forget how Magalena had tormented her over the years. She still wanted revenge. "Oh, then I suppose you know what happens there, and if a man is going to do *that* to me, I want him to be young, hand-some, exciting, and above all, virile."

The "that" had caught Magalena's attention. Her dark eyes were wide with apprehension. Isabel consid-ered telling her the shocking details, then decided against it. Worrying over what horror was in store for her would be enough punishment. Besides, if she told her the truth and Magalena went to her mother with it, Isabel knew she would create an even bigger furor than she already had. Being labeled incorrigible was enough.

Isabel turned and walked away from her cousin, as

regal as a queen. For just a second, she faltered as she caught a glimpse of the duenna from the corner of her eye. Maria, whose stern expression had always seemed to be frozen in place, actually had a smirk on her face!

Later that evening, Isabel's maid, Beatrice, ran into her bedroom, saying excitedly, "Look out the window, mistress! We have visitors. I think it is the same young men who came last week."

Isabel hurried to the small window and looked out at the courtyard through the wooden bars. By the light of the candles the young caballeros held, she could see her uncle leading the visitors to the main *sala*. Several of the men had guitars strung around their necks, and one carried a violin. Isabel knew why her maid was so excited. The young gentlemen had ridden over from the surrounding ranches and asked to dance with the ladies of the house, and her uncle had agreed. There was going to be a fandango, and everyone would join in, including the servants and even the vaqueros and their families. The dancing would spill over from the spacious parlor into the courtyard, then to the outside grounds. Of all the Spaniards' entertainment, the fandango was the most democratic. Young and old, male and female, regardless of class, joined in. Why, back home in Rosario, even the prisoners in the local jail had been temporarily released so they could attend along with their jailers. Isabel was just as excited as her maid at the prospect, for dancing was about the only social activity women could actually participate in. In everything else—the horse racing, the rodeos, the bull-fights, even the games of monte—the women were only spectators. Yes, Isabel loved the fandango, and she could stamp the intricate rhythm with the best of the dancers.

Hurriedly, Isabel slipped into something a little dress-

ier; then her maid placed the big comb at the top of
the bun at the back of her head and draped a lacy mantilla over it. Snatching two gardenias from the pottery
vase sitting on the top of a storage chest, Beatrice placed
them over each of Isabel's ears, and the two rushed off

Isabel never even made it to the *sala*. As soon as she
stepped into the courtyard, she was approached by several eager caballeros who had been waiting for her appearance. Randomly accepting the invitation of one
young man to dance, Isabel stepped into the open area
around the tinkling fountain. Then there was just the
clattering sound of heels on the tile, the fast beat of
the guitars, the flickers of light coming from the candles
each man held. One dance followed another, as did
partners, until Isabel's heart was racing from her exertions and she finally had to beg off one dance.

Standing on the sidelines with a caballero who had
brought her a glass of lemonade to quench her thirst,
Isabel looked about her. She recognized several of the
young men as those whose fathers had asked for her
hand and knew the regretful glances being sent in her
way were genuine. Isabel realized her female cousins or
any of their friends would have jumped at the chance
for such matches. The hidalgos were examples of prime
Spanish manhood, young, vigorous, wealthy, respected
by their peers. Perhaps she was making a mistake, she
thought. If what Magalena had said was true, she was
being sent back to New Mexico, and she had no idea
what future was awaiting her there. Perhaps her father
would match her with some old man, like Magalena.
Would living in her beloved New Mexico be worth that?

"I saw you at the fiesta last week," Isabel's companion
commented, breaking into her thoughts. "I'm sure you
noticed me."

What arrogance, Isabel thought, then responded coldly, "Oh, and why would you think that?"

Undaunted by the iciness in Isabel's voice, the young man answered, "Because I was the best horseman there. I won every race and every rooster pull."

Isabel frowned. She had never seen a rooster pull until she had come to this country. She had never told anyone, but she had always felt rather sorry for the rooster, buried wattle-deep in the earth and waiting for some horseman to come racing down on him and yank him up by his neck. Often the frightened fowl was decapitated on the spot, and Isabel had wondered if there wasn't a better way to exhibit horsemanship than the needless slaughtering or terrorizing of some poor creature.

"I can also roll a cigarette with one hand while riding at full gallop," the braggart continued.

"That doesn't impress me," Isabel told the young man with disdain. "I know someone in New Mexico who can do flips in the air while riding at full gallop, who can drop down, then race beside his horse, then remount with only the use of the horse's mane, who can hang by his heels, shoot . . ." Realizing she had almost said arrows, Isabel came to a dead halt. Then she continued, saying, "shoot his weapon from beneath the horse's belly, and never miss his mark."

"I have never heard of such feats. Who is this man?" the caballero asked with a mixture of amazement and disbelief.

"A friend of mine in New Mexico," Isabel answered smugly, then, feeling a wave of terrible yearning engulfing her, turned her back on the astonished young Spaniard and walked away.

Two

After leaving the obnoxious braggart, Isabel wandered through the crowd in the courtyard, turning down several enthusiastic offers to dance and very much aware of a pair of eyes on her. At first, she assumed it was the fierce duenna watching her, but when the feeling of being stared at only became more intense, she turned and found the bold culprit standing across the courtyard from her. Dressed in an army uniform that looked rather drab against the caballeros' ornate *chaquetas* and *calzoneros,* the man was someone Isabel recognized. She had seen the captain at several of the fiestas the family had attended lately and danced with him once or twice. Darkly handsome, seemingly more mature than the young rancheros who hovered around her, yet just as polished and well-bred, the officer might have interested Isabel, except there was something about him that disturbed her, something she couldn't put her finger on. But she did know what she didn't like about him at that moment. His rudeness at staring so openly. How dare he! Isabel glared at the young man. The fact that her displeasure had no effect on him, for he met her heated gaze directly and coolly, only infuriated her more.

At that moment, Isabel's uncle, Don Jose, stepped up

to the young man and addressed him, forcing the captain to break eye contact with Isabel. For a moment the two men conversed. Isabel noted the officer said something that seemed to surprise her uncle; then the two walked to Don Jose's small office, which sat off the courtyard, and disappeared behind the heavy wooden door. Isabel frowned, thinking it odd that her uncle would leave his duties as host for what must have been business, since she knew he and the captain were not personal friends. Then, dismissing the officer's rudeness and her uncle's peculiar behavior, Isabel shrugged her shoulders and turned back to the dance.

Less than fifteen minutes later, Isabel's dancing was interrupted by a servant's telling her Don Jose wished to see her in his office immediately. Isabel was both piqued at having her fun interrupted and curious. But her curiosity won out, and she hurried to obey. She couldn't imagine what was so important that he had to talk to her right then.

As soon as Isabel stepped into her uncle's dimly-lit office, she saw the captain sitting in a chair beside Jose's desk and knew the summons had to have something to do with him. Then, before she could speculate further, her uncle said to her, "I believe you have met Captain Villagria."

Isabel hadn't been able to pin a name on the officer earlier, but now remembered it in full. Diego de Villagria. "Yes, I have," she answered, giving the captain a curt nod of the head to remind him she hadn't forgotten his earlier rudeness.

The captain rose to his feet, bowed slightly, and said, "Good evening, Miss Espejo."

"Good evening," Isabel answered, still retaining her cool demeanor.

"Sit down, Isabel," Don Jose said, motioning to another chair by his desk. "I have something to tell you."

As Isabel sat and the captain reclaimed his chair, Don Jose began by saying, "As you probably know, Captain Villagria is stationed at El Paso del Norte."

Isabel hadn't known, but had surmised as much. The presidio was the only military establishment for hundreds of miles around. She nodded her head.

"He tells me a military train to Santa Fe will be passing through sometime soon," Don Jose continued. "As you probably realize, this only happens about every three years, so I thought perhaps we should take advantage of the opportunity."

"I'm afraid I don't understand. What opportunity?" Isabel asked.

"Perhaps I can explain," Diego interjected. "It isn't at all unusual for military trains to take civilians with them, particularly if traveling through dangerous country is involved."

"I'm afraid I got ahead of myself," Don Jose said, not particularly liking the captain's audacity in answering the question that had been directed to him. "You see, I planned on sending a letter to your father telling him I would be sending you back on the next trading train coming from Chihuahua, but when I asked the captain if my letter could be included with the next military dispatch to Santa Fe, he told me about the military train, and suggested I send the letter with them, since he had no idea when the next dispatch might go out. Then it occurred to me that the protection the military train would offer you would be much better than the trading train. You'd be in the company of thirty dragoons, all trained soldiers and all very well armed. After all, that's what the train is carrying, munitions for the forts in New Mexico. The Apaches will think twice be-

fore attacking them. Besides, the trading train won't be
making its return trip to New Mexico for another three
months," he added.

Isabel finally realized what was afoot. She was being
sent home! Not months from now, but immediately!
She could barely contain her excitement. "Then I'm
going home?" she asked.

"Yes," Don Jose answered. Then realizing some explanation should be made, he said, "I suppose this
comes as a surprise, but I . . ." Don Jose stopped in
mid-sentence. He had been about to say, *assume you don't
object, since you didn't approve of any of the marital matches
I attempted.* Then he remembered the captain was present and caught himself. His pride wouldn't allow anyone to know he didn't have full control over the females
of his family, nor did he want the officer to know why
he was sending Isabel home. There was no need to
shame the girl. Jose continued, ". . . since I know you
have been wanting to return to New Mexico for some
time."

Isabel realized what her uncle was about and was
grateful for it. No one needed to know the real reason
he was sending her back—that he was disgusted with
her—nor did any one need to know why she wanted so
badly to go—because some strange yearning was drawing her back to her homeland—particularly not a total
stranger like the captain. She smiled at her uncle with
genuine warmth and answered, "Yes, I have been homesick for some time now. Thank you."

The smile took Don Jose aback, for in his dealings
with Isabel, her mouth had usually been set with obstinacy. She was always a beautiful girl, even when stubborn, but to him, her present compliance lent her a
new mellowness that made her particularly lovely. Her
aristocratic nose, high forehead, rather prominent

cheekbones, and firm chin were classical Castilian features, but the mouth had a fullness and softness about it that hinted strongly of a deep-seated passion. And those eyes, Don Jose thought, feeling a twinge of jealousy. Why couldn't any of his daughters have inherited those searing blue orbs? They were, after all, a trait of the Montoyas, his family, yet further proof of their Castilian purity. No Moorish blood ran in their veins. Yet, every one of his seven daughters had their mother's brown eyes, as well as her dowdy looks. Had they looked like his niece, with her classic features, seductive mouth, striking eyes, smooth, ivory skin, jet black hair, and winsome figure, he could have made much better matches for them, but he had had to settle for what he could get, while, ironically, turning down excellent offers for Isabel. Why should the good looks in the family be wasted on her, he wondered resentfully. Spinsters and nuns had no need of beauty, and the girl seemed to have some strange aversion to marriage.

"How soon will I leave?" Isabel asked when her uncle made no further comment and just stared at her with an unsettling intensity.

Don Jose turned to Diego for the answer.

"The train is expected anytime during the next week," the captain informed them.

"That will give you plenty of time to pack," Don Jose told Isabel, then added as an afterthought, "And I will send Maria with you."

Isabel frowned. She had hoped to be free of the hawk-eyed duenna. "But what about your daughters? Don't you need her services for them?"

"I am more concerned that you have a proper chaperone on your trip back," Don Jose answered.

"Excuse me, sir," Diego broke in, very careful to be polite, for he'd noticed Don Jose's displeasure with him earlier, "but as I said, there will be other civilians with the train, settlers on their way to New Mexico. If you like, I could talk to one of the women about serving as your niece's chaperone."

Don Jose had seen the captain staring at his niece earlier. The look on his face had been a little too heated for Don Jose's comfort, and served as a reminder of the kind of men his niece would be exposed to. Soldiers and adventurers, men with no roots and little morals. No, he would choose her protector. "I would prefer a chaperone of my own family," Don Jose answered stiffly.

"But my chaperones on the trip down here weren't family," Isabel objected.

"No, but they were the wives of your father's employees, not total strangers," Don Jose countered. "Besides, I was not in accordance with your father on that decision. My wife and I both found it quite shocking that you weren't accompanied by a proper duenna, a woman of your own class, and since you are my responsibility until you are once more in your father's hands, I will see that the same error is not made. Maria will accompany you."

Isabel offered no more resistance, for fear if she did, her uncle would change his mind about sending her home. She could put up with the rigid, overbearing woman for a little longer, just as long as she knew her freedom was near. And she would be free, Isabel vowed, as free as she had been before she came here. She'd see to that. Oh, she knew her mother would probably want her to keep the *duenna,* but she'd throw her mother's preferences askew. She'd beg and plead with her father until she got what she wanted. Not only did he have a weakness for her, but he was a much more reasonable person. Isabel smiled agreeably and rose from her seat, saying, "Then if everything is settled, I think I would like to retire. I'm going to have a busy day tomorrow making my preparations for the trip."

Don Jose nodded in consent and murmured, "Good night, Isabel."

Isabel turned to Diego and said coldly, "Good night, Captain."

Diego rose to his feet and bowed deeply. "Good night, Miss Espejo."

After Isabel had left the room, Diego stared at the door she had walked through thoughtfully for a moment, then turned to Don Jose and asked, "Has your niece's hand been spoken for?"

The blunt, unexpected question took Don Jose aback. Then he wondered if there was gossip going around about how many marriage proposals he had refused. He brought himself up to his full height and asked tightly, "Why do you ask that question?"

Diego knew Don Jose was on the defensive. He also knew why. There *had* been gossip at the local cantinas about an entire string of young men out to drown their disappointment in drink. But the handsome officer was astute enough not to mention that. "Forgive, me, sir," he answered smoothly. "I realize my question sounds impertinent, that it is not proper for me to speak on my own behalf, however, my father is in Mexico City and cannot do so. I am quite taken with your niece, and would be honored to have her as my wife."

When Don Jose made no comment, but just stared at him, Diego continued, "Please do not think I am not an acceptable match. I assure you, I am of pure Spanish lineage, and my family is one of the most respected in Mexico City. However, unfortunately, I am not due to inherit my father's estate. I am the fourth of four sons. That is why I chose the army, to earn a land grant for military service to His Majesty, and I am pleased to say

I have already accomplished this, for my part in putting down a small rebellion in Yucatan."

The captain had earned a royal grant, Don Jose thought in amazement. It was no small accomplishment for one so young. The grants weren't being handed out as freely they once had. "Oh? Where is it?"

"I haven't decided yet, since my enlistment won't be up for another three years. I can have my pick of any unclaimed royal land in Texas, or California, or New Mexico, or even Florida."

All Spanish frontiers, Don Jose observed. But then, that was to be expected. Spain counted heavily on its tough ex-soldiers to hold the dangerous ground for them. But if the man had his own land and was from a good family, why. . . . "You are not betrothed to anyone?"

"No. In view of my perilous occupation, my father felt it was best to wait to pick a bride for me until I was ready to settle down."

A wise decision, Don Jose thought. He wasn't in favor of making the marriage contracts at such early ages himself. Anything could happen to either of the parties, often leaving the survivor in a predicament. Just look at what had happened to Isabel. The thought reminded him of Diego's original question. Should he act on Isabel's behalf just one more time, he wondered. He was reluctant, after making the decision to wash his hands of her. Besides, he only had this young man's word. What if he wasn't what he claimed to be? "I'm afraid I can't answer your question. You need to talk to her father. I have no idea what arrangements he may have made for her."

Diego knew Don Jose was lying, and there was only one reason he could imagine. "Sir, if you don't trust my word on my eligibility, I can have proof here within a few weeks. Would you take the Bishop of Mexico City's voucher of my good name and position?"

The Bishop of Mexico City, Don Jose thought in surprise. My, the captain did circulate in high places. Perhaps he should reconsider, but then. . . .

"Sir, what is the problem, if it is not my credentials?" Diego prompted.

The captain was a bold, direct man, Don Jose thought. Maybe he should be just as direct. Don Jose sighed deeply, then admitted, "I'm afraid Isabel is the problem. She has been most resistant to any marriage propositions I have put before her. I'm afraid the only person she will obey in this matter is her father, and unfortunately, he is in New Mexico."

So the rumors were true, Diego thought. The lady was particular. Everyone had thought it shocking, but Diego was intrigued. He liked challenges. And he was determined to have Isabel. Ever since he'd laid eyes on her, he'd burned for her. It was a sexual desire that had only grown with time, so intense none of the local *putas*, no matter how skilled, had come anywhere near quenching it. He'd have her, he vowed fiercely. Come hell or high water, she'd be his. "Then I will just have to go to New Mexico," Diego answered calmly.

"You'll ask for a leave for just that purpose?" Don Jose asked in astonishment, thinking the young man really was smitten.

"That won't be necessary. I'll simply ask for a transfer there. I'm sure my commanding officer won't object. There aren't many officers who volunteer to serve in New Mexico."

Indeed not, Don Jose mused. It was considered a hell-hole by the military, with its excess of wild Indians and inhospitable terrain, for what wasn't mountains, was desert. Of all the Spanish frontiers, New Mexico was the worst, the most desolate, the most isolated, the hottest, the driest, the most overrun with savages. No sane Spaniard would choose to live there. Unfortunately, his brother-in-law was not one of those. Becoming aware that Diego was saying something, Don Jose tore himself from his thoughts and said, "What did you say?"

"I said this is turning out to be most fortuitous. I can travel with the military train and give Isabel my personal protection. It will also give me an opportunity to win her over before we reach New Mexico."

And what else, Don Jose wondered suspiciously, remembering the hungry look he had seen on the captain's face. Yes, it was a good thing he had decided to send Maria with the girl. Even if the officer's intentions were honorable, he was a man, wasn't he, and one couldn't be too careful with the virtue of the females in his family. But would the captain be successful in his quest to win Isabel's approval, Don Jose wondered. It might be to his personal advantage to have someone with high connections in Mexico City in the family. Why, it might even open some better marital opportunities for his other daughters. Perhaps the captain could use a little help. Yes, Don Jose decided, he would instruct Maria to give the young man some license with Isabel in his courtship. But not too much. It was still imperative that Isabel go to her marriage bed a virgin.

Three

Isabel clenched her teeth to keep from biting her tongue as the wobbly *carreta* bounced over the rutted trail that was absurdly called *El Camino Real*—The Royal Road. Sitting between Maria and the boy driving the cart and prodding the oxen with a long stick, she found the heat and the closeness suffocating. Yet, despite her misery, she was thankful. The worst of the trip, the searing desert and the dangerous *Apacheria,* was behind her. She could actually see the mountains in the distance. She was almost home!

"Why is it so hot?" Maria complained, breaking the long silence and dabbing her forehead with her damp handkerchief. "It's springtime, not summer. And why doesn't it rain? We have not seen a drop the entire trip."

"It will be cooler when we reach a higher altitude," Isabel reassured the older woman. "And this is our dry season. Our rain comes in the summer. Then all the wildflowers will burst into bloom. Here in New Mexico our seasons are reversed to yours. We have summer, then spring."

Isabel took a close look at the duenna. Despite the thick coating of flour paste Maria had smeared on her face to protect it from the sun, Isabel could still see the

burned skin, as well as the deep lines of exhaustion.
The long trip had been difficult for everyone, but particularly arduous for the older woman, who was accustomed to inactivity and the comforts of life. Maria had
dropped a good fifteen pounds and was beginning to
look alarmingly frail. And Isabel knew every muscle in
the older woman's body must be aching from the rough
ride. Her own were. Every night when she undressed
for bed, she discovered a new bruise. But she was young
and hardy. Maria wasn't. Why, there had been a time
there in the desert when she had feared the duenna's
heart was going to fail her. The poor woman shouldn't
be making this trip, Isabel thought. Don Jose had been
cruel to send her on this horrendous trek with no concern for her personal welfare, or if not cruel, then totally thoughtless.

Isabel took the handkerchief from Maria and wiped
a rivulet of sweat from her forehead, saying, "Don Jose
should never have sent you. This is too hard on you.
One of the older women with this train could have
chaperoned me."

Maria was unaccustomed to other people's caring for
her needs. She had always been the one doing the min-
istering. The reversal of their roles made her feel uncomfortable. She hastily retrieved her handkerchief
and answered, "No, Don Jose did the right thing. These
women are mestizos. Their ways are not our ways. I have
seen how their daughters behave, flirting with the soldiers, sneaking off with them. Their parents are much
too lenient. They have very little honor."

Honor. It was a word Isabel had heard as far back as
she could remember. "Honor" determined the Spanish
hierarchal rankings, with each social class having limits
to how much "honor" they could possess. The pure
Spanish—who had possession of the land and wealth

almost exclusively—naturally had the most "honor," the highest public esteem. Respect from others was their birthright. In New Mexico, they were called *cayotes;* in the rest of the Spanish new world, *espanoles.* Below them were the mulattoes—mixed Spanish and African—, the mestizo—mixed Spanish and Indian—, the *pardos*—mixed African, Indian, and European—and at the very bottom of the social structure, the *genizaros*—the freed Indian slaves—who had no "honor" at all, and never could possess it.

While Isabel appreciated the "honor" bestowed on her by virtue of her ranking, she would have loved to have the freedom to come and go that those mestizo girls had. But she had to admit, the trip hadn't been as bad as she had expected. Much to her surprise, Maria had been far less restrictive with her on this trip, allowing Diego to come visit her in the evenings, then sitting at a discreet distance from them while they talked. Isabel had been amazed. Then Maria had actually allowed Isabel to ride with Diego—Don Jose had given Isabel her own horse as a going away present—as long as they stayed within sight. Everything had been going fine, until yesterday, when Diego had coaxed her away from the train for a while. When they returned, Maria had been furious, and the rides had been abruptly terminated. Well, thank God, the trip was almost over, Isabel thought. She didn't think she could take too many more days of bouncing on this hard seat and breathing the choking dust the oxen were kicking up.

Isabel's thoughts drifted back to the day before, and she reluctantly admitted that perhaps Maria had been justified in being upset. Although Isabel had sworn to the duenna that nothing had happened, it wasn't true. Diego had taken her behind a boulder and kissed her. Then he had done something that had come as a surprise to her. He had fondled her breast. She'd had no idea that was a part of mating with people. She had assumed humans did it just like the animals, and nothing more. And since she didn't know just how serious the liberty Diego had taken was, Isabel had lied to Maria about it, for fear the duenna would insist Isabel marry him if she knew the truth. Isabel had become very skeptical about marriage to Diego.

Isabel had known from the beginning that Diego was wooing her. He'd told her the first night out he intended to ask her father for her hand. Realizing she was going to have to marry someone, and since he promised her he would ask for his land grant in New Mexico and she'd never have to leave her beloved homeland, Isabel had allowed Diego to court her. She found that besides being handsome and polished, he was intelligent, hard-working, and ambitious, traits admired by her people. But there was still that vague something about him that deeply disturbed her, nor did she feel any excitement in his presence. Why, even his kiss had been boring, and his touching her so intimately had only revolted her. She wondered how both would have affected her had it been Spotted Coyote who had done them to her.

For the hundredth time, Isabel shook her head in self-disgust. Why did those foolish thoughts of him always slip in? Why couldn't she forget him? Had he cast some strange spell on her? Indians were very adept at casting spells. She had seen that herself when she had watched the Indians at the Santo Domingo Pueblo near her home perform one of their forbidden rain dances. The Indians had actually danced with diamondbacks— the most venomous of all the rattlers. Why, the Snake Priest had even held one of the hideous reptiles in his mouth! Supposedly, the priest's guide kept the snake

from coiling and striking by stroking it with an eagle
feather, but Isabel's father had called it sorcery, and
Isabel had believed his explanation over the Pueblos'.
Yes, Indians knew how to cast spells, but Isabel was
forced to admit that notion about Spotted Coyote was
ridiculous. They had been nothing but children. Surely,
he had possessed no magical powers at that young age,
certainly not evil ones. Wouldn't she have sensed there
was something wrong, just as she did with Diego? No,
there had to be some other explanation, but just what
that might be continued to elude her. She did know
one thing for certain. She didn't want to marry Diego.

Isabel forced her attention back to the scenery. The
road followed New Mexico's main waterway, called Rio
Bravo del Norte—the Brave River of the North—in
Mexico, but simply Rio Abajo here in lower New Mexico, and Rio Arriba in the upper. Here the river valley
was wide and fertile, but at this arid time of the year,
the river itself narrow and as red as the dry earth
around it. Only by use of the *acequias,* the irrigation
ditches, could anything be grown, and even then the
foot-tall corn plants looked terribly limp. Isabel knew
the colonists were better off where she lived a little farther north, even though the ground was rockier, for
their rivers received some snow melt, and it was water
that was the critical element in cultivating anything here
in New Mexico. She felt sorry for these settlers, living
in their pitiful little red-gold adobe jacals and trying to
wrest a living here beside the river. They struggled to
grow their parched crops, then just as likely would see
them swept away by floods when the heavy summer
rains came.

"The wind is picking up again, just like it did yesterday," Maria commented.

"That's usual for this time of the year, too," Isabel responded.

Except, today, the wind was worse, steadily increasing until it seemed to shriek and driving stinging particles of red dirt through the air. Soon it was impossible to see more than a few feet through the dust storm, and Isabel and Maria felt as if they were being suffocated by the burning sand, despite the scarfs they had wrapped around their noses and mouths. Through the swirling dust, Isabel saw a figure coming towards them, then recognized it as Diego and his horse.

"We are stopping the caravan. It's pointless to try to proceed in this storm," Diego yelled to be heard over the storm. "The animals cannot see where they are going. Pull the cart around, so its side faces the wind," he instructed the boy driving the *carreta*. "Then get down beside the wheel and cover yourselves with a blanket."

"What about the oxen?" the boy asked Diego after he had turned the heavy, awkward cart.

"Forget them! They are just dumb animals," Diego answered impatiently.

Dumb, but still feeling creatures, Isabel thought, for she had a tender heart when it came to animals. She shot Diego a hard look, then said to the boy, "Remove their yoke and bring them around to the protected side of the cart. I intend to do the same with my horse."

Overhearing her as he helped Maria down from the cart, Diego snapped, "I said that is not necessary!"

Isabel glared at him, then answered, "Those oxen belong to this boy's family, and that horse is my property. We will decide what to do with them, whether you consider it necessary or not."

A furious expression came over Diego's face. Isabel ignored it, pushed his hands aside, and scurried down from the cart without any help from him. As she headed to the back of the cart where her horse was tied, Diego followed her, saying in a hard voice, "Isabel, I . . ." He stopped in mid-sentence when Isabel paid him no attention, caught her arm with one hand, and spun her around. "I am talking to you!

"How dare you! Let go of my arm!"

Momentarily taken aback by her fury, Diego dropped his hand. Then regaining his composure, he said, "I will not have you defying me. It is my right to expect respect and obedience."

"You're not in charge of this caravan!" Isabel reminded him bluntly. "You're just riding along with it."

"I'm not talking about that kind of authority. I'm talking about my rights as your future husband."

They weren't even engaged, and he was trying to dictate to her, Isabel thought resentfully. Why, he was just as domineering and arrogant as the rest of the males she'd encountered. "We are not betrothed," she informed him coldly.

"No, but we will be," Diego answered with supreme confidence. "You know I intend to ask your father for your hand."

"That doesn't mean he will agree," Isabel answered, vowing she would do everything in her power to convince her father not to agree to such an arrangement.

"He would be a fool not to," Diego answered. "Once I get my land grant, I will be one of the biggest landholders in New Mexico. I seriously doubt if he could do better for a son-in-law."

Isabel found Diego's pompous answer even more irritating because it was true. The land would belong to him, and not his father, as was the case with many of the eligible young men in New Mexico. He would not have to wait for his father's death to become wealthy.

As an added boon, he had influential connections in Mexico City. Considering this, along with his military service, he could even become governor of the New Mexican Providence, or so he had suggested. But Isabel wasn't thinking of those things. She was thinking of her own feelings, something that apparently never even occurred to Diego. She raised her chin defiantly and answered, "Perhaps *I* will not agree to such a marriage."

Diego's black eyes flashed. His voice vibrated with menacing undertones as he said, "Don't play games with me. I know of your obstinacy with your uncle, of how you have avoided your duty to marry and bear children, but neither I, nor, I think, your father, will tolerate such behavior any longer, not after you deliberately led me on, allowing me to woo you, even allowing me to kiss you. You have gone too far to turn back. You will be mine."

"Too far?" Isabel asked in disbelief. "Just because of one kiss?"

"Do you make a habit of allowing men to kiss you?" Diego asked in a condemning tone of voice. "What about touching you, as I did?"

My God, Isabel thought, it *was* a serious infraction! The color drained from her face, then she asked, "You're not going to tell him about *that*?"

"If I have to, I will. If necessary, I will tell him that things went much further than that, that you are no longer a virtuous woman."

"You'd tell a deliberate lie?" Isabel asked in shock.

He'd lie for her, cheat for her, even kill for her, Diego thought, his lust for Isabel having attained raging proportions. It had taken all of his control to keep from throwing her to the ground the other day and raping her, and once she was his, that was what he would do, take her in every possible manner, break that infuriating spirit of hers, show her once and for all who was master. Yes, Diego liked a challenge, but he always had to be the victor, and he'd do anything—*anything*—to accomplish that end. That was why he had been so successful in putting down the revolt in Yucatan. Other officers had hesitated to randomly slaughter innocent civilians in an effort to kill the instigators of the rebellion. Diego had had no qualms. He could be utterly ruthless. Under his command, village after village of mestizos and *Indios* had been indiscriminately wiped out. And the Crown had rewarded him for it, proof of what a good Spaniard he was. Diego looked Isabel in the eye and answered calmly, "Yes, I would lie. That is how much I want you. You are no longer dealing with a callow youth, or a weak uncle. I am a man. You will be mine. Mark my word."

Isabel heard the fierce determination in Diego's voice, and for the first time had doubts. What if her father did agree, despite her pleas, she wondered. It had been five years since she had seen him. Perhaps he was no longer vulnerable to her whims. She had been a child then. Now she was a woman. Perhaps he would insist she do her duty.

Isabel's bleak musing about what her future might hold was interrupted by Maria's sticking her head around the corner of the cart and saying, "Hurry with your horse, Isabel, and get under the blanket with me. The storm is getting worse."

Isabel suddenly found new courage. "And I say I shall never marry you, Diego," she answered bravely. "You mark *my* words."

With that last piece of defiance, Isabel turned her back on Diego, hurried through the blinding sand, untied the miserable horse, and led it to the side of the *carreta* where the oxen were already standing. Giving the reins of the horse to the boy so he could wrap them around the axle of the cart, Isabel slipped under the blanket beside the heavy wooden wheel with Maria. A moment later the boy squatted beside them, pulling his serape over his head for protection.

The storm lasted for hours, the swirling, shrieking wind making the blanket over the two women flap wildly. Despite the covering over them, the dust still filtered in, just as Isabel knew it would somehow penetrate their trunks and get into their clothing. She had been in dust storms like this before. But she had never had to sit one out beneath a hot blanket, struggling for every breath of air and drenched with sweat, her neck cramped from bending over and her legs numb from where she had drawn them up against her chest. Sand was everywhere. In her ears, in her nose, in her eyes, in her mouth. She had never been so miserable in her life.

Towards sundown, the wind finally died down. "Do you think it is safe to go out now?" Maria asked, breaking the long silence between the two women, for air had been too scarce to waste with talking.

"Regardless, I'm getting out from beneath this hot blanket," Isabel answered, pushing the heavy, sand-laden object from her.

Isabel rose stiffly to her feet, then helped Maria to hers before looking around. Dust still hung heavily in the air, making the twilight lurid and the setting sun look like a faint red disk on the horizon. The pack animals that had lain down on the ground were almost buried with sand, and there were deep dunes on the windward side of the settlers' carts. Then all around them, people appeared, seemingly rising from their graves as they shrugged off their protection and the piles of dust that had settled on them.

Camp was made. The settlers dug down through the sand piles on their *carretas* for their pots and pans and food. Wood was unloaded from one of the burros, and a fire started. While supper cooked, everyone worked, sweeping off sand, shaking out clothing and blankets making their own miniature dust storms. But despite all their efforts, they couldn't remove the fine sand that had permeated the food. Everything tasted gritty. Only the water was still pure, and only because it had been stored in heavy stone jars.

Night fell; the stars came out, and even they looked a little hazy. Lying beside Isabel on her blanket, Maria commented, "That storm was a terrible ordeal. I feared we were going to be buried alive. Do you have many of them?"

"There's hardly a spring I can remember, where we didn't have at least one," Isabel answered.

"I cannot understand why you wanted to come back to this godforsaken land."

"You'll see when we reach the foothills of the mountains, where my home is. It's much nicer there, much cooler, much greener, at least after the summer rains." Isabel paused. She felt closer to the duenna after the long trip. Sharing ordeals like the one that day, facing danger, being in one another's company almost continuously, had a way of breaking down barriers, even barriers of propriety. For that reason Isabel ventured to ask, "How did you feel about Don Jose's sending you with me? You must have resented it."

Maria was silent so long Isabel thought she wouldn't answer. Then she said, "To be honest, I had mixed emotions. In a way, I welcomed the opportunity to get away from Dona Angelina. She has never been an easy person to please. And her being my younger sister always made it more difficult for me to take orders from her. She never let me forget I had her to thank for the roof over my head and the food in my mouth. She never acknowledged that I did anything of any value. I thought perhaps your parents might appreciate me more. On the other hand, I knew I would miss the little ones. And I have," Maria continued sadly. "Much more than I ever dreamed I would."

The "little ones" were Don Jose's and Dona Angelina's younger daughters, and Isabel could understand why Maria missed them. Too young to resent her authority or feel contempt for her, they allowed Maria to be a mother to them, for Dona Angelina was much too busy with her large household and active social life to pay much attention to them. "I noticed they're very fond of you, too. They probably can't wait for you to get back."

"Get back? Make this horrible trip the second time?" Maria asked in horror. "Absolutely not!"

"But what will you do, after I'm married?" Isabel asked. "I'm an only child. There won't be anyone else to chaperone in my family."

"I suppose it would be too much to ask your parents to let me live the rest of my life in their household," Maria admitted. "After all, we're not blood kin." She sighed deeply before speculating, "Perhaps one of the other hidalgo families would have use of my services."

Isabel's heart went out to the woman. She was being moved pillar to post for everyone else's convenience until she was no longer needed. Then no one wanted her anymore. Isabel thought it terribly unjust. Maria had never had a life of her own, her own home, her own children. It was the latter that Isabel thought particularly sad. To be able to bear children, love them, nurture them, was the only reason she was choosing marriage over life alone. It was the only thing that would make marriage worthwhile. Yet Maria had been deprived of that joy in life. The closest she had come was her sister's children, and that wasn't the same. After giving up so much, was it too much to ask for a place to live out her life in peace, a place where she would be appreciated for just herself? Then Isabel made a decision. "You can come live with me when I get married."

Maria was both surprised and deeply touched. She hadn't thought Isabel was particularly fond of her, however, she had come to realize the girl had a kind heart. "That's very considerate of you to offer, but do you fully realize what you're saying?"

"Yes, I do. Oh, I realize we've been a little at odds, but only because you're my chaperone. It's only natural that I'd resent your watching me like a hawk. But after my marriage, that will change. Then we could be more like companions and friends."

That was the kind of relationship she'd hoped she'd have with her sister, but it hadn't turned out that way, Maria thought sadly. "There is still your future husband to consider. He may not want me."

"Well, I'll just insist!"

Maria smiled. She had always secretly admired Isabel's spunk. And she thought they could be friends. "Thank you, but . . ."

"But what?" Isabel prompted when Maria's voice trailed off.

Maria hesitated, then threw caution to the wind and said, "But I do not think I would care to live with Captain Villagria."

"Neither do I!" Isabel answered pertly. "That's why I'm going to do everything in my power to keep from doing just that." Then cocking her head, she asked curiously, "What is there about him you don't like?"

Maria wondered if she should be speaking so frankly

with the girl. Who she married was her father's concern, not hers. The duenna's duty was to see she behaved in a lady-like manner and to protect her virtue. Yet, Maria still felt an obligation to protect the girl, herself, to spare her from pain or heartache if she possibly could. She had already passed the boundary of duenna and stepped into the role of friend. So she ventured to say, "I can't tell you exactly what it is. Oh, he's arrogant and domineering, but all men are. That just seems to go along with manhood. But there's something about him that makes me . . . uneasy," Maria finished for lack of a better word.

It wasn't just her imagination, Isabel thought. There was something terribly wrong with Diego, something that went even deeper than his being willing to lie to have her. Knowing Maria sensed it also only made her more determined to get away from the captain. No, she vowed fervently, she would not marry that man, even if she had to run away and marry the first commoner who'd have her.

Four

Over the next few days, as the caravan moved closer and closer to Santa Fe, Diego kept his distance. But Isabel knew it wasn't because he had taken her rebuff seriously. No, he had simply set it aside. After all, what the woman thought or said in these matters was inconsequential. Marriage contracts were men's business. Women were simply pawns to be manipulated for their gain. Isabel strongly suspected Diego thought he was punishing her for her misbehavior by showing her how angry he was with her. The fool, she mused with contempt. She was more than happy to be rid of his company.

When the Jemez Mountains came into view, Isabel stared at them hungrily. They looked even more beautiful than she remembered, the blue peaks soaring against an azure sky. "Rosario is over there," she told Maria.

"In the mountains?"

"No, they're across the Rio Arriba from my village, and some distance away. But they are always there to see, looking so beautiful. The turquoise mines are there."

"And the capital? Where is it?"

"Over there," Isabel answered, motioning to the east

in the opposite direction. "Santa Fe is cradled in the foothills of those mountains."

"And what is their name?"

"Most New Mexicans call them the Sierra Madres, but my father has always called them the Sangre de Cristo Mountains."

Maria looked at the snow-capped mountains and asked, "The blood of Christ? Why that?"

"Father said a priest named them that, because when the sun is setting, they turn blood red. I've never seen it myself. We've never stayed that late in the day in Santa Fe. Perhaps today I can see it. Surely we'll stay overnight, since we're arriving so late. Oh, Maria, I can't believe I'm almost home!" Isabel smiled. "We should reach Santa Fe in a few hours. Then, by tomorrow evening, we'll be in Rosario."

"Providing your father is in the capital to meet us," Maria answered.

"I thought you asked Diego to send a message to him, telling him when the caravan was expected to arrive in Santa Fe."

"You should not be calling him Diego if you do not intend to marry him," Maria pointed out, then added, "and I did ask him to send a message, yesterday, along with the letter Don Jose wrote your father. But your father may not be able to just drop everything and come."

Isabel remembered her father's adoration as a child and answered confidently, "Yes, he will. He'll be as anxious to see me as I am to see him."

Santa Fe sat beside a tributary that fed the Rio Arriba, and the road pretty much followed the small river. Both Isabel and Maria relished the shade of the tall cottonwoods, interspersed here and there with irrigated fields of corn, oats, barley, melons, and beans. On the hills

in the distance were peach and plum orchards and vine-
yards, while even higher, they could see goats and sheep
grazing.

Taking note of Maria looking around appreciatively,
Isabel commented, "See? Didn't I tell you it would be
prettier here?"

"Yes, I'll have to admit it's quite pleasant. Tell me,
what are those trees over there with the long, narrow
leaves."

"Peach trees."

"Really?" Maria asked in amazement. "The only
peach I have ever eaten is a dried one. They don't grow
back home."

"No, I think they need more cold than you have. We
have snow here, you know."

Maria's brown eyes grew wide. "It actually snows? I've
never seen snow."

"Well, it doesn't fall nearly as heavily as it does in the
mountains, but it is rather pretty. Unless we have a blizzard, but that doesn't happen very often in Rosario.
See? You have something else to look forward to."

Maria looked around her once again and said, "The
crops seem to be doing well enough with the irrigation,
but the grass seems dry. I'm surprised the sheep get
enough nourishment from it to thrive."

Isabel smiled. An ordinary hidalgo woman wouldn't
even have noticed. Worrying about grass or crops was
men's business. But Isabel had always paid close attention to everything going on around her, including nature and the land. She was glad to see Maria was so
observant. It was yet another sign that they could be
friends, "Oh, there's plenty of nourishment in our
grass," Isabel informed the older woman. "Even when
it's bone dry, it's nourishing."

"If the grass is that good, why don't you raise cattle?"

"I don't know how well they would do here. Some of these hills are pretty steep, and sheep and goats are much more sure-footed than cattle. Besides, have you forgotten our Indian problem? Cattle are easy to drive, easy to steal. Sheep and goats aren't."

Maria had been looking at the grazing herds in the distance. "Now I know what's missing. It's springtime. Where are the lambs and kids?"

"They don't come until after the rains, in June. Remember I said our spring and summer are reversed? Even the wild creatures don't give birth until then. That's one reason I'm so happy to arrive home now. We'll be here for the lambing season. Oh, Maria," Isabel continued, her beautiful blue eyes sparkling with happiness, "there is nothing as soft and sweet as a lamb. Just wait. You'll see."

They rode by one of the outlying pueblos. It was not the first they had passed, but the other Indian settlement had been sitting so high on a butte Maria had been able to see very little. She had no idea if Isabel was truly serious about her offer of a place to live, but Maria did know she wasn't going back to Mexico. If this was to be her new home, she needed to know more about it, and there was much about it that seemed strange. Noticing several Indians making adobe bricks for building, she commented, "I suppose the Franciscans taught the Indians how to build their homes."

"Why do you think that?" Isabel asked.

"Because they make their adobe the same way we do, mixing grass and mud."

"I'm afraid it was us who learned from them," Isabel informed the woman. "They have been building their homes like this for centuries, long before we arrived."

"I thought Indians lived in brush shelters."

"The Apaches do, and the Comanches live in hide

tents that look like cones. But these are Pueblos. They're farmers and settled, and therefore much better builders. Look how each house is built on the top of the other, leaving just a small bit of the roof below it for a terrace. That's where they do most of their work, on the terrace, where it's cooler."

"I suppose it is hot inside," Maria observed. "What windows there are, are terribly small. Why, the ground story doesn't even have any windows." Maria took a closer look, then added, "Or doors, either."

"That's to keep out their enemies. They go in and out through a hole on the roof, and the only way you can get to the roof is by those ladders. If they're attacked, they simply pull the ladders up, and the entire settlement becomes a bastion. Quite ingenious, I think."

Maria nodded in agreement, momentarily occupied with watching an Indian woman firing clay pots in a hearth on the ground as they rode by. Then glancing upward at one terrace, she noticed a crude loom stationed there. "Is that a man weaving?" she asked in surprise.

"Yes, the men do all of the weaving and spinning. Amazing, isn't it? And that's not the only thing just the opposite from our people's customs. Their women own the homes, and when a man marries he becomes a member of his wife's family and lives with them." Isabel paused, then said, "See those turkeys? You'll never guess what they use them for. They make blankets out of the feathers."

Maria was peering up at the roof of the uppermost apartment. "Is that a turkey up there?"

Isabel laughed and answered, "No, it's an eagle that's been tethered there. It's kept for symbolic purposes."

Maria was still peering at the roof. "My eyes must be

deceiving me. That looks like a cactus growing up there."

"It is. The roofs are made of brush and two feet of dirt laid over the timbers. All sorts of things grow, either from seeds in the dirt, or seeds blown up there. Why, there's even grass growing on the roof of the governor's palace in Santa Fe."

"You seem to have considerable knowledge of these Indians," Maria commented, returning her gaze to eye level.

"There's a pueblo to the south of Rosario. Santo Domingo. Every time Father went to do any trading with those Indians, I went along. Once we went in August, when they were celebrating the feast day of their patron saint. It was a very strange ceremony, not at all like what we're accustomed to. Oh, there was the mass, and the solemn procession to the small booth where the little red-robed *santo* of Saint Domingo was kept, and the lighting of the candles below it. But after that, the missionaries just seemed to fade away, and the Indians performed their ancient rain dance, with their drums and gourd rattles. Everyone wore ceremonial costume, and they drummed their feet on the ground to make it sound like rain. Then the Koshares came, their faces and bodies grotesquely smeared and spotted, half black and white, and their hair all matted with clay. They're supposed to symbolize the spirits of their ancestors, their souls leaving the earth and ascending into the sky to become rain clouds, or at least, that's what Pedro said. He's the head shepherd's son who always used to go with us. He made friends with one of the Indian boys who told him all this. The boy also confided that the Indians still have their hidden *kivas* below ground, where they still worship their ancient gods."

A shiver ran through Maria. She glanced around her

nervously and said, "Why, they're still heathens. Are they dangerous?"

"Not now. They're perfectly tame. They even act as our allies against the other Indian tribes. Of course, we don't allow them to have guns or horses. They have to fight on foot with their bows and arrows. But they did revolt twice, before the turn of the century. The first was a very bloody uprising, which I suppose is proof enough that they're not cowardly. Hundreds of Spaniards were killed, and those who did escape with their lives had to flee all the way to El Paso del Norte. For years, there wasn't a Spaniard in all of New Mexico. Then we reconquered them."

"What caused the uprising, or do they even know?" Maria asked, still feeling uneasy.

"My father said it was because the early settlers were using them for so much forced labor, but the Indian boy told Pedro that wasn't true, that the uprising had been for religious reasons, because the missionaries wouldn't let them perform their rain dance. Perhaps that's why the Franciscans turned a blind eye to what was going on that afternoon at Santo Domingo." Isabel paused for a moment, then continued, saying, "Yes, it was a strange ceremony, a strange afternoon. But what was the strangest of all, was after the rattlers were released to go back to the desert, it actually began to thunder, and there was lightning. I don't know if it rained at Santo Domingo that night, but it did at Rosario. It was as if the heavens had opened up and a lake had been dumped on us."

Another shiver ran through Maria. "You must not say such things. That's heresy."

"I didn't say I believed. I just said it was strange."

The two women fell silent. Shortly thereafter, they passed a New Mexican leading a string of burros carrying firewood from the mountains. Isabel breathed deeply of the scent of piñon left hanging in the air, relishing it. She vowed she would get a sack of freshly roasted piñon nuts at the open market before she left Santa Fe.

As the caravan moved into the cedar-studded hills where Santa Fe sat and Maria caught her first sight of town, she asked in dismay, *"That* is The Royal City of the Holy Faith of Saint Francis?"

"Yes, but no one here in New Mexico calls it that. Just Santa Fe."

"I can see why. The name would be bigger than the town," Maria responded dryly. "I can't believe that is the capital of New Mexico."

"None of our towns are large. Santa Cruz de la Canada is even smaller, and you saw how little Albuquerque was when we passed through it."

Maria had seen. She would have totally missed the little smattering of reddish-gold buildings among the green-studded hills had they not been pointed out to her. And where had they gotten that strange name from, she wondered. She could barely roll it around her tongue.

"I've never been to Taos," Isabel continued, "but it's mainly an Indian trading village. I don't imagine it's very impressive either."

As they entered the outskirts of the town, Maria's first estimation didn't change. Santa Fe had a haphazard appearance with no defined streets, and its houses set helter-skelter. The caravan wove through corn fields and sometimes skirted the cascading little river. They entered the center of the town by a dusty path that twisted and turned through a maze of one-story adobe buildings.

Isabel pointed to a tall building that could be seen

over the roofs of the lower buildings and said, "That's the cathedral. It sits at the end of San Francisco Street."

Maria eyed the twin-towered building. To her, it looked like all the other churches she had seen, both here in New Mexico and back home, except perhaps a little larger. It certainly wasn't golden-domed, with an ornately sculptured facade, like the cathedrals she had viewed in Chihuahua, the only other Spanish capital she had ever seen. She supposed that was the root of her keen disappointment, Maria mused. She had been expecting another Chihuahua.

The sound of the burros' tinkling bells had alerted Santa Fe of the arrival of the train, and, although the pack animals carried no trading goods, they were met with excited shouts of, *"la entrada de caravana!"* as soon as they rode into the *plaza de armas*. Almost everyone in the settlement left what they were doing to crowd around the train, anxious for news from the outside world and curious to see the new settlers who had tagged along with the soldiers. Everyone seemed to be talking at once, creating a terrible noise. The burros had become alarmed at all the excitement and added their hysterical braying to the din. While Isabel anxiously glanced around, trying to spy her father in the crush of people, Maria looked curiously about the town square.

The 250-square-foot plaza was surrounded with one-story, flat-roofed buildings, lined with arcades supported by pine logs. In each corner of the plaza was a rusty cannon. Under the shady *portales* and a small grove of cottonwoods in one corner of the square, townspeople and Indians from nearby pueblos had placed their wares on blankets for sale: clay pots, colorful blankets, animal pelts, baskets of dried corn, seasonal fresh vegetables, sacks of cornmeal, round loafs of bread, strings of dried chilies, bundles of firewood, and sacks of corn

shucks to be used for stuffing mattresses. Fresh mutton
hung from the limbs of the trees, and chickens cackled
in their wooden cages. Over the rooftops, Maria could
see trees that marked private courtyards, but no sign of
the governor's palace.

Catching Isabel's attention, Maria asked, "Where is
the governor's palace? Everything has grass growing on
its roof."

"It's over there, on the north side, behind the parade
ground and flagpole."

Maria looked to where Isabel had motioned. The palace was nothing but a continuation of the adobe wall
on that side of the square, looking for all practical purposes like every other building. The only difference was
the shabbily dressed soldier who stood at attention with
his rusty musket beside the palace door.

Shaking her head with renewed disgust, Maria looked
around the plaza once more. Two voluptuous young
women standing in a doorway and smoking corn-shuck
cigars caught her eye. But it wasn't the smoking that
shocked her, nor the low-cut *camisas* and the calf-length
skirts that fully revealed their slender ankles. All commoners dressed in that manner, and all women smoked,
even those in her class. No, it was the girls' seductive
stance and flirtatious looks that took Maria aback. Realizing the poses were for the benefit of the newly arrived soldiers, Maria stared in a mixture of disapproval
and fascination at the first *putas* she had ever seen.

By this time the caravan had stopped in the middle
of the congested plaza. While the boy who was driving
their cart scampered down and began undoing the yoke
that was lashed to the oxen's horns, Isabel stood up
and scanned the plaza, craning her neck to see over
the multistoried cage the chicken vendor standing next
to the cart had strapped on his back. "I don't see my

father anywhere," she commented in disappointment to Maria.

Carefully, Maria came to her feet and looked about also, although she had no idea what Isabel's father looked like. She just assumed he would be dressed like a hidalgo, and that eliminated the majority of the crowd. As she scanned the eastern side of the plaza, her gaze came to an abrupt halt. There, beneath one of the *portales,* stood the most magnificent male she had ever seen. He was unusually tall, broad-shouldered, lean-hipped, and the bronze skin on his bare, muscular chest gleamed in the afternoon sunlight. She knew he wasn't a Pueblo. Not only was he not dressed in the simple cotton garments they wore, but he lacked their broad face and rather flat features. His were sharper, more chiseled, and he wore his raven-black hair in long braids, rather than loose and cut short. Also, there was about him a presence that the subservient Pueblos lacked. His bearing was proud, self-assured, and an aura of power hung over him. While the only decorations he wore were the single eagle feather in his scalp lock and the silver loops that dangled from his earlobes, Maria thought he had to be a chief. He seemed to reek of majesty. For the first time since she had come to New Mexico, Maria was impressed. Very impressed.

Noting the awed expression on Maria's face, Isabel looked to see what she was staring at. She saw the two Comanches, but hardly took note of the shorter, older Indian. Like Maria, her full attention was riveted on the tall, younger man with his rugged good looks and splendid physique. She, too, was very aware of his power, his princely air, but it was his potent sexuality that seemed to reach out and touch her. A shiver of excitement ran through her; her heart suddenly raced.

Isabel saw a smile steal across the Comanche's lips,

and suspected he knew she was staring at him and admiring him. That he seemed to find her fascination with him amusing, irritated Isabel, but she couldn't take her eyes from him. It was almost as if she were hypnotized. Then the Comanche turned his head fully towards Isabel. Their eyes met, and held. There was something about those jet black eyes that seemed so familiar to Isabel. Where had she seen them before? And the magnificent warrior seemed just as puzzled as she, for a quizzical expression had come over his face.

"Isabel!"

Isabel broke eye contact at her father's call and turned. Then seeing him shouldering his way through the crush of people, she called out, "Father! Oh, Father, I'm so happy to see you!"

When Don Augustine reached the *carreta,* Isabel threw herself into his arms, hugging him and kissing his cheek. Don Augustine couldn't help the happiness that seemed to flood his soul at having his beloved daughter back in his arms. He hugged her back. Neither saw the look of shocked disbelief that came over the two Comanches' faces, a look that was replaced with fury when the Indians realized they had been duped.

Finally remembering the danger his daughter might be in, Don Augustine firmly took Isabel's shoulders and set her away, saying, "You should not have come back. You should have accepted one of the offers for marriage your uncle received."

"But I missed you, and Mother, and my home."

Don Augustine hardened his heart to the pleading look in his daughter's eyes and answered in a stern, forbidding voice Isabel had never heard from him, "That is no excuse. I did what was best for you."

Isabel had never expected her father to be truly displeased with her. Bewildered and hurt, she said,

"Please, can't we talk about this later? I'm so happy to be home. Don't ruin it for me."

Don Augustine realized it would do no good to chastise the girl. He should have told Don Jose the truth about why he was sending Isabel to Mexico, so he would never have let the girl return. But Don Augustine had not wanted Don Jose to know of the shocking pact he had made with the Comanches, or of how cowardly he had been not to refuse. Now it was too late. What was done, was done, and he had to deal with it. And the first thing he had to do was get Isabel back to Rosario and hidden as soon as possible. "As you wish," he answered Isabel crossly. "We will discuss this fully when we get home." He looked about him, asking, "Where is the chaperone your uncle sent with you?"

While Don Augustine and Isabel had been greeting one another, Maria had managed to climb down from the cart unassisted. From behind Don Augustine, she said, "I'm here, sir."

Isabel made the formal introductions. Don Augustine then said to the two women, "Ramon and the cart are over there." Seeing Maria's raised eyebrow, he explained, "Ramon is my head shepherd and, more or less, second in command. As soon as he has loaded your trunks on my cart, we'll be off."

"We're leaving today?" Isabel asked in surprise.

"Yes."

"But why? We can't make it to Rosario by nightfall. We'll have to camp out again tonight, and we were both looking forward to a good night's rest."

"You can rest when you get to Rosario!" Seeing the shocked expression on Isabel's face at his uncharacteristically sharp answer, Don Augustine added, "I'm sorry, but we can't tarry here. I have important business to take care of back in Rosario."

In the old days, Isabel would have asked what business, but her father seemed different. Irritable, and, yes, nervous. That was the third time she had seen him looking over his shoulder.

While Ramon was busy loading the ladies' trunks onto the *carreta* the men had brought with them, Isabel showed her father the mare Don Jose had given to her.

"And you can actually ride her?" Augustine asked, for horses were so rare in New Mexico, they were reserved exclusively for males.

"Yes. All the ladies ride in Mexico. Please, can I ride her back to Rosario, beside you? I'm so tired of sitting on that hard cart seat."

"She rides quite well, actually," a male voice said from behind Don Augustine, making the older man almost jump out of his skin.

Whirling around, Don Augustine asked sharply, "And who, sir, are you?"

"Captain Diego de Villagria, at your service," Diego answered smoothly, bowing slightly. "I accompanied your daughter from El Paso del Norte and will be stationed here in Santa Fe for a while, until my enlistment is up and I can lay claim to my land grant," he added to impress the older man. "If I may, I would like to talk to you before you leave Santa Fe, in private. This evening, perhaps?"

"In private? About what?"

Diego ignored Isabel's glare and answered coolly, "About your daughter, sir."

This must be the young man Don Jose had mentioned in his letter, Don Augustine thought. And apparently the captain felt rather assured in pressing his suit for Isabel's hand. There had been an almost proprietary air in his comment about her riding. To Don Augustine, this was neither the time nor place for such a discussion. "Not today! I'm in a hurry to get back to Rosario!"

Diego quickly hid his surprise at the older man's abruptness. Hidalgos usually treated one another more politely, particularly a potential son-in-law of some means and influence, and he knew Don Jose would have told Isabel's father about him in his letter. If he hadn't been so determined to have Isabel, he would have taken affront at the older man's behavior and withdrawn his request. But Diego wanted Isabel badly, badly enough he'd grovel, just this once. He forced a smile and answered, "I understand, sir. It was presumptive of me to assume you could fit me into your busy schedule on such short notice. With your permission, I will visit Rosario at a later date. We can discuss the matter then."

"Yes, yes, whatever," Don Augustine answered distractedly, then taking Isabel's arm said to her, "We're ready to leave, my dear. I'll saddle your horse for you."

As Don Augustine and Isabel rode from Santa Fe a few moments later, with Ramon and Maria following on the *carreta*, Isabel glanced over her shoulder and saw Diego watching them with a deep scowl on his face. She had no idea what was so pressing that her father had to hurry so, but at least it would give her some time to argue her side of the case. Besides, her father had been really sharp with the captain. She had never seen him be so rude. He was known throughout the entire countryside around Rosario for his charm and diplomacy. That's why he had been chosen by the town as their spokesman. Perhaps he had taken an instant dislike to Diego. Maria and she had their reservations about the captain, didn't they? Perhaps her father had sensed something, too. If so, it would make him much more receptive to Isabel's plea to refuse Diego's offer.

Feeling much easier about her questionable future,

Isabel turned back around in her saddle. As she did, her eyes came to rest where the two Comanches had been standing, but they had disappeared. She knew they must have been from a band that was at peace with the Spanish, at least temporarily. Otherwise they wouldn't have dared to show their faces in Santa Fe, where the presidio was. Or would they, she wondered. The tall warrior had had a boldness about him that made her suspect he would dare anything. She wondered if she would ever see the magnificent savage again. He had had the most curious effect on her. Then she realized the likelihood of that happening was almost nonexistent.

Isabel was stunned at the powerful wave of disappointment that engulfed her.

Five

When Don Augustine and his small party left Santa Fe, they traveled in a westwardly direction on a narrow dusty trail that wove its way through deserted hills covered with blue gamma grass and studded with squatty piñon pines.

After a desultory conversation with her father in which Isabel felt she had to pull every word from him, she left him to his dark brooding and concentrated on admiring the scenery she had missed so much, until she eventually became bored with that, too. She glanced over her shoulder to where Ramon and Maria were following on the *carreta,* then fell back to where she could ride beside them and have someone to talk to.

Setting her mare at a walk beside the cart, Isabel said to the head shepherd, "I didn't get a chance to say much to you earlier, Ramon. How is your son, Pedro, faring?"

"He is well," the slender, grey-haired man answered, smiling with obvious pride. "He is a man now, you know. You probably won't even recognize him."

"No, I probably won't," Isabel admitted, then not wanting to leave Maria completely out of the conversation, said to the older woman, "Pedro and I were almost constant companions as children. There weren't any girls my age in the village. Besides, I liked being out-doors."

"I see," Maria responded, really not understanding. The mixing of classes, particularly the very high and the very low, was unheard of where she came from, even among children. It appeared things were much more democratic here, something she was going to have to get used to.

"Has Pedro married?" Isabel asked Ramon.

"Not yet, but he is betrothed to the miller's daughter."

Isabel concentrated hard, trying to remember the miller's daughter. She recalled a day when she and Pedro had been playing beside the log mill, built over one of the irrigation ditches so its water could turn the turbine wheel. The miller's wife had come outside carrying a black-eyed toddler in her arms. Was that the girl, Pedro's wife-to-be? It didn't seem possible. But then, it had been so long ago. They had all been children. "And your wife?" Isabel asked the shepherd. "Is she well?"

A look of profound sadness came over Ramon's weathered face. "I lost Guadalupe four years ago."

"What happened?" Isabel asked in shock, for the woman had been in her early forties and very robust-looking the last time Isabel had seen her.

"There was an outbreak of the pox. We lost several people at Rosario."

Was that when his hair had turned grey, Isabel wondered, for Ramon wasn't that old himself. Her heart went out to the kind, gentle man. "I'm so sorry," Isabel muttered.

Before Ramon could respond to Isabel's words of condolence, everyone's attention was drawn to the sound of pounding hooves coming from beyond the crest of the hill beside them. Then four riders came sweeping over the rise, horses galloping as if all the demons in hell were after them.

For a brief moment, everyone was spellbound by the riders' supreme horsemanship, for even at that tremendous speed, they were in full control of their powerful animals. All Isabel could do was stare in amazement, particularly at the rider at the front of the group, who was leaning forward with his cheek against the sleek neck of his horse and his long braids mingling with the gelding's dark mane. He and the animal seemed to have taken on wings. She had never seen anyone who could ride like that, except a Comanche boy she had once known. It was then that Isabel realized the riders were Indians, but not the peaceful Indians she had known. These Indians' faces were painted black, and they were yelling a blood-curdling war cry.

The roar of a musket was added to the loud cries of the fierce-looking Indians. Turning towards the sound of the explosion, Isabel saw her father's old gun smoking, then dazed by everything happening so fast, watched as he wheeled his horse around and raced back towards her, yelling, "Run, Isabel! Run for your life!"

Isabel never had the chance to respond to her father's frantic call. A split-second later, the lead Indian's horse slammed into hers with such force that the wind was knocked from both animals with a loud "swoosh" and Isabel was unseated. As she flew through the air, a pair of strong hands latched around her waist; then she was sat astride in front of the Indian so hard she bit her tongue.

As her captor pivoted his mount and raced the animal away, Isabel heard her father screaming, "No! You can't have her!" Despite the steel-like arm the Indian had around her waist, Isabel managed to look back and see her father tumbling from his horse, his chest riddled with arrows. Then seeing the Indian who had shot him jump to the ground and pull out his knife, and knowing what he meant to do, she screamed, "Nooo! Please, no!"

"Silence!" her captor hissed in Spanish, jerking her around, and unwittingly saving Isabel the added horror of having to watch her father being scalped.

For several moments, Isabel was too shocked by what she had witnessed to do anything. The sound of Maria screaming in terror only barely penetrated her mind, as did the scenery racing past her in a blur. Then rage filled her, and she came alive with fury, screaming, "Let go me, you murdering bastard! Put me down! Put me down, damn you!" while she twisted, and kicked, and clawed at the arm that held her.

The Comanche dropped his reins and wrapped his other arm around Isabel, pinning her arms to her side. But even then it was all he could do to keep a grip on her while his horse raced up one hill and down the other, with her twisting and kicking so wildly. He'd never dreamed a woman so small could have such strength. Had he not been able to guide his horse with his knees, he would never have accomplished it.

Isabel's strength had been fueled by the panic flooding her veins. Eventually, she was worn down, her screams and curses growing weaker along with her muscles. Between her exhaustion from her futile exertions and the Indian's seriously depleting her air with his tight grip around her chest, she almost lost consciousness and slumped forward. Feeling more in control of the situation, the Comanche dropped one arm, picked up his reins, and brought his mount to a halt. Then he jumped down and pulled Isabel from his horse.

The second Isabel's feet hit the ground, a new surge of energy swept through her. She twisted away to run, but the Comanche caught her shoulder with one long arm and whirled her back around. Then she threw herself at him, pounding on his broad, rock-hard chest and screaming insults.

"Enough!" her captor snarled, then catching hold of the thick bun at the back of her head, he savagely jerked her head back, making her cry out in pain, and captured both of her flying hands in one of his. Then releasing her hair, he whipped a piece of rawhide from his horse's saddle and quickly bound her wrists together.

Isabel still fought, kicking viciously, but it did her no good. The Comanche simply held her at arm's length and let her wear herself down a second time, a look of utter disgust on his face. Finally, Isabel sank to the ground, sobbing in frustration.

Looking up at the savage towering over her, she spat, "I hate you for what you did to my father! You're nothing but a filthy murderer!"

Isabel didn't notice the fleeting look of pain that crossed the Indian's black eyes when she said she hated him. All she saw was the stony expression on his face when he answered, "It was not murder. It was justice."

"Justice?" Isabel shrieked in fury.

"Yes, justice! Treachery deserves no less than death."

"Treachery? What treachery?"

"Your father's treachery!" the Comanche answered, his black eyes flashing with anger. "He did not keep his end of the pact. He used us, then betrayed us."

"What are you talking about? What pact?"

"The agreement that he and my father made for our marriage."

Isabel was so shocked she was momentarily speechless. Still stunned, she finally managed to gasp, "*Our* marriage? Who are you?"

"Stands Alone, but you probably remember me by my childhood name, Spotted Coyote."

Despite his black-painted face, Isabel had recognized the Indian as the same magnificent savage she had seen in Santa Fe. When he identified himself, she realized why he had seemed somehow familiar. He was the same person she had been longing for during all those years of her exile. A spontaneous surge of joy shot through Isabel, before she remembered what had happened to her father. Then she forced it down, summoning all the hate and repugnance she could bring forth. "I don't believe you. It's all a lie."

No one had ever accused Stands Alone of lying. He held his anger at Isabel's insult in check and asked tightly, "Why do you think that?"

"Because my father would never betroth me to a heathen savage!" Isabel answered hatefully. "His honor would never allow it."

"Your father had no honor!" Stands Alone answered her bluntly. "And he did betroth you. There were witnesses on both sides. But he thought to trick us. We know that now. All along, he had no intention of keeping his word. He took our gifts, accepted our protection, knowing all along he would betray us. Tell me, whose grave did he show us, or was it, like his promises, empty?"

"What grave?"

"The grave he took us to see the day my father and I rode into Rosario to claim you as my bride. He told us you had died from the pox and led us to a fresh grave he said was yours. He was very convincing. He even shed tears." Stands Alone didn't tell Isabel that he and his father had been grief stricken also. Oh, what fools Don Augustine had made of them, he thought.

Everyone in the village had probably been laughing behind their backs.

Isabel couldn't believe her father had sunk to such deception. Not her beloved father, the man she had admired all of her life. No, he was a man whose honor was above reproach. She came to her feet and said, "I don't believe you! I don't believe any of this! It's inconceivable, it's . . . absurd!"

"It doesn't matter if you believe or not," Stands Alone answered calmly. "It is true. And the pact will be kept. You will be my bride."

Once again, Isabel was stunned. "That's impossible!" she finally muttered.

"No, it is not. Why do you think you are still alive?"

"I hate you! I could never be your wife!"

Stands Alone shrugged his broad shoulders and replied, "You will come to have different feelings for me, eventually."

"No! I could never have any feeling for you but loathing. Never!"

"You cared for me once. You will care again, but this time even more so."

"I never cared for you!" Isabel denied hotly.

Stands Alone caught her arms and pulled her forward until their chests almost touched. Looking down at her with his dark, compelling eyes, he said, "You lie! We played together, laughed together, shared each other's secrets. We held hands, we kissed."

Isabel was filled with mortification. All was true, and shamefully, the last had been her idea. Spotted Coyote had told her his people didn't kiss, and she had shown him how it was done. "I was just a child! I didn't know any better."

His dark gaze slid from the top of her head to her toes, and slowly back up, lingering on her breasts as he said in a husky voice, "And now you are a woman, and do?"

His look had left Isabel feeling weak in the knees, for it was obvious from its heat that he desired her. It took all of her concentration to answer, "Yes, I do know better. I could never feel anything for you."

Stands Alone's dark eyes rose and met hers. "Nothing at all?"

There was a strong hint of challenge in Stands Alone's voice, and Isabel rose to it, throwing back, "Nothing!"

"We shall see," he muttered. Then, with the same unexpected swiftness he had struck with before, his lips were on hers.

A shot of pure excitement ran through Isabel, until she remembered who she was and who he was. She struggled, pushing at his chest and trying to pull away. Stands Alone put one arm around her and brought her full-force against his powerful body, pinning her bound arms between them. Catching the back of her head with his other hand, he held it firmly while he kissed her.

Helpless beneath his superior strength, Isabel thought just to endure the outrage. But she quickly realized this was no child's kiss, no simple pressing of lips on lips as they had done before. And it was far from boring, as Diego's kiss had been. Stands Alone's lips were soft and warm, and he moved them in the most compelling manner, nibbling, teasing, taunting. When he brought the tip of his tongue into play, letting it slide slowly back and forth over her lips, back and forth, then slip inside her bottom lip, Isabel realized that somewhere along the line, Comanche or not, Stands Alone had learned the art of kissing, and learned it very well. She had never dreamed that kissing could be so delightful, so terribly exciting. When his tongue pressed insistently on her teeth, demanding entrance, she was helpless to deny him. She opened to him, her knees growing weak and her heart pounding wildly as he gently ravished the sweetness of her mouth.

Isabel was lightheaded and as limp as a dishrag when Stands Alone abruptly lifted his head and broke the kiss. Dazed, she looked up at him and saw the smug smile on his lips. "Now you have been kissed as a man kisses a woman, and loved it."

The truth was humiliating. "No, I didn't!" Isabel denied fiercely.

"Lying will get you nowhere; I have already proved my touch is not unpleasant to you."

"That's not true!"

He pulled her even closer, so Isabel could feel every hard plane, every powerful muscle, every tendon of his magnificent body. She trembled; her heart raced. Suddenly, it was difficult to breathe.

Stands Alone felt her tremble, saw the pulse beat in her throat quicken. His dark eyes flared with triumph. "Your body betrays you, Isabel. It yearns for the pleasures my body can give it. For the time being, we will have that. Our passion for one another. Eventually, you will come to care for me again. Someday, you will love me, as is befitting a good wife."

His words sounded so arrogant, Isabel was newly outraged. "No, never!" she vowed fiercely. "Never will you possess me, and never will I have any tender feelings for you! I'd die before I sank that low. I, too, have my honor."

Isabel saw the brief flash of anger in Stands Alone's eyes, before a fiercely determined expression came over his blackened face. "We shall see," he replied tightly; then releasing her, he turned and walked away.

When Stands Alone stopped at the top of the rise a

distance from her, gazing out over the countryside, Isabel thought to flee while his back was turned. Knowing she couldn't possibly escape on foot, she eyed his horse. But before she could even make a move towards it, she heard him say, "You can forget that idea. I have trained my horse so he will allow no one but me on his back."

Isabel whirled about and saw Stands Alone was still gazing out with his back to her. How had he known what she was thinking, she wondered. Could he read her mind? "I was just on his back," she reminded him.

"With me."

Frustrated and angry at having her plans for escape thwarted, Isabel stuck her tongue out at him, for lack of any other way to exhibit her fury. She startled at the rumble of his laughter, then heard him say, "I thought you had outgrown such childish antics."

My God, Isabel thought in dismay. Does he have eyes in the back of his head?

At that moment, Isabel heard the sound of horses approaching. As the other three Comanches rode up, she recognized the one who had shot her father. In renewed outrage, she ran towards the man, screaming, "Murderer! Bastard! I'll kill you with my bare hands!"

As she raced by him, Stands Alone caught her and pulled her back against him with one arm, pinning her to him despite her sobs and fierce struggles as the older man dismounted and walked towards them.

When the man came closer, Isabel recognized him as Yellow Sky. "You killed my father!" Isabel screamed.

Yellow Sky winced at Isabel's fury, then replied solemnly, "He betrayed me, my son, and my band. I had no choice. Your people would have done the same, had I been the betrayer."

Isabel ignored the truth of Yellow Sky's words. Spaniards could be just as vindictive, just as cruel as any Indian, if not more so. "There was nothing to betray! I don't believe your son's wild tales. My father would never have promised me to a . . . *savage*. Never!"

Yellow Sky cringed at the way Isabel said "savage." She made it sound as if they were the lowest, the most despicable people on earth. The proud old man had felt doubly betrayed. He had sincerely believed Don Augustine was his friend. "Are you saying you knew nothing of the pact?"

"That is what she claims, and I believe her," Stands Alone answered. "She could not have pretended such surprise."

"It changes nothing," Yellow Sky told his son. "The agreement still stands."

"I know," Stands Alone answered quietly.

"Not as far as I'm concerned!" Isabel shouted. "There will be no marriage! Not ever!"

Yellow Sky's black eyes flashed. "You have no say in the matter," he answered in an adamant voice. "I know your people's way. The daughter obeys her father's dictates in all things, and you will honor your father's word, even though he did not. This is the only way it can be."

Isabel did not understand the meaning of Yellow Sky's last words. Rather it was his furious look that subdued her. She realized, belatedly, that the chief was a dangerous man.

Totally dismissing Isabel, Yellow Sky switched from the Spanish he had been speaking to Comanche and said to his son, "For this reason, I have let the other woman live, so she can go back and tell the people of Rosario what happened, and that we will no longer trade with them, no longer bring them gifts, no longer protect them. That is their punishment for their part in this. But the rest of the pact is being kept. We have the girl, and she will be your bride."

Stands Alone nodded in agreement. Fulfilling the pact was the only way his band could save face with the people of Rosario, the only way they could regain the upper hand after Don Augustine's treachery. The Spaniards would learn that they could not trick the Comanche and get away with it. It was a matter of Comanche pride. And by Comanche standards, it was generous. Most bands would have taken revenge on the village also, wiped them completely from the face of the earth.

"You go ahead with the girl," Yellow Sky told his son. "In case the soldiers in Santa Fe try to follow, we will lead them away from you."

Yellow Sky turned around, mounted his horse, and the three Indians rode away in the direction they had come from. Stands Alone turned Isabel to face him and said, "We will go ahead alone. If you give me your word you will behave, I will not tie your feet beneath the horse."

Isabel lifted her bound hands. "What about these?"

"No, I do not trust you that far. Perhaps later."

Stands Alone led her to his horse, picked her up by the waist as if she weighed nothing, and slung her on its back. Looking up at Isabel, he asked, "Well? Do I tie your feet?"

Isabel winced at the thought. The insides of her thighs were already chafed from their previous ride. "No, that won't be necessary."

Stands Alone nodded, then flew onto the small Indian saddle behind her and picked up the reins.

As they rode away, Isabel asked, "What was that your father said in Comanche?"

"That he allowed the other woman to live, so she could go back to Rosario and tell the people what happened."

Maria was alive, Isabel thought. Thank God for that.

Then she summoned her courage to ask, "And Ramon, the man driving the cart?"

Stands Alone had not seen what had happened, but he knew. "He is dead."

Isabel felt sick at heart. Ramon had been like an uncle to her, a kind gentle man who had taught her how to feed the orphaned lambs and had entertained her and Pedro with stories from the old country, stories his father had passed on to him. It wasn't fair. Her father, at least, had fired his musket at the Comanches. Ramon had not even possessed a weapon. He had done nothing aggressive. No, he'd always been such a peaceful man.

Grief for both men welled up in Isabel. "I'll never forgive you for this," she told Stands Alone in a furious, determined voice. "Never!"

Stands Alone remained grimly silent and turned his horse towards the mountains, mountains that had turned blood red in the setting sun.

Six

Stands Alone and Isabel traveled through the foot-hills of the Sangre de Cristo Mountains, steadily climbing higher and higher, until nightfall. Isabel paid very little attention to her surroundings. For the time being, she had even forgotten about her captor. She was fully engulfed in her overwhelming grief.

It wasn't until Stands Alone had built a fire and roasted a rabbit that Isabel was finally roused from her heavy sorrow by his shaking her shoulder and saying, "You must eat."

Still dazed, Isabel glanced around her, then seeing the piece of steaming meat he was holding out to her, answered, "I'm not hungry."

"You must be. It has been a long time since you have eaten."

"I should have known a cold-hearted savage wouldn't understand," Isabel answered bitterly. "What do you know about grieving? I just lost my father and a good friend. I'm too upset to eat."

Stands Alone overlooked Isabel's insult in calling him cold-hearted and unfeeling because he knew all whites thought that. Like so many other things about his people, it was a misconception. The *Nema* believed in deep grieving, the women—sometimes even the men, if the dead person was a particularly close friend—wailing, ripping their clothing, cutting their hair, gashing their skin to show the depth of their loss. But they didn't deny themselves food, something critical for life. "Still, you must eat. You will need the nourishment for our long ride tomorrow."

Remembering where that ride would take her, to his home where she would have to live out her life as his wife, Isabel angrily batted the food away with her bound hands and answered, "No! I'll never eat again. I'd rather starve to death than consort with a cold-blooded killer, a filthy" . . . an ugly sneer came over her face . . . "animal!"

For a horrifying moment, Isabel feared her recklessness had been her undoing. The look that came into Stands Alone's dark eyes made her blood run icy. He looked furious enough to kill her with his bare hands, and there was no doubt in her mind that the tall, powerful Comanche could break her in two if he so desired. No, this wasn't the fun-loving, easy-going boy she remembered. He was a stranger, a vary dangerous stranger.

As suddenly as it had come, the furious look in Stands Alone's eyes disappeared. "Don't speak so hastily. It is not easy to starve yourself if food is about. That takes tremendous willpower."

"And how would you know?" Isabel tossed back.

"I fasted for four days while I awaited my vision. I was very aware of the animals about me, the berries on the bushes, the nuts in the trees, all readily available sources of food. It took a great deal of discipline not to succumb to my hunger but rather to concentrate on my quest. At the end of the fourth day, I was weak, but nowhere near dead. That would take supreme willpower, I believe."

"And you don't think I'm capable of that?" Isabel asked in a challenging tone of voice.

"No, I don't," Stands Alone answered candidly, then

he rose to his feet, adding, "But I will not force you to eat. When you are ready, you will."

Stands Alone turned and walked back to the fire. Isabel glared at his back, determined to prove him wrong. She'd starve herself, she vowed, and let him sit by and watch. He'd regret the day he challenged her, she thought, foolishly disregarding how much *she* would suffer.

Through the flickering light of the fire, Isabel watched as Stands Alone tended his horse. She noted he hadn't even tethered the animal to keep him from running away and supposed the Comanche had trained the gelding in that manner also. His efficiency, his calmness in the face of her threats, his total self-assuredness, irritated her to no end. Irrationally, despite knowing he was dangerous, she wanted to rile him. "Aren't you afraid the soldiers from Santa Fe will see your campfire? I'm sure they must be in hot pursuit by now."

Stands Alone scoffed and answered scornfully, "They could never follow my trail. They couldn't track an entire buffalo herd fifteen minutes after it passed. They know nothing of reading sign. Besides, only every third soldier has a horse."

"That would still be ten to one," Isabel pointed out, "and they could use a Ute to track."

Stands Alone frowned at the mention of his enemy. Such had not always been the case. At one time, the Utes and *Nema* had been friends and allies, but no longer. Now the *Nema* and Utes were bitter enemies, and the Spanish played each tribe against the other, only increasing the distrust and hatred. But Stands Alone wasn't worried. That was why his father and the others had stayed behind, to lay false trails, to divide, redivide, and redivide, splitting the enemy into smaller and smaller bands, then regrouping and ambushing them one party at a time. That was the *Nema* way. When the Ute saw what was happening, he would turn back, unless he was as foolish as the white man. Then he would meet his death with his new allies. But Stands Alone did not want to tell Isabel this. He sensed she was trying to taunt him, and two could play that game.

"I seriously doubt that," Stands Alone answered. "They seldom send soldiers after us, even when we have taken captives. I think they are cowards."

"They are not cowards!" Isabel denied hotly, taking insult on her people's behalf. "And this time they will send troops. You'll see."

"Why this time?"

"First, because you have killed a man of some importance in this territory. Second, because there is a new officer at the fort, a man who intended to ask my father for my hand in marriage, a man who will *not* give up."

Stands Alone scowled at this information, then said bluntly, "Your father could not give your hand in marriage to this man. It had already been promised." His dark eyes narrowed, "Who is this man?"

"Captain Diego de Villagria. He knows Indians, and he's not afraid of you. That's how he earned his royal land grant, putting down an Indian rebellion in the Yucatan. He'll come for me. You'll see."

Stands Alone wasn't worried about the captain as a military threat. With typical Comanche arrogance, he looked down on all other Indian tribes, so the Spaniard's victory over them meant nothing to him. Besides, he knew even if the Spanish could manage to raise an army large enough to attack his band, they could never find his village in the rugged, almost impenetrable mountains. But the tall Comanche was worried about the man, himself, and asked, "This captain? He loves you?"

Isabel seriously doubted that. Diego had never mentioned love, just wanting her, and Isabel was wise enough to know that meant lust. But Stands Alone had offered her no better. He had said they would share passion, that in time she would come to love him. Not once had he mentioned any tender feelings for her. The realization brought on a painful pang that only fed Isabel's growing bitterness. Men! she thought angrily. They seemed to be the same regardless of race, thinking only of themselves, . wanting only to satisfy their disgusting, raging needs of the flesh. But Isabel wasn't about to reveal her thoughts to Stands Alone. She wanted him to worry about Diego, and surely a man who loved a woman would be more determined to get her back. "Yes, he does. Very much."

"And you? Do you love him?"

"Yes, I do!" Isabel answered impetuously.

Once again the dark eyes flashed, and Isabel felt a tingle of fear. Then Stands Alone said, "It does not matter. You have been pledged to be my wife. You will forget him."

"You can't make me do that!" Isabel flung back. "You can force me to be your wife, but you can't control my mind and my feelings."

For a long time, Stands Alone just stood and stared at her, his look unfathomable. Then he said with infuriating calmness, "We shall see."

Frustrated, Isabel longed to scratch his black eyes out, then watched as he crossed the campsite towards her with his long-legged, graceful walk. Hating herself for admiring anything about him, she shot daggers at him with her eyes as he hunkered in front of her.

"We have a long day ahead of us tomorrow," Stands Alone told her. "I will untie your hands so you can be more comfortable while you sleep. But don't even consider attacking me again. Then I would be forced to tie them again, this time behind your back."

Isabel didn't doubt his threat for one moment. She sat silently fuming while he untied her hands, then as soon as the rawhide fell away, rubbed her wrists to restore the circulation. Seeing Stands Alone sitting down beside her, she asked sharply, "What are you doing?"

"I'm lying down, to sleep."

"Here? Beside me?" Isabel asked in alarm.

"Yes."

"Why? I won't try to run away. I know I'd just get lost."

"I wasn't worried about that. You would have never gotten out of camp. I'm a very light sleeper when I put my mind to it."

"Then why here?" Isabel asked, becoming more and more panic-stricken for fear he planned to force himself on her. "Why not on the other side of the fire?"

"I had thought to protect you," Stands Alone answered, motioning to the bow and quiver of arrows he had earlier placed on the ground beside her. "Bears and wolves roam these woods at night."

They had camped that night beside a stream in what the Spanish people called a bosque, a thicket of cottonwood trees. Isabel glanced around at the dark trees that surrounded them. She had never been in such a dense woods. With the light from the fire casting eerie, dancing shadows over the rustling leaves and making the thick vines that dangled from the trees look like ropes hanging from a gallows, the place looked frightening and very forbidding. "I thought fires were supposed to keep wild animals away."

"Usually, but there are always those animals that are more daring."

Like some men, Isabel thought, thinking of the man now lying beside her. Gingerly, she lay down, being very careful to keep a distance between them. Then she rolled to her side, putting her back to Stands Alone, staring at the woods.

Despite the crackling of the fire, a sound that should have been lulling, Isabel heard every snap of a twig and every soft whisper of a bush stirring. She had heard that *el oso plateados,* monstrous, seven-foot, silver-tipped bears, roamed these mountains. Just as fast and much more powerful than a *el oso negro,* the little black bear she was familiar with, they had a reputation for having nasty temperaments. Almost every encounter she had heard of, had ended with death of the human, the body often mangled beyond recognition. Fast on the heels of these frightening thoughts, Isabel heard a cry that made her almost jump out of her skin.

"There is nothing to be afraid of," Stands Alone said softly. "That was just a night hawk. Go to sleep. I told you I would protect you."

"Then why don't you get your musket?"

"It has only one bullet. In the time it takes to reload it, I can get off eight arrows, arrows that are just as lethal as any bullet. I'm afraid your white man's gun is much overrated," Stands Alone ended with contempt.

"Then why do you even have one?" Isabel threw back.

"They are handy for distance shooting. But for everything else, we use our arrows."

Isabel bitterly remembered her father's being killed with arrows and knew the truth of Stands Alone's words. Then she asked, "But will an arrow kill one of those big bears?"

Stands Alone knew it was the grizzly she was referring to. "If shot close, and strategically placed, yes. Better than a bullet, which doesn't have near the penetration power. If you can put an arrow through the tough hide of a buffalo bull, you can put an arrow through anything. Now, stop worrying, and go to sleep."

But sleep eluded Isabel, long after she had tired of staring suspiciously at the woods. Then it was the cold that kept her awake, for she had never slept outdoors without benefit of even a blanket. She curled into a tight ball to conserve her heat, but it did no good. She shivered, then almost jumped out of her skin a second time when Stands Alone wrapped a long arm around her and pulled her back against him.

"What do you think you're doing?" Isabel asked in fright.

"You're cold. I'm going to keep you warm."

They were much too close to suit Isabel. She could feel every hard muscle and tendon on his powerful body. "No! Let me go!" she demanded, jerking at his arm.

Stands Alone only tightened his grip and replied, "Relax. I'm not going to do anything but warm you. The other won't come until we are married and you are my wife."

"Why should I believe you?"

"Because I have given you my word, and unlike your people, the *Nema* always honor their word."

Isabel would have loved to have made a retort, but wasn't quite up to the effort. It had been a long, hard day for her, between her grueling traveling and her draining grief. As Stands Alone's body heat insidiously crept into her cold flesh and warmed her, exhaustion came down on her like a hammer, and her eyelids drifted down.

Long after Isabel had fallen asleep, Stands Alone remained awake, thinking. His mind drifted back to the day Isabel's father had told him she had died. Stands Alone had felt more than just a keen disappointment. Half in love with Isabel since childhood and looking forward to sharing his life with someone he thought was his soul mate, he had been devastated by the news. He'd never married, knowing he could find no one to take her place. That was not to say there were not women in his life. He was a healthy, virile male. But they came and went, sexual partners eager to share a few hours of passion with him, both in camp and in the Spanish villages he visited. None had ever come even close to touching his heart.

Then today had come, a day of many revelations and many fleeting emotions. When he had first realized Isabel was alive, the shot of joy that ran through him had stunned him with its intensity. Fast on that, came the realization of Don Augustine's treachery. An anger just as powerful as his joy had filled him, an anger made all the worse by wondering what part Isabel had played in that deception. Learning she had known nothing of the arrangement had been a relief, but that had done him little good. He had even been robbed of the satisfaction he had expected their revenge on Augustine to bring him. Instead he felt regret for having to exact their justice. Had everything gone as he and his father had expected, he and Isabel could have had a perfect life together. Now their chance at happiness was seriously jeopardized. What if she never forgave him, as she had threatened, he wondered bleakly. What if she withheld her love? Was the dream he had carried in his heart all those years still destined to failure, despite Isabel's being very much alive?

Perhaps it had been nothing but a childish dream all along, Stands Alone mused sadly, just fabrications of a life together that held no true substance. Isabel was not at all as he'd remembered her. The sweet, yet vivacious child he had been so fond of was gone. In her place was a bad-tempered, stubborn, exasperating woman, a woman who insulted him at every turn. Did he even want her for his wife?

Finding that question unsettling, Stands Alone's busy mind shifted to a different subject. What of this Diego? he wondered. Did Isabel really love the Spaniard? He had felt a stab of raw jealousy when she had said she did, an ugly emotion he had never before experienced. Then he'd had his doubts. He knew Isabel had been taunting him before, trying to make him angry. Had she been taunting him then? She had to have been, Stands Alone decided. He simply could not accept her loving another man, not after he had carried her memory in his heart so long. It was too painful, even if he didn't know for certain how deep his feelings were for her at the present time.

Isabel stirred in his arms, snuggling even closer to his heat, and Stands Alone felt his body automatically responding to her nearness. That much hadn't surprised him, he thought wryly. He'd always known she would grow up to be a desirable woman. Even in her childhood, the promise of great beauty had been there. At least there was no doubt in his mind of his feelings in that area. Despite her bad temper, her infuriating stubbornness, her insults, he wanted her. Badly. There was no denying that. Which was a good thing, he decided with typical Indian practicality. Regardless of what his feelings for Isabel might, or might not be, regardless of what he might, or might not want, she was destined to be his wife, his only wife, if his father intended to keep their end of the agreement to its fullest. He'd hate to spend the rest of his life sharing his pallet with a woman he found repugnant.

Passion, Stands Alone mused. Yes, it was as he had said, a beginning. Hopefully, something more could grow from it. Maybe his dream wasn't dead after all. With that uplifting thought in mind, he, too, drifted off to sleep.

Seven

The next day, Isabel stubbornly clung to her vow to refuse to eat, but unlike the day before, her mourning didn't keep her from noticing her surroundings. She was a person too full of life to submerge herself in a morass of deep grieving for a long period of time.

Isabel and Stands Alone left the short piñons and junipers behind and traveled through a forest of yellow pine where the grass grew thick and lush, a mute testimony to the greater rainfall. Then they dropped into a canyon where elk and deer grazed on the leaves of large aspen trees. As they climbed higher and higher, sometimes up steep, terrifying rocky slopes that gave them a panoramic view of sweeping lands, leaping waterfalls, and deep river canyons, the vegetation changed. Here towering, 200-foot ponderosa pines grew among the grassy stands on the south side of the mountains, and red-barked Douglas fir with their drooping limbs grew on the northern, both magnificent species that Isabel had never seen. Nor had she ever seen so much wildlife. The area abounded with mule deer, elk, moose, badgers, beavers, rabbits and, high above her on the jagged peaks, mountain goats and bighorn sheep that sometimes took death-defying leaps across deep chasms.

Isabel was so enthralled with the beauty all around

her, she didn't utter a word, until they entered a small mountain meadow blanketed with a flock of thick-billed, green and red parrots making the most ungodly screeches and squawks. She watched as they took to the air, long wings flapping loudly and the flock momentarily blotting out the sun, then asked Stands Alone in amazement, "What are those birds? I've never seen them before."

"I don't know their name. They fly here at this time of the year, then go back south in the fall. Sometimes their flocks are so noisy you can hear them from long distances away, just as you can hear the rams butt horns during mating season."

Isabel could well believe the latter. The rams' horns were huge, in some instances almost dragging the animal's head to the ground. She looked around at the lovely meadow, then commented somewhat begrudgingly, "I can see why you make your home up here. I had no idea the mountains were so beautiful."

Stands Alone glanced around appreciatively before he answered, "Not all of the mountains in New Mexico are this beautiful, nor are those where my people originally came from. I have been told they were almost barren, rocky and forbidding. My people almost starved to death there."

"Then you haven't always lived here?" Isabel asked in surprise.

"No, it wasn't until we attained the horse from your people that the *Nema* moved away from that bleak place. Most of my people moved to the plains, where they could be closer to the buffalo, but my band chose to stay in these mountains and travel to the plains when we have need of the buffalo. With so much game around, that does not happen but once a year or so, usually in the fall when the buffalo are fat from their summer grazing."

"Then these mountains were uninhabited until your people same along?

"No, the people you call Apaches lived here. We chased them away, both here and from the plains to the east and south of here. Now it is all *Nema* territory."

Comancheria, her people called it, Isabel thought. It was an immense stretch of land from the Canadian River in the north, almost to the Spanish settlement of San Antonio de Bexar in Texas in the south, and no telling how far eastward. It seemed unbelievable that the Comanches had gained all that territory in such a short period of time. Why, it hadn't even been seventy-five years since Don Juan de Onate had set out to colonize New Mexico, bringing the horse with him. And her people considered themselves such conquerors. If the Spanish had been anywhere near as successful in overcoming the original inhabitants and establishing settlements in this isolated land as these savages— Shocked, Isabel tore herself from her traitorous thoughts, then for the first time became aware of how close she was sitting to Stands Alone. Preoccupied with the scenery, she had settled against him so that the hard muscles of his chest were pressed against her back and his loins pressed against her buttocks. Horrified, she sat up stiffly, putting distance between them.

Stands Alone pulled her back, saying, so close to her ear that his breath fanned her cheek, "No, stay where you were. I liked it better."

Isabel pulled at his arm, to no avail, and answered, "Well, I didn't!"

"No, stay," Stands Alone repeated. "I think it is an excellent opportunity for you to get used to the feel of my body. That way, it will not seem so strange to you when we are man and wife."

At that moment, Isabel was more worried about how her body was feeling than Stands Alone's. Everywhere their bodies touched seemed to be burning, and a warm coil had formed in the pit of her stomach. It was suddenly difficult to breathe. Almost frantic to get away from him, she clawed at his arm, saying, "Let me go! Put me down this instant!"

Isabel hadn't really expected Stands Alone to respond to her demand, and certainly not with such swiftness. With a quickness that stunned her, he brought the horse to an abrupt halt, whipped her from his saddle, and set her on her feet. Then he was standing beside her, holding out his arm to show her the new scratches she had inflicted upon him and saying, "I warned you what would happen if you attacked me again. Do you want your hands tied?"

"No, but I told you to let me go. I find your touch . . ." Every fiber in Isabel's body screamed *exciting*, but she forced out ". . . repulsive."

Stands Alone's dark eyes narrowed. "I think you lie. I think you liked it. You snuggled against me."

"Not intentionally. I was distracted."

"I still think you lie. I think you are as physically attracted to me as I am to you."

Isabel was acutely aware of every bulging muscle, every hard plane on his magnificent body. His heat seemed to surround her, and for the first time she was conscious of his scent, an utterly masculine scent that made her feel weak-kneed and lightheaded. God help her, she thought bleakly. It was true. She *was* attracted to him, had been from the moment she had laid eyes on him in the square at Santa Fe. But she couldn't let herself succumb to his utter maleness, couldn't let herself surrender to her own body's urgings. He was her sworn enemy. "No!" she muttered weakly. "That's not true."

"Liar."

The word had been spoken so softly, it sounded almost like a caress to Isabel's ears. Then she was in Stands Alone's arms, and he was kissing her, at first with a skilled seductiveness that made her weak with yearning, and then with a passion that set her blood on fire. Forgetting everything, she wrapped her arms around his strong neck and pressed herself against him, glorying in the feel of his hard body against hers and reveling in his fiery kiss. When his hand caressed her breast, then gently massaged it, she was powerless to resist. The tingling of that soft flesh only added to her excitement. She shivered with pleasure, then moaned when his thumb found her nipple and teased it to a hard bud. A shot of pure fire seemed to pierce her loins, leaving her burning there. Hoping to assuage that terrible fire, she unwittingly pressed herself even closer to him.

Then she felt the long, hard proof of his arousal pressing against her thigh, seemingly scorching her with its pulsating heat right through their clothing. Shocked at how far things had progressed with just a kiss and fearing he meant to have her then and there, she managed to push herself away from him. Seeing his black eyes were blazing with the heat of his desire only seemed to confirm her suspicions. "You promised! You lied to me!"

Stands Alone's senses were still spinning. "I have never lied to you. What are you talking about?"

"You promised you wouldn't force yourself on me until we were married."

"And I won't."

"Do you think I'm a fool?" Isabel asked angrily. "Don't you think I know what *that* means!"

Stands Alone saw Isabel's quick glance at his tented breechcloth. "It means my body is ready for love, if I so desire. It does not mean I have to do it. I gave you my word. I will not possess you until we are man and wife."

That will never happen, Isabel vowed. Somehow, she'd escape him before he forced her to become his wife. Then she remembered how she had melted under his fiery kiss, how he had caressed her breast. A shiver ran through her at the memory of the pleasure both had invoked. Hating herself for her response as much as him, she said, "I don't want you to kiss me again, either, or touch me so . . . shamelessly."

"No! I will not promise you that. I will kiss and touch you anytime and . . ." He paused to give his words emphasis. ". . . any place I wish."

As his hot gaze moved over her body, Isabel felt as if his eyes were stripping her of her clothing. "That's forcing yourself on me, too!"

"No, it is different," he answered in a husky voice.

Before Isabel realized his intent, he had taken her back in his arms and was nibbling at her earlobe. She steeled herself against the shiver of delight that ran through her, then as he dropped soft kisses over her jawline, moving closer and closer to her mouth, Isabel felt panic-stricken. She struggled, but his embrace was like a steel vise. "Then what do you call this, if not forcing me?"

"Persuasion. You are like a wild horse, frightened of being touched, fighting my possession. I will accustom you to myself as I do them, to my touch, to my smell, to my company, so you will come to hunger for my attentions. Then, when the ultimate act occurs, I will not have to force you. Your body will welcome mine. You will glory in my riding you."

It was Stands Alone's arrogance as much as his words that infuriated Isabel. "Never! I'll never submit willingly!"

Stands Alone's eyes flashed. Then he released her and stepped away, saying calmly, "We shall see."

Stands Alone picked Isabel up by her waist and tossed her on the Indian saddle. Then he mounted behind her. As they rode away, Isabel scooted as far forward on the saddle as she could, but it did her little good. Although he made no move to touch her or close the distance, she was so terribly aware of his nearness, his heat, his intoxicating scent that she was miserable the rest of the day and welcomed their making camp that evening.

But Isabel soon found herself being tormented by a different source, the smell of meat roasting over the fire. Her stomach rumbled loudly and her mouth watered. When Stands Alone set a piece of meat on a rock beside her, she said spitefully, "Take it away! I told you I wasn't going to eat."

"No, I will give you no opportunity to claim I denied you food. It is there if you want it."

It took all of Isabel's concentration to ignore the meat. The painful pangs of hunger that came later couldn't be ignored. When Stands Alone left the camp to attend to a call of nature, she glanced at the meat. What resistance she had left crumbled. She'd eat it and tell him she had thrown it away, she decided.

Isabel's ruse didn't work. Stands Alone returned to camp while she was in the process of gobbling down the meat. Seeing him watching her, Isabel quickly fabricated, "I decided I needed to keep up my strength to fight you off."

Stands Alone was glad to see Isabel eating. He had begun to worry, for fear she would make herself ill with her foolish stubbornness. But he was wise enough not to tell her that, or further goad her. Instead, he answered, "A wise decision. There is more by the fire, if you want it."

While Stands Alone was attending his horse, Isabel ate a second piece of meat, hating herself for being so weak, then promising herself she *would* fight him, fight him tooth and nail the next time he touched her. That time came soon enough, for as soon as he lay down beside her a little later, Stands Alone tried to take her in his arms. Isabel came alive, stunning him with her strength as she kicked, twisted, and clawed, muttering insults and curses all the while. Finally, Stands Alone subdued her, pinning her to the ground with the weight of his lower body and holding both her arms above her head with one powerful hand about both wrists.

Isabel bucked. "Get off me! You're crushing me."

"No!" Stands Alone answered firmly. "You brought this on yourself. I had only meant to give you warmth, but now I think it is time to do some taming." His free hand slid down her body and back up with tantalizing purpose. Isabel squirmed, to no avail.

Then, to Isabel's horror, Stands Alone yanked her shirtwaist free from her skirt and pushed it up. He looked down at her shift in surprise, for he had never seen the underwear worn by hidalgo women. His sexual encounters with Spanish women had been with commoners, who, like Comanche woman, wore no underclothes. Then he asked, "What is this foolish garment?"

"None of your business! What do you think you're doing?" Isabel shrieked.

"Trying to see what will be mine when we are man

102 off

and wife," Stands Alone answered, catching hold of the flimsy fabric of the undergarment and yanking.

As Stands Alone stared down at her bared breasts, Isabel flushed in pure mortification. "Stop it. Cover me, please. You're shaming me."

Stands Alone's eyes rose and met hers, and Isabel was stunned by the blazing desire she saw in those dark orbs. "Why should you feel ashamed?" he asked thickly. "They are beautiful. The most beautiful I have ever seen." He looked back down. "So proud, so full, as white as the milk they will someday hold. And these," he muttered, his fingers brushing across one nipple, "dusky pink and begging to be kissed."

Isabel gasped as the nipple hardened and strained eagerly for his touch. Her flush deepened. Stands Alone once again lifted his head, saying softly, "But it will have to wait its turn. There is something else I have been wanting to do."

As he lowered his head, Isabel jerked hers away to avoid his lips. Stands Alone cupped her chin and firmly turned her head. His warm lips brushed back and forth across hers with a feather lightness until her lips were aching. When his tongue flicked out at the ultra-sensitive corner of her mouth, an incredibly sensuous act that was rich with promise, an involuntary moan escaped Isabel's lips. He tormented her for what seemed an eternity, his lips and tongue playing at her lips, teasing and tantalizing, until finally his tongue slipped into her mouth, sliding the length of hers, then tasting her sweetness, savoring it, stealing her nectar little by little. As he dropped tender kisses over her forehead, the bridge of her nose, down her cheeks, then the long column of her slender neck, Isabel felt as if she were floating on a warm rosy cloud. Even when his lips brushed across her collarbone, then pressed against the tops of her breasts, she couldn't rouse herself to stop him. In a daze, she felt his hand move from her chin to cup one breast and lift it.

As his warm mouth closed over one nipple, suckling her, Isabel suddenly became alert. Shocked at what he was doing, she cried out, "No, stop!"

Stands Alone raised his head. "You don't mean that."

"Yes, I do. It's . . . it's indecent!"

"Indecent? Why?"

"Because it's against nature. It's what babies do."

"No, first men, then babies. Everything in its order." Stands Alone smiled. "But I would not expect you to know much about lovemaking. You are a maiden. It is your husband's duty to teach you, and this I do gladly."

As Stands Alone lowered his head and recaptured the nipple, Isabel made a valiant effort to resist, valiant, but brief, for Stands Alone's only response to her frantic squirming was to catch the other nipple between his thumb and finger and tease it to a hard aching point, bringing a rush of scalding warmth to her loins. Soon she was awash in pleasure, the hot yearning between her legs growing until it was almost painful.

As Stands Alone's mouth left her breast, Isabel moaned in protest, not wanting the delightful sensations to end. She gasped at the feeling of his cold earring trailing across her chest, then sighed when he took the other throbbing nipple in his mouth, each hot swirl of his tongue, each powerful tug of his lips sending thrills racing through her. When he released her wrists, freeing her, she lifted her hands, not to push him away, but to hold the back of his head, arching her back to give him better access, silently and eloquently begging for more.

Stands Alone would have feasted at Isabel's luscious breasts much longer had he not feared continuing would make it impossible for him to turn back. He had promised her he would not fully possess her until they were married, and every fiber of him was beginning to clamor for release. Reluctantly, he lifted his head and jerked her shirtwaist down.

Dazed at the abrupt ending, Isabel looked up at him with questioning eyes.

"That is enough for tonight. Tomorrow, I shall teach you more," he told her. As Stands Alone slid to Isabel's side, he turned her backside to him, then wrapped his arms around her. "Now, we will go to sleep. Do not fight me any longer. I will only warm and protect you."

The world still spinning about her from Stands Alone's exciting lovemaking, Isabel found it hard to believe his words. Surely he couldn't arouse her, then leave her dangling like that, she thought. Besides, weren't men supposed to be more passionate than women? And she knew he was aroused, also. She could feel the hot proof of that pressing against her buttocks. But to Isabel's dismay—and later, to her relief when she finally regained her senses—she discovered Stands Alone meant what he said. Within minutes, he had dropped off to sleep, his slow, regular breathing fluttering a loose tendril of hair at her temple.

Again, it was a long time before Isabel slept, this time not from the lack of heat to warm her, but from too much.

Eight

The next day, Isabel tried very hard to ignore Stands Alone, but she was not in the least successful. It was bad enough that she was aware of each brush of their bodies as they rode, of his arm thrown lightly around her waist, of his breath on the nape of her neck, but his very presence was almost smothering. It seemed as if he were surrounding her with his powerful masculinity, making her acutely conscious that he was male and she was female. She deliberately recalled the horrifying details of her father's death, hoping to summon a hatred for the warrior that would keep her unwanted attraction at bay. But even hatred wouldn't come to her defense, not the intense loathing she strived for. The best she could summon was anger, and she was hard pressed to decide just who that anger was aimed at, Stands Alone, Yellow Sky, or herself, for being so miserably weak.

When they made camp that evening beside a gurgling mountain brook, Isabel was exhausted from her inner struggle and not in the best of moods. After eating, she walked to the stream to wash her hands in its cold, clear water, then sat on a flat rock beside it. For the hundredth time that day, she brushed at a dangling tendril of hair hanging on her neck. Then, deciding she couldn't stand the loose hairs any longer, she undid the

bun at the back of her head and began trying to comb
the tangles from her long, thick mane with her fingers.
Jerking painfully on a particularly stubborn tangle, she
wished she hadn't lost her tortoise-shell comb in her
struggle with Stands Alone when he'd captured her. Although it was meant primarily as a hair decoration, she
could have used it.

Taking note of her almost futile efforts, Stands Alone
asked from where he was tending his horse, "Would
you like to borrow my hairbrush?"

Isabel whirled around and asked in surprise, "You
have a brush with you?"

"Yes, of course. A warrior would never travel without
his hairbrush. I have it in here." Stands Alone bent and
picked up a small leather bag.

Isabel had seen the bag hanging from Stands Alone's
flat Indian saddle. She knew it held his flint and steel,
but had no idea what else was in it, except it couldn't
be anything too large. "It's been in there all along?"

"Yes, except when I've used it every morning."

Isabel had no idea what Stands Alone had done in
the mornings before she had awakened, other than the
first morning when she had risen to find he had washed
the paint from his face. Knowing he had been grooming
his hair every day, while hers had slowly become more
unkempt and tangled only added fuel to her irritability.
"Why didn't you offer it to me?" she snapped.

Stands Alone shrugged. "You didn't ask."

"How could I have asked, if I didn't know it existed!"

"There is no reason to get so angry. Do you wish to
borrow it?"

"Yes!"

Stands Alone frowned at Isabel's sharp answer. Yes,
the sweet child was gone, he thought, and in her place
was a waspish woman. In view of her ugly mood, he was

tempted to withdraw his offer. A warrior didn't loan his brush to just anyone. It was a prized and very personal possession. She should feel honored. But despite his thoughts, he walked to her, withdrew the brush, and handed it to her.

Isabel thought the crude brush looked like some medieval torture instrument. Why, she'd likely scalp herself. "What are the bristles made from?"

"Porcupine quills."

Gingerly, Isabel drew the brush through her hair and discovered it wasn't nearly as rough on her scalp as she had feared. As she sat and brushed the long hair hanging about her shoulders like a lustrous black cape, Stands Alone sank to his haunches across from her and watched intently. Suddenly her grooming her hair in his presence seemed an intimate act. She stopped midstroke, glared at him, and asked, "Don't you have something better to do?"

"No. I'm enjoying watching you. Your hair is really quite beautiful. You'll be the envy of every man in my band."

"You mean every woman," Isabel corrected him.

"No, every man. With my people, it is the male who lets his hair grow long and takes such pride in it. That is why we never travel without our brush. The longer and thicker the braids, the prouder the man is. Why I've even known warriors to beg widows to give them the hair they've cut off in mourning, so the men can make their braids appear thicker."

It occurred to Isabel that she had never seen a Comanche woman. The warriors had always come to Rosario alone. She had just assumed the Comanche women wore their hair like the Pueblo woman did, long and loose. "How do your woman wear their hair?"

"Cropped short, and I'm afraid they pay very little

attention to it. They're much more vain about their painting."

"What do they paint?"

"The parts in their hair, the inside of their ears, their faces, sometimes other parts of their bodies," he answered, his eyes dropping to her breasts. "But you will not need to do that. Yours couldn't be more beautiful."

A warm flush stole over Isabel, a heat that had nothing to do with embarrassment, but rather the memory of Stands Alone's exciting ministrations to her breasts the night before. She felt her nipples hardening in anticipation. Horrified for fear Stands Alone might notice, she quickly turned away on the pretext of looking for her long wooden pins.

As she started to roll her hair into a ball, Stands Alone caught her hand and said, "No, leave it down."

"It's too hot."

"Not at night." He rose to his feet in one smooth movement, then caught her arms and brought her to her feet. Running his hands the length of her hair, he muttered, "It is so silky and soft." Then taking a handful in one hand, he commented, "And so thick."

His touch and the husky timbre of his voice made Isabel tremble. Fearing he might be on the verge of making further overtures, she quickly mumbled, "Thank you," then turned and hurried away.

Isabel sat down on the other side of the fire and, once again, attempted to put up her hair. But her hands were shaking so badly she couldn't manage it. Deciding to leave it down for the night, she lay down. Shortly thereafter, she was joined by Stands Alone. Knowing it would do her no good to demand he sleep elsewhere, she rolled to her side, putting her back to him, acutely aware of his removing the medicine bag from around his neck and carefully placing it beside his bow and quiver of arrows. She waited expectantly as he stretched out behind her, then jumped when he smoothed the hair lying over her shoulder.

Stands Alone picked up a long strand and held it to his nose, breathing deeply of its essence before he dropped it and whispered in her ear, "You will not cut it, like *Nema* women do. In the daytime, you can wear it up, for coolness, but at night, in our tepee, you will wear it loose, like this, so we can wrap ourselves in it while we make love."

A shiver ran through Isabel at Stands Alone's provocative words. Remembering what he had told her the night before, that he would teach her more about making love tonight, she held her breath, her heart racing in anticipation. When he softly kissed her neck through her hair, she thought for sure it was the prelude to yet more unknown delights. She waited, and waited, and waited, all in vain. When she finally realized he had gone to sleep, tears of frustration stung her eyes. She had finally worked up the emotion that had eluded her earlier; she hated Stands Alone for disappointing her, and hated herself for being so utterly shameless.

Isabel was awakened the next morning by the sound of splashing. Groggily, she rose on one elbow and looked about her. Seeing Stands Alone standing nude in the stream, she was suddenly very much awake. Even though he stood with his back to her, the sight of his broad back, tight buttocks, and long muscular legs was electrifying. She had never seen so much exposed male flesh, much less so magnificent. She gasped, then seeing him turn at the sound, jerked her head around.

"You awakened early this morning," Stands Alone commented.

"What do you think you're doing, standing there stark naked?"

Stands Alone frowned at the almost hysterical pitch of Isabel's voice. "I'm bathing."

"In the wide open?"

"That's where the streams usually are," Stands Alone replied dryly. "Where do you bathe?"

"My people bathe inside, in tubs of water."

"That is not completely true. I have seen your people bathing in rivers."

"The poor, those who cannot afford tubs, but not my class. We have more modesty."

"And you consider it immodest to bathe outside?"

"I certainly do. It's indecent."

"Why?"

"Because you're naked, that's why! Anyone could see you."

"There is no one else here but us," Stands Alone pointed out, then asked, "Is that why you are so upset? Because I am naked before you, and we are not yet man and wife? I did not mean to offend you. I only meant to stay close, to protect you in case a wild animal came for water. Besides, I did not expect you to wake up so early. You slept through my other baths."

"Are you saying you bathed every day?" Isabel asked in horror.

"Yes."

"That's unhealthy."

"I doubt that. My people all bathe frequently, daily if possible, and we are the healthiest people on earth." He paused, then asked, "How often do you bathe?"

"Once or twice a month." From the corner of her eye she saw the shocked expression on his face. Mortified that he might think she was dirty, she quickly added, "Of course, I freshen up each morning with a cloth and a pan of water."

"And for this you are naked?"

"No, I'm in my shift."

"That silly garment I discovered the other night? Why do you wear that?"

"Because it's indecent to walk around naked! That's what I've been trying to tell you."

"Even indoors?"

"Yes."

"I think your people make too much of nakedness." With that, Stands Alone turned back around, picked up a handful of sand, and began scouring himself.

Glancing in his direction from the corner of her eye and seeing him, Isabel asked in dismay, "Aren't you going to clothe yourself?"

"Not until I finish my bath. You've already seen me."

"No, I haven't. Not really. I turned my back."

"Then keep your back turned."

Isabel did just that as Stands Alone finished his bath, sitting rigidly with her back to him to show him her disapproval of his outrageous behavior. But she couldn't resist sneaking glances and marveled that he didn't rub his skin off with all the scouring he did. But when he rinsed off, she had to admit he certainly hadn't done any damage. His smooth copper skin had taken on a rosy glow. Then seeing him turn to walk from the stream, she quickly jerked her eyes away, mortified that he might have caught her spying on him.

Isabel heard the soft rustle of clothing, then Stands Alone saying, "You can turn around now. I'm covered."

Isabel turned and gasped. Wearing just his breech-cloth, Stands Alone was still revealing too much bare skin for her comfort. She could see his powerful legs and lean hips, and for some unknown reason, the bare skin around the covering over his privates just seemed to emphasize that very masculine part of him. "What about your . . . your—"

"Leggings?" Stands Alone furnished for her. "I won't need them today, since we won't be doing that much traveling through the woods. That's their purpose, you know, to protect the legs from scratches."

As he turned and walked away, Isabel realized the leggings had covered a good deal of his buttocks also, and the sight of those powerful twin muscles did strange things to her. It was a decided relief when he sat down and picked up the small bag with his brush in it.

"Perhaps you like to . . . What did you call it? Freshen up?" Stands Alone said to her.

Did he think she looked dirty, Isabel wondered. She glanced down and saw her ragged dress, splattered with mud from where they had splashed across shallow streams, then became acutely conscious of the desert grime coating her legs. Knowing what he seemed to be insinuating was true was mortifying, particularly when the savage was so glowingly clean himself. "Yes, I would. I think I'll walk upstream a bit and do that."

"Why leave our camp? If you're going to wear that silly garment, I won't be able to see anything, and that seems to be what bothers you. Besides, I have already seen the top half of you."

Isabel flushed hotly at his reminder. But what was worrying her was the shortness of the shift. It revealed too much of her legs, something he hadn't seen. "I'd still prefer more privacy."

Stands Alone shook his head in disgust, then answered, "Then go ahead, but only around the bend. Many animals water at this time of the day. Most are not dangerous, but a few could be."

Isabel wasn't in the least deterred by his warning. She

would rather face a wild animal than risk exciting the man who aroused such perplexing feelings within her, dangerous feelings against which she seemed to have no resistance. She hurried around the bend, then shooting a quick backward glance to make sure Stands Alone couldn't see, kicked off her slippers and stripped to her shift. She glanced down and saw the ripped garment no longer covered her breasts. Cursing the Comanche for his careless destruction, she swiftly bathed her face, neck, arms and legs, then since she was exposed anyway, splashed some water on her chest. Donning her clothing, she made the return trip, feeling damp, but much refreshed.

When she walked into the clearing where Stands Alone was saddling his horse, she came to an abrupt halt. Besides his moccasins, he had donned silver arm bands and several claw necklaces, and wrapped the ends of his braids with beaver fur from which a dozen black-tipped eagle feathers dangled. But what startled Isabel the most were the red and yellow geometric paintings on his chest and the streak of yellow paint in the part of his hair.

"Is something wrong?" Stands Alone asked her when she just stared at him.

"Why are you dressed like that?"

"Because this morning we will reach my village. I am returning victorious, with my bride-to-be. It's expected for me to look festive. This is the best I can do, under the circumstances." The last was said with a twinge of bitterness, as Stands Alone remembered the beautiful wedding garments his mother had laboriously made for him. Of the softest doeskin, his breechcloth, leggings, and moccasins had been elaborately beaded, and each quill on his breastplate had been dyed, then painstakingly arranged in a beautiful thunderbird pattern. He had worn his finery the day he and his father had gone to pick up Isabel. Even his horse and the one he had taken for Isabel to ride had been handsomely arrayed, colorfully painted, with feathers and bits of metal braided into their manes and tails. He had returned home empty-handed and heart-broken. He had never seen the clothing again. He assumed his mother had burned it.

Isabel had no idea what was going on in Stands Alone's mind. His announcement came as a shock to her. She had thought to have more time to plan an escape. Suddenly, she seemed to have come face-to-face with her future, a future being forced on her and not at all to her liking. She was in a daze as Stands Alone placed a piece of cold meat left over from the evening before in her hand, saying she could eat on their way, then tossed her on the back of his horse.

As they rode though the woods, Isabel wondered how long she had before the ceremony would take place. She couldn't summon the courage to come right out and ask Stands Alone. He might become suspicious, or worse yet, think she was anxious to become his wife, arrogant savage that he was. She did know one thing, though. Any attempt to escape would be folly as long as he was near. She'd have to wait for him to leave her alone, then for the right opportunity.

A nagging little voice at the back of her mind asked, and where will you go if you do manage to escape? You could never find your way back to Santa Fe. But Isabel chose to ignore the voice. She simply wasn't ready to accept her fate.

Nine

When Isabel first saw the mountain valley where Stands Alone's village lay, it took her breath away. Nestled between two majestic peaks, it stretched a good ten miles in length and several across and was dotted with stands of towering ponderosa pine and covered with a lush, knee-high grass waving in the breeze. At the upper end of the valley, stretching for miles on the banks of the small river that ran through it, were the tepees, scores and scores of them, most tan colored with blackened tops, a few painted red. With the smoke from the tepee fires curling lazily into the air and the wind scuttling fat, fluffy clouds across an azure sky high above them, it was the most lovely, peaceful scene Isabel had ever seen.

It wasn't until they were descending the heights surrounding the valley, winding lower and lower over a rocky, treacherous trail, that Isabel finally got a good look at the southern end of the valley. Once again, she sucked in her breath. Her eyes widened in disbelief. There, grazing on the lush grass, were thousands and thousands of horses, seemingly of every color: roans, bays, blacks, duns, greys, whites, but mostly the painted horse that her people called pintos. Isabel had never dreamed there were that many horses in the entire world. She remembered her father telling her the Co-manches had attained most of their horses in the twelve years Spain had vacated New Mexico after the disastrous Pueblo revolt. It had been a simple matter of helping themselves to the animals, since the settled Pueblo farmers had never had any use for the horse. But there couldn't have been even a thousand of the steeds in the entire territory at that time, and Stands Alone's band weren't the only Comanches that had seized that golden opportunity. Isabel had known the little Spanish horses were a hardy breed—supposedly because of the culling that had taken place on the long sea voyage from Spain—but apparently they were also very prolific.

Stands Alone was aware of Isabel's astonishment. "Our band has one of the largest and most impressive herds among the *Nema,*" he informed her proudly. "Not only does every warrior own at least one horse, but every warrior's wife. You will not see some poor woman carrying her household possessions on her back in this band."

"How many horses do you own?"

"Over three hundred."

"Three hundred horses?" Isabel gasped in astonishment.

"That is not so many for one man. My brother owns five hundred, and my father over a thousand. But I am not as interested in number, like the others, as quality. I breed racing horses, animals much more valuable as trading goods than the average animal. That is what I was doing in Santa Fe. The commandant at the fort there had expressed interest in one of my racers."

Isabel thought it sounded so typically New Mexican. The Indians stole horses and took captives from the Spanish, and the Spanish, even those high in govern-ment, bought them back. Of course, they had been commanded by their king to ransom the captives, even Indian captives, who the Spanish in turn enslaved, but the livestock was a different matter. In that case, turning a blind eye to how the animals had been attained was a matter of greed, for the Indians asked much less in trade than the original owner would have.

Then Isabel's mind took a different turn. She remembered Stands Alone as a child racing his mount over the hills above Rosario. It had been a beautiful sight, boy and animal blending into one swift, fluid, powerful entity. At that time, he had done it for just enjoyment. Now, he did it solely for gain. Or did he? She turned in the saddle and looked up at him. "Do you ever just race them?"

"I prefer that to trading them." An appealing grin spread over his handsome face. "Then I get to keep the horse, as well as the goods wagered."

The grin was the first sign she had seen of the boy she had become so fond of and brought a different type of warmth to Isabel, a warmth that seemed much more threatening than the physical attraction she was fighting tooth and nail. Disconcerted, she turned back in the saddle and answered rather sharply, "No, I meant just for the enjoyment of it."

"Only here in my village." Stands Alone shrugged. "To be honest, it's the only way anyone here will race me. My horses always win. But when I race the New Mexicans or the other Indian bands, there's always heavy wagering, not only by myself, but by everyone in my band. My horses have improved everyone's lot."

"Are you saying you never lose?" Isabel asked with obvious skepticism.

"Very rarely."

By that time they had finished their descent into the valley and were riding into the village. Curious Comanches crowded around them, all seemingly chattering in their native tongue at once, many rudely pointing at Isabel. The lanky camp dogs barking furiously—for they knew Isabel was a stranger—only added to the din and confusion.

Feeling very self-conscious, Isabel glanced nervously around her, noting that the young boys were totally naked and the girls wore only breechcloths, as did almost every man in the camp, young or old. Only the women were fully covered in their beaded and fringed dresses. Now she knew why Stands Alone had said the Spanish made too much of nakedness. A good three-quarters of the village were bare or half-naked.

As they passed a cluster of women, Isabel saw their black hair was short and rather shaggy looking, the part painted red. With the insides of their ears painted the same color and the bright reddish-orange circles on each cheek and yellow stripes on their faces, they looked more ridiculous than beautiful to Isabel. Then she noticed the color of one of the women's eyes. It was a decided green, and her skin coloring was much lighter than the other women's. "That woman is Spanish, not Indian," she blurted in outrage.

"Yes, we have several of your people among us, all adults. But they have been assimilated into the tribe, and are *Nema* now, just as you shall be. The only difference is they came to our village as children and slaves, and you as an adult and my wife. You are more fortunate than they. You will not have to earn your place in the band."

"In case you have forgotten my feelings on the matter, I don't consider myself at all fortunate," Isabel answered bitterly, then added, "I'd rather be a slave than your wife."

If Isabel had thought to bait Stands Alone, she wasn't

successful. "You know nothing of what you speak about," he answered calmly. "A slave's life is very hard. That is why we keep only the most hardy, and trade the weaklings."

"Or kill them," Isabel answered angrily.

Stands Alone frowned. Why was she dragging him into this pointless argument, he wondered. He couldn't change the nature of his people, any more than she could hers, and the Spanish were not renowned for their kindness to their enemies. "We are kinder to our captives than your people are to their Indian slaves. We adopt the children, something your people would never think of, and for the better part, marry the women, rather than use them just for labor or our sexual enjoyment. As for adult men, we do not take them captive. We have learned they do not adapt to our way of life. They are killed on the spot, and I would rather be dead than slowly tortured to death in one of your heinous mines, starving, choking on dust, my wrists and ankles bleeding and festered from the chains, laboring until I drop, then being beaten until my back is raw and my bones are laid bare, all the while never seeing the light of day again. A quick death, no matter how violent, is more merciful."

Isabel was horrified. She had no idea of a slave's life in one of the mines. "Are you talking about the turquoise mines in the Jeméz Mountains?"

"No, I have heard they are not quite as bad," Stands Alone admitted. "I am talking about the silver mines, near Chihuahua."

"How do you know what goes on down there?"

"Through the Indian grapevine. Every now and then, but rarely, someone escapes. It does not matter if he is a *Nema,* or a Ute, or an Apache, or some other tribe, the news of those hellholes' existence has spread like wildfire through all the tribes and bands. In all cases, the escaped man was but a shell, a walking skeleton, permanently blinded, horribly scarred, often crippled." Stands Alone paused, then said emphatically, "No, I would rather be dead, than condemned to that."

Stands Alone brought his horse to a halt in front of a tepee in the center of the village. "This is my father's lodge."

To Isabel it looked like any other tepee in the camp. The only difference she could see was the standard before it, its eagle feathers fluttering in the breeze. Stands Alone jumped to the ground, then swung Isabel down, saying, "We are expected."

"How do you know that?"

"The flap is open."

He guided her to the tepee, bent to enter, then pulled her in behind him. Coming from the bright light into the dim interior, Isabel's eyes took a moment to adjust. She found herself facing Yellow Sky. Her response was immediate. She longed to curse him, to throw herself at him and claw his flesh, but in his home surroundings, the chief looked much more imposing and dangerous than he ever had before. Judiciously, she fought down the urge to do him harm. Instead she just glared at him.

Yellow Sky ignored Isabel's hot look. He had done what he had to do, what his powerful Indian honor had demanded of him. The girl's personal opinion of him was regretful, but irrelevant. He greeted his son by clasping his upper arms. "What took you so long?" he asked in Comanche. "We returned yesterday."

Stands Alone clasped his father's upper arms and answered in the same tongue. "I took my time, in hopes Isabel would become more reconciled to our marriage."

"And has she?"

"I'm afraid not."

"It doesn't matter. She'll adjust." Then switching to Spanish, Yellow Sky said, "Sit down."

Yellow Sky turned and walked to the pallet at the back of the tepee, and Stands Alone walked to the right. Isabel started to follow him, but Stands Alone turned and pushed her back, saying, "No, you sit over there, with the women."

Isabel glanced to the left, having not even noticed the three women sitting in the shadows. If the women had taken any note of her, they didn't show it. They were all staring straight ahead. She stepped over to them, sank on her knees, then sat back on her heels like they were doing.

While Stands Alone sat cross-legged beside another warrior, Yellow Sky sat on his pallet and leaned back on his willow back rest. "It was just as well you did not arrive until today," he told Stands Alone in Spanish. "That gave me time to discuss everything with the council. I told them I wished to consider this betrayal as a family matter, not tribal, and that I was satisfied with the revenge we had extracted. Of course, there were a few young hotheads who wanted to satisfy their blood lust and raid Rosario. As you know, it is the *Nema* way, that anyone who wants to lead a raid can—"

"Raid the village?" Isabel interjected. "You just said you were satisfied!"

Yellow Sky's dark eyes bore into her. "We are conducting a family council here. Women are allowed to observe, but do not speak unless spoken to. Since you are new to our ways, I will overlook your transgression this time. You did not allow me to finish. Your village has not been attacked, nor will it be. The elders talked the young warriors into respecting my wishes."

"The elders? I thought you were chief?" Isabel asked despite Yellow Sky's stern admonishment.

"I am the principal peace chief of this village, but all important decisions, such as making war, are made by the council, not me." Yellow Sky turned his attention back to Stands Alone and said, "By making this a family matter, I had hoped to make it easier for Isabel. It will be difficult enough for her to adapt to our ways without having undue resentment from the others."

Stands Alone knew Yellow Sky's words were more for Isabel's benefit than his and hoped she would take note of them and appreciate his father's efforts in her behalf in making the matter an insult to his personal honor, rather than his station. Stands Alone knew how much personal pride his father had and that he was risking ridicule by the others. Some would call him weak for being so generous. Others would call him foolish. Only the truly wise would realize it took a noble man to set his pride aside for another. He gave Isabel a pointed glance and answered, "Thank you, Father."

Yellow Sky nodded, then said, "Now, I think you should introduce your future bride to the others."

Stands Alone came to his feet and motioned to the warrior sitting next to him, saying to Isabel, "This is my brother, *Asenap.* Then realizing he had given her his name in his native tongue, Stands Alone, added, "Greyfoot."

Isabel leaned forward and peered at the man. He was a good ten years older than Stands Alone, and just as ruggedly built, except shorter and a little heavier. Then she recognized him as one of the men who had taken part in the murders of her father and Ramon, and her look hardened, her blue eyes shooting daggers.

Stands Alone drew Isabel's attention away from his

brother by saying, "And this is my mother, Beaver Woman."

A slender woman at the far end of the seated women came gracefully to her feet. Had Isabel been told to pick which of the three was Stands Alone's mother, she would have picked the woman next to Beaver Woman, for she looked much older and more matronly, until Beaver Woman came to her full height. Like her son, it was quite obvious she was taller than the others. Then Isabel noticed the look in the woman's black eyes. It was just as hard as the looks Isabel had given Yellow Sky and Greyfoot, and came as a shock to Isabel. When the woman nodded curtly in acknowledgment, Isabel was too stunned to even respond.

"And these are Greyfoot's wives, Corn Woman," Stands Alone continued, motioning to the older, stern-faced woman, "and *Tekwitchi*. Perhaps it would be better if you call her that. The name does not translate into Spanish well. It means skinny and wrinkled."

Isabel looked at the woman Stands Alone had called skinny and wrinkled, wondering why she was called such an unflattering name. Smooth skinned, chubby, and rather pretty, she was much younger than the other two women and seemed much friendlier as she gave Isabel a shy, but warm, smile, until the older woman next to her gave her a sharp nudge in the ribs with her elbow and the smile disappeared. Isabel agreed with Stands Alone. The Spanish translation did sound insulting.

Seeing her husband pull his pipe from his smoking bag and knowing it was time for the women to leave, Beaver Woman announced in Spanish so perfect it stunned Isabel, "We will go to Stands Alone's tepee now."

Dutifully, the other two women came to their feet and followed Beaver Woman to the door. When she came to Isabel, Stands Alone's mother stopped in front of her and said, "You will come with us."

A tingle of fear ran through Isabel. Were they going to do something unpleasant to her, she wondered. As much as she hated to look to Stands Alone for protection, she shot him an apprehensive look.

"Go with them," he told her. "We have men's business to discuss. I will come later."

Isabel was turned by Beaver Woman and shoved towards the door. Feeling she really had no recourse, Isabel ducked her head and stepped through the small, oval opening, quickly followed by the other three.

As soon as she stepped outdoors, Isabel saw a crowd of women had gathered around the tepee. They followed them through the camp as Beaver Woman led the way to Stands Alone's tepee, giggling and making remarks in Comanche that Isabel sensed were crude and aimed at her. She was actually relieved when they reached the tepee and Beaver Woman threw back the flap. Then, as she started to step into the hide lodging, she was jerked back and asked by the older woman, "Are you having your woman's flow?"

Isabel was shocked at the very personal question. Beaver Woman shook her arm and demanded, "Answer me! This is very important. If you are, you cannot enter Stands Alone's tepee. You will endanger his medicine."

"His medicine? What are you talking about?"

"The power his guardian spirit gave him. He keeps his medicine bundle in there, the things his guardian spirit gave him. It must be protected from grease and women's blood at all cost."

"I thought his medicine bag is that pouch he wears around his neck."

"No, it contains only a small part of his medicine. Are you flowing?"

"No, but why didn't that matter when I entered Yellow Sky's tepee?"

"My husband keeps his medicine in a separate tepee, both because he is chief and so many people come and go, and since Corn Woman and Tekwitchi come to our tepee when they are flowing. Their parents are dead, and they can no longer go there. It is where you will come, too, when your time is upon you," Beaver Woman answered, motioning for her to enter Stands Alone's tent.

When the four women were standing inside the tepee, Beaver Woman drew the flap shut, then turned and said to Isabel, "We will help you don your new clothes."

"I'll keep the ones I have on, thank you," Isabel replied stiffly.

"No, you will not," Beaver Woman persisted. "You will wear the clothing we brought for you." Then taking a more critical look at Isabel, she added, "After we have taken you to the river to bathe."

Why did everyone think she was dirty, Isabel wondered in dismay. Then glancing down at her clothing, she said, "Only my clothing is dirty. I won't need to wash up. I did that this morning."

"Still, she should bathe," Corn Woman commented, entering the conversation, and both Beaver Woman and Tekwitchi nodded in agreement, making Isabel sense there was some particular meaning in her words, but just what eluded her.

"We will take you to the river," Beaver Woman said.

"You don't seem to understand," Isabel replied irritably. "I don't want to bathe, and I don't want any new clothes. I'll stay just as I am."

"No, *you* do not understand," Beaver Woman told

her firmly. "You will bathe and don fresh clothing. We will take you to the river."

Isabel knew by the adamant expression on Beaver Woman's face that she was going to have to comply. But bathing in the wide open, with every woman in the camp watching, was something she couldn't accept. "I prefer to bathe here. If you'll just bring me a bucket of water and some soap."

"Like we bathe in the winter?" Corn Woman asked with a look of disgust. "You cannot get yourself really clean that way."

"I'm not used to bathing in the wide open, where others can see me. My people consider that immodest."

Beaver Woman considered modesty imperative for a maiden, and this maiden was to become her son's bride. For that reason, she relented. "We will do it your way." She turned to the other two and said, "Fetch water, while I help her disrobe."

"I don't need any help," Isabel objected.

"No, we will help you bathe and dress," Beaver Woman answered firmly. "It is our way."

Isabel wondered if this was a strange hospitality of some kind, assisting a stranger in her first bath and offering her clean clothing. In any case, she was going to have to obey. There were three of them, and one of her. If they put their minds to it, they could easily overpower her. Besides, if she put up too much resistance, they might decide to take her to the river after all, and that really would be humiliating, forced to strip and be bathed in front of God and everyone.

Isabel endured her bath, flushing with embarrassment the entire time, both at being naked in front of virtual strangers, and at their frank comments.

"She is slender, but her hips are wide enough," Corn Woman remarked, as she poured a hide bucket full of water over Isabel to wash off the Indian soap the Spanish girl had lathered herself with. "She should bear children well enough."

"She has nice breasts, with big nipples for babies to latch onto," Tekwitchi commented, then added with unconcealed awe, "And her skin is so white. The only thing I have ever seen so white is the cactus flower that blooms at night on the desert. What is it called?" she asked Beaver Woman.

"We have no name for it. The Spanish call it the queen of the night, because the flower is so large and fragrant."

"She needs a *Nema* name," Corn Woman said. "Maybe we should call her that."

Reina-de-la-noche? Isabel thought in disgust, then fed up with everything, cried out, "No!"

"Flower Woman, then," Tekwitchi suggested.

"I have a name! It's Isabel."

"That is a Spanish name," Corn Woman pointed out.

"I *am* Spanish, and I always will be!" Isabel retorted hotly.

The three women exchanged sharp glances; then Beaver Woman said to her daughters-in-law, "That is enough discussion about names. We will dress her now."

After Isabel was dried off with a piece of trading cloth, Beaver Woman slipped the short, poncho-like doeskin blouse over Isabel's head. Then the skirt was added, and the two laced together with leather thongs. A decorative doeskin peplum, richly beaded with the same pattern that ran down the sleeves, came next, its points dropping to Isabel's thighs. Soft, beaded moccasins, made of the same buff-colored doeskin, completed the ensemble.

After Isabel was dressed, Beaver Woman looked her over critically, then said, "Now, we will groom her hair."

Isabel glanced at the three women's cropped hair in horror, then said, "You won't cut it. Stands Alone doesn't want it cut."

"He told you that?" Beaver Woman asked in surprise.

"Yes."

"Maybe she is lying," Corn Woman suggested.

Isabel shot her a furious look. "I am not lying!"

Beaver Woman studied her quietly for a moment, then said. "I believe her. We will just brush it."

"I prefer to do it myself."

"No, we will do it today. It is our way."

Isabel was led to the pallet at the back of the tepee and told to sit. Then her long hair was taken down and brushed by Corn Woman. Noticing Tekwitchi pulling some paints from a skin bag, Isabel said, "I'll let you brush my hair, but I won't let you paint me." Seeing Beaver Woman start to open her mouth, she hastily added, "And don't tell me it's your way. I'm not Comanche. I'm Spanish. It's—" Isabel had started to say, *it's stupid and silly*, then thought better of it. She was astute enough to know not to insult these women, not when she was virtually their prisoner. "—It's not accepted. Among my people only the lowest women paint their faces."

"Lowest?" Beaver Woman questioned.

"Yes. Women who make a living by selling their bodies to satisfy men's lust."

There was no such thing as a whore in the Comanche culture, but unmarried women who were too free with their sexual favors were looked down on, and maidens were prized. Again, Beaver Woman bowed to Isabel's culture, saying to the other women, "We will not paint her if it will shame her, nor shall she paint herself, until she admits she is of The People. Otherwise she would shame Stands Alone by proclaiming she was a low woman."

Isabel longed to scream that she would never admit to being a Comanche, nor did she care if she shamed Stands Alone or not, but she held her tongue. For the time being, she'd go along with them, she decided, even if she didn't understand what was going on.

"Are you hungry?" Beaver Woman asked her.

"Yes, but I can wait until mealtime."

"That won't be necessary," Beaver Woman answered, "We always have a pot of food simmering for unexpected guests, or anyone who might be hungry. Tekwitchi, go and get a bowl of your stew for Isabel," she directed her youngest daughter-in-law.

Within minutes, the chubby girl was back with a steaming bowl of stew and a spoon made from a buffalo horn. As soon as Isabel took a bite, she said in surprise, "Why, this is good. What's in it?"

"Venison, wild onions, peas, and a dried root we call *yep,*" the girl answered, pleased at Isabel's complimenting her cooking.

Beaver Woman started for the door, saying, "We will leave you now. I don't know when Stands Alone will join you. Until then, you can take a nap."

"I would advise you to do that," Tekwitchi chimed in with a little smirk.

Isabel wondered at the smirk, but not for long. Seeing Beaver Woman leaving with her dirty clothing alarmed her. "Where are you taking my clothes?" she asked.

"You no longer need them. There is another dress for you in that *nat-sakena,*" Beaver Woman answered, pointing to a rawhide case sitting to one aide of the tepee.

"I don't want any more Indian dresses. My clothes will be just fine once they're washed."

"I said, you no longer need them."

Beaver Woman's voice was so adamant, the expression on her face so forbidding, that Isabel made no further objection. She watched as the three women left the tepee, closing the flap behind them, then heard Beaver Woman say something sharply in Comanche to the women still standing around the tepee. She knew by the sounds of many shuffling feet that they were all leaving.

Then there was nothing but silence, and Isabel wondered apprehensively what would happen next.

Ten

After the three Indian women left Isabel in Stands Alone's tent, she had a great deal of time on her hands. She would have spent at least a part of it putting her hair back up, but she discovered, to her disgust, that Beaver Woman had taken her wooden hairpins along with her clothing. As she waited, Isabel studied the tent, seeing its framework was comprised of twenty-two poles set three to four feet apart and that it was held together at the top by large wooden pins. Besides the buffalo hides that covered the framework, there was an inner wall of hides hung on shorter poles. From these poles dangled water skins, coiled rawhide ropes, a bow and quiver of arrows, a lance, several small bags whose contents were unknown, Stands Alone's smoking bag, and a pair of strange, oblong objects with interwoven rawhide that Isabel had never seen before. Curious to see what was between the inner walls and the exterior wall of the tepee, she lifted one of the skins and peered in, seeing it was a storage area containing several parfleches. For a moment, she considered opening one of the large hide bags to see what it contained, then she suppressed the urge, for fear Stands Alone would walk in and find her snooping.

Returning to the pallet, Isabel saw it consisted of buffalo hides that rested on a low platform. Sitting once more on the bed, she decided it was as comfortable as her corn husk mattress in Rosario had been, or more so. And it didn't smell at all bad, she thought, bending over and sniffing cautiously. To the contrary. Apparently some fragrant herb had been sprinkled on it. Then spying the blanket at the end of the pallet, she picked it up. She knew immediately it wasn't a Pueblo blanket. It was much heavier and softer. She stood and shook it out, admiring its intricate Indian design and vibrant colors.

Stands Alone entered the tepee, stepping in so silently that he startled Isabel. Feeling ridiculously nervous, Isabel said, "I was just admiring your blanket. I didn't know your people wove such beautiful blankets."

"We don't weave cloth of any kind. Our blankets are made of buffalo hides. That's a Navajo blanket."

Isabel dropped the blanket as if it had suddenly turned red hot. "You stole it, then, in a raid?"

Stands Alone frowned. "Why do you think that?"

"I know the Navajo are your enemies."

"That's true, and so are the Ute, the Apache, the Pueblo, the Kiowas, and the Pawnee, especially the Pawnee. There is hardly any Indian tribe who are not our enemies. The *Nema* are such skilled warriors, we do not need allies. But we do not raid for something as trivial as blankets. We raid for horses."

"Then how did you get the blanket?"

"By trading, at the annual fair in Taos."

Isabel knew of the Indian fairs where the various tribes gathered at the Taos pueblo and traded. They had been going on for hundreds of years, since long before the Spanish had arrived on the scene. Friends and foes alike gathered and peacefully traded, then left and resumed their raids and warlike behavior as if the brief period of harmony had never existed. At first, it had been a puzzle to the Spaniards how the tribes could be such fierce enemies yet get along well enough and long enough to trade, until the New Mexicans had realized the material advantages of the practice and joined in. "I didn't realize your people took part in the fair."

"Some years we do. Some years we trade at the fair on the Pecos River, or at Spanish Fort, in Texas. That is where we go when we have need of guns or ammunition."

"A Spanish fort in Texas trades you guns and ammunition?" Isabel asked in shocked disapproval.

"No, not the Spanish," Stands Alone answered in disgust. "They will not trade guns and ammunition to any tribe. That is just the name of the place. It's a trading center run by Wichitas who have access to French goods."

"I've never heard of the Wichitas. I assume they're Indians, too."

"Yes, but they are strange. They live in grass huts, instead of tepees."

"But your people are friendly with them?"

"Yes."

Isabel wondered if it was because the Wichitas controlled a valuable avenue to French arms that the Comanches stayed on good terms with them, or if the Texas tribe was too far removed from Stands Alone's band to be considered a threat.

She watched while Stands Alone built a small fire in the center of the tepee. "I understand you have already eaten," he commented, rising from the fire and coming to sit on the pallet beside her.

"Yes, I have," Isabel answered, inching away from him. Then, hearing the sudden sound of drums, she almost jumped out of her skin. "What's that?" she asked suspiciously.

"It's just the drums warming up for the dance."

Had Stands Alone been lying all along? Had she been brought here for a sacrifice of some kind, Isabel wondered wildly, her heart suddenly racing. Had that been why she had been dressed in these Indian clothes? Then another possibility occurred to her, one just as frightening. Maybe a ceremony was about to take place. A wedding ceremony! "What kind of dance?"

Stands Alone wondered at the wild look in Isabel's eyes. "Just a dance. Like your people, my people dance almost every night."

Isabel had not known that Indians danced for pleasure. The only dancing she had seen the Pueblos do had been ceremonial. Feeling a little foolish, she laughed and said, "Oh, I see. Can we go watch?"

"Not tonight."

There was a huskiness in Stands Alone's voice that caught Isabel's attention. She shot him a quick look and saw him openly admiring her. Suddenly the threat she had felt earlier returned, not coming from outside, but from the man sitting beside her.

"I am glad you left your hair down," Stands Alone said softly, reaching to run one hand down its silky length.

Isabel jumped as if she had been burned and wiggled away, saying, "I didn't have any choice. Your mother took my hairpins with her."

Stands Alone moved closer, and Isabel was panic-stricken. Frantically searching for something to say—anything—she asked, "Where did your brother get his name? Greyfoot?"

Stands Alone scowled, then answered, "Some of his

friends named him that, after he walked through the ashes left by a forest fire."

"His friends named him that? Not his parents?"

"It is common practice among my people for warriors to give their friends their adult name, something that distinguishes them from all others."

"And Tekwitchi? Why would anyone call her something so unflattering as skinny and wrinkled?"

"I understand when she was born, she was very skinny and wrinkled."

"She was born too early?"

"No, too late."

Isabel frowned. She had never heard of too late. Then she remembered that the late lambs were often the scrawniest and prone towards sickliness. Perhaps it was true with humans, too. Then seeing Stands Alone moving even closer, Isabel roused herself from her thoughts and quickly asked, "And you? Who named you?"

"No, no more questions!" Stands Alone answered in an adamant voice. "You are just trying to distract me."

With the swiftness of a striking snake, Stands Alone caught Isabel's shoulders and lowered her to the pallet. "No! Don't!" she managed to get out before his lips covered hers.

Grasping her head firmly with one hand and holding her down with the weight of his body, Stands Alone kissed her at leisure, first coaxing and wooing, then hard and demanding, then wooing once more, switching back and forth from furious ardor to sweet, melting seduction so quickly that Isabel was left reeling in confusion. When his free hand cupped one of her breasts and massaged it through her Indian dress, Isabel was flooded with sensation. The brush of the soft doeskin across her swollen, tender nipples was a delicious agony. She tried to steel herself against everything his lips and

hand were making her feel, but found herself as helpless as a grain of sand in a wind storm. The hands that
were pushing against his rock-hard chest weakened,
then slipped around his neck. Her tongue, as if it had
a will of its own, swirled around his, and as if from a
far distance, Isabel heard him groan in pleasure and
felt him shudder.

She was gasping for breath when he bathed her face
with soft kisses, floating somewhere above the earth on
a warm, rosy cloud. The tip of his tongue traveled the
length of her throat, making her shiver; then he supped
on the sensitive skin at the crook of her neck. She ran
her hands down the length of his bare back, relishing
the feel of the powerful muscles there.

Stands Alone shifted his weight, and Isabel felt his
hot arousal pressing against her thigh, the hard, searing
flesh making a mockery of their clothing. Or rather, his
clothing. Somehow or another, her dress had gotten
pushed up to her hips. The realization that her lower
body was totally exposed was like a dash of cold water
on Isabel's heated senses. In a movement that took
Stands Alone completely by surprise, she pushed him
away and rolled away from him, saying as she frantically
pushed her skirt down, "What do you think you're doing?"

Stands Alone reached out and caught her shoulder.
"I'm making love to you."

She looked over her shoulder and glared at him. "I
said no, and I meant it!"

Stands Alone glared back. "Your mouth says one
thing, your body another. You kissed me back. You were
twisting your hips, pressing yourself against my thigh,
begging for more."

Isabel remembered kissing him back. Horrified that
she might have been doing the other, also, and desper-

ate to get away from him, Isabel hotly denied, "No, I didn't!" then jumped to her feet to flee.

Stands Alone sprang to his feet, reached out with his long arms and caught her shoulder, dragging her back against his chest, holding her firmly around the waist and pinning her arms to her sides.

Isabel squirmed wildly and felt, to her horror, him lengthening yet another inch where his erection was pressed against her lower back. "Let me go, or I'll scream!"

"Go ahead. Do you honestly think someone would invade my privacy to investigate? Besides, they would probably think you are screaming from pleasure."

To Isabel the Comanches thinking that would have been even more mortifying than what Stands Alone was trying to inflict upon her. Sobbing in frustration, she said, "You promised you wouldn't force me until we were married."

Stands Alone wondered if he should tell her this was their wedding night, and that he had come to the tepee with full intentions of claiming what was his. But deep down, he didn't want to force her. He wanted her to want him as much as he did her, to enjoy it to the fullest. What frustrated him was her denial of her feelings. "Why do you persist in denying us the pleasure we both crave?"

"Because I don't crave it. Only you do!"

"You lie!" Stands Alone answered angrily, jerking her even closer. "And I will prove it to you."

Horrified, Isabel felt him inching up her skirt. She squirmed to no avail, demanding, "Stop that! You're exposing me!"

Totally ignoring her, Stands Alone tucked the skirt under his arm around her waist, then smoothed his free hand over her bared stomach, brushing her groin, before he caressed her thigh. Dropping his head, he kissed and nibbled the length of her neck, then took her earlobe into his mouth and sucked on it.

Ordinarily, Isabel would have been enthralled with the feelings Stands Alone's accomplished mouth was invoking, but she was too occupied with his hand. His stroking the inside of her thigh ever so lightly was making her skin tingle and a slow warmth build between her legs, an ache that seemed to be begging for his touch. As his hand moved slowly upward, a shiver of anticipation shot through her, then as he touched her there, she felt as if a bolt of fire had run through her. Horrified at her own body's betrayal, she twisted away, saying, "Stop that! It's indecent!"

"It's part of making love," Stands Alone answered in a husky voice against her ear, right before his tongue shot into it as true as one of his arrows.

Isabel twisted her hips wildly, but it did her no good. If anything it just intensified the feelings his fingers were invoking as they teased and titillated her there. As the hot waves washed over her, making her knees so weak she could barely stand, she finally gave herself up to sensation, arching her hips and pressing against his hand, throwing her head back and moaning as the sweet ripples grew into powerful undulations of pleasure.

When it was over Isabel would not have been able to stand had it not been for Stands Alone's holding her up. Her legs felt incredibly weak and were quaking like the leaves of an aspen in a wind storm. She was still dazed when she heard Stands Alone whisper in her ear, "See? You craved and enjoyed it. It will be even better when it is this,"—he pushed his erection against her lower back so there would be no doubt in her mind what he was talking about—"that pleasures you."

Isabel knew the truth of his words. She had craved and enjoyed it. She was sick with self-disgust and remorse. "I hate you!" she spat angrily.

Stands Alone flinched at her strong words, but astutely suspected she hated herself as much at the moment. She was fighting her passionate nature with everything she had, but it was as futile as a dry leaf's struggling against the winter wind to stay on its branch. What was meant to be, was meant to be. Eventually she would learn that and accept it. Until then, he would try to be patient. But it wasn't going to be easy. Exciting her had excited him, and every fiber of his being was clamoring for release.

With supreme will, Stands Alone dropped Isabel's skirt and released her, saying, "I told you that love will come later. For now, it is enough that you crave my touch." He pulled her back down on the pallet with him. "Now, we will go to sleep."

As soon as they were once more prone on the skin mattress, Stands Alone placed her head on his shoulder and possessively wrapped his arms around her. Isabel hated him for forcing her to endure his embrace, even in her sleep. Feeling her stiffness, Stands Alone said softly, "Relax. Nothing else will happen tonight."

"Then take your arms away. It makes me feel like a prisoner."

Stands Alone didn't want Isabel feeling as if she were his prisoner. He wanted her willing in all things. He considered her request, then decided against it. A husband slept with his wife in his arms, and this was his wedding night. He had been cheated of his rightful pleasure by Isabel's stubbornness. This much, at least, he would have. "No. We will sleep this way."

Stands Alone lived to regret his decision. Long after Isabel had fallen asleep, he lay awake. With her soft curves pressed against him and the memory of his touching her moist womanly delights so fresh in his mind, his body still clamored for release. He wasn't accustomed to denying himself in such a manner. There had always been a warm, willing woman about when he was aroused, and he had never been this aroused. He was sorely tempted to break his word and take her. Their union was inevitable. Why not now, and save himself this torture? But a deeper emotion, one born and nurtured in his childhood, tempered his raging need, and he fought down the urge. Finally, he fell asleep, his last conscious thought, *No, it wasn't going to be easy.*

The next morning when Isabel awakened, Stands Alone was gone from the tepee. She recalled the night before and the humiliating way her body had betrayed her, still betrayed her, she realized with self-disgust, for just thinking about what Stands Alone had done to her made her feel warm and tingly all over. She had to escape him, she decided, now, before he further eroded what little honor she had left.

She rose from the pallet and walked to the door, then cautiously lifted the flap and peered out. Her hopes that there would be no one about were quickly dashed. Although the morning light was still dim and the night mist still floated on the ground, the camp was a beehive of activity with women starting outside fires or already cooking the morning meal, their young children playing around them, while the older girls lugged water from the river and gathered more firewood. There weren't any men about that Isabel could see. Were the lazy creatures still sleeping, she wondered. But where had Stands Alone disappeared to?

Isabel stepped from the tepee and scanned the camp,

seeing no sign of Stands Alone. But she did note that no one seemed to have even noticed her. Then she saw Stands Alone's horse staked beside his tepee. Recognizing her, the gelding whinnied a welcome. She remembered Stands Alone telling her that the horse would allow no one but him to mount him. But maybe the gelding had become so accustomed to her on his back, that had changed. Slowly, she approached the horse, saying softly, "Good morning, boy. How are you today? Would you like to go for a little ride?"

"Good morning."

Isabel jumped at Stands Alone's greeting and whirled around, her face flushing with guilt. "Where did you come from?" she asked in a rush of words.

"From the river," he answered, nodding his head to the rear. "I brought Runs Uphill a bucket of water."

"Is that his name, Runs Uphill?"

"Yes."

"I didn't think Indians named their horses."

"Only our favorites. This is my war horse, and my buffalo pony. He's very valuable. That's why I keep him here, beside my tepee at night, so no one can steal him."

"You mean, someone from another tribe?"

"Ordinarily, yes."

Isabel knew from his words and his expression that Stands Alone knew what she had been up to. The color drained from her face.

Stands Alone set the bucket down in front of the gelding, then turned to her and said softly, "Do not attempt to escape. Even if you are successful in getting away from this camp, it will do you no good. I will follow and bring you back. You are my wife. What is mine, I keep."

There was a dangerous glitter in Stands Alone's black

eyes that made a shiver of fear run through Isabel. "I'm not your wife," she said. "Not yet."

"You are mistaken. As of last night, you are my wife."

Isabel couldn't believe her ears. "That's impossible! There was no ceremony."

"My people do not have a ceremony. We spent the night together in my tepee in full sight of the entire band. We are married in my people's eyes, and mine."

Isabel thought to remind him the marriage hadn't been consummated, then decided against it. She knew he'd be only too happy to correct that oversight. For that matter, for all she knew, the Comanches might not even consider consummation a necessity for the marriage to be valid. "You tricked me! I didn't know that!"

"You knew when I brought you here you were to be my wife. It is done. We are married. The sooner you accept it, the better."

His arrogance, his total disregard for her feelings infuriated Isabel. "I'll never accept it! I'll never consider myself your wife. Never!"

Isabel had no idea how hurtful Stands Alone found her words. His face revealed nothing when he calmly replied, "Never is a long time. In the meanwhile, remember what I said about trying to escape."

He turned, took a few steps, then whirled back around. "My mother will teach you everything you need to know to be a good *Nema* wife. She does this as a favor to me. Listen to her and obey her."

"And if I don't?" Isabel tossed back recklessly.

"That would be very foolish. Your survival in this camp depends upon it. If you wish to eat something other than raw meat, you will learn to cook and gather. If you wish to wear clothes and have shelter over your head, you will learn to tan hides and sew them. If you wish a fire to warm you, you will collect the wood and learn how to build it. The wives provide these things, not the husbands. You can expect nothing from me but fresh meat and protection."

Stands Alone turned and walked away, and Isabél knew he meant every word of what he had said. He'd never allow her to escape him, nor would he coddle her. If she wanted to survive, she'd have to learn the Comanche woman's skills. But did she want to survive, she asked herself. Isabel had already been down that road when she tried to starve herself and failed. She wanted to live. Even if she had to spend the rest of her life among savages, she wanted to live.

Eleven

When Beaver Woman came to Stands Alone's tepee later that morning, she stood before Isabel and said without preamble, "Come with me."

Isabel knew where she was taking her—to begin her lessons on how to be a Comanche wife. Filled with bitterness and anger, she answered, "No, first I have something to say! Now I know why you and the others insisted upon bathing and dressing me yesterday, to prepare me for my wedding night. Perhaps the others didn't realize, but you knew full well I didn't know what was going on. Out of common decency you should have warned me, but you didn't."

Beaver Woman's facial expression revealed nothing. "Did Stands Alone hurt you?"

"Hurt me?" Isabel blurted in puzzlement. Then realizing what Beaver Woman was thinking, she blushed furiously and answered, "No, he didn't . . . do that."

Beaver Woman was surprised. As Isabel's husband it was his right, and *Nema* men were lord and master in their tepees. Did he really love this stranger enough to put his physical needs aside until Isabel became more reconciled to the idea, Beaver Woman wondered. If so, Stands Alone was showing remarkable consideration. She remembered how broken-hearted he had been when he had thought the girl dead. Hoping to ease his pain, Beaver Woman had used a considerable amount of her deer power to try to help him find a new love. But it hadn't worked. Apparently the only woman Stands Alone wanted was this one standing before her. Why that should be was totally beyond Beaver Woman's comprehension. Then, becoming aware Isabel was awaiting an answer, she tore herself from her musing and said, "If he didn't do that, then what should I have warned you about?"

"About your marriage custom. I expected a ceremony of some kind. He claims we're married in the eyes of the band, just because we spent the night together in his tepee."

The band assumed something happened other than the two sleeping together, but Beaver Woman wasn't going to tell the girl that, not if Stands Alone had not seen fit to enlighten her. Some in the band might think him weak for not asserting his husband's rights, but what happened, or didn't happen, in the privacy of his tepee, should be Stands Alone's business and no one else's. Besides, it was an assumption, not a necessity. By spending the night together, the couple officially announced their intentions to live together as man and wife. "You are married."

"You should have warned me. I would have left the tepee if I had known. You're just as underhanded and sneaky as he is."

Isabel saw the fleeting flash of anger in the older woman's eyes before her facial expression returned to its usual unreadable one. Having elicited no verbal response, Isabel continued, asking, "Doesn't it bother you that I didn't want to marry your son, that all of this is being done against my will?"

"Your father made the arrangements for this marriage. It is my understanding that it is your people's custom, and that the daughter obeys her father's wishes."

"I don't believe my father did that," Isabel answered with firm conviction.

"Still, it is true."

"My father would never betroth me to a savage!"

The look of fury that came over Beaver Woman's face stunned Isabel with its intensity. "Don't you ever call my son a savage again," she told Isabel in a menacing tone of voice, "not in my presence, or to any of the others. If I hear of it, I will not be held accountable for what I might do to you." Pausing to let Isabel absorb the full import of her threat, she continued, "I will tell you this, and it is only for your ears. I did not approve of this arrangement from the very beginning. I wanted my son to take an Indian bride, a strong, capable woman, a caring woman, a woman who would put him first, before everything, as is befitting a good wife. And he could have had his pick. There is not a marriageable woman in this camp, or among any of the bands we mingle with, that would not feel honored to be his wife. He is strong in body and spirit, quick in mind, wise in counsel. He is an excellent provider. He always brings back more loot from a raid, and shoots more game than any of the others. He is brave in war, generous to the poor, hospitable to strangers, cool and fearless in danger, ardent in friendship, loyal to the tribe, and respected by all. He is everything a good *Nema* should be. He deserves much better than you."

Isabel had known from the beginning that Beaver Woman didn't like her, but being told so frankly stung her pride. "If you dislike me so much, then why don't you help me escape?" she responded bitterly.

"Because my son wills this marriage, because my husband wills it, and we are women. It is our duty to obey their wishes. The same is true for your people. I suspect the same is true for all the peoples of the earth. Since the beginning of time, it is the woman's place to follow, to obey without question, to strive to please, to labor unceasingly for her man and her family's comfort, without expecting anything in return, except the knowledge they have done well. It is the woman's lot. So, you see it is pointless for you to appeal to me. I will not go against my son's and husband's wishes."

Although Isabel knew everything Beaver Woman had said was true—for Spanish women were as much slaves to their husbands' wishes as the Indian—she still wasn't prepared to accept her fate gracefully. "It's wrong what they're doing. It's unjust!"

"That is not for me to judge," Beaver Woman answered stubbornly. Then seeing how frustrated and angry Isabel was, she felt a twinge of compassion and said quietly, "I suggest you do what wise women before you have always done, accept your lot and try to make the best of it."

With this sage advice, Beaver Woman turned and stepped from the tepee. Tears of exasperation glittered in Isabel's blue eyes. It wasn't that easy, she thought. She couldn't just accept. It would be a betrayal to her father.

Beaver Woman stuck her head back into the tepee and asked, "Are you coming?"

For the moment, Isabel was resigned. "I'm coming," she replied bleakly.

Beaver Woman took Isabel to her tepee and pointed to several dead rabbits lying to one side of it, saying, "Stands Alone shot those this morning. I told him to bring small game at first, so you will not feel overwhelmed. We will start with teaching you how to skin rabbits, butcher them, build a fire, and make rabbit stew. That should be simple enough."

What Beaver Woman thought simple, Isabel found difficult. She had never butchered anything. That had always been the servants' job. She forced herself to endure the bloody chore of skinning and gutting the rabbits, her stomach threatening to expel its contents the entire time, thinking she would never be able to bear eating the meat, or any rabbit, ever again. Then Beaver Woman took her into the woods beside the river to gather firewood, teaching her how to recognize the different woods, the special properties of each, how to pick the right length and thickness, and how to tell dry from green.

Isabel had never started a fire. That, too, had always been the servants' job. On her hands and knees with her flint and steel, Isabel worked and worked and worked to try to spark the small pile of dry leaves and kindling, wondering why it had looked so easy when Stands Alone had done it. Then, her back aching from bending over and blowing ever so carefully on the small flame, she got the kindling going, only to extinguish her fire by adding too much firewood too quickly.

After the fifth try, and much furious mumbling, Isabel was finally successful in building her fire. As she sat back and proudly admired the flames, Beaver Woman remarked, "Fire making takes more patience than skill. It also consumes much time. That is why we always save an ember for the next day's fire."

"Are you saying I could have started this fire with an ember from yours?" Isabel asked, then realized that was probably how the servants back home had done it, using yesterday's ember to start today's fire.

"Yes."

"Then why didn't you let me start it that way and save me all that time and trouble?" Isabel asked irritably.

"Because you needed to learn how to start a fire from the beginning. Sometimes, even the most carefully protected ember can be extinguished, and when we travel, you cannot carry one with you."

"Can I start my fire with a hot coal tomorrow?"

"No, for the next few days, you will start from the beginning, until you become more adept and faster. It is slow work, but not usually that slow," Beaver Woman remarked with a strong hint of scorn. "It took you half the day. You will have other things to do than build a fire."

Cooking was the easiest of her chores, Isabel thought. The meat was simply thrown into a pot of boiling water—water she had to lug from the river—along with dried vegetables and a pinch of herbs that Beaver Woman took from a small leather bag.

While the stew was simmering, Beaver Woman helped Isabel set up her Comanche kitchen, giving her another, larger pot, an assortment of knives—a few made from bones and not metal—several wooden bowls, hide platters used for eating just meat, half a dozen spoons and cups made from buffalo horns, and two hide buckets. Leather bags of dried staples—peas, Indian potatoes, wild onions, sliced prairie turnips, pumpkin, sego lily bulbs, piñon seeds, sunflower seeds, and herbs—were also added until Isabel could learn how to prepare and store her own. Feeling something critical was missing, Isabel asked, "What about cornmeal? Isn't that a staple?"

"We do not use it, except to make a drink," Beaver Woman replied.

Isabel didn't know if she could spend the rest of her

life without a corn tortilla. She dearly loved them. "What about bread?"

"Sometimes we make little cakes from a flour made from mesquite beans. That is what we use to make the drink also. The beans are very sweet. But I do not have any. If you want them, you will have to gather the beans yourself."

"There aren't any mesquite trees around here," Isabel pointed out.

"No, but there are on the prairie where we go buffalo hunting. You will have to wait until then, to gather both them and the cactus leaves."

Isabel thought mesquite beans sounded revolting, but her people often ate the fruits of cactus. "You mean the cactus fruits?"

Beaver Woman shrugged. "Those, too, as well as the leaves."

"But how can you eat the leaves with all those thorns on them?" Isabel asked in horror.

"You singe the thorns off, then peel the leaves," Beaver Woman answered as if it were the silliest question she had ever heard. Then she admitted, "But we in this band are not that fond of them. They are Apache food, poor man's food. Who would want to eat them when you have plenty of meat, as we do?" Not waiting for a response, Beaver Woman handed Isabel a small sack, saying, "This is crushed sumac, to mix with your tobacco when Stands Alone buys more from your people."

"He smokes real tobacco?" Isabel asked in surprise.

"Yes. Isn't it what your people smoke?"

"Only the very wealthy. It's controlled and taxed by the government, you know. Most of the colonists here in New Mexico smoke a pale, native plant that's much milder, rolled in a corn husk."

Beaver Woman knew of the plant the Spanish called

punche. It wasn't even of the tobacco family. She wrinkled her nose in distaste, then answered, "Most of our people prefer pipes. Those who smoke cigarettes roll them in cottonwood leaves, but we all smoke real tobacco, we did even before your people came. Then we traded with the tribes to the east for Indian tobacco." She handed Isabel two sacks and said, "The smaller one contains sage to sprinkle on your pallet to freshen it. The larger is your sewing bag. I will show you how to use everything in it later."

Beaver Woman looked down at Isabel's dress and shook her head in disgust. "I cannot believe how dirty you got with just the little work you did. You look as if you rolled in the dirt."

It didn't seem like a little work to Isabel, and she had lain in the dirt, when she was trying to start that damn fire.

"I will bring you a brush to clean your clothes with," Beaver Woman announced.

"You don't wash them?"

A horrified expression came over Beaver Woman's face. "No! Never!"

"Then that's the only way you clean them? Just brush them?"

"They are skins. Dirt does not penetrate them, like cloth. When they are very soiled, you smear wet clay on them, then after it has dried, brush it off. They will look like new. Even the grease stains are gone."

Beaver Woman turned to leave, then pivoted and asked, "After I bring you the brush, I am going to the river to bathe. Do you wish to come along?"

"No, I'll wash up here in the tepee."

"Suit yourself, but you will have to tote your own water this time. I think after a few days of that, you will find it easier to go to the river, than to bring the river to you."

That evening, when Stands Alone and Isabel were eating her stew in their tepee, she was acutely aware of him. He had donned a buckskin breechcloth that was dyed blue, handsomely beaded with white, red, black, and a lighter blue, and wore fringed moccasins that matched. The tails of his thick, lustrous braids were covered with red trading cloth from which raven feathers dangled. On his braided scalp lock was the usual lone black-edged eagle feather, and around his neck was a necklace made of pieces of polished obsidian and studs of silver, the skinny black and glittering metal emphasizing the powerful muscles on his broad chest. With the light of the fire playing over his chiseled features, he looked very masculine and very appealing. Isabel was so engrossed in admiring him from under the fringes of her lashes that she jumped when he said something to her, then asked, "What did you say?"

"I said your stew was very tasty."

Despite thinking she would never be able to eat rabbit meat again, Isabel had. Her rather heavy activity that day had worked up a hearty appetite. She, too, had thought it tasted good, but Stands Alone's compliment brought a warm glow deep down inside.

"You have learned much today," Stands Alone commented. "You must be very proud of yourself."

Isabel could have pointed out they were things she hadn't wanted to learn, but didn't. With Stands Alone mentioning it, she realized she *did* feel proud of her accomplishments.

When Isabel didn't respond verbally to his observations, Stands Alone asked, "What meat would you like me to bring tomorrow?"

Something small, Isabel thought, remembering what Beaver Woman had said. But she was beginning to get a little tired of rabbit. That was all they had eaten on the trail. She longed for lamb or goat meat, but knew that was out of the question. It had to be wild game. "What about a turkey?"

A horrified expression came over Stands Alone's handsome face. Then he answered sternly, "No, the *Nema* do not eat turkey. The only use we have for them is for feathering our arrows. We do not eat fowl of any kind. Their meat makes you cowardly."

Isabel thought it was a ridiculous notion. She considered a moment, then smiled and said, "What about fish? I saw some beautiful trout in the shallows of the river this afternoon."

"No, fish is taboo also, as is dog and coyote."

Isabel would have never dreamed suggesting the latter two, but she was curious. She had heard some tribes of Indians ate dog. "Why not dog?"

"That would be like eating your grandmother." Then seeing the baffled expression on Isabel's face, Stands Alone explained, saying, "It is said that long ago, when the *Nema* returned from a hunting trip, they found the camp dogs had eaten one of the old women. From then on it has been taboo to eat them; to do so is to eat your grandmother. We also do not kill them."

Well, that explained why the camp was so overrun with the surly animals, Isabel thought. And the Comanches apparently associated eating dogs with cannibalism. She was relieved to know they did not approve of *that* barbaric practice. She had heard some of the Texas tribes were cannibals. Apparently, the Comanches were more civilized.

"Have you decided what meat you would like?" Stands Alone prompted.

Isabel was weary of trying to guess the Comanches' dietary taboos. "Just bring anything."

"Squirrel?"

"That will be fine."

Stands Alone reached to one side and pulled out a hide sack, saying, "I brought you something."

Isabel wondered where the sack had come from. It hadn't been there when she and Beaver Woman had set up her kitchen. Stands Alone must have brought it in and changed clothes while she was away toting water. She accepted the heavy sack and asked, "What's in it?"

"Honey for your kitchen. My mother said she did not have enough to spare. My father has a terrible sweet tooth." An appealing grin spread over his face. "I'm afraid all of my people do."

Isabel fought off the tender feelings the grin was eliciting. "How is it used in cooking?"

"I believe my mother mixes it with fat marrow and brushes it over roasting meat. We also like to dip dried meat into it."

Isabel imagined the dry meat needed something to make it more attractive. Beaver Woman had given her a piece of jerky to chew on that day, since the Indians didn't make a practice of eating a mid-day meal. It had been satisfying, but boring.

The sudden sound of drums once again startled Isabel. Then she asked, "They're dancing again tonight?"

"Yes, would you like to watch?"

Isabel jumped at the opportunity to escape the close confines of the tepee. Stands Alone was much too pleasant and appealing. She was finding it difficult to remember she hated him. "Yes, I would."

"You are not too tired? You are not accustomed to

the labor you did today. It is a considerable walk to the other end of the camp, where the dance is taking place."

Probably a good two miles, Isabel thought, remembering how the camp was stretched out along the river. Ordinarily, she wouldn't find that long a walk appealing, even when not already a little weary, but Stands Alone's consideration seemed even more threatening than his physical appearance. "I'm not too tired," she assured him.

As Stands Alone led her through the camp, Isabel noted practically everyone was going to the dance, young and old alike, weaving their way through the maze of tepees whose fires made them look like glowing candles in the darkness. When they reached the center of the village where the dance was taking place, she saw a huge bonfire had been built, sending red-hot cinders floating high in the air, and beside it were the musicians with their drums and hand rattles made of gourds. A wide circle had formed around the fire, many of the Indians sitting, apparently having come just to watch. As the music settled into a steady rhythm, both men and women stepped inside the circle, standing side by side, beating their feet against the ground, slowly moving towards the center, then back, over and over, as they moved clockwise, then counter-clockwise. That dance having ended, a score or more of couples stepped into the circle. Facing each other, with their hands on each other's waists, they performed what was essentially the same dance. Isabel noticed that most of the dancers were young and, for the better part, seemed much enthralled with one another. "Are they courting?" she asked Stands Alone.

"No. This dance is for married couples only. We have very strict courting rules. Public intimacy, even touch-

ing one another while dancing, is strictly forbidden."
He glanced towards the deep shadows of the woods and
added, "Of course, there's much clandestine activity going on. As long as the couple is discreet, the band turns
a blind eye to them."

While the dance was much tamer than what Isabel
was accustomed to, the primitive music did have an appealing rhythm. She soon found herself tapping her
foot to the beat. Taking note of this, Stands Alone
asked, "Would you like to dance?" Seeing the stunned
expression on her face, he said, "It's permissible, you
know. We *are* married."

His reminding her of their intimate status was almost
enough to make Isabel refuse. Almost. But she didn't.
She loved to dance. She nodded her head.

Stands Alone took her hand and pulled her into the
circle. Facing her, he lightly placed his hands on her
waist, and she did the same to him. "Look into my
eyes," Stands Alone commanded.

"Why?"

"Because that is how this dance is danced."

Isabel thought the steps incredibly simple, compared
to the wild fandango she was accustomed to, but she
found the dance much more intimate, even though she
and Stands Alone stood just as discreet a distance apart.
The fandango was passionate, while this dance was
more sensuous. Stands Alone's hands on her waist
seemed to burn even through her clothing, and she
was acutely conscious of his smooth, naked flesh beneath hers. Their gazes locked, his dark eyes bore into
her, intensifying the almost mesmerizing sway of their
bodies. Despite the distance between them, they
seemed as one, their heartbeats beating in unison to
one another and the throbbing drums. They seemed
to be locked in some strange vacuum where the world

had ceased to exist and there was only them and this steadily growing, almost painful awareness of the other.

Then abruptly, it was over, leaving Isabel feeling dazed, with her breathing strangely ragged and her pulse racing, reactions that had nothing to do with the physical activity of the dance. She still had not completely recovered when they returned to their tepee a short while later. The small fire in the lodge, used strictly for light at this time of the year, had burned down and bathed the interior with a rosy glow, a glow that seemed to mirror the heat Isabel was still feeling. When Stands Alone pulled her into an embrace and kissed her, she offered no resistance.

It was a long, sweet, incredibly sensuous kiss that made Isabel feel as if her spine was melting. Then, just as abruptly as the dance, it was over, and Stands Alone was pulling her down with him to their pallet.

Suddenly very much alert, Isabel stiffened.

Stands Alone frowned, then said, "No, it is not what you think. I will not claim what is mine tonight. You have had a long day. We will just sleep."

As they lay prone on their pallet, Isabel remained tense and expectant. But she discovered Stands Alone was a man of his word. Hearing his steady deep breathing and knowing he was asleep, she told herself she was relieved he had not forced the issue, that she'd had a reprieve from the inevitable. But deep down, there was not relief. There was just that terrible yearning.

Twelve

Over the next several days, Isabel continued her Comanche housekeeping lessons under the direction of Beaver Woman, then at night she was confined in the tepee with Stands Alone, a time that was both heaven and hell. It was heaven because she found she could hardly wait to see him, to be with him; hell because he tormented her, touching her at will with featherlike caresses, holding her close at night, so close she had memorized every hard plane, every corded tendon, every bulging muscle on his magnificent body. And he kissed her, sometimes with such sweetness, she ached, sometimes with such fiery passion, she burned for want of him, then left her hanging and having to deal with something she had never even known before—sexual frustration.

When Isabel had been in the camp a week, Stands Alone brought her her first deer. Beaver Woman taught her how to skin and butcher it, then how to roast the choicest cut on a spit over a fire and how to cut the rest into thin strips to dry in the sun for jerky. It was the hardest, most backbreaking chore Isabel had yet performed, until the next day, when Beaver Woman announced it was time she learned how to tan a skin.

"I will let Tekwitchi teach you," Beaver Woman told

Isabel. "She is younger and more agile than I, and just as much an expert."

Tekwitchi showed Isabel how to stake the deer skin to the ground, flesh side up, then with a metal blade with an elkhorn handle, how to scrape the remaining bits of flesh from the skin. When that tedious chore was finished, the skin was turned and the hair scraped from it with another instrument made from a buffalo bone. As the two young women worked, Tekwitchi asked Isabel, "What are you going to make from your new buckskin?"

Isabel sat back on her heels and gazed out at the camp. Her eyes came to rest on a group of women walking to the river. She had to admit they were a graceful sight with the long fringes on their dresses swaying with every step and the brilliant patterns of beading on their peplums glittering in the sunlight. "A dress, I suppose," she answered. "I only have two."

"I don't blame you. Two is adequate, but Stands Alone is such a good hunter, you can certainly have more."

Isabel bent and resumed her scraping, then said, "I've been curious about something. How did you and Corn Woman and Beaver Woman learn to speak Spanish so well? The other women can't. Either that, or they're pretending they can't."

"Most of those who have had much contact with the Spanish captives can speak a little. That's where Corn Woman and I learned, from the Spanish woman my father captured for a chore wife. She claimed she couldn't learn our tongue, that it was too difficult, so we had to communicate in Spanish. My mother always said she was just being stubborn, but Corn Woman and I didn't mind. We were young, and your tongue came easy to us."

"Corn Woman is your sister?" Isabel asked in surprise, for the two looked nothing alike, nor did they have similar temperaments.

"Yes. You did not know that?"

"No, I didn't."

"Well, we are," Tekwitchi answered with a casual shrug of her shoulders, then continued, saying, "But to finish answering your question, Beaver Woman learned Spanish from the same woman. When my parents died, Yellow Sky took the captive into his household, so Beaver Woman could learn Spanish, since she was to have a Spanish daughter-in-law."

"I haven't seen this woman," Isabel commented.

"No, she died last year."

Having had that puzzle solved, Isabel said, "There's something else I've been curious about. When I knew Stands Alone as a child he was called Spotted Coyote. He told me that males are given an adult name that usually denotes something different about that person. I can't imagine why he was named Stands Alone. He's not at all aloof. Do you know how he got such a strange name?"

"Oh, yes. Everyone in the band knows that. One day, when a group of our warriors were hunting elk, they split into two groups. The group Spotted Coyote was with was ambushed by a raiding band of Pawnees in one of the river bottoms. There was a fierce fight. Our men were outnumbered four to one. By the time the other group of our warriors came to the rescue, almost all of the ambushed group were dead or wounded. There was only Spotted Coyote left standing in the midst of them, firing his arrows at the enemy. They said he was a fearsome sight, his eyes blazing with fury as he brought down one Pawnee after the other, while the enemy's arrows whizzed all around him. He was hardly more than a boy, yet to make his first raid, but the warriors were so impressed with his bravery that they gave him his adult name, Stands Alone, then and there. Everyone of those wounded men owe him their lives. It was a deed not to be forgotten by this band."

Isabel wasn't particularly surprised to learn Stands Alone was a hero. She had already come to realize he was a cut above other men. There was about him an aura of fearlessness, of immense strength and fierce determination. She had also come to realize he was much liked and respected by all. Everywhere he went he was greeted with a smile. Even the old men, who Beaver Woman claimed had a tendency to be jealous of the younger successful warriors, seemed to admire him. And the maidens and widows of the band absolutely adored him, casting yearning looks in his direction that made Isabel long to scratch their eyes out. Knowing that he was *almost* the paragon of virtue his mother had claimed—in Isabel's opinion, no mortal could be *that* perfect—made it all the more difficult for her to maintain her hard feelings towards him.

Isabel and Tekwitchi worked all day on the deer hide, applying a revolting tanning mixture of brains, grease, liver, basswood bark, soapweed, and water, then rubbing it in with stones, then drying it, stretching it, rubbing it again with their hands, pulling it back and forth across the limb of a tree, trampling on it, beating it against a rock, then repeating everything, until Tekwitchi finally declared it soft enough.

Exhausted, Isabel sank to the ground and murmured, "Well, thank goodness, it's done. Now, at least I'll have another dress, when it's sewn, that is," Isabel added, wondering how much work that was going to be.

"No, you still need to smoke it to make it darker, and

that will only make a blouse. You will need two more skins for the skirt and another for the peplum."

Horrified, Isabel asked, "It takes four skins to make a dress?"

"Yes, but you can also get a pair of moccasins out of the skin you cut the peplum from."

"Is it always that much work, or was this skin particularly tough?"

"This was usual. A buffalo hide is much more difficult. If you have absolutely nothing else to do, you might be able to tan one in three days."

"How in the world do you do it, with all the other work you have to do?" Isabel asked in frustration, thinking she would never be able to perform all of her chores in a timely manner.

"If it is shared with two or three women, the work is not too hard. That is why we do not mind our husbands' taking other wives. It is even better if you are chief wife. Then you can make the others do the hardest work."

Since Isabel had come to know just how arduous the Indian woman's work was, she could appreciate their viewpoint. From that light, polygamy didn't seem all that terrible. A proficient hunter could well work one wife to death. Isabel knew Corn Woman was the chief wife in Greyfoot's tepee. Curious, she asked, "Don't you resent having Corn Woman ordering you around?"

Tekwitchi shrugged her shoulders and replied, "I am used to it. As my older sister, she has always ordered me about. It is customary for our men to take their first wife's younger sisters for additional wives for that reason. We grew up together and are used to one another. Sisters are not as likely to bicker or be jealous of one another. Also, it makes it easier for the man to take care of his wife's parents, as is expected of him. This way, there is only one set of parents."

"But your parents are dead?" Isabel asked for confirmation.

"Yes, they died from the pox eight years ago, as did many more in this camp, including Beaver Woman's daughter."

"Beaver Woman had a daughter?" Isabel asked in surprise.

"Yes, but you must not mention her to Beaver Woman. We do not talk of the dead, for fear it will make those who loved them feel bad."

"I'm sorry. If I had known that, I wouldn't have mentioned your parents."

"That's all right. I do not mind. And I did not grieve my loss as deeply as Beaver Woman did her daughter. They were very close."

Isabel wasn't very fond of Beaver Woman. The older woman had maintained a coolness that clearly told her she still did not approve of her. But knowing that she had lost a close loved one, too, made Isabel feel a little less hostile towards her.

"My other sister, Greyfoot's second wife, also died then," Tekwitchi informed Isabel. "That is when I went to live in Greyfoot's tepee, although I did not become his true wife for three more years. I was not yet a woman." Tekwitchi fell silent for a moment, then confided, "It has been hard on Corn Woman and me. Greyfoot is a good hunter, and there is much meat to butcher and many hides to tan and sew. We asked him to take another wife, but he did not feel at liberty to do so. Then, when things changed with Stands Alone, he considered it, but so far had found none of the women to his liking. Now, he says he will try to get us a chore wife on the next raid, but not of your people. An Indian woman. It was a Spanish captive that brought the pox to us. Since then, the council has decided we will take no more Spanish captives, even though your government will buy them back. It is not worth the risk. They are too diseased."

Isabel had been about to ask what things had changed with Stands Alone and why it should have anything to do with Greyfoot's taking another wife, but the Indian girl's insults towards her people took precedence in her mind, and she asked in a caustic tone of voice, "Are you saying *you* don't have diseases?"

"Not like the white man's," Tekwitchi answered calmly. "Before the white man came, we never had the spotted disease, the pox, the choking disease, the sores on men's penis disease that makes the brain rot. There were more of the *Nema* then. Many have died."

Isabel knew the spotted disease was the measles and the choking disease diphtheria, but had no idea what the latter disease was. She wasn't about to ask for any further clarification. Tekwitchi's frankness had embarrassed her.

"Stands Alone will have to get you some chore wives, too, since he is not allowed any other wives," Tekwitchi commented. "But not Pawnee. You do not want one of them in your tepee. They are treacherous."

"Why is he not allowed any more wives?" Isabel asked.

"Because that is what Yellow Sky agreed to with your father, that Stands Alone would take no other wives, that he would share his pallet with only you. Your father said it was your people's way."

Isabel was stunned. Surely her father wouldn't have made that stipulation to the marriage, because he wouldn't have agreed to the marriage at all, she thought. Then where had the notion come from?

She looked up and saw Stands Alone walking across the camp towards her. For a second, she admired his graceful stride and striking manliness, then seeing a young boy walking beside him, asked, "Who is that little boy with Stands Alone? I've seen him with him before."

A warm look came into Tekwitchi's eyes. "That is Red Feather. He is Greyfoot's and Corn Woman's son."

"I didn't realize they had children."

"Yes, they have two sons. Jumping Rabbit is still in his cradleboard."

"Do you have any children with Greyfoot?"

A sad look came over Tekwitchi's face. "No, but I am hoping. And I love Red Feather and Jumping Rabbit like they are my own, just as I will your children. You are my sister, too."

Strangely, even though the girl's father had held a Spanish woman captive, Isabel found that she didn't mind Tekwitchi calling her sister all that much. The chunky girl had a winning personality. To be perfectly honest, she liked the Indian girl better than any of her female cousins. As Stands Alone and Red Feather passed nearby, Stands Alone barely nodded to her. Isabel didn't take offense at his almost ignoring her. She had discovered that Comanche couples treated each other very formally in public. Then hearing the Indian boy address Stands Alone as *ap,* Isabel asked Tekwitchi, "What does *ap* mean? Uncle?"

"No, Father."

Isabel sucked in her breath sharply, then said in an accusing tone of voice, "I thought you said he was Greyfoot's son."

"He is. All *Nema* children call their father's brothers that."

"But why?"

"Because someday the brother could very easily be their father. That is why the warriors treat their brother's children as their own from the very beginning."

"I still don't understand."

"*Nema* brothers always assume responsibility for each other's families if the other is killed, and many of our men are, in war, on raids, in hunting accidents. The brother marries his dead brother's wife and takes her and the children into his tepee. It is his duty. That is why it is not uncommon for brothers to share their wives, particularly if one is gone for a long while."

"Are you saying what I think?" Isabel asked in a shocked voice. "That brothers take each other's wives to their pallets?"

"Yes."

"That's terrible!"

"Why?" Tekwitchi asked in puzzlement.

"Because they're not married!"

"But they may be one day."

To Isabel, the custom seemed all one-sided, in the lusty male's favor, as usual. "How do your women feel about that?"

"We do not mind. As I said, the brother might someday be our husband, and it is a small price to pay for security, for knowing there will be always be someone to take care of you, even if you are older and no longer desirable."

Isabel was thinking of how strongly she disliked Greyfoot for his part in her father's death. "But what if you really hate the man?"

"*Nema* women scrutinize their future husband's brother as much as the man himself. If the brother is known to be particularly cruel, a woman might refuse. But that does not always work. Sometimes our fathers and brothers insist on the match. But most wives simply accept it, and I have heard some say they are glad for it, that it relieves their hungers when their husbands are gone for long periods of time."

A horrifying thought occurred to Isabel. Had Tekwitchi not been talking so frankly, herself, she would never have had the courage to ask something so personal. "Has Greyfoot ever shared you or Corn Woman with Stands Alone?"

"No, although I would not mind sharing Stands Alone's pallet," Tekwitchi answered with total, unabashed honesty, her eyes sparkling at the thought. "He must be a splendid lover." When Isabel made no response to her observation, the Indian girl continued, saying, "Greyfoot has never offered either of us, since he knows Stands Alone can never reciprocate."

Isabel was immensely relieved on both counts, then asked curiously, "Why not?"

"Because that was part of your father's and Yellow Sky's agreement, too, that Stands Alone would not share you with his brother, or any man. He said your people do not do that, that it would shame you. Is that true?"

Again, Isabel was stunned at the information Tekwitchi had given her. "Yes," she muttered, distracted with trying to make sense of it all.

"Stands Alone has promised Greyfoot that if anything happens to him, he will take care of Corn Woman and me and our children, just as if we were his wives, except for that," Tekwitchi continued. "That is why Red Feather still calls him father. And of course, if anything happens to Stands Alone, Greyfoot will do the same for you. But that is why Greyfoot does not wish to take more wives. He says he does not feel right giving Stands Alone so much responsibility, for so little in return. So, instead, he will get a chore wife. Brothers are not obligated to take responsibility for them. They can be sold."

Isabel realized then that the question she had forgotten to ask had been answered. Stands Alone's marriage to her was what had affected Greyfoot's taking another wife. When the Comanches had thought her dead and the pact dissolved, he had felt at liberty to marry again, since Stands Alone could also take as many wives as he wished. But now that had all changed once more.

Later, in Stands Alone's tepee, Isabel was mulling over everything Tekwitchi had told her. She had already recognized the practicality of polygamy in the Indian culture, and the more she thought about wife sharing, the less shocking it seemed. Over and over, Tekwitchi had used the word responsibility. Apparently, the warriors thought of their brother's wives and families as an extension of their own, and reasoned that certain privileges came with that responsibility. Considering the custom was a means of assuring that widows and orphans were taken care of, Isabel was surprised Yellow Sky had agreed to her father's demands, since it affected Greyfoot as well as Stands Alone.

Isabel's mind came to a dead halt. My God, what was she thinking? Surely her father hadn't really made those demands as part of a marriage agreement. He wouldn't have dishonored her that way, betrothed her to a savage, not even as a trick, would he? But she was becoming more and more doubtful of his innocence. She couldn't imagine the Comanches making up something that was so much against their way of life.

"You are very quiet tonight."

Stands Alone's observation startled Isabel from her thoughts. "Oh, I was just thinking."

Stands Alone hoped she wasn't thinking about her father's death. He wished she could forget, or at least forgive. He turned her to face him.

Anytime Stands Alone touched her, Isabel became nervous. She never knew if it was just a touch, or a prelude to something more. "What's wrong?" she asked.

"Nothing. I just wanted to look at your eyes. They're beautiful, you know. I have never seen anything so very, very blue." He smiled. "Did you know blue is my people's favorite color? In view of that, you would think Our Sure Enough Father would have given a few of us blue eyes."

Isabel was glad Stands Alone didn't have blue eyes. Dark as the obsidian necklace he wore, they were the most expressive eyes she had ever seen, flashing when he was angry, twinkling when he was amused, penetrating when he was thoughtful or intense, shimmering when he was pleased with something, and smoldering when he was aroused. Then, just as his head dipped, she realized that *that* was what they were at that moment, smoldering. She didn't have the strength to turn her head to avoid the kiss. Nor did she have the will. Her lips ached for his.

As he had done so often in the past, Stands Alone kissed her lingeringly, sweetly; his warm lips playing at hers, his tongue darting out to lick one corner, then the other, in a sensuous promise that left Isabel trembling. Finally, his tongue slipped into her mouth, tasting her honeyed sweetness, before plunging in and out in a passionate kiss that brought Isabel to her toes and flush against him.

His mouth still locked over hers in that fiery kiss, Stands Alone dropped to his knees on the pallet, taking Isabel with him. He caressed her shoulders, her back, then ran his hands down her hips, before he cupped one breast, his thumb teasing the nipple through her buckskin dress and making her moan. Then, catching her totally by surprise, he caught the hem of her dress by both hands and whipped it over her head.

Stunned, Isabel tried to cover her breasts with her hands, but Stands Alone caught her wrists and pulled them away, saying in a husky voice, "No, let me see. They are so very beautiful." Then his eyes dropped, and Isabel flushed hotly as he boldly drank his fill of her there.

When he laid her back on the pallet, she was shocked to see his eyes were blazing with the heat of his desire. "You are my wife," Stands Alone muttered in a husky voice. "Let me give you pleasure."

Isabel wanted to say no, but the word wouldn't come. Slowly, over the past days, Stands Alone had readied her for the act of love. Her body would not be denied any longer. The inevitable had finally come. She knew she had lost. She squeezed her eyes shut and a single tear ran down her cheek. "I hate myself," she muttered.

"Why?" Stands Alone asked in astonishment.

"Because I'm so weak, because I can't fight you any longer."

"You are not weak," he answered, kissing away the tear. Then he looked her in the eyes and smiled a little, self-derisive smile that tugged at her heart. "No adversary has ever held me at bay so fiercely. I feared you would drive me mad, before I could wear down your resistance. I never dreamed a man could want a woman so badly. And you will not be sorry you submitted to me. You will see how right it is for us. I will give you only pleasure."

He caressed her, his hands stroking her arms, her sides, her breasts, his mouth dropping butterfly kisses over her face and shoulders all the while. Ever so slowly, his head descended, his warm, wet tongue laving the soft mounds on her chest, his teeth nipping gently, until Isabel's nipples were straining and throbbing for want of his mouth. Then his lips closed over one turgid peak, and she sighed in pleasure, giving herself up to sensation.

When Stands Alone's hand brushed across the dark curls at the juncture of her thighs, before slipping between them, Isabel made no effort to escape his teasing, slender fingers. She knew the pleasure that was awaiting her, pleasure that exceeded even the magic of his mouth on her breasts. She arched her hips to give him even better access. Suddenly, it seemed as if every nerve-ending in her body had shifted to that part of her body, as if a flaming torch had been set to her, searing her clear to the soles of her feet. Sweet ripples rushed over her, followed by powerful undulations that left her limp and breathing raggedly.

When she recovered, she saw Stands Alone smiling down at her. "I believe you liked that."

Isabel knew she would look foolish to deny it. "Yes."

"There is more that is even better."

He kissed her softly, and Isabel realized he was naked. Briefly, she wondered when he had slipped off his breechcloth and moccasins, but didn't dally over the question. All thought fled at the feel of his body pressing against hers, so hard, so male, so very different from her own. Then she became acutely aware of his erection pressing against her hip. Bare of all covering, it felt enormous and seemed to sear her skin with its heat, and she could feel it throbbing. A twinge of fear ran through her, to be quickly replaced with excitement. An answering throb began between her legs. She pressed her hip against him in a silent but eloquent plea.

Stands Alone knew the time he had been waiting for had finally come. He kissed Isabel, a deep, demanding kiss that gave full rein to his passion and sent both of their senses spinning. Between the wild kiss and the feel of his hands seemingly everywhere and his hot, exciting scent, Isabel felt as if every nerve in her body was on fire. Finally, the aching between her legs became unbearable and she sobbed, "Please, oh, please."

Knowing what she wanted, what she needed, Stands Alone rose over her and positioned himself between her legs. As he entered her, he forced himself to go slow, steeling himself against her scalding heat. Then, feeling the barrier, he hesitated before plunging in.

Isabel stiffened and cried out as she felt a sharp pain tear through her. The cry affected Stands Alone more strongly than any sound of distress he had ever heard. With a tenderness he hadn't known he possessed, he soothed her with gentle caresses and soft endearments in Spanish and Comanche. Not until he felt Isabel moving her hips tentatively and knew she was trying to relieve the burning in her loins, did he continue, moving at first slowly, then faster and faster.

As he began his movements in earnest, Isabel clung to his shoulders, marveling at the entire new world of wonderful sensations he was introducing her to. As his masterful strokes became bolder, deeper, stronger, she felt herself spiraling higher and higher, her senses expanding, her heart pounding as if it would jump from her chest right through her skin. An intense, unbearable pressure began to build in her. She writhed beneath Stands Alone, her fingernails digging into his shoulders as the strange tension grew, and grew, and grew. Isabel didn't think she could stand it. She feared she would burst at any second. Then there was a blinding flash in her brain, and her body convulsed as wave after wave of exquisite pleasure washed over her. She was totally oblivious to Stands Alone's following her a split second later in his own explosive release.

When she recovered, Isabel's first awareness was of Stands Alone's head pillowed on her breasts. Dreamily she stroked his damp shoulders, thinking she had never felt anything so absolutely wonderful.

Stands Alone rose, resting his upper weight on his forearms and asked, "Did I hurt you?"

The sincere concern she saw in his face touched Isabel more than anything he had ever done or said. "Not really. There was just a brief pain."

"I'm sorry. It couldn't be helped. But from now on, there will be only pleasure. But not tonight, or you will be sore tomorrow."

He kissed her forehead, relieved her of his weight, then brought her close to his side. Lying in the protective circle of his strong arms, with his powerful heart drumming in her ears, Isabel knew she had burned her bridges. Now, she was truly Stands Alone's wife, and he would never let her go. The white world was closed to her forever. Perhaps she should do as Beaver Woman had suggested, accept her lot and make the best of it.

But Isabel's fierce Spanish pride wasn't ready to yield completely. She decided she would give Stands Alone her body and perform her duties as his wife, but she would never surrender her love. Unlike her treacherous body, she could control that. Yes, she could still salvage a part of her honor.

Thirteen

The next few nights were ecstasy for Isabel as Stands Alone proved what an accomplished lover he was, and untiring, for once was never enough for the virile warrior after Isabel had recovered from her initial soreness. Not that Isabel really minded performing this wifely duty. She discovered, somewhat shamefully, that she was just as hungry for the sensual delights as he and gloried in his recuperative powers and endurance. Her demeanor during the daylight hours, however, was entirely different. Then she was decidedly cool and brisk. It was her way of protecting her heart and trying to keep a clear-cut delineation between passion and caring.

One day, while she was collecting wood, Isabel's period began. Remembering what Beaver Woman had told her, Isabel went to the older woman's tepee and told her of her condition. "That is good," Beaver Woman responded. "Tekwitchi is here, too. You can keep each other company. Perhaps, she can begin your sewing lessons."

When Isabel entered the tepee, she saw Tekwitchi sitting to one side, sewing beads on a smoking bag she was making for Greyfoot. The girl didn't look at all happy.

After Beaver Woman had given Isabel a piece of trading cloth to wear like a breechcloth and some padding made of cattails, she pointed to a darkened area of the tepee and said, "You can put it on over there. But before you do, there are some other instructions I have for you. While you are flowing, you will not wash your face, cut your hair, or eat any meat, and before you can go back to your husband, you must bathe completely, in the river, and not just wash off, as you have been doing. That is only allowed in the winter, when there is snow on the ground."

When Beaver Woman said "go back to your husband," Isabel knew she meant resume sexual relations and blushed furiously, telling the older woman something she had suspected from the glow on the Spanish girl's face the last several days. Beaver Woman had mixed emotions. A part of her was glad her son had asserted his male rights. She had feared the others might realize what was going on and think him weak. But another part of her was disappointed that the two had come to an agreement on at least the physical part of marriage. She had been harboring hopes that Stands Alone would get disgusted with the girl and take her back to her people.

After Beaver Woman had left the lodge, Isabel sat next to Tekwitchi and asked, "What's wrong? It's not at all like you to look so unhappy."

"But I am unhappy. I am terribly disappointed. This means I am not with child—again."

Like all the girls in her class, Isabel had been told very little about sex and pregnancy. Those things were usually learned by experience, after the fact. What she did know she had learned from observing animals. "Are you saying you stop flowing when you are pregnant?"

"Yes. Didn't you know that?"

"No, I didn't. My people don't approve of talking about such intimate things to young girls."

"Then how do you know what to expect?"

"Unless you can figure it out on your own, you don't."

"That's stupid," Tekwitchi observed candidly.

"Yes, I suppose it is," Isabel agreed. "Are there any other times your flow stops?"

"Yes, when you are too old to have children and when you are nursing a baby. That is why you will not see Corn Woman here. She is still nursing." Tekwitchi paused, then giggled.

"What was that for?" Isabel asked.

"I am thinking ordinarily I would be pleased to be here. Corn Woman will have to do all the work while I am gone."

"You don't do your chores while you're flowing?" Isabel asked in surprise.

"Not if there is another wife, or even another woman in the family, like Beaver Woman, who can do them for you. It is a time the women look forward to, when they can escape the heavy work and just do something light and pleasant, like sewing and beading."

"Beaver Woman said you would teach me to sew. Would you mind?" Isabel asked, much preferring the good-natured girl to the aloof woman.

"I would be happy to. We can start on the blouse for your dress."

"The skin is in Stands Alone's tepee. I can't go back there."

"Beaver Woman will fetch it for you."

Isabel smiled. After having Beaver Woman order her around and work her to death, she rather liked the idea of the older woman having to wait on her for a change.

The rest of the day, Tekwitchi taught Isabel sewing,

using a buffalo bone needle to penetrate the tough buckskin and sinews peeled from the spinal column of a buffalo for thread. As the day progressed, Isabel couldn't imagine why the Indian girl had said the chore was light. The wrist had to be held at just the right angle to get the correct thrust, and it took considerable strength to penetrate the skin. Finally, Isabel remarked in self-disgust, "I've only sewed one seam. I hate to think of how long it would take to sew an entire tepee. Buffalo hides are bound to be even tougher." Isabel glanced around at the tepee. "Why, there must be at least twenty skins here."

"No, every tepee has seventeen, but you don't have to worry about sewing your own tepee. No one does. That is entrusted only to an expert tepee maker, and then every woman in the band helps sew it, under her direction."

Isabel glanced at the tepee door and knew by the slant of the light that it was growing late. The day hadn't been too bad, but she dreaded sleeping in the same tepee with all the others, particularly Yellow Sky. Even if she hadn't hated him, it would be awkward sleeping in the same room with a man who wasn't a husband or close relative. "Where will we sleep?" she asked Tekwitchi.

"Over there," the girl answered, motioning to one side of the tepee.

"And Beaver Woman and Yellow Sky back there?"

"Just Beaver Woman. When I am here, Yellow Sky sleeps with his other wife."

"He has an entirely different household for his other wives?" Isabel asked in surprise.

"Yes, but he has only one other wife. Many of the wealthier men do that, particularly if their wives are not sisters."

"Do you stay with his other wife sometimes?"

"No."

"Oh, I think I see. You stay with Beaver Woman because she is Greyfoot's mother."

"She is not Greyfoot's mother. Greyfoot's mother is dead. She is just Stands Alone's mother, now that her daughter is dead."

Well, that explained why Greyfoot and Stands Alone looked nothing alike, Isabel thought. They had different mothers. Then something occurred to her. "Does Yellow Sky have any children by this other wife?"

"No, she has never conceived," Tekwitchi answered, and Isabel knew by the sad sound of her voice that the girl was thinking of herself.

Upon reflection, Isabel realized that none of the Comanches in the band had big families, certainly nothing like the majority of the Spanish. The most she had seen any Comanche woman have was three children, and that was unusual. Despite their hardiness, they didn't seem to be particularly prolific. "I'm curious about something. If neither Beaver Woman nor this other woman are Greyfoot's mother, why do you only stay with Beaver Woman?"

"Because the other woman did not make the offer. Beaver Woman is much kinder, and not lazy. Woman Runs Slow did not want to do our chores. After our parents died, she said to let me and Corn Woman go to the women's hut, with the others who have no parents here."

Isabel wasn't surprised at Yellow Sky's other wife's name. She had learned almost every female had "woman" in her name and that both men and women often had names that were phrases. But what did surprise her was Beaver Woman's extending her courtesy to her, when she didn't care for her and there was another place she could have gone.

At that moment, Beaver Woman stepped into the tepee and said to Isabel, "Stands Alone is outside. He wishes to speak with you."

"I guess I should have told him I was leaving . . . and why." Isabel flushed, wondering how one approached something so personal with a male. She was just getting used to discussing it with females.

"He knows why you are here," Beaver Woman informed her with her usual candor. "He still wishes to speak with you."

Isabel stepped out of the tepee and saw Stands Alone standing a few feet away. Not knowing if she was still supposed to keep her distance, she asked, "Is there something you wanted?"

Stands Alone walked up to her and said, "Yes. I want you to come back to my tepee."

"But it's my understanding I can't, that I will ruin your . . ." She frowned, then asked, "What do you call it?"

"Puha," Stands Alone answered in Comanche. "My power, or medicine. But it is not necessary for you to go away. I have hidden it in the woods."

Isabel knew Yellow Sky had moved his medicine someplace else. Beaver Woman had told her that. But Isabel sensed this wasn't ordinary. Greyfoot had not accommodated his wives in such a manner. "Why did you do that?"

Stands Alone didn't feel he could admit the real reason, that he simply wanted her close to him. It sounded so weak. As a rule warriors didn't go out of their way for their wives, even women they were very fond of. It was always the woman who had to bend. "I know you are not accustomed to sleeping with others and how strongly you feel about my father."

Isabel could have pointed out that Yellow Sky would not be there, but didn't bother. She didn't feel all that comfortable around Beaver Woman, either, and much preferred to sleep where she had been sleeping. Common courtesy told her she should thank Stands Alone for his unusual consideration, but Isabel found that impossible. Being grateful didn't fit in with her daytime demeanor, nor did she feel it should. After all, he had forced this position on her. Therefore, without a word, Isabel turned and walked to Stands Alone's tepee.

Stands Alone scowled at her back, then followed.

Several days later, when Isabel and Tekwitchi were once again on their knees tanning another deer hide, Isabel saw a fringed pair of moccasins step up to her. Recognizing them as Stands Alone's, she looked up and saw he was holding a string of horses and smiling down at her. Having no idea what was going on, she rose to her feet and asked, "Is there something you want of me?"

"No. I have brought you your bride's gift."

Astonished, Isabel looked at the string of beautiful mares, then muttered, "These are for me?"

"Yes. Ordinarily, they would have been given before the marriage took place, but I wanted to pick the best from my herd. That took a little time and consideration."

Recovering from her astonishment, Isabel remembered she wanted nothing for which she would have to thank Stands Alone. "No, thank you," she replied haughtily. "I do not want them."

Tekwitchi gasped, then jumped to her feet and said

in a low voice, "No, Isabel. You must not refuse. To do so would openly insult Stands Alone."

Isabel glanced around and saw practically everyone in the village was watching. She looked at Stands Alone. His face was a thundercloud. She wondered if insulted Comanche husbands punished their wives, and if so, what that punishment might be. So far, Stands Alone had been kind to her, but she had never seen him looking so angry. A little shiver of fear ran through her. Maybe she should reconsider.

Hoping to smooth things over, Tekwitchi said in admiration, "Oh, Isabel, the mares are so beautiful." She leaned over and looked down the long line. "And so many. The usual bride's gift is only five or six, you know. How many did you bring her, Stands Alone?"

"Twenty."

He must love her very much, Tekwitchi thought in astonishment, with just a twinge of envy thrown in. But Tekwitchi wasn't the kind to remain envious for long. "If you like, I will teach you how to care for them," she said to Isabel.

"Care for them?" Isabel asked in a shocked voice. "I have to care for them?"

"Of course. They are your horses. Every woman cares for her own string."

Isabel's objection to the gift took a different path. She already had entirely too much work to do. "With everything else I have to do, why do I need so many? One or two, perhaps."

"Are you mad?" Tekwitchi asked. "It takes two horses just to carry your tepee long poles. What will you use for the other poles, and the cover, and all of your belongings, and where will you ride? No, you can make good use of every one of them."

Thinking Isabel's objection had been to the work involved all along, and not personal, Stands Alone let his anger slip away. Pulling a beautiful bay forward, he said to Isabel, "This is your riding horse. She has the smoothest gait of any horse I've ever ridden."

Isabel suspected what Stands Alone was thinking, and while she wasn't foolish enough to insult him publicly, was determined she wouldn't let him get off that lightly. "Do your people mark their horses, as mine do?"

"You mean, cut notches in their ears? No, everyone recognizes each horse by the horse itself."

"This horse has notched ears. She has been stolen from my people. I will not ride a stolen horse," Isabel replied frostily. Then seeing the furious expression coming over Stands Alone's face once more and fearing she was again pushing him too far, she quickly added, "I will ride that horse." She pointed to a red roan further down the line.

"The *ekaesi?*" Stands Alone asked, so upset he lapsed into Comanche. "She is a mustang, and still half wild. I just captured her this spring. She will do for a pack horse, but not for riding. She would need to be saddle-broken.

And surely that must be men's work, Isabel thought, then answered, "Still, that is the one I want."

Stands Alone scowled. Others might think Isabel's wanting another mare for her riding horse was just a whim, but he knew better. She was being deliberately difficult. He called himself a fool for thinking Isabel would be appreciative of his gift. He should have known she would be just as cold and thorny as she had been all along. Oh, he knew why she was behaving that way. She was still angry at him for abducting her and forcing her to be his wife. This was her way of punishing him. But Stands Alone was finding it difficult to deal with Isabel's fluctuating behavior. He felt like he was married to two women: the nighttime woman warm, passionate, eager, incredibly exciting; the daytime woman frigid, cutting, exasperating. He longed for a compromise, a blending of the two, so to speak, even if it meant having to give up some of the unbelievable pleasures of the night, for he had never known such ecstasy was possible. He would rather have a woman who was civil than one who ran hot and cold and kept his emotions in a constant turmoil. Then, remembering his Indian teaching that all things came to those who were patient, he forced a smile and said to Isabel, "If that is what you wish."

A smug smile spread over Isabel's lips. She noticed that Tekwitchi was watching her expectantly, and her smile disappeared as she realized the girl anticipated a certain response from her. As much as she hated to say thank you, Isabel realized it would be currish to refuse, and she didn't want Tekwitchi to think badly of her. She dropped her head and muttered, "Thank you."

Stands Alone heard what she said, but it was *his* turn not to let her off so lightly. "I'm afraid I didn't hear that. What did you say?"

Isabel knew better. Her blue eyes flashed. "I said thank you!" she snapped.

Stands Alone felt ridiculously happy. He knew it was but a small victory, and not even genuine at that, but every one counted. "You're welcome."

The warm, shimmering look in Stands Alone's dark eyes made Isabel's insides melt. She knew she had won, only to lose. For just a second, the infuriating warrior had slipped past her defenses, and touched her heart.

Fourteen

Instead of Tekwitchi's teaching Isabel how to care for her string of horses, Stands Alone decided to do that himself, much to Isabel's frustration. She knew it would force her to be in his company during a good part of the daylight hours, and judging from her nighttime capitulation to his masculine charms, she didn't know if she could maintain her distance at such close, continuous proximity.

Early the next morning, Stands Alone took Isabel to the pasture where her string of mares were grazing beside his herd, leading the war horse that had been staked beside their tepee behind him. As they walked, Runs Uphill kept nuzzling Stands Alone's shoulder, and the warrior kept patting his muzzle and stroking his cheek. Remembering Tekwitchi's telling her that many of the warriors loved their war horse more than their wives, Isabel felt a pang of jealousy, despite herself. Then recalling something else Tekwitchi had told her, she asked, "Is it true the warriors consider the killing of their favored horse paramount to murder?"

"Yes. If it is deliberate, revenge is sought; if accidental, recompense."

"Don't you think that's a little extreme? They're just animals."

"Perhaps to your people, they are, but not to us. A favored horse becomes like family."

"That's silly. They're just useful, nothing more."

"Is it? If I remember correctly, Pedro was very fond of his sheep dog, even if it was only a useful animal."

"Dogs are different. They're more human."

"That is a matter of opinion."

When they reached the pasture, the knee-high grass was still damp with dew, the droplets glittering brilliantly in the sunlight as the golden globe rose over the jagged mountain peaks. Stands Alone released Runs Uphill, and the gelding moved off to graze with the rest of his herd. This was the first time Isabel had seen Stands Alone's herd up close, and she was surprised to see at least a third of it was comprised of small, rather shaggy-looking animals. "I thought you said you bred racehorses," she commented.

"I do."

"Then what are you doing with those pitiful-looking wild horses? They're not good horseflesh."

"Contrary to what your people believe, you cannot judge good horseflesh by appearance. The wild horses are tough, agile, capable of great speeds and great endurance. They can survive on twigs and bark in the winter and go without water for long periods of time. They can sense danger from great distances and are adept at fighting off predators. There is no horse any braver, or fiercer. Like the *Nema*, they have survived everything nature has thrown at them and passed the test of time."

"Well, if you think they're so wonderful, why do you bother to steal Spanish horses?" Isabel asked in a cutting tone of voice.

"For several reasons. It is easier to steal a Spanish horse than capture a wild one, and Spanish horses don't have to be saddle-broken." He grinned. "Your people have already done the work." Then ignoring the sour look she gave that comment, Stands Alone continued, saying, "But for myself, it is the wild horse's qualities that I wish to breed into my herd. I have found that combining these traits with those of the larger, gentler Spanish horse have produced horses superior to both. Runs Up-hill is an example of that. The same will be true for our children. They will be stronger than either of us."

Isabel was stunned. She had never even considered children.

But Stands Alone didn't give her time to think the matter over. He immediately began instructing her on the care of her animals, saying, "We do not hobble our animals at night, but I have hobbled yours, until you can recognize each mare. Then if they wander in with my herd or another's, you can identify them. Therefore, I would advise you to spend as much time with them as you can."

He paused to let her absorb this, then continued, "You will not have to worry about food or water as long as we are here in this valley. There is plenty of good grass and water nearby. However, when we move to our winter camp, you will have to forage twigs and bark for them, particularly when the snow is very deep and they cannot dig down to the grass. You will also forage for my herd."

Isabel had found it shocking to learn she was going to have to wander around in the snow looking for food for her horses, but when she learned she would have to forage for Stands Alone's, too, she was infuriated. "The devil I will! You take care of your own!"

"No, that is the wife's duty."

"You took care of them when you didn't have a wife, didn't you?" Isabel retorted.

"Yes, but that was different. Now I do have a wife."

"A slave, you mean," Isabel tossed back bitterly.

Stands Alone knew that Isabel wasn't accustomed to such hard labor, but in his heart he believed she would adjust to her new life. She was stronger than she thought she was. He had noticed that the New Mexicans were almost as hardy a breed as his people. Had he not believed that, he would not have taken her to wife. Ignoring her barb, he said, "You will not have to worry about protecting your horses. We set sentries at night. Nor—"

"Then why do you stake Runs Uphill next to our tepee, if you are not worried about someone stealing him?" Isabel interjected.

"He is too valuable to risk, and while the herds are guarded at night, that is not a guarantee an attempt might not be made. However, if that should occur, you can be assured that I and every other warrior in the camp will rush to their defense."

"Just as you'd rush to your family's defense?" Isabel asked, still smarting over the idea that some men loved their horses more than their wives.

Stands Alone heard the sarcasm in Isabel's voice and wondered in exasperation what was bothering her now. She seemed to be spoiling for a fight. She *always* seemed to be spoiling for a fight. "Yes, of course."

Isabel was tempted to ask if he would protect her as fiercely as his precious horse, but didn't have the courage. Despite the fact that she was determined to withhold her love, she wanted his. Not just his passion, but his love. It was a matter of female pride.

When Isabel made no further comment, Stands Alone continued his instructions, saying, "Nor will you have to worry about exercising them. The boys perform that duty. That is how they learn their riding skills."

Isabel looked about at the thousands and thousands

of horses in the valley, then asked in disbelief, "Are you saying every horse is ridden every day?"

"No, even though the *Nema* love riding. Sometimes the boys will simply chase them around. That way they can exercise a score or more at the same time. The horses think of it as a game, and it serves to keep them limber and fit."

"Well, if I don't have to feed them, or water them, or exercise them, what do I need to do?" Isabel asked irritably.

"First of all, learn to recognize each one. Also, you should occasionally ride those you plan on riding, so they will become accustomed to you. And every morning, you should check your string, to make sure they are all fit."

"How do I know if they aren't?"

"I will teach you what to look for, also how to trim their hooves when they become ragged and how to toughen them. Also, they should be brushed every now and then. Most *Nema* don't agree with that, but that is what a Spanish captive told me, and it does seem to help their appearance, since that seems important to you. And, if you do brush them, save the mane and tail hairs that fall out for me to make ropes from. They are stronger than those made of rawhide."

Over the following several hours, Stands Alone took her from horse to horse, showing her how to inspect them, an inspection that included looking into their mouths at their gums and teeth, something the animals didn't particularly like. After having forced one particularly stubborn mare's mouth open, Isabel asked in a testy tone of voice, "Are you sure this is really necessary every day?"

"Yes. By the time they stop eating and lose weight,

the gums are already bleeding and swollen. Then they have to be scoured."

Isabel didn't ask how that was accomplished. She strongly suspected it was a messy, disgusting chore. She turned to the horse next to her, then asked, "She's in foal?"

"Yes, she should drop it soon. Of course, it, too, will be yours."

Isabel wondered if baby horses were as cute and appealing as lambs, then decided they couldn't be. You couldn't take them on your lap and pet and cuddle them. It would be just another responsibility, something she was already overburdened with.

As they made the rounds of Isabel's horses, the bay Spanish horse followed them, nudging Isabel's shoulder. "I think she likes you," Stands Alone finally commented.

Isabel thought so, too. The mare was acting almost as foolish over her as Runs Uphill did over Stands Alone. Why, she was nothing but a pest. "I suppose so," Isabel admitted.

"Perhaps you will reconsider using her for your riding horse?" Stands Alone asked hopefully.

"No, I want the roan," Isabel answered stubbornly.

Stands Alone struggled for patience, then said, "There are several others that can be ridden. Perhaps one of them."

"I told you, I like the roan."

"That horse was particularly difficult to capture. She has too much spirit. She will not make a good saddle mount."

"If she can carry a pack, why can't she carry me?"

"She might carry you, but she will never be dependable. Always she will resent you on her back. She will let you down when you need her the most."

"That's the most ridiculous thing I've ever heard. You just don't want to take the time and trouble to break her."

In truth, Stands Alone wasn't looking forward to it. "Why are you being so stubborn?"

"I'm not being stubborn. I just want the roan."

"Why?" Stands Alone demanded.

"Because she's pretty," Isabel fabricated.

"I told you you cannot judge a horse by its appearance."

"I still want the roan," Isabel insisted, then seeing Stands Alone's face darkening, she said, "I don't know why we're arguing about it. As far as I can see, I won't be riding anything. I haven't seen any saddles, either back at our tepee or around here, and surely you don't expect me to ride bareback."

"No, I don't. A saddle maker is working on a saddle for you right now."

"You have people that just make saddles?"

"Women's saddles. The Spanish captives make them, except we no longer have any Spanish slaves. They belong to the tribe now but they still excel in saddle making."

"And the men? They all ride that little padded saddle?"

"The warriors prefer the Indian saddle. It's lightweight and won't slow you down. Many of the women don't use saddles at all. They do ride bareback. However, the woman's saddle is handy for tying a cradleboard on. But you won't be able to ride to the side, as you were doing at Santa Fe. The women's saddles are made like the Spanish men's saddle. Like everyone else, you'll ride astride."

Isabel remembered riding astride when Stands Alone had brought her here and how uncomfortable it had been. She decided she would be doing as little riding as possible.

As she and Stands Alone walked from the pasture later that morning, Isabel watched the boys exercising some of the horses, racing them across the valley and performing tricks much as Stands Alone had done as a boy. Then seeing two boys racing beside one another, then bending down to pick up another boy lying prone on the ground, she commented to Stands Alone, "Someone should stop those boys. It seems to me that game they're playing is rather dangerous. What if they should drop that boy?"

"That is not a game they are playing. None of the tricks they are doing are. They all have a very explicit purpose, used in either battle, or hunting buffalo. Those boys are practicing the first trick every Comanche boy learns, how to retrieve a wounded or dead comrade during battle. As soon as they have perfected doing it with a partner, they learn how to do it by themselves. To rescue a fallen comrade is the highest obligation of the warrior."

"I can see the importance of rescuing a wounded man, but why a dead one? It seems to me that is an unnecessary risk."

"To leave a man to be mutilated and scalped, even if he is dead, is a disgrace to the people."

Stands Alone suddenly jerked Isabel back, keeping her from being run down by a group of horses being chased by two younger boys. "You must always stay alert while you are out here," he cautioned her.

Isabel looked at the band of horses and the boys. Both seemed to be enjoying the exercise, the boys laughing and the horses whinnying and tossing their heads. Then seeing several other animals among them, she asked, "Are those mules?"

"Yes. We don't bother to steal them, but many times they are mixed in with the wild horses we capture. They make good mounts for our captives, as well as capable pack animals."

Isabel knew why the mules made good mounts for the Comanche's captives. They couldn't run as fast as a horse and thus lessened the possibility of escape. She wondered why Stands Alone had given her the string of horses. Was it because he trusted her, or did he think she wouldn't bother to attempt any escape after he had told her he kept what was his. She rather hoped it was the first. The latter made her feel too much like a prisoner.

Several days later, Stands Alone announced he was going to saddle break the roan that day.

"Good," Isabel responded. "Then I can finally try out my new saddle."

"You could have done that on several of your horses," Stands Alone pointed out.

"No, I want to ride the roan first."

Stands Alone's eyes narrowed. He knew she was still being deliberately difficult. Then he said, "I have decided you will go with me to break her."

"You mean, out to the pasture?"

"No, we will have to travel to a place where the water in the river is deeper. Horses are easier to saddle break if they are standing in deep water. They cannot twist and buck as hard."

"How far away is this place?"

"A half-a-day's ride. Bring our blanket and some food and your flint and steel. We will probably have to stay overnight."

"Why my flint and steel? Why not yours?"

"It is the wife's duty to start the fire."

"You started it before," she argued.

"You were not my wife then," Stands Alone replied calmly.

Isabel glared at him as he walked out the door, then put some jerky and a few dried plums into the Navajo blanket along with her flint and steel and her bag with her hairbrush in it. Then remembering that he had said they would be near a river, she tossed in a piece of trading cloth she used as her towel and a piece of soap. Ever since Tekwitchi had taken her to an isolated spot in the river to bathe after her period, Isabel had developed a liking for bathing outdoors, in the nude, as long as she had relative privacy. It most definitely beat trying to accomplish the chore with only a bucket of water.

Stands Alone was waiting for Isabel outside with Runs Uphill and the roan. Seeing the heavy, high-backed saddle on the mare's back, Isabel remarked, "Why, she's already saddle-broken."

Stands Alone snorted and replied, "Hardly. It took me two days to accustom her to that saddle. She knew it felt different from the packs I had placed on her back. She's going to like the feel of a person up there even less."

Stands Alone took the blanket roll from Isabel and tied it on to the back of his saddle. She noted that there were also several heavy ropes tied to the saddle. Then he lifted her on top of his horse and swung up behind her.

They rode through camp, then crossed the shallow river, their horses splashing water on the children playing naked beside their mothers as the women washed their woven blankets by pounding them against the rocks. Isabel noted that the majority of the blankets drying on the nearby bushes looked to be either Pueblo or trading blankets, not Navajo as Stands Alone's was. They

were not nearly as colorful and pretty. Then she made
a mental note to wash hers when they came back.

The ride was made in almost total silence, the two
having become so comfortable with one another that
neither felt the need to keep a conversation going. Isabel enjoyed the quiet and the solitude after the busy,
noisy camp, and being given a reprieve from her heavy
chores that day was a real treat. She just sat back and
enjoyed the magnificent scenery, hardly aware she was
riding astride.

They reached their destination shortly after noon.
Dismounting, Stands Alone said, "I think I'll have a
little to eat before I start."

"You don't usually eat at mid-day," Isabel responded.

Stands Alone shot the roan a sour look, then replied,
"No, but I think I'm going to need my strength today."

Isabel rolled the blanket out on the ground, and they
sat on it and ate a few pieces of jerky. Eyeing a berry
bush nearby, Isabel said, "I wish those berries were ripe.
They'd taste good right now."

"They will be soon, along with the grapes and plums
and everything else. The summer rains should start any
day now."

Seeing him recline on the blanket, Isabel asked,
"What are you doing?"

"I thought I'd take a little rest."

"I've never seen you rest in the daytime. You're just
procrastinating."

"I'm not familiar with that word."

"You're just putting off what you know you have to
do."

"You're right," Stands Alone admitted. "I am." He
sighed in resignation, then came to his feet and walked
to his horse. Removing the two ropes from his saddle,
he walked to the roan and tied them firmly around her

neck. Then he picked up two heavy sticks and a rock and waded into the river.

"What are you going to do?" Isabel asked.

"Drive these stakes into the bottom of the river, so I'll have something to tie her to. Otherwise, she'll just walk away from me."

Stands Alone waded in until he was about waist deep. Then he ducked beneath the water. A few moments later, he emerged, water sluicing down his dark braids and bronzed chest.

He took the roan's ropes and led her to the river. Stopping just at the water's edge, he looked over his shoulder to where Isabel was sitting on the blanket watching, and asked hopefully, "Are you sure you won't change your mind?"

"I'm sure."

Shaking his head in disgust, Stands Alone led the mare into the river until she was belly deep in the water. Then once more he disappeared beneath the surface. Having firmly secured the mare by the ropes around her neck, he resurfaced, then gritting his teeth, caught the pommel and swung into the saddle.

To Isabel, it seemed as if he didn't even hit leather. The mare came alive as if a red-hot torch had been set to her. Wall-eyed, she let out a piercing whinny, and the water churned as she tried to kick, all the while jerking frantically on the ropes around her neck. Then the mare discovered she could still buck. She arched her back and seemed to come straight out of the water, over and over. Water splashed everywhere, and Stands Alone hung on for dear life, his eyeballs feeling like they were bouncing in his head each time he hit the hard saddle. Then, with a particularly fierce buck, the mare threw him, and he went flying through the air and landed with a tremendous splash.

He surfaced and grimly waded back to the mare. This time she knew what was coming, and Stands Alone had a devil of a time even getting into the saddle with all the sidling the animal did. Finally, he made it, and endured another teeth-rattling, bone-grinding ride that ended the same way, with him being thrown into the river.

As he walked to the mare the third time, Isabel said, "You're not going to try again?"

It was no longer a matter of breaking the mare because Isabel wanted it. It had become personal, a contest between man and beast that Stands Alone was determined to win. "I certainly am."

"But she's exhausted."

Isabel's concern for the horse, and not him, didn't sit well with Stands Alone. He shot her a disgusted look and answered, "That's the objective, to wear the animal down."

As Stands Alone walked to the roan he noted she did look exhausted, her chest heaving and her head hanging just enough out of the water to keep her from drowning. He mounted the third time. Having thought the mare was weakening, he wasn't prepared for the violent response he got. Almost immediately, he went flying. When he emerged from the water, he heard Isabel laughing. "If you think this is funny, you can try it yourself," he growled.

"I'm sorry. It's just that the expression on your face was priceless." She tried to suppress a giggle by placing her hand over her mouth. "I've never seen anyone look so utterly surprised." Then despite her efforts, she laughed outright again.

Stands Alone realized it was the first time he had heard Isabel laugh since he had captured her. That was one of the things he had loved about her as a child. Her joyous laughter. It always made his spirits soar. And she looked so beautiful sitting there with the sun picking out the bluish highlights on her hair and her blue, blue eyes sparkling. His anger disappeared and he grinned, admitting, "I was surprised. She's a sneaky one."

He waded to the shore, then untied his breechcloth. As it fell to the ground, and he revealed his full magnificence, Isabel sucked in her breath, thinking she would never become accustomed to the impact of seeing him stark naked. He was truly a beautiful sight. His wet, bronze skin glistened in the sunlight; his muscles rippled with animal strength, and there wasn't an ounce of fat on him, every inch of him radiating power and male virility. Then realizing how hungrily she was staring at him, she guiltily jerked her eyes away.

From the corner of her eye, Isabel saw him walking towards her. She had assumed he had stripped off his soggy breechcloth to keep it from hampering his ride. "Aren't you going to try again?"

"No, I think I'll take a rest first. I'm a little tired."

"What about the mare? Surely you're not going to leave her out there in the water?"

"It won't hurt her. As a matter of fact, that's how we soak their legs when they're sore or strained. Besides, if she has to stand out there for a while, maybe it will give her time to reconsider her ways."

"I doubt that. I don't think she's going to be any more reconciled than she is now."

"You're probably right."

Isabel knew by the sound of Stands Alone's voice that he was close, but she didn't realize he was standing over her until he clasped her arms and brought her to her feet in front of him. She saw his black eyes were blazing. That penetrated her mind about the same time she realized his hot erection was pressing against her lower abdomen. Her heart raced in anticipation, but perversely she said in an accusing voice, "I thought you said you were tired."

"Tired of riding that mare. I'll never be too tired for this."

His strong arms slipped around her shoulders, and his mouth covered hers. As his masterful tongue darted inside her mouth, swirling around hers, Isabel felt a delicious tingling all over. She slipped her arms around his back and, for the first time, boldly kissed him back. Stands Alone was both thrilled and incredibly excited by her unexpected response. Usually, she had to be thoroughly aroused, drugged with passion, before she responded. Not wanting to discourage her, he had to fight the urge to ravage the sweetness of her mouth and unleash his full passion on her. With an iron will, he forced himself to keep his raging need at bay, taking his time with her, teasing and taunting, kissing and caressing, loving her with just the right amount of male aggressiveness and strength, tempered with tenderness.

Stands Alone caught the skirt of Isabel's dress and whipped it off. His mouth closed over the rosy crest of one breast, his tongue flicking erotically while his other hand massaged its twin. Catching the back of his head, Isabel arched her back, her breath coming in tiny gasps, her legs growing weaker and weaker with each powerful tug. When his hand left her breast to smooth across her abdomen, then lightly stroke the inside of her thigh, Isabel thought she couldn't feel any greater sensation, until his fingers moved upward, then slipped inside her, sliding in and out in an erotic play that made her legs buckle.

When Isabel fell to the ground, Stands Alone lowered himself to the blanket with her. Dazed, with her head resting on his shoulder, she realized her legs were straddling his muscular thighs. She could feel his manhood trapped between their abdomens, hot and throbbing with a life of its own. But that was not where she wanted him, that was not the part of her that was burning for him.

Weakly, she raised her head and looked up. The blazing look in his black eyes only fueled her need. She wondered what he was waiting for. Surely he knew she was ready. Then, to her surprise, he lay back on the blanket, bringing them to rest with her on top and still astride him. Gently, he pushed her shoulders back, relieving him of her full weight. Isabel was acutely aware of his erection springing to attention in front of her as he reached behind her, unbraided the large braid that hung down her back, then smoothed her long hair over her shoulders.

"Take me in your hands," he told her in a thick voice.

Isabel had been longing to do just that for some time, touch and feel the part of him that was the very source of his masculinity. She had thought of it as a shocking, unladylike urge and fought it down. Now he was encouraging her to do it. But here, in broad daylight, with him watching her so intently, it seemed so intimate. Too intimate.

Seeing her hesitate, Stands Alone took her hands in his and wrapped them around him, then taught her the movements. "This, too, is a part of making love," he told her, his breath catching at every stroke. When he moaned, telling her of the pleasure she was giving him, Isabel was filled with an incredible excitement. The burning between her legs became unbearable. Without realizing she was doing it, she rubbed herself against his hard thigh.

"Ride me."

Isabel couldn't believe she heard Stands Alone's hoarse command. She stared at him.

He lifted his head and said, "Ride me, as I have you."

Isabel remembered all the times Stands Alone had had her at his mercy, writhing beneath him, sweetly torturing her by bringing her over and over to a shattering climax, while he retained rigid control. Yes, she would like to have him at her mercy for a change.

Needing no further encouragement. Isabel raised her hips, then lowered herself over him, taking him into her hot depths, inch by inch, her legs firmly grasping his hips. Stands Alone gritted his teeth at the exquisite feel of her muscles surrounding him, then watched enthralled as her long hair fell about them like a shimmering waterfall. At first Isabel's movements were deliberately slow and seductive as she rotated her hips to pull him even deeper into her velvety heat, then faster and faster. As the sensations of pleasure began to wash over her, she threw her head and shoulders back, making her lovely breasts jut out impudently. Unable to refuse what looked like an invitation to him, Stands Alone cupped the soft mounds in his hands, a sheen of perspiration breaking out on his brow as his pressing need grew to an agonizing throb, loath to take his eyes off her as she rode him hard and magnificently. Then he began to buck beneath her, his movements in perfect counterpoint to hers, driving him even deeper into her.

Isabel gasped in shock as Stands Alone penetrated her deeply, sucking the breath from her lungs and sending pinpoints of light flashing in her brain. But rather than retreat from the intense, almost frightening sensations, she rode him harder, slamming her hips down as he came up. Briefly, she wondered if it was the new position, or just the knowledge that she had him writhing, that made this so very exciting. The heat within her had never been so intense. She felt as if she were riding on the edge of a tremendous lightning bolt.

Then a roaring filled her ears, and she was thrown into space in a firestorm of exploding stars.

Stands Alone held Isabel where she had fallen weakly over him, both still trembling in the aftermath, their sweat pooling between their bodies and glistening on their skin in the sunlight. After she had regained her breath and her senses Isabel wondered why Stands Alone had let her be on top. She knew from watching animals that that was the male's place, that nature had delegated them to dominate and the female to be submissive. She raised her head and asked, "Why did you do that?"

Stands Alone knew exactly what she was talking about. It hadn't been just a whim. He was Indian and deeply enmeshed in symbolism. He had done it because he loved her—yes, loved her despite her stubbornness and irritating ways. He had relinquished his age-old male right, made himself weak, so she could be strong. For a man who had grown up in a society where the male was all powerful, it was the ultimate gift. But Stands Alone could not admit this to Isabel. To proclaim his love, while she withheld hers, would leave him too vulnerable. "I thought you enjoyed it."

"I did, but—"

Stands Alone placed his hand over her mouth to silence her and said, "It, too, is a part of lovemaking."

He kissed her forehead, then gently pushed her from him, rose to his feet, and said, "Now, I have some riding to do. Unfortunately, I don't think I'm going to enjoy it near as much."

As Stands Alone walked into the river to the waiting mare, Isabel frowned. She sensed his answer had been evasive.

Fifteen

When Stands Alone and Isabel left the river the next day, Isabel was riding the roan. Although the mare was officially saddle-broken, Stands Alone still didn't feel too easy about the mustang. He kept glancing over his shoulder to make sure the animal was behaving herself.

"Have you thought of a name for her?" he asked Isabel, when he looked back for the twentieth time.

"No."

"How about, She Bucks Hard?" he asked ruefully. Every muscle in his body ached from the beating the mare had given him, particularly the ones he was sitting on.

Isabel laughed, then answered, "That might be appropriate enough, but it's too long. I'll think of something."

Mid-afternoon, Stands Alone dropped back to where Isabel was riding and said, "Let's pick up our speed a little. I want to get out of this canyon before that storm hits."

Isabel looked up at the sky. There wasn't a cloud in sight. "What storm?"

"The one that will be coming over the mountains any minute now. Didn't you hear the thunder?"

Isabel hadn't. But then he saw things she couldn't

see, too. Neither her vision nor her hearing was as sharp. But if he was correct, she was in total agreement. A canyon in the mountains was not the place to be caught in a rainstorm. She had seen arroyos hardly more than a dip in the ground turn into raging streams during one of New Mexico's summer deluges.

They had barely cleared the canyon and were climbing up a steep mountainside, when Isabel saw the towering, purple thunderheads coming over the jagged top of the mountains. Eyeing them also, Stands Alone said, "I think we'd better dismount and find cover. I don't want you on that mare when that thing hits. Even as well trained as Runs Uphill is, he gets skittish during a storm." Seeing a rocky overhang that jutted from the side of the mountain, he pointed to it, saying, "Over there looks like a likely spot."

By the time they reached the spot, the wind that preceded the storm was lashing the limbs of the trees about, and the mare was beginning to get nervous. Stands Alone jumped to the ground and said over his shoulder, "Don't get down yet. Not until I've checked it out."

Isabel looked under the jutting ledge. All she could see was gravel and rocks. It certainly didn't look like an animal lair. "Checked it for what?"

"*Casabeles*," Stands Alone answered, giving her the Spanish name for the reptiles, which meant small bells.

A spontaneous shiver ran over her. "I didn't know rattlesnakes lived in the mountains."

"From what I've observed, they live everywhere," Stands Alone remarked wryly.

Isabel watched apprehensively as Stands Alone used his bow to cautiously turn over the larger rocks, then examined the roof of the overhang. Deciding it was safe, he hurried to her to help her dismount.

As soon as Isabel's feet touched ground, Stands Alone tied the horses securely to a sturdy bush nearby, then grabbing their blanket roll, hurried Isabel beneath the ledge. By that time, thunder was rolling almost continuously and jagged strokes of lightning were flashing across the dark sky.

Isabel had seen some strong storms in her lifetime, but none that even began to compare with this. She huddled beneath the rocky outcrop while the storm rent its fury, the wind whipping the branches of the trees about as if some demented demon had caught them and the water coming down in solid sheets. But it was the thunder and lightning that were so terrifying. Crash after crash of horrendous thunder shook the earth, sending showers of loosened gravel down on them and making Isabel's ears ring, while tremendous bolts of lightning struck over and over and over, so that all around them, there was a pulsating, blinding, white light. A peculiar smell filled the air, so strong it was almost suffocating, and despite the coolness of the rain, the heat from the electrical discharges hung heavily in the air.

Isabel was shivering in fear, even with Stands Alone's powerful arm thrown protectively around her. Then seeing something she had never seen before—balls of what appeared to be fire dancing down the manes and tails of the horses—she cried out, thinking they had been hit by a bolt of lightning. Stands Alone quickly covered her mouth with his hand and urgently murmured, "Sssh!" in her ear.

A moment later, a stroke of lightning hit a towering ponderosa pine that stood less than a hundred feet from them. The trunk of the tree seemed to explode, sending a burst of vanilla scent into the air and burning pieces of wood flying everywhere. Terrified, the horses

whinnied shrilly, frantically jerking on their reins, only
adding to the deafening noises. Isabel wrapped her
arms tightly around Stands Alone and buried her face
in his chest. Her heart was racing. Her stomach felt like
it was tied in a hard knot. There was a heaviness in her
chest, making it difficult to breathe. She knew they were
going to die, and there was nothing they could do to
prevent it. Nature was throwing everything she had at
them, as if she had a personal vendetta against them.
It was just a matter of time before lightning would strike
them, too.

Suddenly, the rain stopped, and it began to hail. Ice
balls the size of Stands Alone's fists began to batter
everything, bouncing like rubber balls on the ground.
The horses began to squeal in pain.

Stands Alone had not tried to protect the animals
from the rain. They were accustomed to that. As for the
lightning, if it struck them, it struck them. He had no
control over that, and he was just as vulnerable as they.
But their shrieks moved him to pity. He peeled Isabel's
arms from around him, rose to his feet, and hurried to
them, braving the bruising hail to untie them and
crowd them beneath the rocky outcrop, where they
might have at least some protection. Isabel's nostrils
were filled with a new odor, the pungent smell of fear
that came from the animals.

The hail turned to rain again, and gradually, very
gradually, as if nature was loath to spare them, the se-
verity of the storm lessened. Finally, it stopped raining,
but Isabel could hear the sound of rushing water pour-
ing down the mountainside from above them, and see
the lightning in the distance and hear the rumble of
thunder echoing among the peaks and reverberating
down the valleys. As Stands Alone took the horses from
beneath the overhang and began to examine them, Is-

abel looked at the blackened shell that had once been the pine. It was still smoldering. She was glad there had been no other trees close to it. The flaming debris could have ignited a forest fire, despite the rain, with the wood itself so very dry. She glanced at the other trees, seeing the deep gouges in the bark the hail had made. No wonder the horses had been squealing, she thought.

"Are they injured?" she asked Stands Alone.

"They've both got a few bad bruises, but nothing broken. On our way back to camp, I'll collect some aspen bark. Boiled, it will help take out the soreness."

Isabel knew that the shepherds in Rosario had chewed aspen bark for fever. "They drink it?"

"No, I bathe their skin with it."

Isabel noticed an ugly bruise on Stands Alone's shoulder where he had been hit by hail. "You'd better put some on your shoulder, too."

Stands Alone walked towards her, saying, "I'm afraid your saddle is ruined. It's full of dents. You'll have to use our blanket to pad it. Good thing we brought the blanket in here where it didn't get wet."

"What about your saddle? Was it damaged?"

"No, it's just rawhide, stuffed with moss. It was the wooden framework on yours that was dented."

Isabel looked back around her. Broken limbs lay all over the ground in mute testimony to both the wind and the hail. Then seeing a blackened area on the ground where the grass had been totally burned off, she noted how close it was to where she and Stands Alone had been sitting. Realizing how very close they had come to being struck, Isabel felt her knees turn weak. "That was the most terrifying storm I've ever been through," she told Stands Alone.

"I've been through worse," he commented.

"Worse?" Isabel gasped in disbelief. "Where?"

"Right here in these mountains. The lightning and thunder is particularly severe up here, even more so than in the other mountains in this area."

Remembering something that struck her as peculiar, she asked, "Why did you silence me during the storm?"

"Because I didn't want you attracting the Thunderbird. The *Nema* are always very quiet during a storm for that reason. If he knows you are there, he will flap his wings and the storm will get worse. It is he who controls the lightning and thunder and shoots invisible arrows that kill people, and he has no pity."

"Is this Thunderbird one of your gods?"

"We do not have gods," Stands Alone answered, placing the blanket on her battered saddle, "or rather we do not call them such. We speak of spirits. Our Sure Enough Father is the supreme spirit. He created everything. He shows himself to us through the sun, who we also call father. The earth is mother, because life came from her. The moon is guardian of the raid and is also sometimes called mother. These are all powerful, good spirits. The Thunderbird is powerful, also, but malicious."

"Are these the same spirits you get your medicine from?" Isabel asked as Stands Alone helped her mount.

"No!" Stands Alone answered emphatically. "These are powerful spirits, too powerful. Humans could never handle that much power. Our medicine comes from animal spirits, and it is they who choose us, and not the other way around. We call them guardians because they give us power to protect ourselves."

Isabel had been taught that any religion other than Roman Catholicism was heresy, but Stands Alone was so intense and sincere when he spoke of his beliefs that she couldn't help but respect them. As he mounted, Isabel asked, "Who is your guardian spirit?"

A closed look came over his face. "I cannot reveal that without my guardian spirit's permission."

"Not even to your wife?"

"No." He looked at her intently, as if measuring her in some manner, then said, "But I will ask."

When they rode into the Indian camp later that day, the sun was setting. The only remaining trace of the horrendous storm was the heat lightning flickering on the rose-colored clouds on the horizon. Even the water puddles had disappeared, absorbed by the thirsty ground.

Despite the late hour of the day, it seemed as if every woman in the camp was busy erecting an open-sided brush shelter beside their tepee. "What are those for?" Isabel asked Stands Alone.

"Now that the summer rains have begun, they will protect their cooking fires. They are also cooler during the daytime than the tepees. Out on the prairies, we sleep under them, but as you know, it is still cool here at night. Beaver Woman will show you how to erect ours tomorrow."

Isabel was glad they wouldn't be sleeping in the open. As shameful as it was to admit, she'd hate for their love-making to be curtailed.

The next day dawned bright and clear, and both Beaver Woman and Tekwitchi helped Isabel erect her brush shelter. By mid-morning a lone cloud had formed out of nowhere, looking as if it were skewered by the mountain peak it hovered over, then was joined by more. Isabel had barely gotten her cooking fire started before the storm came rushing down on them, and it was every bit as terrifying as the one the day before, or more so, since Stands Alone wasn't there to give her reassurance by his mere presence. She was forced to huddle in their tepee alone, the utter silence of the usually noisy camp seemingly intensifying the noises of the storm.

As soon as the storm had passed, Isabel hurried outside to check on her fire. Thankfully, it was still going. Then Tekwitchi walked up to her and asked, "Did you spend the storm alone?"

"Yes."

"That was very brave."

"I didn't have a choice. Stands Alone hasn't gotten back from hunting."

"Neither has Greyfoot. I think they are together. The next time that happens, come to our tepee. It doesn't seem so frightening if there is someone with you."

"How often do you have these storms?"

"Almost every day."

"Every day?" Isabel gasped in horror.

"Yes. Some say it is because Thunderbird lives right up there, above us." She pointed to the highest peak of the mountains. "That way he must pass over us, regardless of where he flies."

Something on the mountainside above them caught Isabel's attention. It was black smoke billowing in the air. "Is that what I think it is? A forest fire?"

"Yes, but it is too far away to be any threat to us." Then a worried frown appeared on Tekwitchi's face.

Taking note of it, Isabel asked, "What's wrong?"

"Greyfoot and Stands Alone are hunting somewhere up there."

An icy hand seemed to clutch Isabel's heart. Then as more and more time passed and the pair did not make an appearance, she became increasingly frightened. The sun went down in a glorious display of colors, and the stars came out. Somewhere in the distance, a coyote let out a series of barks and yelps, followed by a long, drawn-out howl that prompted the camp dogs to answer, then ended with short, sharp raps. Stands Alone had told her that when the song dog, as the *Nema* called the coyote, gave that particular cry he was telling the rest of the members in his pack his location. If only she knew where Stands Alone was and if he was safe. Glumly, she stepped into the tepee and sat down, waiting, her fear growing steadily.

Suddenly, the flap was pushed aside and Stands Alone entered the tepee. An immense wave of relief washed over Isabel. "Where have you been?" she asked.

"Hunting."

"I know that!" Isabel snapped. "I mean what took you so long?"

"There was a storm. We sat it out."

"But no forest fire?"

"No."

"You must have gone a good distance, for it to take you that long to get back."

He shrugged his shoulders. "No, not that far."

"Then why were you so late?"

"We were in no hurry after the storm had passed. We were throwing dice."

Isabel was suddenly furious. Here she had been worried sick, and he'd been enjoying himself—gambling, no less! "Well, don't expect your stew to be hot! I've already banked the fire for tomorrow. And don't expect me to skin whatever you brought back this late. If it can't wait until tomorrow, it can just rot!"

Stands Alone couldn't imagine why Isabel was so furious, but he wasn't going to let a perfectly good deer go to waste. He'd take it to the widow who lived next door. He was sure she wouldn't mind skinning it in the dark. As for eating lukewarm stew, he'd done worse. "That's fine with me!" He whirled around, and left the tepee in a huff, thinking loving Isabel didn't make it any easier to accept her sour temperament.

Later that night, after Stands Alone had returned and eaten the bowl of lukewarm stew Isabel had given him, after they had made love and he had dropped off to sleep, Isabel lay for a long while musing over her fear. She finally decided that it was the possibility of being left with no one to protect and provide for her—she adamantly refused even to consider Greyfoot's caring for her—that had frightened her so badly, and not fear for Stands Alone's well-being. To admit to the latter was to admit to caring, and that was much too close to doing something she had vowed she would never do.

Over the next few days the torrential summer rains continued, but the ground never got soggy and muddy, nor did the weather hamper the Comanches much. They performed their daily duties until the storm came, then emerged from their tepees to continue what they were doing as soon as the storm had passed.

With so much moisture, both preceded and followed by brilliant sunshine, the pastures got even lusher and wildflowers appeared everywhere: graceful columbine, with huge long, spurred blue flowers, clouds of tall yellow and white evening primroses, whose petals were so delicate you could almost see through them, scarlet paintbrush, and in the low, moist areas, streaks of pretty little pink flowers Isabel had never seen before.

The rains also brought on a burst of birthings. Puppies were all over the camp; everyone had to watch that the blinded little balls of fur didn't haphazardly wander into the cooking fires. Almost every bird seemed to have fledglings they were trying to teach to fly. Baby bunnies and squirrels abounded in the woods, as did nimble-footed fawns. Isabel's mare gave birth to a fine stallion. It seemed as if half the mare population dropped foals. New life surrounded them.

Isabel discovered that foals had an appeal of their own, even if she couldn't hold and cuddle them like she could lambs. Checking on her string of horses became her favorite chore, for unlike the vicious mother dogs, the mares didn't mind if you petted their colts. Though they were ever watchful, the mother horses seemed to be pleased that you admired their offspring, and Isabel loved to watch the colts frolicking with their stiff legs and short tails.

One morning, when Isabel was engrossed with watching the colts at play, she felt a nudge on her shoulder. Without even turning, she knew it was the pesky bay mare. She whirled around and snapped, "Stop that! I'm tired of you bothering me!"

The look that came into the mare's dark eyes tore at Isabel's heart. It was so pained, the animal almost seemed human. Moved by pity, Isabel said in a contrite voice, "I'm sorry. I shouldn't have done that. You're just like me, aren't you? Stolen from those who cared about you, forced to endure a life among strange people. You must have sensed a familiarity about me, and I shunned you." Isabel reached up and stroked the bay's cheek, then said, "I promise I won't ignore you anymore. And I'll ride you, just as much as Ruby. I've got to ride her, you know, after I made all that fuss about Stands Alone saddle-breaking her."

"Have you named her yet?"

Isabel started at the sound of Stands Alone's voice. She turned, wondering how much he had overheard. "No, but I think I will ride her . . . occasionally."

With his keen hearing, Stands Alone had heard everything, but he was wise enough to make no comment. "I came to see the new addition to your string."

Isabel beamed with pride. "He's over there with those colts," she told Stands Alone, motioning to a group of small horses a short distance away. "He's the little black one with the white stockings."

Stands Alone nodded in approval. "We will geld him when he is two years old."

Isabel winced at the thought, then said, "Do we have to?"

"Stallions do not make good riding or pack horses. Only the best are kept for breeding purposes." He looked back at the colt, saw he had potential, then said, "We'll see." Turning back to Isabel, Stands Alone said, "I am going on a little trip, to a place where many of the bands gather to race their horses. I have decided you will go with me."

"I didn't know you took your women anywhere with you," Isabel remarked in surprise.

"As long as it is safe, we do. We have even let them accompany us on raids, provided we can set camp at a safe enough distance. But that is usually on raids in which we travel very long distances and are gone months at a time. Greyfoot is going, also, and taking his family."

Isabel wondered if Stands Alone was taking her because he would miss her company. Was he, perhaps, falling in love with her? Her spirits soared.

Stands Alone thought Isabel looked particularly beautiful with her glorious blue eyes sparkling. He was doubly glad he had decided to take her with him. Even though she was still prickly and unpredictable, he couldn't bear the thought of being away from her for that long a time. Then as something else occurred to

him, he said, "It will be a good opportunity for you to
learn how to take down and put up a tepee, before we
make our fall buffalo hunt. We will be traveling at a
much more leisurely pace on this trip. No one will mind
if you slow us down a bit."

Thinking his decision had nothing to do with her
personally, but rather her training as a Comanche wife,
Isabel's soaring spirits plummeted. She turned so he
couldn't see the sudden tears gathering in her eyes and
muttered listlessly, "Whatever you say."

Having no idea what had caused the sudden shift in
Isabel's mood, Stands Alone stared at her back as she
walked away, totally baffled.

Sixteen

Several days later, early in the morning, preparations began for the trip to the races. Following Tekwitchi's and Corn Woman's instructions, Isabel packed everything in the tepee in parfleches, then dragged the heavy bags outside. Then she packed everything in the brush shelter. Then she removed the hide walls inside the tepee, dismantled the short poles that held them, and took them outside, where she rolled the hides into one large bundle and tied the poles securely together. That was as far as she could get by herself.

She walked the short distance to Greyfoot's tepee to observe Tekwitchi and Corn Woman as they dismantled their tepee. To her amazement, she discovered the lodge pins holding the hides together at the top of the tepee were removed by the younger sister standing on the shoulders of the older. Then with the removal of the smoke-hole pole, the entire covering came sliding down to puddle on the ground, leaving only the skeletal framework standing. After the covering was folded, the stakes that secured the long poles were removed, then the poles themselves.

"We will show you how to pack everything on the horses after we have brought your tepee down," Corn Woman informed Isabel.

When they reached Stands Alone's tepee, Corn Woman said to Isabel, "I think it would be better for you to stand on Tekwitchi's shoulders, since you are much lighter than she."

"Me?" Isabel asked in surprise.

"Yes, you. It is your tepee."

"But I don't think I can do that, balance on some-one's shoulders."

"Then you will have to learn."

To Isabel, it looked very tricky. "Maybe she could get on mine."

"No, she is much too heavy for you, and stronger."

Isabel knew both were true, particularly the latter. She had seen Tekwitchi lift and carry things she had thought only a man would be capable of. But, still, her shoulders didn't look all that terribly broad. She glanced at the string of horses the men had brought around before they had conveniently disappeared, then suggested, "Why don't I stand on one of the horses?"

"Because that is not how we do it," Corn Woman answered with obvious disgust.

Thinking Isabel was looking for reassurance, Tek-witchi said, "Don't be afraid. I will hold your ankles very tight. I won't let you fall."

Since she wasn't given any choice, Isabel warily stepped on Tekwitchi's shoulders as the girl crouched before her. Holding the Indian girl's hands for balance as Tekwitchi slowly rose to her feet, Isabel teetered on her perch precariously.

"Don't move around so much," Tekwitchi cautioned her.

"I can't help it. If I don't, I'm going to fall," Isabel answered, thinking not only was she nervous, but she felt stupid squatting like a roosting chicken.

Having fully come to her feet, Tekwitchi said, "Now

you stand, Isabel. Let go of my hands, so I can hold your ankles. Then just straighten your legs."

It seemed to Isabel that her knees had turned to water. Her heart was pounding in her chest, for she seemed to be awfully high and she knew a fall from that distance would be painful, particularly as packed as the dirt was around the tepee. Then she saw a crowd of women had gathered around to watch, and knew she couldn't back out and face their ridicule. Trembling, she slowly rose, waving her arms for balance until she had competed her stand.

"Now just reach over and pull the pins out," Tekwitchi instructed her.

Thankfully, most of the pins just slipped out, except for the last and highest. That one took a little more tugging. Isabel was terrified she would fall before it gave. Finally, it, too, slipped out, and Isabel dropped it to the ground.

"Do you want to jump from there, or for me to crouch a little?" Tekwitchi asked.

Even though Tekwitchi had jumped from Corn Woman's shoulders, it looked much too high for Isabel. "Crouch, please."

Once Isabel was safely on the ground, Tekwitchi smiled at her and said, "You did well."

"Thank you," Isabel replied, knowing she hadn't really done all that well. Everyone knew she was terrified. She was just thankful she hadn't taken a tumble and embarrassed herself and her sisters-in-law in front of the others.

Isabel learned that the real work came with loading the horses. Dragging the heavy packs was one thing; lifting them was quite another. She would never have been able to accomplish that task without the help of at least one person, and it took both women helping her to get the tepee cover to the top of the horse's back. Finally, both households were loaded, and the three women mounted their horses, Corn Woman lashing her cradleboard to the side of her saddle.

They waited patiently for the men to appear. Or rather Tekwitchi and Corn Woman did. Knowing they had been off someplace, comfortably lounging, while the women worked up a storm, irritated Isabel to no end. "We ought to go off and leave them," Isabel suggested and knew by the shocked look on both women's faces that that was unheard of. She might as well have suggested shooting them, Isabel observed, then thought, why not? They were a useless bunch. God, her back was aching.

Then the two men appeared, coming from the pasture and leading their strings of horses. With them was Red Feather on his pony. As the men passed the women, Tekwitchi and Corn Woman smiled at them, but Isabel gave Stands Alone a murderous look that stunned him, before he shook his head in renewed dismay.

The women and their string of pack horses followed the men and their horses through the village, with everyone calling good wishes as they rode by. When they reached the fringes of the Indian town another warrior and string of horses joined Greyfoot and Stands Alone. "Who is he?" Isabel asked Tekwitchi, riding beside her.

"Eye Goes That Way. He is a friend of Greyfoot's who wishes to race his horses, too."

Isabel's nose wrinkled. "Why did they name him that?"

"Because that is what one eye does, goes that way," Tekwitchi answered, crossing one eye.

"And I suppose we're going to have to cook for him, too!" Isabel commented sourly.

"No, he is bringing his wives, also." Tekwitchi turned half-way in her saddle and nodded to the rear.

Isabel twisted around and saw three other women and a string of pack horses falling in behind theirs. Obviously, the family wasn't as well to do. With only six horses between them, two women had doubled up on one horse, and the others were so loaded down you could barely see the animals. Isabel reversed her position and said, "I'm sorry. I shouldn't have made that hateful remark. It's just that I think you women do too much work and the men do too little."

"We are content with our lot," Tekwitchi replied.

Isabel knew it was true. She had yet to see an unhappy woman among the band. They laughed and chattered with one another as they worked, and they never acted tired or complained. They seemed to idolize their husbands and absolutely adored their children. They expected so little in the way of comfort, yet enjoyed life so much. To look at them or talk to them, you would think they had the very best of lives, instead of one just bordering on pure servitude. They were a total enigma to Isabel.

They left the village behind, following a narrow, twisting trail that wound up the mountainside on the opposite side of the camp from which Isabel and Stands Alone had always entered. When the trail reached its highest level in a pass between two peaks, they had a breathtaking view of the magnificent countryside for miles around them, the clouds gathering over the icy peaks looking so close you could almost reach out and touch them, the deep valleys below a verdant green where the sun reached them, purplish in the shade.

Leaving the pass behind them, they traveled through a thick forest. Since the trail was narrow and they had to ride single file and conversation was impossible, Isabel occupied herself with admiring the scenery and watching the birds and the squirrels in the trees. When the daily deluge threatened, the women dismounted and found refuge in a shallow cave, while the men spent the storm with the horses to keep them from panicking and running away.

As thunder crashed and lightning cracked and the rain came down in sheets all around, Isabel became aware of an overpowering smell. "What is that stench?" she asked Tekwitchi, who was standing next to her.

"It's probably left from the bear that uses this cave to hibernate in the winter."

"Left from? They smell that bad?"

"Some do. I have heard some warriors claim they can smell them coming."

Isabel might have thought the claim a gross exaggeration, had it not been that the Indians seemed to have sharpened senses. Curious, she asked, "Can bears be guardian spirits?"

"Oh, yes, and the man, or woman, who has a bear for their guardian spirit has power in curing, but those who have skunks for their guardian spirits, have even greater healing powers."

"Women can have a guardian spirit?" Isabel asked in surprise.

"Yes, after they no longer have their monthly flow, any woman can seek a vision. Most don't though. They are afraid to go off by themselves to wait and fast and pray, like Beaver Woman did. Most just ask their husbands to intercede with their guardian spirit and ask if they can share their power with them. They don't receive as much power, but most women are content with that."

Isabel had sensed Beaver Woman was a cut above the other women, and wondered if it was because her power was stronger since it was attained individually, or if it was a strength that was just inherent. "Do you know what Beaver Woman's guardian spirit is?"

"No."

"Do you know what Greyfoot's is?"

"No, but he has told Corn Woman. She is his first wife, you know. They usually hold a place of confidence. Perhaps someday he will be able to tell me."

Isabel was thoughtful for a moment, then said, "Stands Alone has never told me what his guardian spirit is, but I think it is an eagle. I know your people regard them highly."

"Yes, because eagles have war power. That is why eagle feathers are used on war shields and braided into the war horses' manes and tails. But I do not think Stands Alone has eagle power, even though he is a superior warrior, because he allows others to walk behind him when he is at rest."

"What does that have to do with it?"

"Eagles do not allow anyone to walk behind them. Neither do those that have eagle power. The next time you pass the captive eagles we keep for feathers, notice that. If you try to walk behind them, they will turn to face you."

Isabel frowned. She had thought she had guessed the source of Stands Alone's power, and now she knew she hadn't. Since he had yet to tell her anything, it had become a consuming curiosity.

When the rain ended, the group resumed their ride, the drenched trees dripping so much water on them that Isabel thought the women had accomplished little in seeking shelter. Then, to Isabel's amazement, the women called a halt beside a rushing mountain stream, declaring it an excellent camping spot.

As Tekwitchi helped her unload her horses, Isabel

remarked to the Indian girl, "I'm surprised the men let us stop. There's still several hours of daylight left."

"Where and when we camp is always the women's decision. Besides, we are not in any hurry on this trip."

"Have you gone to the races before?"

"Yes, but not last year. Corn Woman was heavy with child."

Isabel glanced over to where Corn Woman had leaned the cradleboard against a tree, but the baby was asleep. "I noticed Corn Woman didn't take the baby out of the cradle all day, not even to change it."

"You haven't looked closely at the baby, have you?"

"No, I really haven't been near the baby at all, until today. You've been doing most of the teaching. Then, even today, when Corn Woman and I had occasion to ride side by side, the baby was on the other side. Why?"

"Because you would see the baby is wrapped so his penis sticks out."

Well, it wasn't modest, Isabel thought, but typical of the Comanches, it was utterly practical. "And what about . . ."

"There is soft moss inside the cradle," Tekwitchi answered. "It's changed every night, when the baby is cleaned and greased, then put in its night cradle. For girl babies, we fashion a tube to drain off the liquid."

As soon as the women's horses were unloaded, the men took them away to pasture them with their horses. Isabel watched as Corn Woman and Tekwitchi put up their tepee, first setting down a four-pole foundation that was tied together at the top, then placing the other eighteen poles between them three to four feet apart. Short stakes were pounded into the ground several inches above the long poles for greater stability, then, with Tekwitchi on Corn Woman's shoulders, all the poles were tied together at the top. To Isabel's amazement, the seventeen skins that were sewn together were hoisted with a single pole from inside the tepee. Then once again, Tekwitchi stood on Corn Woman's shoulders to pull the skins together at the front, then pin them.

When the women had finished, Isabel frowned and said, "It's tilted to the back a little. Does that matter?"

"It's supposed to be that way, to allow for more room at the back," Corn Woman answered rather sharply.

"Oh," Isabel replied lamely, "I guess I just never noticed."

After Tekwitchi had placed a pole at the back of the tepee that positioned the smoke hole flaps, Corn Woman said to Isabel, "Now we will put up your tepee."

Isabel had been dreading it all day, but the chore seemed to be going surprising well once she got involved in it. She set up the framework as if she had been doing it all her life. She even managed to accomplish her second balancing act on Tekwitchi's shoulders without incident. Hoisting the hides was a little tricky and took considerable muscle, but that, too, was eventually accomplished. It wasn't until she was standing on the Indian girl's shoulders again and trying to pin the covers that Isabel met her downfall. While jerking on the hide to bring it closer together, she lost her balance and fell right into the tepee, taking everything—covering, lodge pins, and poles—with her.

Her breath left her lungs in a loud "whoosh" when she hit, and Isabel winced in pain when one of the falling poles clipped her on the shoulder. But it was her dignity that suffered the most injury when she realized that Eye Goes That Way's wives were laughing at her. Tears of humiliation stung her eyes.

Then to Isabel's amazement, Corn Woman whirled angrily around to face the amused women, giving them a murderous look that sent them scurrying away.

Tekwitchi fought her way through the maze of fallen poles and crouched beside Isabel, asking, "Are you hurt?"

"My pride was," Isabel answered, unconsciously rubbing her shoulder.

Seeing her action, Tekwitchi gently pushed her hand away and slipped the neckline of Isabel's blouse over, revealing an ugly reddened knot on her shoulder. Running her fingers lightly over it, she said, "The bone is not broken, but you're going to have a bad bruise."

"Help her out," Corn Woman told her younger sister. "Then we will put up her tent. After a hard fall like that, it will take some time for her to recover her confidence."

Isabel sat to the side and glumly watched while Tekwitchi and Corn Woman put her tepee up. When they had finished, Tekwitchi walked to her and said, "Those hateful women make me so angry. Who are they to laugh? Did you see how long it took them to put up one lodge?"

Isabel had noticed that it took them much longer than Tekwitchi and Corn Woman, and there were three of them. "Just how long should it take, if you're really good at it?"

"You should be able to dismantle one and put one up in fifteen minutes."

"I'll never be able to do that!" Isabel cried out softly, fighting back fresh tears.

Corn Woman heard the despair in Isabel's voice, walked straight to her, then said firmly, "Yes, you will. You just need practice, particularly with standing on Tekwitchi's shoulders. After we have unloaded everything and have a fire going, I will cook our meals, while you and Tekwitchi go off someplace in the woods and practice."

"Do you think we should do it today?" Tekwitchi asked. "Her shoulder is bound to be hurting her."

"The longer she waits, the harder it will be. It will only give her fear time to grow," Corn Woman answered.

After they had a fire going, Tekwitchi and Isabel slipped away, giving the men the excuse that they were going to look for berries. When they reached a secluded spot, Tekwitchi said, "This looks like a good spot. The grass is thick and soft here."

Isabel remembered all too well how hard the ground was. She glanced at the nearby stream, then said, "Perhaps we should practice in the stream, where the water will break my fall, like the men do when they're breaking a horse."

"And get our clothes wet?"

"We could strip, like we do when we're bathing."

Tekwitchi walked over to the stream and looked down, then said, "The bottom is covered with slippery rocks. I don't think I could keep my footing. We'd better do it the other way."

"Did you have to practice to learn?"

"Yes, but I was just a child. The girls practice that and tumbling just like the boys practice their tricks with their horses. I think it is easier to learn when you're young."

So did Isabel. Children were more daring and more limber, and they didn't have as far to fall.

Isabel and Tekwitchi stayed in the woods throughout the lingering twilight, practicing not just balancing on Tekwitchi's shoulders, but tumbling, so Isabel could learn how to break her fall if it did occur. And it did, three times, but none as hard as the first. Still, Isabel was aching all over when they returned to the camp. It was all she could do to hide her discomfort from Stands Alone and the others.

The next morning, Isabel was partially rewarded for

her efforts when she took down her tepee without mis-
hap. But they all knew the real test of skill lay in putting
it up, so Isabel was apprehensive all that day.

That evening, when they made camp, Isabel was
aware of the other women sneaking glances her way as
she put up her framework. She knew they were just waiting for her to make a mistake. They might not dare to
laugh out loud, not with Corn Woman watching them
like a hawk, but Isabel knew they would take delight in
her failure. It made her twice as nervous, but despite
that, she performed the chore perfectly, albeit slowly.
She even jumped down from Tekwitchi's shoulders
when the last pin was slipped in, something that apparently really took her critics by surprise, judging from
the astonished looks on the three women's faces.

Coming to her feet, Isabel saw both Corn Woman
and Tekwitchi were beaming with pride. "You did very
well," Corn Woman told her.

"I was awfully slow," Isabel replied.

"Speed will come with time. At least, for most it
does," she answered, casting a meaningful glance in
the three women's direction.

When Corn Woman looked back, her eyes directly met
Isabel's. Isabel had never expected the older, sterner sister to come to her defense as she had. She had never
considered her the friend she did Tekwitchi. But Corn
Woman had given Isabel her undivided support and encouragement. Filled with gratitude, Isabel said, "Thank
you."

The older woman knew exactly what Isabel was thank-
ing her for. "That is not necessary. We are family. Sisters. We work together, we play together, we fight
together, if need be. In all things, we are together."

At that moment, Isabel did feel a sense of unity with
the two women. Strangely, it was stronger than she had

ever felt with her own family. Then she looked up and saw Greyfoot standing a short distance away. She had no idea if he had heard what his wife had said. The look on his face was totally unreadable. He might as well have been a statue carved of stone. But Isabel did know one thing. She might be able to accept Stands Alone as her husband, Corn Woman and Tekwitchi as her sisters, but she would never be able to accept Greyfoot as her brother. For him, and for Yellow Sky, she could only feel hatred.

That night, when they were alone in their tepee, Stands Alone said to Isabel, "I was very proud of you today."

Stands Alone's praise always disarmed Isabel, particularly when it was accompanied by the warm look she saw in his eyes. "In what way?" she asked in surprise.

"How well you did putting the tepee up."

"Isn't that what I was supposed to learn on this trip? How to put up the tepee?"

Stands Alone heard the bitterness in Isabel's voice and frowned. Then he replied, "I thought it might be a good opportunity, yes. But I feared after you had fallen the day before, you would not be willing to try again."

"Who told you about that? Corn Woman?" Isabel demanded, then realizing Corn Woman wouldn't betray her, quickly added, "No. It was those women, wasn't it?"

"No, I saw it myself."

Why did he, of all people, have to witness her clumsy humiliation, Isabel thought. He who did everything, no matter how difficult, so easily, so perfectly, so gracefully. "I didn't have any choice but to try again. I couldn't let Tekwitchi and Corn Woman down."

While Stands Alone was glad Isabel was learning re-

sponsibility to her *Nema* family, that wasn't the answer
he had hoped for. "No other reason?"

"Well, I suppose a little for myself. Proving I could
do it helped me regain my pride."

Stands Alone had hoped Isabel had persisted so he
would be proud of her. Wasn't that what loving wives
did, try to please their husbands? He schooled himself
not to reveal his disappointment and smiled.

Isabel wondered at the smile. Even though it
stretched across his handsome face, it didn't reach his
expressive eyes. Those dark, velvety orbs had a strange
wistfulness about them that tore at her heart strings.

Seventeen

The next day, the group left the mountains behind, then the foothills, and moved onto a broad, grassy plain, bisected by high mesas, towering, multicolored buttes that jutted into the air seemingly from nothing, and deep, picturesque canyons timbered with white firs.

On and off throughout the day, Isabel had the opportunity to ride beside Corn Woman and observe her baby. Much to her surprise, she discovered Jumping Rabbit spent the better part of the day awake, alertly watching everything. Since he was always so quiet, she had assumed before that he was asleep. Then realizing he had an audience, the dark-eyed and chubby-cheeked baby began laughing and cooing at her. Isabel's maternal instincts had already been stirring, so that by the end of the day, when they camped beside a broad river, she had fallen in love with the baby and asked to hold him while Corn Woman and Tekwitchi put up their tepee, a request that pleased both women immensely.

After the camp had been set up, the women went hunting for wild plums, grapes, and berries that grew at random in the river bottom. As they carried their treasure back to camp in their peplums, Corn Woman said, "We will probably eat these tonight, since we are all hungry for fresh fruit. Tomorrow we shall start gath-

ering in earnest for that we wish to dry and take back
with us."

"But won't we be traveling tomorrow?" Isabel asked.

"No, this is the place where the races take place. We
arrived early, which pleases our group greatly. Not only
did we get the choice campsites, but we can get a head
start on the gathering before the others get here."

Curious as to where they were, that night Isabel asked
Stands Alone what the name of the river was.

His name for the Canadian River was given in Comanche.

"No, I mean, what is its Spanish name?"

"I do not know if it even has a Spanish name."

Was she seeing territory that had never been seen by
a white person, Isabel wondered. A little thrill ran
through her as the thought aroused her spirit of adven-
ture. Was this what her conquistador forefathers had
felt? This excitement? If so, she understood better what
drove them. And what other strange new lands would
she see in the future? Perhaps her new life did have
some advantages, she mused.

All the next day, taking turns carrying Jumping Rabbit on their backs, Isabel and Corn Woman and Tekwitchi gathered green plums, tart black grapes,
reddish-orange chokeberries, and purple mulberries.
Then they went out on the prairie and dug up *yep*, the
Indian potato, which could be eaten raw, like an apple,
or cooked, or sliced and dried. When they returned to
the camp later that afternoon, they discovered two new
bands had arrived and were making camp across the
river from them. To Isabel's surprise, Corn Woman
elected to delay starting their evening meal so they
could watch the women putting up their tepees.

"See, it takes them longer," Corn Woman remarked.

Isabel glanced over and saw Eye Goes That Way's

wives were watching with a critical eye, also. Apparently, the Indian women considered the speed and skill with which a woman put up her tepee as a measure of her success as a wife and homemaker. She was doubly glad she had persisted and learned. "Are they *Nema,* too?" she asked Corn Woman.

"One band is. The other is . . ." Corn Woman stopped in mid-sentence and frowned. Then she said, "I do not know the Spanish name. We do not even have a name for them. We never saw them before, until two years ago. They come from the north, in hopes of trading, as well as racing. They do not have many horses, like our people. They are . . ." She held her hand pointing straight up, palm facing Isabel.

"Is that supposed to mean something?" Isabel asked.

"Yes, it is sign language. That is how the different tribes talk to one another. This signifies that tribe's name."

"Do the *Nema* have a sign name?"

"Yes." Corn Woman placed her arm, bent at the elbow parallel before her, then moved it backwards while wiggling her hand. "It means 'snake going backwards.' "

"But why are the *Nema* called that?"

"I do not know. You will have to ask Stands Alone."

"They do not even put up their tepee the same way we do," Tekwitchi observed, watching the second Cheyenne tepee being assembled. "See? They use a three-pole base, instead of four."

That night, Isabel asked Stands Alone why the *Nema* were called "snake going backwards."

"This is the story I have heard," Stands Alone answered. "When a band of *Nema* left the mountains from which my people came, a group of the people became afraid and wanted to turn back. The leader called a

council, but the group could not be persuaded to continue. In a fit of anger, the leader compared them to a
snake backing up in its track. Since then, that has been
our sign."

"But your band didn't turn back," Isabel objected.
"You're here."

Stands Alone shrugged his magnificent shoulders,
then replied, "Still, that is our sign."

Isabel shook her head, thinking sometimes the Comanches made very good sense, and sometimes none
at all.

Over the next few days, more and more bands of Indians arrived, pitching their tepees on both sides of the
river, and soon the camp was as busy and noisy as the
one they had left, if not noisier. Many of the bands had
brought their dogs with them, and there wasn't an hour
that passed that a furious dog fight didn't take place,
the Indian women having to wade into the cluster of
snapping, vicious dogs and break it up with a big stick.

As they waited for the last of the bands to arrive, a
festive air hung over the gathering, with the Indians
making social visits with one another as well as taking
the opportunity to do a little trading. Seashells from
the beaches on the Gulf of Mexico were exchanged for
obsidian and turquoise from New Mexico, Spanish
knives traded for French gun powder, colorful trading
blankets from the British far to the north and east bartered for beaver skins, and horses changed hands right
and left, each Indian firmly convinced he had out-
smarted the other.

One evening, their band was invited to a feast by another *Nema* band. Sitting in a circle around the campfire, they were served heaping platters of steaming

venison and antelope. But no one touched a morsel until their host cut off a piece of meat, raised it as an offering to Our Sure Enough Father in heaven, then buried it in the ground next to him. To Isabel, the meat tasted particularly good. She didn't know if it was because the other women were actually better cooks, or if it was because she had not had to labor to cook it. Even when she found out that their band was going to have to reciprocate the next night, Isabel didn't mind the added work. It had been nice to be waited on for a change, if only for one night.

Finally, the day the races were to begin arrived. The dew wasn't even off the ground when the preparations began, the warriors walking their horses in the smoke of the campfires to give the animals' hooves some last minute toughening, then grooming them and braiding their manes and tails, then painting bolts of lightning on their legs for speed. The betting was fast and furious and, in Isabel's opinion, a little insane as men wagered their tepees and their wives' household goods as well as their own personal property.

Isabel was standing beside Stands Alone and his mount before the first race began when an Indian from another tribe walked up to them, pointed to Isabel, then asked Stands Alone something in sign language. From the corner of her eye, Isabel saw the sudden flare in Stands Alone's eyes before a forbidding look came over his face and he shook his head.

The Indian said something else, and again, Stands Alone shook his head. For the third time, the man's hands moved frantically. Suddenly, Stands Alone slammed his fist into the palm of his hand in what Isabel assumed was an emphatic, no! A furious expression came over the Indian's face. Then he turned and walked away in a huff.

"What did he want to gamble for?" Isabel asked, already suspicious, for she had seen the man pointing at her.

Stands Alone wondered if he should tell her, then answered reluctantly, "You."

"That's the most indecent proposal I've ever heard!" Isabel said indignantly. "His tribe must be an utterly shameless people."

"I'm afraid his tribe isn't the only one in which warriors sometimes wager their women, whether they be wives, sisters, or daughters. Some of the *Nema* do it, too."

"That's disgraceful!" Isabel retorted, her eyes spitting blue sparks. "Women are human beings with souls, not animals. It's bad enough that you gamble away their property, but to wager them, as if they are nothing but chattel. . . . You have no right!"

Stands Alone took Isabel's "you" literally. "I didn't. You saw me refuse his offer. A very generous offer, I might add. He was willing to wager six hundred horses for you."

If Stands Alone had thought Isabel would feel complimented, he was sadly mistaken. "Generous?" Isabel spat. "You'd set my worth at six hundred horses?"

"I didn't say that," Stands Alone answered in exasperation. "I said that's what he offered. I refused, remember?"

"That has nothing to do with it!" Isabel answered irrationally, so outraged she wasn't even listening to Stands Alone. "I'm talking about the demeaning way you treat your women."

She was doing it again, Stands Alone thought in frustration, attacking the ways of his people in general, blaming him for things he couldn't change, refusing to judge him simply for the man he was. Was it just Isabel, or did all whites have this blind spot, he wondered. Bands were often blamed for things other bands or tribes had done. They were all deemed the same, regardless of what they did, or didn't do. Over and over, the Spanish refused to judge the bands by their individual merit, just as Isabel persisted in doing. He hadn't accepted the wager, even though he knew full well his horse would win. He had refused on principle. Isabel was his soul mate, his other half. He would no more dream of wagering her than his arm or leg. To do so would have been an abomination against nature. Then he glanced around and saw they were attracting attention. "We will discuss this later."

"No, I—"

"I said later."

The words were said softly, but there was steel beneath them, and the expression on Stands Alone's face was adamant. Suddenly, Isabel realized she was creating a spectacle and had the good sense to be embarrassed. She nodded and stepped away.

Stands Alone turned and flew into the saddle. As he pivoted his horse and rode off in the direction of the prairie where the races would take place, Isabel's embarrassment turned to shame. She realized she had overreacted—again! It wasn't Stands Alone's fault that the Indian had made the indecent offer, she admitted. And he had refused it. She couldn't even blame the other man, not if it was the Indians' way and they didn't consider it wrong. She didn't know why, but there was this part of her that rebelled against male domination, rebelled so strongly she sometimes lost her powers of reason. And it wasn't just restricted to Indian males. She had felt just as strongly about Spanish men. She wished she could learn to accept as Beaver Woman and the others had. If she could content herself with her lot, set her warring soul at peace, life would certainly be easier.

* * *

A little later, Isabel, Corn Woman, and Tekwitchi walked to the open area where the races were to take place. Throughout the day, the Indians raced their horses, one contest following the other in such rapid succession that the dust didn't even settle between runs. And the Indians, although reserved in so many other things, were every bit as enthusiastic over their racing as the Spanish people. They rooted their favorite on with cheers, jumped up and down and screamed, and generally went berserk when their horse won. They even got into a few shoving matches when there was a disagreement over whose horse cleared the finish line first.

Stands Alone didn't participate in every race, but in those he did, he always won, sometimes by such a wide margin it was almost embarrassing, except Isabel was always too excited to feel anything except that. Then there was a pause before the final and most important race, not so much to give the riders a rest as to sweeten the anticipation.

Isabel had taken refuge from the hot sun beneath a small cottonwood tree that grew on the fringes of the field where the horses were being raced. She had never gotten a good look at the horses Stands Alone had brought with him, so when she saw Stands Alone leading the horse he planned to race from the remuda of his other horses, she was shocked. Obviously a mustang, for it was much shorter and smaller than the other horses, it was the most miserable-looking creature she had ever seen, its long hair falling out in unsightly patches, its thick shaggy tail dragging on the ground, its head drooping listlessly as it plodded along. Then she noticed something else. The animal was limping!

Stands Alone walked up to her, smiled, and said, "I

saw you rooting for me that last race. Do I dare hope you've forgiven me for earlier?"

"Yes. I'm sorry I got carried away. But I'll never forgive you for what you're about to do."

"What's that?"

"Race that thing you call a horse. You must be insane. You're going to lose everything you won, to say nothing of the ridicule you'll have to endure." She glanced around, then said, "Why, everybody is already laughing at you."

"Good. Then they'll wager more."

"You *are* insane! What difference does it matter how much they wager, if you lose?"

"I won't lose."

Isabel's look was incredulous. "Won't lose? Riding a lame horse?"

Stands Alone lowered his voice so no one else could hear and said, "Do not be deceived. He's not lame. He just limps."

With that, Stands Alone walked away, leaving Isabel to stare at his broad back in puzzlement. As he walked to the starting line, Stands Alone was besieged with warriors who held the same low regard for the mustang as Isabel, all wanting to make big wagers. After Stands Alone had agreed and walked on, the men smirked behind his back. Having never seen anything but the highest regard being shown to Stands Alone, Isabel was sickened by the contempt.

As the warriors mounted their horses at the starting line, Isabel felt doubly sure Stands Alone would lose. All the other animals were splendid specimens of horse-flesh, many eagerly pawing the ground in anticipation of the race. The mustang appeared to have fallen asleep. And Stands Alone looked ridiculous seated on the little horse, his long legs almost touching the ground and the other warriors towering over him. Isabel heard several women in the crowd around her snickering and knew why. Then she saw them glancing at her. Isabel's first instinct was to cower in shame. Then, remembering that Stands Alone was her husband, a man much superior to all others, she squared her shoulders and raised her chin proudly in defiance.

The race began with a suddenness that caught everyone but the riders by surprise. Through the swirling dust left by the others, Isabel could see the mustang trailing. But the little horse clung to the pack. Isabel was surprised that he could even begin to keep up with his long-legged, sleek competitors. Isabel was so absorbed watching the mustang that she didn't pay any attention to which horse was in the lead, but she knew by the loud cheers all around her it must be the favorite. Then, when the race was about three-quarters of the way through, the ground shaking from the pounding hooves, there was the most amazing transformation in the mustang. Suddenly, the animal flew forward, as if shot from a cannon, his long mane floating out on both sides of him as if it were wings, his sweeping tail trailing as if it were a banner. The mustang raced past one horse, then another, and another. A stunned silence fell over the majority of the crowd. But not Isabel and the others in their band. They began to cheer and call encouragement as the valiant little horse left more of the competition to the rear, the riders' looks of total astonishment as the mustang flew by making Isabel laugh out loud. Then the race was down to the lead horse and the mustang, and even then there wasn't any contest. The little horse streaked by. Then to everyone's surprise—and Isabel's total delight—just before the mustang crossed the finish line, Stands Alone flipped around in the saddle, riding backwards and grinning impishly at the others bringing up the rear.

The crowd roared in approval. When Stands Alone jumped from his mount, he was surrounded with warriors congratulating him and clapping him on the back. Even those who had wagered against the mustang and lost didn't seem to mind. Indians admired craftiness almost as much as courage, for it played a big part in battle strategy.

After all the hubbub had settled down, Stands Alone walked to where Isabel was anxiously waiting, leading the mustang behind him. With the glow of victory still on him, Isabel thought he looked incredibly handsome, and she was so proud of him she thought she would burst. When he stepped up to her, she couldn't hold back. She threw her arms around him and hugged him, saying, "That was the most exciting thing I have ever seen."

Stands Alone didn't even notice Isabel's break in Comanche etiquette. Knowing she was pleased with him was even more heady than winning the race. When she stepped back, he said, "Didn't I tell you looks were deceiving?"

"But he *was* limping. How did you get him to do that?"

"I didn't teach him that trick. It was his own." He took her arm, saying, "Walk with me to where my horses are pastured, and I'll tell the story."

Isabel fell in beside Stands Alone. As they walked, he said, "The first time I saw Lightning Strikes he was standing with his herd of mares. Like you and everyone else, I thought he was a sad-looking horse. But he had the biggest herd of mares of all the stallions in that valley. I was curious as to why that was, since he didn't look all that powerful and valiant. I decided to stay and observe him. A few days later, another stallion entered that part of the valley and grazed his herd near Lightning Strikes.

I saw Lightning Strikes eyeing the other stallion's herd. Then, looking just as pitiful as he did today, he limped over to it. The stallion saw him coming and became immediately alert, holding his ears straight up in warning. Lightning Strikes laid his ears back, like the mares do in submissiveness. The stallion decided Lightning Strikes was so miserable-looking, he wasn't any threat. He went back to his grazing. Before he knew what had happened, Lightning Strikes had cut three splendid mares from the herd and driven them into his own."

"Didn't the other stallion try to get them back?"

"Ordinarily, one would, or better yet, challenge the interloper for his entire herd. But I think the Lightning Strikes' clever deception made the other stallion wary. Perhaps he was afraid Lightning Strikes had more tricks. He simply drove what was left of his herd away."

"Then Lightning Strikes doesn't limp all the time?"

"No, only when he's around other males. He doesn't know they're gelded and would offer no threat. But if there had been any mares in that race, he wouldn't have run. He'd have been too busy stealing them."

Naturally, the racehorses had been geldings. Isabel had learned the warriors never rode mares. They were for women and children, Even the female horses were held in low esteem. Then, taking more careful note of something Stands Alone had said, she asked, "Are you saying Lightning Strikes isn't gelded?"

"No. That's one reason I haven't trimmed his coat and have left his tail so thick and long. All wild horses have unusually long and thick manes and tails. They also have longer hair all over, particularly farther north, where I found Lightning Strikes. I was hoping the others wouldn't notice what was beneath all that hair. Then they might have become suspicious. They'd wonder what breeding qualities he had, if it wasn't his looks."

"Then you intend to breed him?"

"The way he runs? I certainly do."

Isabel remembered the way the mustang had run. She had never seen anything so swift. "Why did you wait so long to let him run? Up until almost the end of the race, I just knew you were going to lose."

"If I had given him his head from the very beginning, there wouldn't have been any contest. Then no one would have had any fun. This way, it was more exciting."

As they approached the enclosure where Stands Alone had his horses roped in, Isabel saw warriors leading the horses they had wagered towards it. Without actually counting, Isabel knew Stands Alone had won several hundred horses. "What are you going to do with all the horses you've won?"

"If the mares and stallions look like good breeding material, I'll keep them. If not, I'll give them away with the geldings. I told you, I'm more interested in quality than quantity."

Isabel took a good look at Stands Alone's remuda and remarked, "You didn't bring many horses for wagering."

"No, I didn't. In each race, I wagered the horse I rode. Everyone knew it would be equal to anything they could put up. As I told you before, I have something of a reputation as a horse breeder."

"Then why did they bet on the last race, if everyone thought the mustang was going to lose? Surely, no one wanted him."

"No, they wanted revenge, just to be able to say they beat me and walked away with one of my horses." He reached back and patted the mustang's cheek, saying, "But we fooled them, didn't we, boy?"

Isabel looked over her shoulder and saw the sleepy look in the mustang's eyes turn to one that was absolutely diabolical. She glanced at Stands Alone and saw the devilish grin on his face. She had never dreamed that man and beast could be co-conspirators, but that's what these two obviously were. Cunning co-conspirators.

Recalling the snickers and smirks the others had directed at Stands Alone and her, she couldn't help but laugh.

Eighteen

As Isabel and Stands Alone were walking back to the camp after corralling Lightning Strikes, Isabel saw Corn Woman and Tekwitchi hurrying towards them.

When the two women reached them, Tekwitchi said breathlessly, "Here you are, Isabel. We have been looking all over for you."

"I went with Stands Alone to put up his horse," Isabel answered.

Corn Woman turned to Stands Alone and said to him, "Congratulations. That was the most exciting race I have ever seen."

"And the most profitable for Greyfoot," Tekwitchi added. "He won a hundred horses betting on that mustang."

"Then he knew about the limp?" Isabel asked Stands Alone.

"No, he just had faith in me."

Isabel felt a twinge of guilt, knowing she hadn't. But she hadn't let the others shame her, she remembered, taking consolation in that, at least. "What did you want with me that was so important?" she asked Tekwitchi.

"I didn't want you to miss the women's races, since I am going to participate," Tekwitchi answered, her dark eyes alive with excitement.

"The women race, too?" Isabel asked in surprise.

"Of course. You don't think we came just to work, do you?"

That was exactly what Isabel had thought, that they had been brought to provide the men with the comforts of home. "I didn't know the women raced horses at all."

"How silly," Tekwitchi answered. "I know you've seen us racing back home."

"I thought you were just exercising your horses."

"Well, we weren't," Tekwitchi replied a little tartly. "We were racing. If you'd take a little time away from your chores, you'd know that."

Isabel had always felt she needed every possible moment she had to complete her chores and had never dallied when she was attending her horses, except to watch the colts for a moment or two. And here she had been feeling sorry for the Indian women, because she thought their lives all drudgery.

"Isabel is new to our way of life," Corn Woman reminded Tekwitchi in a censoring tone of voice. "If she did not know we have activities to amuse us, it is our fault." She directed her next words to Isabel, saying, "Many of the women enjoy racing horses. Others prefer foot races. Still others prefer our kickball game, but we play that mostly in the fall, when it is cooler." She looked back at her younger sister and said, "Tekwitchi is quite good at racing horses."

Tekwitchi blushed at her sister's censure as much as her compliment and said to Isabel, "Forgive me, Isabel. Of course, you do not know all of our ways yet. I do race, more for the fun of it than anything. It's really exciting, much more so than just watching."

"I imagine it is," Isabel answered. "Spanish women aren't allowed to play games or participate in any kind of competition, particularly anything physical. It's considered unladylike. We always had to just sit and watch, except for dancing."

Stands Alone knew how much Isabel loved dancing. "Why don't you race today?" he asked her.

"Me?" Isabel responded in surprise. "I don't know anything about racing."

"You don't have to do it to win," Tekwitchi told her. "Just do it for the fun of it, like I do."

Stands Alone saw the spark of interest in Isabel's eyes. When she hung back, he said, "Come on. Let's go back and pick out a horse for you."

Ordinarily Isabel would have resented Stands Alone's taking the initiative from her, except his decision was in perfect accord with hers. "All right."

"Oh, I'm so happy you're going to!" Tekwitchi cried out softly. Turning, she called over her shoulder, "I'll meet you at the starting line."

When Isabel reached the spot where her mares were corralled, she slipped beneath the rope and looked over her riding horses, trying to decide which one to use. Spying Ruby and remembering how fast Stands Alone's mustang had been, she walked towards the roan mare. Then she felt a familiar nudge on her shoulder. She turned and saw the bay mare, an almost pleading expression in her soft brown eyes. "Oh, all right, I'll ride you," Isabel said softly. "We're just doing it for the fun of it, like Tekwitchi said."

Stands Alone waited while Isabel slipped an Indian bridle over the mare's lower jaw and then saddled her. He knew the high, bowed saddle would slow the horse down, but kept his thoughts to himself, not wanting to discourage Isabel before she even began. It wasn't until he was walking her to the starting line that he began to have reservations. Sometimes the women's races could get pretty rough, even more so than the men's. Theirs was a no-rules, no-holds-barred competition that some-times amazed even the most hardened warrior with its viciousness.

As they stepped up to the starting line, Tekwitchi and her horse were waiting, as were a score or more of other women and their mounts. Tekwitchi moved closer to Isabel and said in a lowered voice, "Let me warn you of a few things. Don't let any of the women crowd you. They may try to push you off your horse. And if you see any of them carrying switches, keep your distance. They're not above using them on you."

Stunned, Isabel wondered what she had gotten herself into. Seeing the expression on her face and even more worried for her safety, Stands Alone said, "You don' have to do this. You can just turn around and leave."

And have everyone, including him, think she was a coward and a weakling, Isabel thought. Especially him. "No, I said I would, and I will," she answered with de-termination, valiantly trying to suppress her fear and anxiety.

Isabel turned and mounted, then looked around her and noted that everyone else was riding bareback. See-ing the sneers directed at her saddle, she knew she had made her first mistake and wished Tekwitchi had warned her about that, too. Then, she realized that if Tekwitchi had pointed that out, she wouldn't have agreed to race at all, since she couldn't ride that way, with nothing between her and the horse but a thin blan-ket. No, she would just have to remember she was doing this for the fun of it. Since she wasn't truly competing, what difference did it make how she rode?

When the starting signal was given, all the horses bolted, including the bay mare, with no encouragement from Isabel. Isabel had decided to race just for the fun of it. Apparently, the mare had different ideas. She sped from the starting line with a burst of speed Isabel had never dreamed she possessed. Isabel found herself in the thick of the racing horses, surrounded by swirling dust and seemingly enveloped in a steamy cloud of heat generated by the animals' exertions, the sound of pounding hooves almost deafening. She had no choice but to hang on for dear life, her heart racing for fear she would fall.

Suddenly, Isabel found herself being crowded, not by just one horse, but by one on each side. As her legs brushed the legs of the woman beside her, Isabel saw the switch being raised from the corner of her eye. She cowered in anticipation, and endured several stinging lashes. But when she heard her mare whinny sharply in pain, a fury filled her, totally crowding out her fear. She turned to face the woman, took several lashes full on the chest as she reached across, then caught the switch and yanked it from the woman's hand. Seeing the furious look on Isabel's face and afraid she would use her own weapon on her, the woman veered away sharply, leaving Isabel to contend with the woman on the other side. Then as Isabel turned to her, and she, too, saw the switch, the second woman also decided retreat was the better part of valor.

Isabel's fury brought forth her keen Spanish competitiveness. No longer was she racing for the fun of it. She wanted to win. She bent over the mare's neck and yelled encouragement. What the mare lacked in racing expertise, she made up in heart by giving it everything she had. The wind rushed by Isabel, flapping her clothing wildly about her and loosening the thick braid that hung down her back, leaving her long hair to trail behind her like a lustrous black banner. As they passed one horse, then another, and another, Isabel's excitement grew and grew. Before her, she recognized Tekwitchi, racing in the dusty wake of another rider. Everything else was a blur as the scenery flew by. Then the crowd of spectators roared, drowning out even the sounds of the pounding hooves.

Isabel knew the race was over. She hadn't won, but she wasn't displeased with herself. She knew she and the mare had put up a good fight. And it *had* been terribly exciting. She slowed the mare, then brought the animal to a stop beside Tekwitchi's mount.

Seeing her, Tekwitchi jumped from her horse and said with total exuberance, "Did you see that? I came in second!"

"Yes, I know," Isabel answered, also dismounting. Although she hadn't been able to see much of Tekwitchi's race because she was so busy with her own, she said, "You rode superbly."

"Thank you. I'm afraid I didn't get to see you, but you must have done well, even to finish your first race." Tekwitchi glanced around, saying, "I wonder who came in third."

"Isabel did," a deep voice said from behind them.

Isabel turned and saw Stands Alone and Greyfoot. Both men had looks of pride on their faces, but it was Stands Alone's that took Isabel's breath away. He was positively glowing. Stunned, and feeling a little answering glow deep down inside her, Isabel muttered in surprise, "I did?"

"Oh, Isabel, that's wonderful!" Tekwitchi cried out, not waiting for further confirmation. As she embraced her, Isabel saw Greyfoot smiling at them over Tekwitchi's shoulder. As their eyes met, he said to Isabel, "I understand this is your first race. You rode remarkably well."

Isabel still hated her brother-in-law, but she knew it would be currish to refuse to at least be civil. "Thank you," she replied a little stiffly.

"We have done well for our band, don't you think?" Tekwitchi asked the two men, her round face still glowing from her victory. "Both of you won all the raccs you were in, I came in second, and Isabel came in third in the women's race."

"We certainly have," Greyfoot agreed readily. "We have honored our band."

Having finally realized how well she had done, Isabel felt a victorious rush and said, "We'll do even better next year, Tekwitchi. We'll take first and second place."

Isabel was so excited, she didn't realize the import of her words, but Stands Alone and Greyfoot did. They exchanged a meaningful glance, both men feeling relief that Isabel was accepting her new life well enough to anticipate the next year.

"What did you name your mare?" Stands Alone asked Isabel.

Isabel had completely forgotten the mare and the important part she had played in winning the race. She whirled around and said to the horse, "I'm sorry, girl. I forgot to thank you. You did well. Really well." Then becoming aware that Stands Alone was awaiting an answer, she stroked the mare's cheek thoughtfully, then said, "I'm going to name her Golden Heart, because she put her whole heart into that race."

Stands Alone nodded in approval and answered, "That is perhaps the best trait a horse can have, a valiant heart."

"Or a person," Greyfoot observed wisely, showing Isabel a side of him she had never guessed.

That night, there was a feast to celebrate a successful gathering and friendship, old and new. Isabel and Stands Alone attended only because it was expected of them. The excitement of their victories that afternoon had triggered their passion. Their only desire was to make love. Throughout the feast, and then the dancing, they were both so anxious to get away alone they could hardly sit still, the waiting only increasing each's hunger for the other.

Finally, they escaped, and hurried through the camp to their tepee, almost running in their excitement. They had barely stepped into their tepee when Stands Alone took Isabel into his arms and kissed her fiercely, molding her soft curves to his hard, muscular body as if he intended to absorb her right through his skin. Whirling from the passionate kiss, Isabel barely had the presence of mind to loosen the belt to his breechcloth, and then her hands were so weak from longing she could barely manage the task. Finally the cloth fell away, and she eagerly took his hot length in her hands. Stands Alone groaned in pleasure, broke the kiss, lifted the hem of her dress and tossed it over her head.

Then, seeing the red welts on her chest in the light of the small fire they had left burning, he froze.

"What's wrong?" Isabel asked, then glanced down.

"Where did you get those?"

"This afternoon, in the race."

Isabel had told Stands Alone about the woman's hitting her horse. She had asked him to show her how to prepare a potion to put on the mare's injury. But she had mentioned nothing of the injuries she had received. A furious expression came over his face. "She hit you, too?"

"Yes, before I got the switch away from her." Then when it dawned on her that Stands Alone looked angry enough to kill, she said, "They're nothing. Forget them." She slipped her hands around his neck and pressed her naked body against his, whispering, "We have better things to do."

The feel of Isabel's soft skin, her nipples like hot darts against his chest, tempered Stands Alone's anger. But the hot passion that had been driving him had also been tempered. He arched her back, bent his head and tenderly kissed the entire length of each welt, then ran his tongue over them. It was a ministration that brought tears to Isabel's eyes as well as tingles to her skin. But she wanted more. She cupped her breast and offered it to him.

It didn't take long for their passion to build to the cutting edge it had had before. Isabel moaned and wantonly rubbed herself against his readiness, her nails gently raking his back. Then, to her surprise, she felt herself being lifted from the ground and her legs being wrapped around Stands Alone's hips. As straight as an arrow, he penetrated her, making Isabel feel as if she had been impaled on a red-hot lightning bolt.

If Isabel had had any fears that Stands Alone might drop her, they were quickly dispelled. He was in full control, each magnificent, deep thrust an ecstasy, each withdrawal an agony of anticipation. They didn't kiss, but looked deeply into one another's eyes, the awareness of the wondrous sensations they saw there multiplying their pleasure. Then as Stands Alone increased his thrusts, driving deeper and harder into her hot depths, seemingly reaching for her soul, Isabel threw her head back and gave herself up to sheer sensation, each powerful wave of rapture washing over her stronger than the last, until she climaxed in a final explosion that plunged her into a deep, black void.

When Isabel came to her senses they were lying on the pallet and were drenched with sweat. Stands Alone took a wet rag and washed her body with it, then cooled his own in like manner. Then they extinguished the fire and rolled the bottom of the tepee up a foot or so to allow for better ventilation, since it was much warmer here on the prairie than in the mountains.

As they lay on their pallet, in the light of the full moon that streamed down on them, Stands Alone once again saw the welts on Isabel's chest. Again, he bent and kissed them tenderly, wishing he could take the pain from her.

Isabel caught the back of his head in her hands and brought it to lay in the valley between her breasts, then said softly, "Stop worrying about them. They don't hurt that much. I just wish I could have given that woman some of her own medicine for what she did to Golden Heart. If she hadn't gotten away, I would have gladly thrashed her."

It appeared Isabel could take care of herself with the women, Stands Alone thought, give tit-for-tat, if necessary. She wasn't about to be intimidated or beaten, not without a fight. His beloved captive also had a valiant heart. He went to sleep with his head still pillowed on her soft breasts, a proud smile on his face.

Nineteen

Two months after Isabel and Stands Alone had returned to the Comanche village from the races, Isabel was sewing with Tekwitchi when she heard the village crier making an announcement as he wove through the maze of tepees. Since Stands Alone had brought her to the camp, Isabel had been slowly learning the Comanche language, so that she understood much of everything that was said and was beginning to speak a few words. But that day, the crier was calling words she had never heard, and she asked Tekwitchi, "What is he saying?"

"That the council has decided we will leave for our fall buffalo hunt in three days, and everyone should start preparing."

"Are you saying the entire village goes on the hunt?"

"Yes."

"How far is it?"

"That depends upon where we find the buffalo. Sometimes they are not in the usual places and we have to search for them. It could take weeks."

"In that case, wouldn't it be better to leave the children and elderly behind? All that moving around must be exhausting."

"They are going to have to move anyway, to our winter camp. Besides, everyone looks forward to this."

Over the next few days, the camp was in a frenzy as everyone prepared for the move. On the morning of the third day, the village was ready for its trek. Household goods and everyone's personal belongings were piled on the horses, and, if there weren't enough animals, on travois, some were pulled by dogs if the load were light enough. Everyone but the infirm was mounted. Those who were unable to sit a horse rode on the travois, sandwiched in amongst the packs in most cases, while young children often rode two and three to a horse.

The band moved out in single file, the men first, looking dignified and grave and, because an unexpected encounter with an enemy tribe was always a possibility, they carried their prized weapons: the three-foot-long, osage orange-wood bow and a quiver of dogwood arrows thrown over their shoulder; a musket, if they owned one, tied to their saddle, along with a bison-hide war shield, decorated with bear's teeth or horses' tails or rimmed with feathers; a battle ax; and perhaps a long, feathered lance. Behind the men came the women, keeping a watchful eye on the pack horses, and the children. Behind them came the massive herd of horses, driven by the boys of the band, overseen by several warriors. And here, and there, and everywhere, were the village dogs that hadn't been called into service, yapping and nipping at the horses' hooves.

For three days, the band moved down from the mountains, passing through canyons where the aspen and maples displayed their fall foliage in splashes of spectacular color. Each night, they pitched camp, unloading everything; then they disassembled the tepees and loaded everything back up each morning, the Indians' efficiency, organization, and speed surpassing that of the best-trained army and amazing Isabel, who had to scramble to keep up.

When they moved out on prairie, Isabel knew the band had taken a different direction from the one they had taken to the horse races. That prairie had been gently rolling and broken by wide rivers and rushing streams. This grassland was as flat as a pancake, totally barren except for the seared grass and tall yucca plants that looked from the distance like stakes driven into the ground.

After they had passed over the second shallow-banked, sandy creek where only a trickle of water flowed, water that was undrinkable and reeked to high heaven, Isabel's apprehension grew. She said to Tek-witchi, riding beside her, "Maybe we shouldn't have come to this desert, or whatever it's called. There's no water here."

"It's here. You just have to know where the water holes are. There's the proof right over there," Tek-witchi answered, pointing at something in the distance.

Isabel could see something moving in the huge, swirling cloud of dust. "Is that buffalo?" she asked in excitement.

"No, but this is buffalo country. That's a herd of antelope you see. They're all over out here. They wouldn't be able to survive if there wasn't any water."

The Comanches were one of the few southwestern tribes who did know of the secret water holes in the arid, forbidding territory the Spanish called the *Llano Estacado*. The band camped that night in a lightly wooded area beside a small crystal-clear stream. As soon as camp was made and the evening fires going, the women took advantage of the opportunity to pick the reddish-orange fruit of the persimmon trees that were scattered amongst the cottonwoods, as well as sweet thistle stalks and milkweed buds that grew amongst the grass. A few even went out onto the arid prairie to gather the paddle-like leaves of the cactus and the dried, brown beans from the mesquite that grew here and there in squat, thorny thickets. That night, buffalo skulls were laid out in a circle around the camp in hopes of attracting a herd, the bleached bones looking eerie as they reflected the moonlight.

The next morning when the scouts rode in and reported there were no signs of buffalo, the band packed up and moved on. Day after day, they traveled across the high tableland, choking on the dust raised by their own horses, the hot autumn sun beating down on them unmercifully, the perpetual wind rattling the stalks of the dried grass. At night, they camped near streams where willows grew, so they could add the wood to the campfires to produce smoke to keep the hordes of mosquitoes and gnats away. For two days, they camped near an old buffalo wallow, the huge, bowl-like indentation so dry the earth was cracked and peeling, in hopes the buffalo would return; then when that produced no results, they moved on once again.

On one particularly hot day during the second week of their search, Isabel saw Tekwitchi looking intently at the ground, first on one side of her mount, then the other. "What are you looking for?" Isabel asked.

"A horned toad. It's said if you ask a horned toad where the buffalo are, he will lead you to them. That is why we call him *kusetemini*, 'asking about the buffalo.' "

"So will a raven point to a herd," Corn Woman interjected from where she rode on the other side of Isabel. "If it circles your camp four times, then flies away, it will lead you to the buffalo."

Isabel looked up and saw a bird circling high in the sky. "Is that a raven? It's black."

Corn Woman looked up, then replied, "No, I think it is a hawk. Ravens don't fly that high."

"Why didn't we stay where we were?" Isabel asked, feeling hot, sticky, and very discouraged. "We had plenty of meat there. Or why don't the men attack one of those antelope herds we've seen so many of."

"Antelope is suitable, and sometimes our men do hunt them," Tekwitchi replied. "But the hunt is never as exciting as with the buffalo. The warriors drive the antelope into brush pens, like the wild horses they capture, then slaughter them."

"Are you saying we're running around out here, getting our faces burned to a crisp in this hot sun just because the men think hunting buffalo better sport?" Isabel asked angrily.

"No, of course not," Corn Woman answered. "Our people have a craving for buffalo meat that just can't be satisfied by any other meat, to say nothing of all the other things we use the animals for. How many deer hides do you think it would take to make a tepee? Many too many, I can assure you. Even then, buckskin is not nearly as thick and durable. And nothing is warmer than a buffalo robe, with the hair left on. Four heavy trading blankets can't give you that much protection from the cold. There is not one thing on the buffalo that we do not make good use of. You will see and learn."

Tekwitchi bent forward and took a closer look at Isabel's face, then said, "I did not realize you were so burned."

"Yes," Isabel answered, the tender tip of her peeling nose feeling as if it were on fire, "and we don't have any flour for me to make a protective paste from."

"Maybe we can fashion you a sunshade from a buffalo hide platter," Tekwitchi suggested, "until we have more bull hides to work with. It has the thickest and toughest hide, you know."

"A sunshade?" Isabel asked, then scoffed, saying, "I've never heard of anything so ridiculous."

"No, it is not," Beaver Woman commented from where she rode on the other side of Corn Woman. "There is a group of *Nema* who live on this prairie who carry pieces of hard buffalo hide to protect them from the hot sun. They are called the Sunshade Band. We will just have to figure out how to attach a stick to the platter, so you can hold it over your head."

Two days later, when the noonday sun was blazing down on them and a yellow haze hung over everything, the scouts returned. Even before they reached the column, Isabel and everyone else knew they had been successful by the joyous acrobatics they were doing on their horses. A loud cheer rang out, so loud Isabel feared it would frighten the buffalo away, until she learned the herd was still a good ten miles in the distance.

Camp was made at the first likely spot that provided both wood and water. The rest of that day and the next, the Indians prepared for the upcoming hunt in a frenzy of activity: the men sharpening their arrows and lances, restringing their bows, and grooming their horses; the women grinding their butcher knives and scouring the huge kettles they had brought with them; the children gathering fuel for the fires that would be built to boil the meat.

When Isabel first saw the dried buffalo paddies the children were bringing from the prairie, she was shocked and said to Tekwitchi, "Someone should stop those children. They shouldn't be playing with . . . ," she made a face, "that."

Tekwitchi laughed and replied, "They are not playing with it, silly. They are gathering it for fuel. It burns much hotter and longer than any wood, even mesquite. Before we go home, we will all go out and gather it, to take back with us."

"You might, but not me. I'm not about to pick up that disgusting stuff," Isabel answered indignantly.

"Yes, you will," Beaver Woman replied, overhearing the conversation, "and you will be glad you did when snow has covered the ground and the only wood you can find is still on the trees. It is much easier to collect fuel now, than when your hands are blue and frozen."

Stands Alone had been appointed the hunt leader, an honor afforded only to a respected warrior and a man of good judgment, so Isabel had seen little of him since the beginning of the search. Most of the time, he returned to the tepee long after she had fallen asleep and was gone before she arose. When he appeared the night before the hunt earlier than usual, she took the opportunity to ask some questions, starting with, "Just what does the hunt leader do?"

"Until tomorrow, not much. I give general directions for the conduct of the hunt, although that's really not necessary. Everyone in this band knows what's expected of them and they work for the common good, unlike some plains tribes that actually have to have groups of warriors to police their people, so no one will sneak away and attack the herd on their own."

"If you don't have that much to do, why have you been away so much?" Isabel asked, irritated at having been unnecessarily cheated of his company.

"As long as the council stays up, I'm expected to be with them. Naturally, they were concerned, since it took a while to find a herd this year."

Isabel had been with the Indians long enough to know that the men consumed an unbelievable amount of time discussing things. Nothing was ever just decided.

It had to be approached from every conceivable angle, and a decision wasn't made until everyone was in agreement. It seemed to her that they were always "in council." They talked and talked about things, while the women simply did things. "And what will your duties be tomorrow?"

"I will signal the attack, since all the hunters charge simultaneously, and I will decide when the hunt is finished."

"Then you don't just kill until all the herd is dead, or have escaped?"

Stands Alone smiled when Isabel said "until all the herd is dead." He knew she had no idea of how many animals they were talking about. Then he answered, "No, we will take only what we can cure for the time being. And we will kill as quickly as possible. The meat spoils before it can be cured if the animal is overheated before it is slain from being run too long." He paused, then said, "Another of my duties is mediate any arguments over whose kill a buffalo might be. If the difference can't be resolved, I make the decision."

"But how can you tell whose kill is whose?"

"We will be using marked arrows, which is precisely why we don't use guns. Bullets can't be marked. Every man's arrows are different, either in how they are notched or how they are feathered. If two men's arrows are found in the same animal, ownership is determined by the position of the arrows. If both arrows inflicted a mortal wound, and the men are not willing to divide, I will make the ruling."

"How will you decide that?"

"In all fairness, you can't. Therefore, I will declare the animal be set aside as part of the portion for the old people, the widows and orphans, and those less fortunate, including a hunter who may have been unfortunate enough not to make a kill."

Isabel gazed off thoughtfully. Her people, too, talked of the common good, of charity to those in need, but in her heart she knew they didn't always practice what they preached, not when they built elaborate churches within spitting distance of the hovels of the poor. Yet, it was the Indians who were called savages.

The next day, everyone in the camp was up long before daybreak, making last minute preparations, and the excitement was so intense you could almost taste it. Finally, the column of hunters moved out, buffalo horses and warriors alike brilliantly painted, some of the animals half-spotted and half-striped, some carrying the varied marks of their masters. The men were stripped down to their breechcloths, and most rode bareback, carrying only their bows, or perhaps a long lance, their quiver of arrows hanging around their mount's neck so as not to encumber them in any manner. In almost every instance, a rope hung from the horse's neck and dragged on the ground, in case the hunter lost his seating, a line that could be lifesaving. Caught, the man could be dragged to safety by his well-trained horse, rather than crushed beneath the hooves of the stampeding herd.

Behind the hunters came the older boys making their first buffalo hunt, so filled with excitement they could hardly sit still, even though their quarry would be the calves, and then only after the rest of the herd had abandoned them. They called to the younger boys, relishing their envious looks, glorying in their first test of manhood.

Bringing up the rear were all the able-bodied women, mounted and leading strings of horses with travois to haul the meat back to camp. Left behind were the children and the elderly, the old women to tend the children and keep the fires going, the old men to sit and sadly remember hunts from long ago.

Isabel was with the women. Much as it was for the boys, this would be her first real test, the act of butchering, and even though she didn't relish the chore, the excitement of what was about to take place was contagious. To her, it seemed an eternity before they reached the herd, and when she caught her first sight of it, she gasped in disbelief. The entire prairie before her seemed to be covered with the shaggy, reddish-brown beasts. She had never dreamed there were that many buffalo in the entire world, nor had she any idea how large an animal they were. The bulls stood well over six feet tall and weighed more than a ton.

"Why don't they run?" she asked Beaver Woman in puzzlement. "If we can see them, surely they can see us."

"No, they are very nearsighted. And their hearing is not that good either. The only keen sense they have is that of smell. That is why we approach them from downwind." She glanced around, then said, "This is as far as we go."

"Can't we get a little closer, so we can see better?"

"No, it is too dangerous. The hunt is about to begin."

"I wish there was at least a hill to watch from," Isabel commented to an empty space, for Beaver Woman had already dismounted.

Unlike the other women, Isabel stayed on her horse, to at least give herself the advantage of height, and stood in her stirrups, squinting against the bright sunlight and looking for Stands Alone. As usual, he had been gone when she awakened that morning. The only thing she had seen of him had been when the column of hunters had moved out and as usual, with that typical

Comanche reservation that could sometimes irritate her to no end, he had acted as if he hadn't seen her. Then she spied him among the hunters, not so much because he sat taller in the saddle than the others, but because of his commanding air.

Isabel watched as Stands Alone gave instructions, and the group of hunters split into two columns, one going to the left, the other to the right. When the men were riding parallel to the herd, Stands Alone gave a signal, and the Comanches began firing their arrows. A buffalo fell, and another, and another. The huge beasts were dropping like flies, their demise apparently totally un-noticed by the others grazing just feet away. Isabel was filled with disgust. This wasn't a hunt, she thought. It was a slaughter. What was all that talk about skill and speed and danger?

"What's wrong with the stupid things?" she asked Beaver Woman. "Why don't they run?"

"They still have not realized the danger. They prob-ably won't until they catch the scent of man."

By the time the buffalo did catch the scent, the Indians had almost circled them. Then the herd bolted as if it were one huge entity. Isabel was stunned. She had never dreamed anything that immense could run that fast. Even their top-heavy head and shoulders didn't slow them down. The herd was a blur as they raced away, and the ground shook from thousands of pounding hooves. "They're going to escape!" Isabel cried in alarm.

"No, the lead riders in both columns are rushing in to turn the lead buffalo," Beaver Woman told her. "Soon they will be milling."

"How do you know that? I can't begin to see the front of the herd."

"I know because that is how it is done."

Within minutes the herd *was* milling, chasing itself

in circles in total confusion, while the Comanches encircled them, racing beside the terrified herd, then picking their prey and darting in for the kill. Isabel strained her eyes, looking for Stands Alone in the kaleidoscope of swirling dust and blurring, moving animals. She spied him just as he swerved his horse for the kill, then watched in terror as he rode up to the monstrous bull from the rear, coming in close on its right side, so close his leg brushed the animal's side, then shot his arrow deep down into the animal, aiming it at the soft spot between the protruding hip bone and the last rib. She gasped as she saw the wounded beast turn its head to gore Stands Alone's mount, the wicked horns looking as if they were mere inches from the gelding's belly as the buffalo horse swerved away. Seeing Stands Alone had gained a safe distance, she looked back at the still running buffalo. He must have missed, she thought. Then the huge animal suddenly fell forward, tumbling head over heels, tripping another buffalo following him. She looked up and saw Stands Alone had ridden ahead without a backward glance and was in the process of shooting another shaggy beast.

As exciting as it was, Isabel couldn't watch any longer. Her fear for Stands Alone was too great. Her stomach was tied into what felt like a million knots, and there was an iciness in her chest. She averted her eyes, but could have saved herself the trouble. By that time, none of the women could see; their view totally obscured by the thick cloud of dust. But they knew the hunt was still going on from the pounding hooves and the hunters' victorious cries that punctuated the air. Then, after about fifteen minutes, the sound of the hooves seemed to be fading into the distance, and the dust settled enough for them to see. In that brown haze, Isabel saw fallen buffalo scattered all over the prairie. A thundering cheer broke out from the women, a cheer that was answered by the victorious hunters, waving their bows and spears over their heads.

When the hubbub had died down, Isabel saw several of the hunters had dismounted and were walking among the fallen beasts, approaching them very cautiously. "What are those men doing?" she asked Beaver Woman.

"Looking for those that are just wounded. There is nothing more dangerous than a wounded buffalo, particularly a bull. They will charge even when they are riddled with arrows, even when they are taking their last breath."

Isabel had always thought that the Comanche men had the easy life, since they did no chores to speak of. Today, she had seen them performing their duty and was forced to change her mind. Each and every one of them had put their lives on the line to provide the necessities for living for their families. True, their work was done in a brief period of time, but what an intense, dangerous work it was. And not one of them had cowered or run from it. They had faced what they had to do with determination and bravery. She could no longer look upon them with contempt, but only with a newly born respect.

As the hunters who were checking the buffalo moved further away, Beaver Woman saw Stands Alone signal to the women and said to Isabel, "Come. Now it is time for us to do our work."

New respect or not, Isabel still dreaded what lay ahead of her. She dismounted and followed her mother-in-law in grim resignation, her sharp butcher knife glittering in the bright sunlight.

Twenty

As Isabel walked with the other women among the fallen buffalo, she saw Stands Alone. He was grinning from ear to ear, his dark eyes still dancing with excitement. A quick look about her confirmed the same was true with every warrior, one even standing on the buffalo he had slain and dancing a little jig. She realized they weren't just feeling victorious, although that was a part of their exultation. To the man, they had loved every dangerous moment of what they had done, absolutely thrived on it. But knowing they enjoyed their work, while she hated hers, couldn't rob her of her new appreciation. What they had done had been brave and daring, and—yes, now that it was behind her—incredibly exciting.

Isabel stopped and looked at the dead beasts all about her, feeling totally overwhelmed, then asked Beaver Woman, "Where do we begin?"

"We don't. Not yet. The *Nema* are one of the few tribes whose men do the hardest part of butchering the buffalo. With most plains tribes, the men leave as soon as the hunt is finished, and the women do all the work. But our men will skin them and disjoint them. Then we take over, cutting the meat into smaller, more man-

ageable pieces, and loading it in the skins to take back
to camp with us."

Isabel watched the men placing the cows on their
sides and heaving the bulls over to set them on their
bellies with all four legs spread. In many cases, it took
several men to position the monstrous bulls for butchering, and Isabel wondered how women, any women,
could possibly handle that backbreaking chore.

When the carcass had been skinned and disjointed,
even the rib steaks broken off, and the bare spine and
the rump and head were all that remained, the women
moved in, cutting the meat into smaller chunks and
bagging it in the hides, then loading everything on travois, including the bones, the head, and—to Isabel's
revulsion—the entrails. All that was left behind was the
heart, to help the mystical power regenerate the depleted herd.

All day long, beneath the blistering sun, Isabel labored with the others, her arms covered with blood up
to her elbows, her back aching from lifting the heavy
loads onto the travois, her fingers numb from wielding
the heavy knife. Exhausted, and sick to her stomach
from the brassy smell of warm blood, she rose from
finishing one buffalo and looked about her. Spying a
bull in the distance that had yet to be skinned and
butchered by one of the men, she wove her way through
the maze of fallen animals and Indians, treading carefully so as not to slip on the wet, sticky ground, thinking
her nausea might not be so bad if there were not so
much blood and guts all about her. No one noticed her
wandering off, everyone intent on their work.

When she was about three feet from the buffalo, Isabel stopped, thinking just to wait until one of the men
got around to skinning the bull and give herself a brief
rest. She was so weary she didn't even notice the faint

blowing sound that came from the buffalo, nor did she see his nostrils dilate when he caught a whiff of her scent, or his eyelids flutter. What happened next occurred so fast, it remained a blur to Isabel for the rest of her life. Suddenly the monstrous animal was on its feet, eyes glowing red as it lunged at her, fetid hot breath hitting Isabel as if a furnace door had been opened. She screamed and jumped back, but not soon enough. The tip of one wicked horn tore across her chest, ripping the buckskin blouse as if it were tissue paper. But Isabel was too terrified to feel the stinging pain. Seeing the enraged animal lunging again, she acted on sheer instinct, grabbing the horn as it was thrust at her and yanking it to the side with all her might. The mortally wounded bull was just weak enough that she was able to deflect the jab. Then she hung on for dear life while the buffalo bellowed in fury at not having full control of his master horn and shook his head, tossing her about as if she were a rag doll.

When Stands Alone heard Isabel scream, he whirled about to see what was happening. He acted as fast as lightning, leaping on his buffalo horse and racing to her, frantically swerving to avoid bowling over other warriors who were running to her aid. Sweeping past the bull, he leaned down and caught her waist out of mid-air with one steely arm, almost ripping Isabel's arm from her shoulder joint due to her death grip on the bull's horn. Finally freed, the bull twisted his head and lunged at Stands Alone's horse, missing the animal's flank by a fraction of an inch. Then a hail of arrows hit the bison from every direction, and he dropped, the impact of his massive weight shaking the ground.

Safely away, Stands Alone slowed his horse, then jumped down from it, taking Isabel with him. Standing her on her feet, he scanned her anxiously; then seeing the ripped buckskin, his knees buckled. "Have you been gored?"

Stunned by everything happening so fast and her brains a little scrambled by the bull's thrashing, Isabel looked down at herself, muttering, "Gored? Where?"

"Your chest!"

Through her muddled senses, Isabel finally felt the long sting that halfway circled her chest. With trembling hands, she parted the severed buckskin and peeked in, saying, "No, I think it's just a scratch."

Stands Alone looked and saw the wound was barely bleeding, but knowing how close she had come to certain death made him feel incredibly weak. He had been afraid before, for himself and others, but never had he experienced a fear that was so powerful it was crippling, a fear that left him feeling helpless. An irrational anger came over him. "What were you doing off by yourself? Why didn't you stay with the others? A wounded buffalo is the most dangerous animal on earth!"

"I thought he was dead," Isabel answered. "He was positioned for skinning and butchering."

Stands Alone realized the animal must have fallen in that position, and everyone had assumed what Isabel had. But he couldn't forgive her for scaring him so badly. "No, he just fell that way! That's why the hunters do the skinning, to prevent accidents like this from happening. A mortally wounded buffalo can live for hours, barely clinging to a thread of life. Even the hunters that check the herd can miss it."

Stands Alone didn't realize he had raised his voice, but Isabel was very aware of it. Her ears were ringing. "Well, stop yelling at me!" she shouted back. "I didn't know that."

"No, she didn't," Beaver Woman said, rushing up to them. "If it was anyone's fault, it was mine. I should have been watching more closely." She turned Isabel to face her and asked, "Are you hurt?"

Tears pooled in Isabel's eyes, but not in pain. The attack had unnerved her, and Stands Alone's unfairly blaming her had hurt her feelings. "I think it's just a scratch."

"Even so, it should be tended to. We will go back to camp and see to it. Corn Woman and Tekwitchi will finish up here."

Not wanting her sisters-in-law to have to take on her share of the work, Isabel said, "It can wait. It's not that serious."

"No, it can't wait. It needs to be cleaned immediately. Buffalo dig in the dirt with their horns."

Later, back in the camp, after Beaver Woman had washed the deep scratch and applied an herbal ointment to the wound to keep it from getting infected, Corn Woman and Tekwitchi visited Isabel.

"We were so frightened, Isabel," Tekwitchi said, her brown eyes wide in remembrance. "Everyone was. Especially Stands Alone. I have never seen him so terrified."

"He wasn't terrified. He was angry!" Isabel tossed back, fresh tears welling in her eyes.

"No, he was afraid" Corn Woman corrected her. "I saw his face when he saw what was happening. It turned as white as snow."

"Well, he might have been frightened at first, but he wasn't later. He yelled at me!"

"And that alone should tell you how frightened he was," Corn Woman countered. "I have never seen him lose control. Never! Not even when he was furious. It is not our way."

Isabel had been around the Comanches long enough

to know what Corn Woman said was true. She had never seen one raise his voice in anger.

Before Isabel had time to ponder that profound truth, Tekwitchi remarked, "You were so brave. We are all so proud of you."

"Brave?" Isabel asked in astonishment. "I was terrified!"

"It didn't look like it from where we were standing," Corn Woman said. "The other women have given you a new name. They are calling you 'She Who Dares To Rattle Buffalo Horns.' "

"I wasn't rattling his horns," Isabel replied candidly. "He was rattling me."

Both women smiled. That was one reason they liked Isabel so well. There was nothing pretentious about her. Then Corn Woman said, "If you prefer, we will still call you Isabel, instead of your new name."

"Yes, I would." Then not wanting her new sisters to take offense, Isabel added, "But not because it's an Indian name. Because it's not true."

Again the two women smiled at Isabel's honesty; then Tekwitchi changed the subject, asking "Do you feel recovered enough to come to the feast tonight?"

"Feast?" Isabel asked in surprise. "I thought we were going to take the meat back with us, to last us through the winter."

"Not all of it, and this is the only time we can eat fresh buffalo meat, the day of the hunt," Tekwitchi answered. "Tomorrow we will start drying it and making sausage from what is left of the boiled meat tonight."

Isabel couldn't imagine where the Indians would find the energy to feast and celebrate, but if they could, she could. "Yes, I'll go."

An hour later, Isabel was sitting with her female relatives around a huge bonfire, her platter piled high with buffalo meat. Even though she was eating the hump ribs, the choicest cut, next to the tongue—which she adamantly refused—and supposedly the tenderest, she found the meat tough and much stronger tasting than the other game she had eaten. She glanced around her and saw the others didn't share her opinion. They weren't just feasting, they were gorging themselves.

Stands Alone sank down beside her. Immediately a platter of steaming meat was set before him. As he picked up a piece and began eating, Isabel decided she would ignore him, at least until he apologized. But the apology didn't come forth. Finally, when he had finished the food with ravenous haste, she said coldly, "I thought perhaps you weren't going to attend, you were so late."

Stands Alone knew Isabel was angry with him. He wasn't so happy with himself. He had never lost his temper. Even knowing that it had been triggered by an intense fear didn't make it easy to accept. He had known he loved Isabel, but not until he saw her life endangered had he realized just how much, and from that had stemmed his crippling fear. Of course, these were not things he could speak of. He couldn't even apologize, for that would demand explanations he couldn't give. If only he knew her true feelings for him. Instead, he said, "I couldn't leave until all the meat had been butchered and transferred here. Then I had to bathe."

Isabel glanced at his long braids and saw the water drops still trapped in them glistening in the firelight. "Then you're through for the night?"

"Yes."

Stands Alone turned his head and looked her directly in the eye, and Isabel couldn't hold on to her anger. It slipped away like a wisp of smoke in the wind. She knew what he was thinking, and she wanted it, too. After three weeks of abstinence, she wasn't just hungry for his love-making, not as beautifully and skillfully as Stands Alone did it. She was desperate.

Without a word, Stands Alone stood and offered Isabel his hand, helping her to her feet. If anyone took note of them slipping away, the couple didn't notice. They were totally absorbed with one another.

Once inside their tepee, they quickly stripped, tearing off their clothing with an urgency that would have been comical had they not been so intent. Isabel's breath caught at the sight of Stands Alone, tall, bronzed, magnificently male, and totally aroused. Then she became aware that he was staring at the wound on her chest, fully revealed to him for the first time. Gone was the blazing passion that had been in his eyes just moments before. What she saw was abject fear, coming from a man she considered totally fearless. She was stunned to realize he cared that much.

Stands Alone didn't give Isabel long to contemplate her discovery. He took her into his powerful arms and kissed her, long, sweetly, deeply, his hands caressing as he laid her back on their pallet. Then he adored every inch of her body, from the tip of her head to the soles of her dainty feet, his lips kissing, his tongue laving, his teeth ever so gently nipping, leaving a trail of fire in his wake and Isabel trembling with need.

Throughout the night, Stands Alone made love to Isabel, telling her with his body what he didn't dare to speak, and by the time it was over, there was a lump in Isabel's throat and tears in her eyes. Stands Alone's loving had been so achingly sweet and exquisitely tender, so cherishing, she knew, without a shadow of a doubt, that he loved her.

But, to her dismay, Isabel discovered it wasn't a knowledge she could exult in. It could have been, had she been able to return that love. But her fierce, unrelenting Spanish pride wouldn't allow her to listen to her heart. Instead, she felt the knowledge of Stands Alone's love a heavy burden.

Over the next several days, the women kept busy from dawn to dusk cutting the buffalo meat into strips for drying and making sausage by mixing boiled meat, marrow fat, wild onions, and sage, then stuffing it into the washed buffalo intestines. The hides were fleshed, then put aside to be tanned later, for there was more immediate business at hand. Then, when every morsel of meat was preserved, and every other part of the buffalo set aside for other uses, another hunt took place, and the procedure was repeated, over and over, until the council deemed the hunt closed.

The night before the band left the prairie, there was another great feast and celebration. Because he was being honored for having conducted a successful hunt, Stands Alone did not sit with Isabel and his other relatives. Instead, he sat with his father and the rest of the council, made up mostly of the heads of the different families, men who were almost without exception middle-aged or older. Isabel looked at her husband across the distance that separated them. Stands Alone stood out in any crowd, but he looked particularly handsome and virile among the older men. She couldn't give him her love, but she was proud of him, and justifiably so. Other than her incident, which thankfully the Comanches had not held against Stands Alone, and the loss of one horse, there had been no accidents or further losses, something she had been told was quite remarkable.

"Are you sure you will not have some more meat?"

Tekwitchi asked, drawing Isabel's attention away from her husband.

"No, thank you. I think I could go the rest of my life without tasting another morsel of buffalo."

"I hope not. We're going to eat what we preserved this winter. And we can always hunt more buffalo if we want. The herds do not migrate down here."

"You have buffalo hunts in the winter?" Isabel asked in dismay, having thought the ordeal was over for that year.

"Not like this. But sometimes the men get hungry for fresh buffalo meat. They know the canyons where the buffalo winter. Sometimes two or three men will go and shoot one. Stands Alone and Greyfoot did last year. The meat was frozen, so we didn't have to do anything to preserve it. When cooked, it tasted just like fresh meat."

"The horses can travel in that deep a snow?"

"Oh, no, they do not take their horses. They walk on their snow moccasins and bring the meat back on sleds made of buffalo ribs."

"What are snow moccasins?"

"I'm sure you've seen Stands Alone's in the tepee. They're oval-shaped wooden frames, with a middle made of woven deerskin thongs."

So that's what those peculiar looking things were, Isabel thought, then asked, "But how can they walk on those? They aren't even woven solid. The snow would go right through the web."

"You would think so, but it doesn't. We will have to make you a pair before winter sets in. The women use them, too."

"Where in the world did you learn about something like that?"

"My people came from the mountains to the north,

where the snow is much deeper than even here. We have always used them."

"*Pia.*"

The small voice saying *mother* in Comanche drew both women's attention away from their conversation. They looked up and saw Jumping Rabbit had been taken from his day cradle, cleaned, and was toddling to them on wobbly legs. "Look! He's walking!" Isabel exclaimed in surprise.

"Yes. He's been taking a few steps in the tepee before he's put in his night cradle the last few nights," Tekwitchi answered with pride.

Both women watched as the chubby baby carefully made his way to them, holding out his little arms for balance. Then he fell, right into Isabel's lap, and laughed with glee. Isabel snuggled his warm, naked little body against her.

The baby looked up at Isabel, then grinned, and said, "*Pia.*"

"See?" Tekwitchi asked, totally without any sign of jealousy. "He knows you are his aunt and mother, too."

Feeling a rush of love, Isabel snuggled the baby closer. But even that wouldn't satisfy her need. She wanted her own baby to cuddle and love, but not just any baby. She wanted a very special baby. She wanted Stands Alone's baby.

Isabel looked up, her eyes seeking the man on whom her deepest desire was focused, and saw Stands Alone watching her, his look so intent she knew he wanted it, too.

Twenty-one

When the Comanche band returned to the mountains after the buffalo hunt, they didn't go back to their old camp. Instead they went to a place where they wintered each year in a deep canyon at a lower altitude. Here, they were protected from the north winds, as well as provided with water and plenty of wood, but not just any wood. The trees were almost exclusively cottonwoods, whose bark could be eaten by the horses.

For the first several weeks after their arrival, the women were busy with tanning the buffalo hides they had brought back with them. Isabel had thought the job might not be as tedious as tanning buckskin, since the hair did not have to be removed for making buffalo robes, and fortunately, that was all she and Stands Alone needed. She soon found out differently. Besides being much larger, the skin was much tougher and took more beating and pounding and rubbing than the deerskin. Each night she went to bed with her arms and back aching, feeling as if it were she, and not the hide, that had taken a beating.

When that work was finally done, the women finished their preparations for winter: collecting big piles of firewood to supplement the buffalo chips they had brought back; and collecting fall nuts and berries, but never the *chiltipines,* the little, pea-sized hot peppers the mocking-birds and turkeys and New Mexicans loved. In fact, the Comanches had no use for chili peppers of any kind, unlike the Pueblos and Apaches and other Indians of that area. Isabel sorely missed the peppers in her diet, and found the Comanche food much too bland for her taste.

But despite the last minute preparations, this was a time of relaxation for the Indians. The autumn days were cool enough that what labors they did were not taxing, and the women often spent the mornings working and the afternoons racing their horses and playing several different ball games they dearly loved. The first time Isabel watched the women playing shinny, she was shocked at how very physical and rough the game was. There was a lot of pushing, shoving, and misaimed strokes—some unintentional, some not—to try to get the hair-stuffed deerskin ball to the goal at their team's end of the field by means of a curved stick each player carried. The first few times Isabel played the game, she was covered with bruises and scrapes. But she soon became adept at it and at kickball, a variation of the game that took extraordinary balance and dexterity, for the player had to hop on the left foot, while dribbling the rag ball in the air with the instep of the right foot. It was soon acknowledged that Isabel was the best kickball player in the camp, something she took pride in, for Isabel had discovered not only did she have a competitive spirit, but an athletic side, and loved participating in sports.

Stands Alone was proud of her, too, and would sit with the others in the band watching her while she played. It was one of the few times he could stare at her in public, and he found that he could never get enough of just looking at her.

One day, when Isabel was leaving a particularly fierce

game, Stands Alone was waiting for her when she left the field. "Our family is very proud of your ball playing," he informed her, "particularly my mother. She says you could well be a daughter of her band, the Water People. They're renowned among all the *Nema* for their skill in ball playing, you know."

Isabel was glad her mother-in-law thought she did well in something. While she wasn't as forbidding as she had been at first, Beaver Woman still seemed to be judging her in some way. Then Isabel's mind shifted to another subject, and she said to her husband, "I'm glad I have an opportunity to talk to you. Tekwitchi came to me with some distressing news this morning. She told me one of the women had given birth to twins, a boy and a girl, and that she offered the girl to Tekwitchi, since she has no children."

"Yes, Greyfoot told me the same."

"How can that woman do that?" Isabel asked in outrage. "Give one of her children away? Why, it's . . . it's unnatural!"

"No, it is unnatural to give birth to two babies. In many bands, one is abandoned for that very reason. At least this mother is looking for foster parents for her child."

Isabel had come to accept many of the Comanche beliefs, but this was one she knew she would never be able to accept. And she found it puzzling and contradictory. Otherwise, the Comanches had a very high regard for life, all life. "Are Greyfoot and Tekwitchi going to take the infant?"

"Greyfoot is leaving the decision up to Tekwitchi, since she is the one who is childless and so urgently feels the need. Greyfoot has already fathered two children."

What did Stands Alone mean by that, Isabel wondered. Did Greyfoot think his manhood was not being ques-

tioned because he had fathered two children, while Tekwitchi's womanhood was? Did Comanche men take
pride in their ability to reproduce? She knew Spanish
men did. Large families were considered a silent testimony to their manliness. But surely that couldn't be what
was bothering Tekwitchi in not being able to conceive.
Like her, Tekwitchi just wanted a child. She wasn't worried about proving her womanhood. Or was she, deep
down?

Later, Isabel was sewing outside her tepee and watching a group of nearby children play "grizzly bear." On
a mound of sand which represented "sugar" was a child
designated the "grizzly." Surrounding him, in a circle
marked by a line drawn in the dirt, were the children,
the first child in the line called "mother." As the bear
tried to grab a child, the "mother" would swing the line
back and forth, and while the "bear" was busy trying to
catch another child, the other players rushed in to try
and steal his "sugar." The game ended with all the children either being captured by the "bear," or all the
"sugar" stolen. If a child was caught, he was eaten by
the "bear" by being tickled, and Isabel could never help
but laugh right along with the captured child.

Then spying Tekwitchi hurrying towards her, Isabel
put down her sewing, jumped to her feet, and rushed
to meet her, asking without preamble, "Are you going
to take the baby?"

"Oh, yes," Tekwitchi answered, her brown eyes sparkling with happiness. "We are all so excited, even Red
Feather. He says he has wanted a little sister. Greyfoot
has already talked to the medicine man about the naming ceremony."

"How does Corn Woman feel about this?" Isabel
asked out of curiosity.

"She is excited also, particularly since it is a girl. She

will be someone to help us with our work when she is older."

Well, at least someone appreciated the child, Isabel thought, even if it was for the labor she would later provide. The band in general valued males higher than females because they would become warriors to protect the band. That was why the female twin had been given away, and not the male.

"We are making her day cradle right now," Tekwitchi continued. "We thought you might like to help, particularly since you have become so good at beading."

Even though she couldn't share the other's enthusiasm for the new member in their family, Isabel was more than willing to help. "I'll be right with you. Let me get my sewing bag."

Several days later, Isabel stood with Stands Alone and the rest of the band at the naming ceremony. She watched as the medicine man lit his feathered ceremonial pipe and blew smoke to the heavens, the earth, and the four directions, then offered a prayer for the welfare of the child. He picked up the infant in her beautifully beaded cradle and held it aloft, four times, to symbolize his wish for the child to grow up. Then he proclaimed, "Her name is Elk Woman."

Isabel frowned at the name everyone had been so anxiously awaiting, but she had enough sense not to mention her displeasure until she and Tekwitchi were alone in her tepee. She asked the new mother, "Why did the witch doctor name the baby that? Elk Woman? Why not something dainty and pretty, like Deer Woman or Flower Woman? Elk are so big, so ungainly with those huge, ugly horns of theirs."

Tekwitchi's face turned deathly pale, and she glanced

nervously around Stands Alone's tepee. Then she leaned forward and said in a hushed voice, "No, Isabel, you must not say that. The elk spirits might take offense."

"Elk spirits? What are you talking about?"

Again Tekwitchi glanced around, then asked, "Are you sure Stands Alone's medicine bundle is not here?"

"I'm positive, but what does that have to do with it?"

"Greyfoot picked that name, and Corn Woman and I think he did it to honor Stands Alone. We were very pleased when the medicine man was in agreement. Elk Woman is a strong name, and we would much rather our daughter be strong than dainty and pretty."

"You said Greyfoot picked it to honor Stands Alone. Are you suggesting Stands Alone's guardian spirit is an elk?"

"We do not know, of course. Corn Woman and I just suspect it. Those who have elk as their guardian spirits are exceptionally strong men. They excel in everything they do. They are good warriors, good hunters, good horsemen, good leaders. But even more important, they have a strong character. They are unshakable in their beliefs and totally incorruptible. It is truly an honor to be chosen by the elk spirit."

Isabel had to admit that Stands Alone was all those things. "Does Greyfoot suspect this, too?"

"We think he knows. Brothers tell one another everything, you know. They are even closer than husband and wife. When he suggested this name, it just confirmed our suspicions." Tekwitchi grinned. "Our men do not give us credit for being able to make deductions. They would be surprised at what we know. Sisters tell sisters everything, too."

Isabel had learned that, too, was true. Comanche women were far from stupid, nor were they disinterested in what was going on. When they were around the men, they kept their mouths shut and observed. It was amazing what could be learned from observations and from what was overheard. Then those things were passed along by the female grapevine. Often, the lowly women knew the decisions before the council even announced them to the rest of the village, but they were smart enough to give no hint of their knowledge. It would have been a terrible blow to the men's vanity.

The first signs of winter came. Frost covered everything in the mornings, then was burnt off by noon. The leaves fell by the millions, blanketing the ground in yellow and bronze and providing the children with a new toy to play with. For hours on end, they would dive into piles of leaves, scattering them everywhere amongst gleeful gales of laughter. Isabel was forced to admit she had never seen such happy, carefree children.

A new entertainment was also added to the nighttime festivities, this one for the adults. Huge bonfires were built to ward off the chill of the evening air, then two sides of men and women lined up for the gambling game. While the players sang the gambling song to the accompaniment of drums, one player took a bone and, with many gestures and movements of hands, might keep it, or pass it to another on his team. Then he would thrust his closed hands forward for a member of the opposite team to guess which hand the bone was in, if any. If the player guessed right, his team scored one point and gained possession of the bone. Many of the players were quite skilled in deception, causing intense excitement; others were simply entertaining with gestures that bordered on ridiculous, bringing much laughter from the others. It was a classic display of the Comanche's fun-loving nature, and Isabel embraced

284 *Lauren Wilde*

the game with enthusiasm. It was yet another outlet for her own zest for living.

Winter came, softly, silently in the night. The band arose one morning to find the ground covered with snow. Just like their human counterparts all over the world, they greeted this first snow with excitement. Snow mocassins were strapped on for an invigorating walk in the woods; children romped in the fluffy white stuff and tossed snowballs; old men and women sat outside their tepees wrapped in their buffalo robes, simply admiring the scenery or watching the activities.

Isabel donned her snowshoes for the first time, and with Stands Alone beside her, made her first clumsy steps. "Now I know why a duck waddles," she told him. "It's hard to walk with big, spread-out feet." Then as if to prove her words, she took a tumble into the soft snow.

Stands Alone laughed and helped her to her feet. Brushing the snow off, Isabel glanced up, then said to him, "Aren't you cold with nothing on your chest? I should think you men would wear a shirt of some kind."

"No, my buffalo robe keeps me warm," he answered, pulling the robe made from two buffalo hides sewn together closer around him.

Isabel was amazed. She, too, wore a robe over her dress, and winter mocassins lined with fur that came to her knees. Still, she felt the chill. But the only change the men had made in their dress was to add knee-high winter boots.

In the weeks that followed, more and more snow fell, and the enthusiasm the Indians had felt for the first snow wore thin. For the better part the Comanches stayed in their tepees, which Isabel discovered were much warmer than her home in Rosario had been. Of course, the women still had their outside chores to do, fetching firewood and stripping the bark from the cottonwood branches the horses couldn't reach. Isabel became adept at climbing the huge trees for this purpose, being dumped more than once in the deep snow when a brittle branch broke beneath her, however the other women were always quick to rescue her, rushing to her on their snowshoes as if they had been born with the awkward contraptions on their feet.

While the Comanches spent most of their time indoors, their social life didn't suffer. They were inherently a gregarious people. Much visiting was done back and forth, sometimes even during a howling blizzard. As many people as possible would crowd into a tepee. Often a storyteller would entertain them, while they munched on roasted piñon nuts. But most often they played gambling games. If Isabel were to say the Indians had any weaknesses, it would have been that of gambling. They thrived on it, so much so that it was almost compulsive. Fortunately, none were very skilled, which meant what was lost one night was more often than not regained the next.

And so the winter passed in leisurely fashion, and since almost all outdoor activities were curtailed, what Isabel enjoyed the most was Stands Alone's company. They spent a lot of time talking, by silent mutual agreement avoiding anything controversial or upsetting, such as her capture. He helped her improve her Comanche, she his Spanish. She educated him about her world, he about his. But what Isabel loved the most were the long, lazy sessions of lovemaking every afternoon, sessions in which Stands Alone revealed his inventiveness. Isabel was amazed at the many moods of lovemaking, sometimes fiercely passionate, sometimes light and teasing, sometimes with laughter, sometimes with such aching sweetness it brought tears to her eyes. Then, when it was over, she would feel guilty for being so passionate, until Stands Alone assured her everyone else was spending their afternoons doing the same.

When winter ended, with the sound of the ice breaking in the streams and the snow falling from the trees in big, wet "plops," everyone was as glad to see it over as they were to see it begin. They stepped from their tepees and turned their faces to the warm sun. All except Isabel. She emerged heavy-hearted. As much as she and Stands Alone had made love, she had not conceived. Her deepest desire had not been fulfilled.

It was a profound disappointment she kept close to her heart.

Twenty-two

In late spring, while the mountain streams were still swollen with snow melt, the Comanches moved to their summer camp higher in the Sangre de Cristo Mountains. Then, several weeks later, Stands Alone surprised Isabel one night by saying, "I have decided to make a trip to Taos to trade some of my racehorses, and would like you to go with me."

"I thought the trading fair was in the fall," Isabel commented.

"It is. I would not dream of taking you then. There is too much potent Spanish whiskey to be had. Some drunk might mistake you for one of the women brought for the men's enjoyment, and I would have to kill him. The trading fair is no place for a respectable woman."

"Are you saying the men bring their women for that reason, for other men to slake their lust on? That they deliberately prostitute their own wives and sisters?" Isabel asked in shocked outrage.

"Some bands do, yes," Stands Alone answered, hoping they weren't going to get into another one of *those* discussions.

"And how do the women feel about that?" Isabel asked in a challenging tone of voice.

They were, Stands Alone thought glumly, then answered, "Some are willing, some even anxious for the trinkets they might receive, and some are not."

"And those that aren't willing are raped?" Isabel asked angrily, her blue eyes blazing.

Stands Alone flinched at Isabel's furious question, then answered, "Yes." Then, seeing she was about to explode, he quickly interjected, "May I remind you, I said our band does not do this. We do not approve, but we cannot change what the others do, just as some of your missionaries often have no control over what your soldiers do to the Indian women under their protection."

Stands Alone's counterattack was effective. Isabel knew many Indian women were raped by the soldiers at the pueblos, despite the Franciscans' efforts to protect them. The priests were helpless to punish the offenders, since the men were fully under the control of their commandant, and not the Franciscans. All the soldiers had to do to escape punishment was claim the woman had been willing. Of course, the woman's word was worthless in Spanish courts of law. Isabel was forced to redirect her anger at men in general, rather than just the Indians.

Two days later, Isabel and Stands Alone left the village, followed by the string of racehorses he wished to trade and a pack horse carrying their camping supplies. Isabel was very excited about the trip, for it gave her an opportunity to see Taos and a vacation from her hard labors. She also felt very honored, for Tekwitchi and Corn Woman had assured her it was rare for a warrior to take his wife along, simply for the company.

For several hours, they traveled in silence, both enjoying the spectacular scenery all around them, rugged mountain peaks that seemed to pierce the sky. Finally

Isabel broke the silence, asking Stands Alone, "How long will the trip take?"

"It can be made in two days, if you travel hard, but we are in no hurry."

As if to prove his words, they camped early that day beside a murmuring mountain stream whose crystal-clear waters danced over a gravelly bed. As soon as she had unloaded the pack horse, had a fire going, and had tended the horses, Isabel looked at the stream long-ingly, then said, "I think I'll have a bath before I start my meal and it gets too cool."

Stands Alone grinned from where he was tending the horses and answered, "I was thinking the same thing."

The grin should have warned Isabel, but it didn't. Slip-ping a soft bar of Indian soap and a piece of trading cloth from one of the parfleches, Isabel walked to the stream, stripped, then walked into the knee-deep water, carrying her soap with her. Hearing splashing behind her, she turned and saw Stands Alone wading into the stream behind her in all his male glory. The sight of his magnificent physique had its usual breath-stealing effect on her. Then she asked sharply, "What are you doing here?"

"I'm going to bathe."

"Then go downstream, where you belong."

"There's no reason for me to go to a separate place to bathe. We aren't in camp, with the men's bathing area and the women's at opposite ends of the stream. There's no reason we can't bathe together."

For all of their intimacy, Isabel found bathing to-gether, particularly in the wide open, shocking. "It's indecent."

"Why? We're man and wife. We've certainly seen each other naked enough before. And there's no one else to see. You can wash my back, and I can wash yours.

Here," he said, reaching for the soap, "give me the soap. I'll wash you first."

Isabel had no recourse. Before she could even respond, Stands Alone had taken the soap from her, dipped his hand in the water and started lathering her back, then her buttocks and her legs. He turned her to face him and washed her front. But no longer were his ministrations businesslike. He dallied much too long on her breasts, circling and massaging, then flicking the nipples with his thumb, and then lingered on washing her upper thighs, teasingly close to that part of her that was beginning to ache. Isabel knew he was no longer simply bathing her, but making love to her. She saw his manhood stir, then rise, and reached for him.

Stands Alone deflected her hand and said in a husky voice, "Let me rinse you first."

He tossed the soap aside, cupped his hands, and poured water over her. Then he swept her up in his arms and carried her from the stream.

"What about your bath?" Isabel asked.

"It can wait until later."

Isabel was vastly relieved. His bathing her had excited her unbearably, and each time he made a step she felt the brush of his hot tip against her buttocks, only increasing her need. She was so weak she doubted if she could have reciprocated.

Stands Alone lowered himself and Isabel to a blanket that had been spread beside the fire. For a moment, he hovered over her, drinking in her naked beauty with his eyes. Then, spying a drop of water on the tip of one nipple, sparking like a diamond in the sunlight, he bent his head and licked it away. Isabel gasped, feeling as if a bolt of fire had shot to her loins. He raised his head and his mouth closed over hers in a long, demanding kiss. As his tongue softly plundered the nectar of her mouth, Isabel answered his kiss ardently, her tongue an instrument of exquisite torture as she drove him wild and made every powerful muscle in his body tremble with intense anticipation.

Pulling his mouth from hers, Stands Alone broke the fiery kiss, then dropped soft kisses over her face and eyes, down her silky throat to her breasts. There he dallied once again, licking the moisture away, the rasp of his tongue making the soft mounds tingle and the nipples grow to hard points. He followed a trickle of water down across her rib cage and flat abdomen, to lap at the small pool of water that lay in the indentation of her navel.

Isabel thought making love in the wide open particularly satisfying. The feel of the warm sun and gentle breezes on her naked skin, the sound of the murmuring stream, the smell of the crushed grass beneath the blanket, made it seem so natural and beautiful. And this was her husband, her man, she thought dreamily, running her fingers over the hard muscles on his shoulders. What could be more right? When she felt Stands Alone placing tiny, biting kisses on the tender insides of her thighs, the burning between her legs became so intense, she couldn't bear another minute. She desperately wanted him inside her. "Now! Please, do it now," she begged in a ragged voice.

Stands Alone slipped his hands beneath her buttocks and lifted her. Isabel eagerly arched her back to receive him. Then seeing him lower his head, his silky braids brushing the inside of her thighs before he kissed her there in the most intimate of all places, she stiffened in shock, then cried out, "No! Stop!" when his tongue flicked out like a fiery dart.

Stands Alone lifted his head, his dark eyes blazing with the heat of his desire, and asked thickly, "Why not?"

Isabel's rigid Spanish sensibilities were shocked to the core. "It's indecent! It's forbidden!"

"No, it is not indecent," Stands Alone answered, holding her firmly while she tried vainly to twist away. "And nothing is forbidden between a man and his wife. My body is yours, and yours is mine, and I have waited so long to taste your sweetness there. You have been my wife for a year now. I will not be denied any longer."

Stands Alone dropped his head, ignoring Isabel's frantic pleas for him to stop. His tongue laved the damp lips, swirled around the bud of her desire, then dipped to taste her sweetness, before returning to tease and tantalize the burning core of her womanhood. Isabel tried to fight the ripples of pleasure he brought her, but she was helpless against his exciting erotic ministrations and his artful tongue. When the ripples turned to waves of sheer ecstasy, she surrendered and spread her legs, whirling in a maelstrom of sheer sensation as he mastered her. Her blood felt as if it had caught fire; every tingling nerve in her body seemed to be expanding. There was a roaring in her ears and a red haze over her eyes. As he brought her to that shuddering peak over and over, Isabel moaned and writhed beneath him, thinking she would die if he didn't stop, yet not wanting him to stop. It was heaven and hell all rolled into one, an utterly delicious agony.

Then, when Isabel was still convulsing from the last climax, Stands Alone gave up his erotic play and entered her with one powerful, deep thrust that seemed to explode behind her eyes in a blinding white light. He took her with a tender savagery, as if he were determined to place his seal on her very soul, leading her up those glorious heights, bringing them both to that mindless, searing explosion of passion that hurled them into a firestorm of flaming colors.

When it was over, their muscles still trembling and their breaths still rasping in the air, Stands Alone held Isabel tenderly in his arms. He was a patient man, but he was beginning to despair of Isabel's ever loving him. Sometimes, when he caught her looking at him at an unguarded moment, he would think she did. Then the look would disappear, and he would be plagued with doubts, fearing he was imagining things. He longed to have her say the words, to positively confirm what he so desperately wanted, just as he yearned to say them to her, so much it was sometimes a painful ache in his throat. Would she see the significance of what he had done that day, Stands Alone wondered. By bathing her, he had shown his willingness to care for her totally, that no task was too menial for him to undertake in her behalf. Surely she knew by now that *Nema* men did not pamper their wives. And he had loved her in a manner in which he would never have dreamed of loving another woman, with an intimacy that surpassed all intimacies, taking her woman's nectar into his body as she took his seed into hers. Would she realize their lovemaking had reached a higher plane?

Stands Alone would have found some consolation if he had known Isabel was also experiencing despair at that moment. His unsettling lovemaking had shaken her to her roots, and in its wake, she knew she was losing her battle against herself. God help her, she thought in dismay. She was beginning to fall in love with her husband!

The next day, after traveling through a rugged passageway Stands Alone identified as Apache Pass, they came upon a man dressed in a buckskin shirt, leggings, and moccasins and wearing a fur cap. Standing in the middle of a stream, he was pounding a stick into the bottom of it. Isabel knew he was a white man, not because of his long, straggly hair, but because of his bushy beard. Indians plucked what little facial hair they had.

Startled, the man looked up, a glimmer of fear coming into his eyes when he saw Stands Alone. Then when Stands Alone made no overt movement, he nodded solemnly.

Stands Alone nodded back curtly, and he and Isabel crossed the stream, their horses splashing water and sending the rainbow trout madly darting here and there. When they were out of the man's hearing, Isabel said, "That man was white, but I'd stake my life that he's not Spanish."

"No, he isn't. He's a French trapper."

"What is he doing here? The Spanish government prohibits foreigners from doing any kind of business on Spanish soil, particularly Frenchmen. Why, he'd be shot on sight, if caught."

"That might be true anywhere else in New Mexico and Texas, but not around Taos. Many French trappers winter there, and no one bothers them. In the first place, there are no soldiers to enforce the law; in the second, no one wants it enforced. The trappers bring trade to the town, just as the Indians do."

Isabel knew what Stands Alone said about the Indians was true. That was why he dared to go to Taos to trade after murdering her father and Ramon and taking her captive. The Spanish merchants might have heard of his crimes against the crown, but that wouldn't keep them from doing business with him, as usual. Taos sat on the very fringes of civilization. The Spanish settlers there cared nothing about the law. It did nothing to protect them, nor did it encumber them. They survived by their wits and had only one interest—trade, and they would trade with the devil himself, if it were profitable.

As they were riding upstream, and through the trees, Isabel could see the trapper had resumed his work. "What is he doing with that stick?"

"Anchoring a steel trap to the bottom of the stream. Then he will smear some of the musky secretions from a gland taken from a beaver on it to lure another beaver to his death."

Something in Stands Alone's voice made Isabel look across at him. Seeing him scowling, she said, "You don't approve?"

"I don't."

"Why not? Indians trap, too."

"Yes, but we only take what we need. The white trappers take more than they need. I have been told by some of the northern tribes that in some places the white trappers have completely depleted the streams of beavers because of their greed. That is a crime against nature. You must always leave some to replenish the supply. Even a fool should realize that. Nor do I like the foreigners wanting our women. They come into the *Nema* camps, asking for them for their wives. But they do not want them as true wives, women to be given a respected place. They want them only to satisfy their manly needs and to slave for them, tanning their pelts, cooking for them, caring for their comfort."

Isabel had to bite her tongue to keep from saying, Well, isn't that what Indian men do, too?

"They are not true husbands," Stands Alone continued scornfully. "They do not care that their wives live hard, lonely lives in the wilderness, without the companionship of others, that they are unprotected for long periods of time while the trapper is away. And even worse, in most cases, when the trappers return to their people, they abandon the women, and the children, if there are any. Then if the woman wants to survive, she has to go back to her people, feeling shamed and broken-hearted.''

Isabel knew the Indian scorned the white man's wastefulness of natural resources. Until she had lived with them and learned how to appreciate nature's gifts, she, too, had thought there was no end to this new country's bounty. Now she knew that had been a stupid, irresponsible assumption. But Stands Alone's remarks about how the trapper treated his Indian wife gave her new insight. Indian women worked hard, but their men went to great lengths to protect them, even planning their raids hundreds of miles away so as not to endanger their families. Indian women were never left alone. When their men were gone, they had the company of the rest of the band. Loneliness was not a burden they had to endure. And despite everything, they did have a respected position in a group where they belonged. They labored hard, seemingly without appreciation, but no one questioned their importance to the group. It went without saying that survival without them would have been impossible. And abandonment by their husbands was unheard of. To shun responsibilities of any kind, particularly one so important as providing for his family, was thought unmanly and totally scorned by the others.

For a long time, Isabel silently mused over these profound truths.

Two days later, Isabel and Stands Alone looked down on the beautiful valley of Taos, shimmering in the sunlight like a green jewel, then wove their way down the rugged foothills studded with evergreens to the valley itself, following one of the gurgling streams that fed the Rio de Taos.

When they passed the Taos pueblo, some of the adobe dwellings towering six stories in the air, Stands Alone said, "These Indians call themselves the Red Willow People, and this is where the trading fair takes place." He motioned about the broad plain, saying, "At that time, all this is covered with the camps of *Nema*, Utes, Apaches, Wichitas, Sioux, Navajo, as well as those of French trappers, hoping to pick up some prime pelts cheap, and New Mexican traders, with their knives, axes, cooking pots, bridles, trading cloth, tobacco, and whiskey. From the mountains at night, you can see hundreds of fires burning, looking like stars in the heavens.

"But where is the town?" Isabel asked, anxious to see civilization again.

"Further on. That is where I will do my trading."

They covered the three miles that separated the pueblo and the town, and entered San Fernandez de Taos. Isabel saw the town itself was a small plaza surrounded by crumbling, one-story houses whose windows were filled with panes of mica, a shiny mineral that had been split into thin, transparent sheets. The town was even sleepier than Santa Fe. Cottonwoods spread shade above lazy burros dozing at hitching posts. Between the cracks in the adobe Isabel could see the residents' cool patios and beehive ovens.

A tantalizing smell drifted in the air, the aroma of freshly baked bread. Getting a whiff of it, Isabel lifted her head and drank in the almost-forgotten smell, then said, "Oh, please, can we get some bread before we leave?"

Stands Alone smiled, then said, "I thought you might want to do some shopping while I traded. I was thinking of the usual trinkets our women are so fond of, but you can buy whatever you like. Here are some of the coins your people use, and if that is not enough, tell the merchant I will arrange for a trade."

As Isabel accepted the coins Stands Alone gave her, he said, "I will be trading across the way. Take your time. When I am ready to leave, I will find you."

After Stands Alone had ridden across the plaza, Isabel dismounted, tied her horse to a hitching post, then hurried to one of the patios, where she asked an Indian servant there if she could buy one of the loafs of bread cooling at one side of the oven. Since she sold her master's bread for him on market day, the woman quickly consented, stating her usual price. A moment later, Isabel was walking away with a warm loaf of round bread that made her stomach rumble in anticipation.

Looking around her for a place where she might sit and enjoy her bread, Isabel spied a bench under the cottonwood beside the church. She hurried to it and, beneath the rustling tree, consumed the entire loaf of bread, relishing each and every bite.

Suddenly, she had the uncanny feeling that she was being watched. She quickly glanced around, but saw no one other than two boys playing *pitarrilla*, a type of checkers, beneath another cottonwood, but they were intent on their game. The feeling persisted, and Isabel made another quick scan of the plaza.

As her eyes swept over the storefronts, a rickety sign hanging over one caught her eye. It read, *Curato*. Isabel stared at it. She knew the Spanish healers had potions for everything, even infertility. Did she dare try something so drastic? She had heard that some of the potions could be dangerous. But Isabel's desire to conceive Stands Alone's child overroad everything. She rose and hurried to the store.

If the bent, old woman inside the dim, musty store

thought it unusual for a Spanish woman to be dressed like an Indian, she showed no signs of it. Like everyone else in business in Taos, she asked no questions. She listened while Isabel explained what she wanted, then handed her a small leather pouch, instructing her to simmer the contents in water for two hours, then drink it.

Isabel held out her hand and opened it, saying, "This is all I have. I hope it's enough."

Without comment, the woman took every single coin.

Isabel rushed back out and stood, savoring the heat of the sun, glad to be away from the hideous things she had seen in the darkened store: dried scorpions, spiders, bat wings, toads, snakeskins, spiderwebs, and grotesquely shaped roots, things that the woman used to make her potions. She almost jumped out of her skin when she heard Stands Alone say, "There you are! I've been looking everywhere for you. Where were you?"

Suddenly Isabel remembered what Stands Alone had said about Greyfoot's fathering children. She had bought the potion because she feared she was infertile. If she told him where she had been and what she had done would he think she was questioning *his* fertility? That would never do. Quickly slipping the pouch beneath her peplum, she turned and said vaguely, "Oh, around."

Stands Alone thought Isabel was acting strangely. "Well, did you find anything you liked?"

Knowing she might have to produce anything she said she bought, Isabel said, "I'm afraid I spent all my money on bread."

"All of it?" Stands Alone asked in astonishment.

Isabel had never lied to Stands Alone. A guilty flush stained her cheeks as she answered, "Yes. I was very hungry for it."

Stands Alone saw her flush and wondered what she could possibly be hiding. Then, thinking maybe she had bought a surprise for him, he buried his suspicions.

"Are you through with your trading?" Isabel asked, anxious to get off the subject of how she had spent her money.

"Yes."

"Did you make a good trade?"

"Yes. The merchant is loading the goods I traded for right now. You'll be happy to know that one of those things is another Navajo blanket."

Isabel was glad. Despite its warmth, she hated sleeping beneath a buffalo robe. She couldn't seem to get the smell from it no matter how much sage she sprinkled on it. She much preferred a blanket she could simply wash.

"Would you like to look around more while we're waiting?" he asked her. "Surely you will find something you like. I do have more coins," he patted a bulging leather pouch that hung from his belt.

"You got all that and trading goods?" Isabel asked in surprise.

"Yes. I told you my racehorses were highly valued. Usually, I am not that interested in accepting coins, but they are easier to use in trading with the French. Greyfoot and I thought to make a trip to Texas for more gunpowder."

"When?" Isabel asked.

"In a week or two."

"How long will you be gone?"

"Several months."

"Will the women go along?"

"No, this trip will be much too dangerous."

A tingle of fear ran through Isabel. Then she remembered that Stands Alone was very capable of taking care of himself. Another concern came quickly to mind. She frowned and asked, "How soon did you say you would leave?"

"In a week or two."

Isabel knew she didn't have much time. She couldn't bear to wait several months longer to achieve her goal. She said a silent prayer that the potion would work quickly.

Twenty-three

Stands Alone took Isabel through the shops in Taos
while they were waiting for his trading goods to be
loaded, but the only things Isabel bought were some
beads and ribbons for Beaver Woman, Corn Woman,
and Tekwitchi and some new wooden hairpins for herself, since Corn Woman had never returned hers.

As soon as they stepped outside under the *portica,*
Stands Alone said to Isabel, "You are not going to start
wearing your hair up again, are you?"

"I certainly am."

"I like it hanging down your back in that big braid."

"You don't have to work with it that way. Even braided,
it's hot on the back of my neck," Isabel answered, having
found out for herself why the Comanche women chopped
their hair off short. Then seeing Stands Alone scowl, she
said, "It's either that, or I cut it."

The scowl deepened. *"Nema* wives do not give their
husbands ultimatums."

"Neither do Spanish," Isabel answered pertly, "but
I'm neither."

"Then who are you?"

"Isabel."

As she turned and walked away, Stands Alone's frown
gave way to a smile. Despite his strong *Nema* beliefs,

there were times when he found Isabel's independence refreshing. At other times, he found it utterly exasperating. But he loved her for it. It was one of the unique things about her that made her so special.

He hurried to catch up with her, then stopped her, saying, "I noticed you did not buy anything pretty for yourself, so I did." He held out his hand and unclasped his fist.

Isabel looked down at the silver necklace and knew it was Spanish, and not native crafted. From the chain, an ornately filigreed cross hung, encrusted with small stones. She strongly suspected it had been stolen, then used by some Indian for trading purposes. The old Isabel would have refused to accept it on principle, but for once, she looked past where the necklace came from to who was giving it to her, and more important, why. She knew Comanche men did not pamper their women by giving them gifts and was touched.

"I do not know what the stones are," Stands Alone said, "but they reminded me of your eyes."

If there had been any doubts in Isabel's mind about the depth of Stands Alone's feelings for her, she knew then. His black, velvety eyes were filled with love. A lump came to her throat, and she answered, "I believe they're sapphires. Thank you. It's beautiful."

As she started to put the necklace on, Stands Alone took it from her, saying, "Here. Let me."

He stepped behind her, draped the necklace around her neck, and fastened the clasp. The feel of his warm fingers brushing her neck made a sudden hunger rise in Isabel. She couldn't wait to make camp and be alone with him, to experience the heaven only he could give her. She reached over her shoulder, caught one of his hands in hers, and asked, "How soon can we leave?"

Stands Alone had become attuned to Isabel's needs;

he knew what she was yearning for, and he was in perfect agreement. "Soon," he answered in a husky voice.

Ten minutes later, they left Taos. They passed the Indian pueblo, then threaded their way up the steep foothills, the late afternoon sun casting long shadows and turning the mountains ahead blood red. Suddenly, as they rode out of a narrow canyon, they were surrounded by six Spanish dragoons. Isabel was stunned by their unexpected appearance, but Stands Alone reacted quickly, reaching for the bow strung across his shoulder.

"Put it down, or we will shoot your woman!"

Stands Alone saw the muskets pointed at himself and Isabel. Not for one minute did he doubt the threat. The Spanish thought nothing of killing innocent Indian women. He lowered his hand.

Isabel thought she recognized the voice that had called the command to Stands Alone. While Stands Alone obeyed and two dragoons rushed in to disarm him, she looked about her. Seeing the officer riding from behind a boulder where he had been obscured from her view, she gasped, "Diego!"

Stands Alone recognized the name of the man Isabel had said loved her and wanted to marry her. He also remembered her claim that she loved the Spaniard. He gave both her and the officer a sharp, questioning glance. Diego saw the look, sensed Stands Alone's insecurity at that moment, and immediately seized the opportunity to play on his vulnerability. "Yes, my dear, it is I. Thank you for your help in capturing this murdering savage."

"What . . . what help?" Isabel sputtered in surprise.

"There's no need to pretend, Isabel," Diego answered. "He can't hurt you now. You're safe." He turned to Stands Alone, who was being roughly tied to his horse by one of the dragoons, and said, "You can't imagine how surprised I was to see Isabel in Taos. I thought I would never see her again. And she thought she would never see me. But I didn't want to attempt to capture you there. That would have endangered so many people, so we planned—"

Finally, Isabel realized what Diego was up to. She looked at Stands Alone, saw him glaring at her, and interjected, "No! I didn't have anything to do with this!"

Stands Alone scoffed and answered, "Do you think me a complete fool? I guess this explains why I couldn't find you, and why you looked so guilty when I questioned you."

"No, I—"

"Silence, Isabel!" Diego said harshly. "The savage deserves no explanation on how we planned this trap." Then sidling his horse up to hers, he put his back to the others and said in a lowered voice so no one else could hear, "Keep your mouth shut, and I may let your savage live."

Isabel's objection was made softly, but it was an anguished cry that came from the depths of her soul. "But he thinks I betrayed him!"

"And that is exactly what I want that bastard to think!" Diego hissed. "So hold your tongue, or I will kill him right here and now."

Isabel saw the fury in Diego's eyes and knew he wasn't making idle threats. Stands Alone's life depended upon her cooperation. She nodded her head in grim resignation.

A smirk crossed Diego's handsome face. "Good! I am glad you have come to your senses." He whirled his horse around and said to his men, "Take the savage back to Taos and put him in chains. But be careful. He is a sly one. Be warned. If he escapes, you will pay with your lives."

The color drained from each and every dragoon's face at Diego's threat, for the soldiers had learned their commanding officer was a hard, cruel man who delighted in thinking up heinous punishments. It wasn't death that frightened them so much as the torture he might first inflict upon them.

Then one of the men broke off from the others and rode up to Diego. Handing him Stands Alone's pouch of coins, he said, "We found this on him, Captain. It was probably stolen from some poor Spaniard."

Diego nodded and took the sack. As the man rode away, Isabel said, "It wasn't stolen. Stands Alone was paid that in Taos for the horses he sold."

"It doesn't matter. It is mine now," Diego answered, slipping the pouch into a pocket on the inside of his dusty jacket.

It was he who was the thief, Isabel thought in disgust. She turned away from Diego and watched in silence as the soldiers took Stands Alone away, two dragoons riding at the head of the column, two beside the Comanche, and two behind him. She noticed Stands Alone didn't even cast her a backward glance, and his being so willing to believe her guilt hurt her deeply. But her hurt didn't stand in the way of her fear for him. She turned back to Diego and asked, "What will you do with him?"

Diego saw the deep concern in Isabel's eyes. It infuriated him. He hated her for caring about the dirty savage, so much so that he longed to put his hands around her neck and choke the life from her, but he also still desired her. She was even more attractive than before, despite her slenderness, her tanned skin, her red, roughened hands, her loss of innocence. There was about her a maturity that enhanced her beauty, a touch of seductiveness that had not been there before. He was determined to have her, not just possess her once or twice, but have her helpless in his power forever. Before he had wanted her to pay for spurning him. Now she would pay double, for that and for caring for another, particularly someone as low as an Indian. Diego looked Isabel straight in the eye and answered coldly, "That depends totally upon you."

"In what way?"

"If I agree to let him live, you must agree to marry me."

Isabel had suspected Diego wanted her body. She had always known he lusted after her. Shameful as it might be, she would give it. She would do anything to save Stands Alone. But marriage? No, that was going too far. "I can't marry you. I am already married."

"To that heathen?" Diego thundered. "No, that is impossible! Marriage is a sacrament. It must be blessed by a priest."

Diego couldn't make Isabel feel any less married. She and Stands Alone had bonded, giving themselves to each other as no ceremony, no priest ever could. They were man and wife in their own eyes, in the eyes of his people, and yes—in the eyes of God, for Isabel knew her God and his Sure Enough Father were one and the same. "I would still consider it a sacrilege."

Diego reached across the distance and caught her arm, his fingers biting painfully into the flesh as he said, "Regardless of what you consider it, you will marry me. If not, he dies."

Despite the furious glitter she saw in Diego's eyes, a look that would have warned even the bravest of men away, Isabel flared out, "Why are you insisting on this? You only want my body. That's all you've ever wanted.

Well, you can have it. I'll be your mistress, your whore, whatever!"

Diego didn't want Isabel to know what a life of misery, of degradation he had planned for her. And he didn't want to take any chances of her escaping him. As his wife, she would legally belong to him, to use as he saw fit. But there were other reasons. He also wanted vengeance on the savage who had known her body first. "That is not enough. I want the savage to suffer. I want him to think that you came to me of your own free will, that you love me, that you've always loved me."

There was a diabolical gleam in Diego's eyes when he said these words that made Isabel realize what she had always sensed about him. He was a cruel, vindictive man, a man who took pleasure not only in causing physical pain, but in mental torture. A shiver ran over her. She knew if she agreed to his demands, her life would be sheer hell. But what choice did she have? Cautiously, she asked, "If I agree to this, what will happen to Stands Alone? Will you set him free?"

"Free?" Diego scoffed. "Are you insane? So he can come back and murder us in our sleep?"

Isabel knew what Diego said was true. Stands Alone would never let the insult pass. Hadn't he said he kept what was his? But he wouldn't sneak in and do it under the cover of darkness. He wasn't a coward. He'd attack in the wide open, probably even hand Diego a weapon to defend himself, if need be. That was more her daring husband's style. "Then what will you do to him?"

"Send him to the mines."

Isabel remembered what Stands Alone had told her about the silver mines in Mexico and how he had said he would rather be dead than have to slave in one. The color drained from her face. "What mines?" Then hopefully, she asked, "The turquoise mines in the Jemez Mountains?"

Diego was a very observant man. "Yes, of course."

Isabel gazed off thoughtfully for a moment, then said, "I will have to think on this."

A hard look came over Diego's face. "You have until tomorrow morning. Then, we will either leave Taos to take my prisoner back to Santa Fe, or he will be executed. Hanged, I believe. I understand the Comanches have a particular aversion to that kind of death."

Isabel grimaced. She didn't know how Diego knew, but it was true. The Comanches thought death by strangulation of any kind prevented the soul from escaping the body and finding its way to heaven. Yes, she thought morosely, Diego did possess an unusual cruelty to seek vengeance even beyond death.

When they were riding back to Taos, Isabel said to Diego, "I'm curious. How did you happen to be in Taos? I was under the impression that the army never patrolled it."

"They didn't, until I came to New Mexico. I found it shocking that they allowed Taos to become a haven for those running from Spanish justice, both Indian and Spanish. When a man committed a particularly heinous crime in Santa Fe, I finally convinced my commanding officer to let me come to Taos to bring the man back, or any other criminals I might happen to find here."

Diego didn't mention that his commanding officer had finally agreed to his badgering just to get him out of his hair for a few weeks. The captain's superior attitude and criticism about how things were done on the frontier were wearing on the colonel's nerves. The young man had yet to learn that the army was essentially powerless in the face of so many hostiles. If the young fool wanted to go on a wild goose chase, let him. All of Santa Fe would be glad to be rid of him for a while.

"Did you find the man you were looking for?" Isabel asked.

A flush rose on Diego's face. "No."

"Did you find any of the criminals you were looking for?"

The flush deepened. "Until today, no, although I am sure the entire village of Taos are thieves and murderers."

"Including the merchants?"

"Especially the merchants! They deal with the murdering savages, don't they, buying and selling stolen goods to line their own pockets?"

Isabel could have pointed out that was only the trade the merchants could deal in, that the Spanish government had prohibited trade with any other country, even regulated what the territory could sell to Mexico and California and Texas. The settlers were only trying to survive in a very harsh land beneath an oppressive government.

"But my mission has not been fruitless," Diego continued, breaking into Isabel's musings. "My commanding officer will take an entirely different viewpoint after he sees the prize I have brought back, the most wanted criminal in all of New Mexico."

"Is that who Stands Alone is?"

"Yes, of course. Not only did the savage murder one of the most respected men in the territory, but he did so practically within hearing distance of the capital. His audacity was not to be tolerated. The governor was absolutely furious!"

Typical Spanish arrogance, Isabel thought. They were more angry at being made to look the fool, than about the crime. Then a sudden, terrifying thought came to her. "Perhaps the governor will demand Stands Alone's death."

"No, as arresting officer, I will be allowed to set the punishment. He and I agreed on that when I first set out to find Stands Alone. I assured him that death would be too swift, too merciful."

It wasn't as much Diego's words as the way he said them that alarmed Isabel. "But you will send Stands Alone to the turquoise mines?"

"If you agree to marry me, yes."

Isabel didn't notice that Diego broke eye contact before answering.

Isabel and Diego made the rest of the trip to Taos in silence. When they rode into the village, there was no sign of Stands Alone, but Isabel knew the villagers knew of his capture and imprisonment. The expressions on their faces were even more noncommittal than before, clearly telling Isabel they would interfere in no manner. As usual, they were keeping in the middle of the road, taking no sides. Any hopes she might have been harboring of any of them helping Stands Alone to escape were quickly forgotten.

Isabel spent that night in the home of a merchant, under guard herself. Then, when the sun had barely risen over the mountain tops, Diego knocked on her door and demanded a decision. Exhausted after a sleepless night of tossing and turning and fruitlessly searching for another way out, Isabel knew she had no recourse. "I will marry you," she told him in a flat voice.

A victorious smirk spread over the officer's face. Then he said, "A wise decision, my dear." His eyes swept over her, his expression turning to one of total disgust. "Now, get out of those heathen rags. I will have the merchant bring you some decent Christian clothing. We will leave for Rosario as soon as we have eaten."

"Rosario?" Isabel asked in surprise. "I thought you said you would take him to Santa Fe."

"By way of Rosario. The village is just a day's ride off the main road. It will be worth the added time and trouble. I want the people there to be the first to learn your father's murderer has been captured and that Don Augustine's death will be revenged. Also, we will announce our engagement. Perhaps we will even marry before we leave."

"Aren't you getting a little ahead of yourself? What about asking my mother's permission and the church banns that have to be posted?"

"The bans will be waived at my insistence. That stupid little parish priest would not dare defy me. As for your mother, she is not there. She has gone to northern Mexico for an extended visit with her sister. But she would not object. I told her when I went to pay my condolences that I had spoken to your father about offering for your hand before he died, and that he had agreed."

"You didn't talk to him! He cut you off!"

"Yes, but she doesn't know that."

"Why did you lie to her?"

"I should think that would be obvious. In the event that you escaped or were rescued, it would already be established that you were my betrothed. Your resistance to the match would be pointless. Besides, I do not think she would object under any circumstances." He sneered. "You are soiled. No one else would want you."

Isabel felt his contempt like a slap in the face, yet she knew it was true. Women who had been rescued from Indian captivity were scorned by her people. They were considered dirty and sinful for having cohabited with an Indian. Even if they were raped, the women were blamed. Maybe that was why so many Spanish women simply accepted their captivity. They knew there was no respectable place for them in their society any longer, that they would be treated better by the Indians than their own. "Aren't you worried about what the others will think of you, for marrying a soiled woman?" Isabel asked bitterly.

"Why, they will all talk about how noble I am, of course, to take my previous commitment to you so seriously. Every one in New Mexico will be impressed with my Christianity, which should be quite advantageous for me when I make my bid for governor."

She should have known Diego would have some ulterior motive for marrying her, Isabel thought. Not only was he lustful, cruel and vindictive, but dangerously ambitious. He would sink to any deceit to get what he wanted. She shuddered to think what would happen to New Mexico under the control of such a corrupt man.

Later, after she had changed into some Spanish clothing and eaten, Isabel walked from the merchant's house and out into the plaza. Then she came to a dead halt, seeing they had put Stands Alone into a sturdy wooden cage and he was manacled there, hand and foot. To see him caged as if he were some wild animal infuriated her. She whirled around and angrily asked Diego, "Is that necessary? Just how dangerous can he be? You already have him chained."

Diego's eyes flashed. He clenched his fists to keep from hitting her. "Silence! I will decide how to handle the prisoner."

As Diego ordered the cage put on a *carreta* that the back had been removed from, then paraded around the plaza, Isabel knew why Diego had caged Stands

Alone and was exhibiting him before the townspeople. To humiliate him. To try to rob a man as fierce as Stands Alone of his pride, seemed the ultimate cruelty. Tears came to her eyes. Then she saw that Diego had not been successful in his ploy. Stands Alone stood in the cage, humped over, swaying from one side to the other, but proud and defiant, every inch the magnificent creature he was.

When Diego saw that no one was making sport of Stands Alone, but that the townspeople were watching with either compassion or showing admiration for the Comanche's defiance, he ordered a halt. Isabel had to bite her tongue to keep from laughing at the fury she saw in his eyes.

Automatically, Isabel's eyes rose to seek out Stands Alone's, to silently share, as they had done so often in the past, something they thought amusing, but she was stunned by the look Stands Alone gave her. It was filled with such unmitigated hatred, she recoiled from it as if he had dealt her a physical blow.

As they rode from the plaza, Isabel had never felt so low or so dispirited. Her world had suddenly collapsed all around her. She had lost Stands Alone forever and made a pact with the devil himself. Her future couldn't look any bleaker.

Twenty-four

The narrow road from Taos to Santa Fe followed the Rio Grande. Here, the river leaped over rocky ledges, creating shimmering rainbows in the bright sunlight, and rushed through deep, rugged, windswept gorges topped with spruce and fir, the roar coming from below sounding like the stampede of wild horses. But Isabel didn't even take note of what was some of the most spectacular scenery in the territory, nor did she notice the next day when the turbulence was left behind, and the river flowed placidly beneath a canopy of cotton-woods and willows through a broad valley made of sand hills covered with lush grass, an equally lovely land-scape. She was too enmeshed in her own misery.

It wasn't until they rode into Rosario the afternoon of the third day that Isabel was finally roused from her almost stuporous state by the soldiers' firing their mus-kets into the air to gain the villagers' attention. Startled by the loud noise, Isabel's mare reared, and it was all she could do to maintain her seat on the sidesaddle Diego had found for her in Taos and insisted she ride. Then, as they recognized her, she heard the settlers yell-ing, "Isabel! It's Isabel! She's been rescued!"

Diego jumped from his horse, caught Isabel's mare's cheek strap, and helped her dismount as the crowd surged towards them. Motioning the excited villagers back, Diego said, "I know you are thrilled to see Isabel alive and well, but I have brought you something even more exciting. The savage who abducted her and cold-bloodedly murdered her father." With a broad, dramatic sweep of his hand, Diego motioned to the cage that was being unloaded from the *carreta* and said, "Did I not promise I would bring you this heinous criminal, the man who betrayed your friendship and murdered your good friend, Don Augustine?"

The villagers of Rosario knew nothing of the agreement between Don Augustine and the Comanches. At the don's request, the two Spanish witnesses had kept the pact a secret. Therefore the villagers believed it was the Comanches who had betrayed them by killing Don Augustine, a man much respected and admired by all, by abducting his virtuous daughter and violating her, and, something that angered them even more, by removing the village from their protection and causing them to suffer two disastrous Apache attacks within the past year. With an enraged roar, the townspeople swept down on Stands Alone, furiously picking up rocks and bombarding the cage, yelling insults and curses.

"No! Stop it!" Isabel screamed to be heard over the noise.

"Shut up!" Diego hissed, a furious look on his face. "You are supposed to hate him for what he has done to you. Do not think for one minute that I will bear the humiliation of having them know you care for him. Keep your mouth shut and act appropriately—or I will release him and let them tear him limb from limb!"

Isabel looked back at the cage and saw that the villagers, frustrated at being unable truly to harm Stands Alone with their rocks, had taken up sticks and were jabbing him, spitting on him, still cursing him. The soldiers, rather than protecting their prisoner, joined in. Stands Alone stood as still as a statue, stoically enduring everything. Isabel was filled with a strange mixture of compassion and pride.

Then a tall, slender young man rushed forward, yelling to the people, "Stop it! You are behaving like animals!" Fast on his heels was the village priest, admonishing the crowd for their violence. Only then did the furious townspeople begin to back away.

Isabel's attention was drawn away from the drama taking place in the center of the small plaza by someone saying, "Isabel!" then turning her.

"Maria!" Isabel cried out in surprise when she saw her old duenna.

"Mother of God! It is you!" the older woman answered, then embraced Isabel.

After all she had been through, Isabel couldn't hold back the tears any longer. They burst from her like a dam had broken, and Maria held her while her slender body was racked with deep sobs.

Diego shot Isabel a furious glance, then said to Maria, "She is distraught. She has been through much."

Maria's low opinion of Diego had not changed. She gave him a cutting look and answered coldly, "Of course, she is upset. That is only natural."

Gaining some semblance of control, Isabel said between sobs, "I didn't expect you to be here. I thought you had gone back to northern Mexico with my mother."

"She wanted me to, but of course that was impossible. A married woman belongs with her husband."

Isabel's head shot up. "Married?" she asked in surprise. "You're married?"

"Yes, Ramon and I have been married for six months now."

A look of total shock came over Isabel's face. "Ramon? Then he's not dead?"

"No, he survived, but he was very weak for some time. He lost much blood. I stayed in Santa Fe and nursed him back to health. That was how we got to know one another, and love one another."

There was a soft look that came over Maria's face when she said the latter, a look that transformed her face to actual prettiness. Isabel remembered Diego's referring to the murder of her father only. She had thought he had just discounted Ramon's life, since he was a commoner. "Oh, I'm so glad he lived. I don't think I've ever heard of a scalped man living."

"He wasn't scalped. The Comanche who shot him didn't even attempt it."

Isabel wondered at that. She had thought the Comanches always scalped their victims.

"Come, Isabel," Maria said, gently moving her away. "You look exhausted. We'll go to my home."

"No," Diego interjected, stepping in front of them. "I will take her to her own home."

"The house is completely closed and there are no servants there. Isabel needs attention. She will stay with me."

Maria used her duenna tone of voice and her old authoritarian stance. Without another word, she sidestepped Diego and started leading Isabel away.

"Wait!" Diego called.

Maria turned. "Surely you do not intend to interfere with my seeing to Isabel's comfort, Captain?"

Diego cringed. Damn the woman, he thought, with her icy voice and haughty airs. She made him feel like he was a child. Regaining his composure, he said, "There is something I wish to announce to the villagers first."

"Then announce it," Maria replied bluntly, once more starting to turn away.

"No, I wish Isabel to be present, since it concerns our marriage."

Maria cast Isabel a sharp questioning look. Unable to look her friend in the eye, Isabel said, "It's true. We are to be married."

"Come, Isabel," Diego said smugly, walking up to her and taking her arm. "We will go over here where everyone can see and hear." Then, when they were out of Maria's hearing, he hissed, "Smile, dammit!"

Filled with dread and knowing the announcement would seal her fate, Isabel forced a smile onto her face. Diego led her through the crowd and then stood her before the cage that held Stands Alone. Isabel could feel the warrior's hate-filled eyes boring into her back and wished the ground would open up and swallow her.

Calling out, Diego said, "Please, everyone, may I have your attention?"

The crowd became quiet and moved closer to hear better. Drawing Isabel to his side possessively, Diego said, "I would like you all to know that Isabel and I still plan to marry, just as her father and I agreed before he was so vilely murdered."

There was a moment of shocked silence, and Isabel imagined the villagers' surprise that the well-bred officer would be willing to take soiled goods. Then a cheer of approval rang out.

"Thank you," Diego responded with pleasure, knowing his ploy to gain their esteem had worked. "You will all be invited to the ceremony that I hope," he shot a pointed glance at the priest, "will take place very soon. In the meanwhile, my men will take the prisoner on to Santa Fe, where I assure you, he will be severely punished."

"Kill the murdering beast," someone yelled.

"Yes! A life for a life!" someone called out.

"Chop off his head!" another yelled.

"After you've gelded him!" came yet another vicious cry.

"See, my dear," Diego said to Isabel in a lowered voice. "Aren't you glad I'm not going to turn him over to them? My, what a bloodthirsty lot they are." A satanic smile crossed his face. "Men after my own heart."

Diego dismissed the crowd with renewed assurances that Stands Alone would be severely punished. Then, he turned Isabel to face Stands Alone and said to the Comanche, "Did you hear? Isabel and I are to be married. You see? True love always wins out."

There was just a crack in Stands Alone's stony demeanor, but Isabel saw the fleeting look in his dark eyes. She had thought nothing could touch her as deeply as his unmitigated hatred had, but she was wrong. To betray him for her freedom was one thing. To betray his love and give what he had sought so avidly, so tirelessly to another man, was quite another. The terrible pain she saw tore at her heart and reached deep inside her to shred her soul into a million pieces. But she knew she dare not reveal what she was feeling. With super-human effort, she turned and quickly walked away.

But not Diego. He wanted to torment Stands Alone even further. "Think of us when you are slaving in that dark pit, of Isabel writhing in ecstasy beneath me, of her whispering love words in my ear, of her belly swelling with my child. You may have known the sweetness of her body first, but I will have it, and something you never had—her undying love—for eternity."

Diego heard a snarl, then suddenly two manacled hands flew out between the bars on the cage, caught him by the neck, and slammed him into the hard wood. Of course, Diego's soldiers were there in a flash, to beat Stands Alone's forearms with their muskets until they were bloody, then when that failed, to pry the tenacious fingers loose from the captain's throat, but not before Diego saw stars and knew the cold terror of thinking he was about to meet his maker.

When he was finally snatched from the hands of death, gasping for breath and trembling all over, Diego's lieutenant asked, "Do you want him punished, Captain? We could hang him right now. The villagers would more than welcome it."

Diego was so furious, he had to fight down his instincts to do just that. "No, I have a better punishment for him, a slower, more agonizing one," Diego answered in a hoarse voice. He withdrew a missive from his jacket and handed it to the officer. "When you reach Santa Fe, give this to the colonel. It contains the punishment I have chosen. Tell him to follow the instructions exactly as I have laid them out and make no substitutions. Both he and the governor should be well pleased. There is no better hell for this bastard than my uncle's mine outside Chihuahua." He smiled, a smile that made his men's blood run cold. "They say I take after him."

A frown crossed the lieutenant's face. "But surely you don't expect us to leave now. We've been on the road three days. The men are weary and in need of a rest."

"No, now! The sooner I get this murderer to Santa Fe and locked in the prison there, the easier I'll feel. As for the men, they are soldiers. They should be willing to stay on their feet until they drop dead. See to it!"

* * *

Isabel had not seen Stands Alone's attempt on Diego's life. Maria had rushed her into her modest home.

As soon as the bedroom door had closed behind them, Maria had turned Isabel to face her and asked, "Why are you marrying Diego? Have you changed your mind about him?"

"No. He's cruel and vindictive, a thief and a liar. I hate him, but I have no choice. If I didn't agree to marry him, he would have killed Stands Alone, and I couldn't bear that. Oh, Maria, I love him!" Isabel cried out in anguish. "I love him with all my heart and soul."

Maria heard the pain in Isabel's voice and took her into her arms, cradling her head on her bosom and rocking her while she cried, until the emotional storm finally passed.

With the words out in the open, Isabel knew she could no longer deny her feelings. She had always loved Stands Alone. That love had only grown as she had come to know him better. She could not dictate to her heart, any more than she could to her body. She raised her head and asked Maria. "Does that shock you?"

"That you love an Indian? Absolutely not! I have learned much since I came to New Mexico, about living, about loving. I, too, love a man who is supposedly beneath me." She scoffed. "Where did we get this . . . this stupidity, this impossible arrogance, this belief that wealth and station make a person superior? It couldn't be farther from the truth. It's what's inside a person that makes a person special. Ramon is a wonderful man, a good man. I have never known such happiness, such contentment."

Isabel had forgotten that others might think Stands Alone beneath her. She knew just the opposite was true. He was a man a cut above others, not just his own kind, but all men, a man of superior caliber. But wasn't that just what Maria had said? It was what was inside a person that made him or her special. "I was happy, too, but I didn't know it, or rather, I wouldn't admit it. But that's not what I meant when I asked if you were shocked. I'm talking about my betrayal of my father. It's wrong to love your father's murderer."

"Stands Alone did not kill your father. I was there, remember."

"I know. It was his father who did it. But, still, he took part in it."

A closed expression came over Maria's face. Her voice was guarded as she said, "Perhaps it was not murder, not in the strictest sense." Her dark eyes rose to meet Isabel's directly. "Ramon tells me that the Comanches feel as strongly about betrayal as our people, that betrayal and treachery are considered synonymous and those found guilty deserve punishment by death. Perhaps what we saw was an execution, just, but terribly sad." Maria took Isabel's hands in hers and said, "I am going to tell you something. Ramon may not like my divulging this, but you deserve to know the truth. Don Augustine did betray the Comanches. He did betroth you to Stands Alone when you were but a child. Ramon, and another man, since deceased, were witness to the agreement. True, your father felt under duress at the time, but if he had been honest and forthright with the Comanches from the very beginning, none of this would have happened. Having made the agreement, he set out to trick them, sending you away, then claiming another's grave as yours. What's worse, he accepted their gifts and protection as if it were his due, knowing all the while he was betraying them. All these things Ramon disapproved of, but he held his silence, forever loyal to your father."

Isabel had already suspected her father's guilt, but coming face-to-face with his dishonesty, his cowardice, his dishonor cut deeply. No one wanted to hear such terrible things about someone she had loved and respected. Tears glittered in her eyes.

Seeing them, Maria said, "I'm sorry. I know this hurts you, but you must realize you did not betray your father. You see, I have no blind loyalty to him, like Ramon. I clearly see the truth. It was he who betrayed you. He deceived you as much as the Comanches. As for his death, it was his own arrogance that killed him. He thought he was too clever to be caught. So put aside any guilt you might be feeling."

Isabel opened her mind and heart to Maria's words and felt as if a tremendous burden had been lifted from her shoulders. But she couldn't love Stands Alone any more for finally knowing and accepting the truth. That had come despite the knowledge, rather than because of it. "Thank you, Maria. I'm glad you told me. And I assume the others in Rosario don't know the truth, since they treated Stands Alone so horribly."

"No, they don't, despite the fact that Chief Yellow Sky directed me to tell them why they were being punished. That's how I got wind of the betrayal, by what the chief instructed me. Ramon only relented after I insisted on being told the entire story. Then he requested that I not tell the townspeople of the betrayal. He thought it better that they just think the Comanches had betrayed them at whim. He saw no purpose in ruining your father's good reputation. From that standpoint, I had to agree with him. It seemed nothing would be accomplished by revealing the true story. It wouldn't change anything. And I certainly never expected to see you again."

"Then no one else knows the truth?"

"Your mother knew, and I suspect she told Diego. They became thick as thieves after your father died. Of course, I knew your father had not agreed to betroth you to Diego, as he claimed to your mother. I was there when Don Augustine spurned him. But again, I thought it didn't matter. Diego could never make you his wife. You were gone. Even when he went looking for you, I wasn't concerned. I didn't think he'd ever find you."

"Went looking for me?" Isabel asked in surprise. Then, remembering something, she frowned and said, "That's right. Diego did say something about when he first set out to find Stands Alone."

"Yes, shortly after your abduction. He kept taking patrols out to search for you, until winter forced him to remain in Santa Fe. That's how he endeared himself to both your mother and the villagers. Pedro said he could have saved himself the trouble. He would never find you in those rugged mountains. That's why I never thought to see you again."

"He didn't find the Comanche camp," Isabel informed the older woman. "He stumbled across us in Taos by chance."

"Oh? Then Pedro was correct, after all. He is the only other person that knows the entire truth. Like me, Pedro insisted on it after the attack. He said he knew Stands Alone too well to believe he would sink to such treachery without cause, that a righteous child does not grow up to be an unjust man. And he was already suspicious. He was in the graveyard visiting his mother's grave the day Don Augustine brought Stands Alone and Chief Yellow Sky there and showed them another grave. He was too far away to hear what was said, but he never forgot the look on Stands Alone's face when he left. Pedro said he looked utterly devastated. It was Pedro who insisted that I should not worry about you. He said Stands Alone would not harm you, that he loved you, that he loved you even as a child."

"He did love me," Isabel answered bleakly. "But not anymore. Now, he hates me. Diego made him think I helped plan his capture and willingly agreed to marry Diego, that I even love him. Oh, Maria, I'd give anything if Stands Alone could know the truth, particularly that I love him with my whole heart and soul."

"Then he knows nothing of why you agreed to marry Diego, to save his life?"

"No. Diego forbid that. He wants Stands Alone to think it's because I love him, that I've always loved him. It's Diego's way of making Stands Alone suffer for my caring for him, except Stands Alone doesn't know how deeply I care. I would never admit to my love for him because of my fears of betraying my father."

"Are you saying, if anyone tells Stands Alone the truth, the bargain is off? He will be killed outright?"

"Yes. Diego wants him to suffer mentally as well as physically."

Maria shook her head sadly, thinking what a terrible cycle of deceit Don Augustine had started, a cycle that was causing so much pain and suffering. "What is to be his punishment?"

"He's to be sent to slave in one of the turquoise mines. I've been told they are not as terrible as the mines in Mexico."

"Perhaps someone in Taos will send word to his band about what has happened and they will rescue him."

"Even if someone was willing to do that, they could never find their camp. And by the time his band becomes alarmed and comes looking for him, it will be too late. He will already be incarcerated in one of the mines."

"Then there's no hope for his escape?"

Isabel carefully considered the question for a moment, then replied, "No, I wouldn't say that. His father

and brother are very determined men. Somehow they
will find out what happened, then do everything in
their power to try and rescue him. I don't think Diego
realizes that."

"Then we must do everything in our power to delay
your marriage to Diego."

Isabel saw where Maria's thoughts were leading, that
if Stands Alone could be rescued, he would rescue her
in turn. "That's not very likely. Diego said he is going
to get the banns waived, that the priest would not dare
defy him."

Maria laughed, then said, "He doesn't know Father
Cruz. That little bandy rooster doesn't bow to anyone
but God, Himself."

For a brief moment, Isabel allowed herself to have
hope that she and Stands Alone might have a future
together, after all. Then her rising spirits plunged to
the ground and she said glumly, "It doesn't matter. I
gave Diego my word. Marriage to him in exchange for
Stands Alone's life. I won't go back on my word. There's
been enough dishonor in my family."

Maria stared at Isabel, thinking there was nothing
sadder than a noble fool.

Twenty-five

The next day, Diego went to Father Cruz and found that what Maria had said was true. Threats had no effect on the fierce little priest, nor did Diego's attempts at bribery change anything, except to anger the priest further. Even Diego's false claim that Isabel was pregnant and he wished to spare her and the child from scorn by making it look as if the child was his, did not deter the priest. Church law was church law. Father Cruz firmly declared that Diego and Isabel would wait the usual three weeks for the banns to be announced from the altar each Sunday.

While Diego fumed at the priest's dictate, Isabel was greatly relieved. She dreaded the marriage and didn't know how she would ever survive Diego's touch. Just the thought of his making love to her, doing all those intimate things Stands Alone had done, made her quite ill. Every morning she woke up retching.

One night, after Diego had left from his evening visit with Isabel, Maria said to Isabel, "Won't you reconsider? I can't stand the thought of you being in that horrible man's clutches."

"I can't either, but, no, I won't go back on my word." Seeing Maria scowl, Isabel smiled at the older woman, then said, "Please stop worrying about me. I'll manage.

I'm much tougher than I look. I survived Indian life, didn't I?"

"That was an entirely different kind of difficulty from what you will be facing," Maria pointed out. "You told me yourself you were not demeaned or humiliated or scorned by the Indians. Mental abuse, while much more subtle than physical, can be much harder to bear. Believe me, I know. I lived most of my life under those conditions. It erodes the very center of your being, your self-esteem. Everyone deserves to be valued, particularly by themselves."

"I won't let Diego do that to me. He'll never break my spirit!" Isabel vowed fervently.

Still unconvinced, Maria answered, "I would feel much better if you let Pedro handle the matter."

Ramon's son, Pedro, was the young man who had come to Stands Alone's defense when the villagers were attacking him. Isabel's old playmate had grown into a strong-willed young man with a mind of his own and the courage to act on his convictions. Isabel had come to the conclusion that it was the influence of his many Indian friends that made Pedro so fiercely independent. As a rule, commoners were subservient, blindly following those above them on the social scale. Proof of Pedro's divergence from the norm had come shortly after the two had been reunited and Pedro had demanded to know why Isabel had agreed to marry "that pompous hypocrite." But despite her admiration for what Pedro had become, Isabel could not approve of what he had suggested as a solution to her dilemma. "No, Maria, that would be murder. I can't believe you would condone that."

"Pedro didn't say he would kill Diego. He said he could arrange for an accident to happen. You didn't even give Pedro the chance to explain."

"What possible explanation could there be? It would still be murder."

"Not if the man seeks it out himself. Diego has been begging Pedro to show him where the Silver Devil lives. The fool thinks he can kill it."

"The Silver Devil? Are you talking about that huge grizzly that has terrorized the area around Chaco Canyon for years?"

"Yes. Pedro said it has killed at least twenty men over the years, to say nothing of the livestock it has destroyed at a nearby pueblo. Pedro says the search parties that were sent against it either returned empty-handed, or didn't return at all, causing much speculation about what happened to them."

"A grizzly couldn't kill an entire search party, no matter how notorious it might be."

"No, but Pedro suspects the Utes who live in that area consider the bear sacred and eliminated the search parties that disappeared. So you see, Pedro wouldn't have to lift a hand against Diego. All he would have to do is take Diego to the canyon and leave him to his fate. Diego does not want his help. He's convinced he can bring down the grizzly single-handed."

It sounded so much like the egotistical Diego, to think he could succeed where hunters so much more accomplished than he had failed. Isabel was tempted, but couldn't agree. "No, it would still be wrong."

Maria shook her head in disgust, then said, "Well, perhaps Diego will tire of asking Pedro and find someone else to take him."

Isabel secretly hoped so. Then she would feel that the matter had been taken out of her hands. Or was hoping for someone's death just as wrong?

Isabel was still struggling with this moral dilemma when she went to the kitchen for a bite to eat before

she retired later that night. She almost jumped out of
her skin when Diego stepped from the shadows of one
corner. Recovering from her surprise, she asked angrily,
"What are you doing here?"

"I was hoping to have a moment alone with you,"
Diego answered sullenly, for Maria had been protecting
Isabel like a hawk, insisting upon chaperoning them
every moment they were together.

"Even if we're betrothed, you know that is not appropriate," Isabel answered icily.

Diego slammed his hand on the table and said angrily, "To hell with propriety! What do you think you're
protecting? You're no virgin!"

A flush rose on Isabel's face. Then she said, "That
may be true, but I am still a chaste woman."

"Chaste?" Diego made an ugly, scoffing noise. "You
fornicated with a savage, an animal. You're nothing but
a whore!"

Furious, Isabel drew herself up to her full height and
answered, "You cannot shame me. Stands Alone was
my husband, and I was his wife. What we did was an act
of love, and not lust. Nothing could ever make me be
ashamed of that."

"I cannot believe the depths to which you have sunk,"
Diego answered with a sneer. "You whore and dare to
call it love?"

"I *do* love him! I will always love him," Isabel answered fiercely. "You can possess me a million times,
and it will never change that."

Diego's hand flew out and caught Isabel's wrist. Jerking her to him, he said, "No, but I can make you regret
it." His eyes glittered with malice. "And believe me, I
will make you regret. I will make it so agonizingly painful, you will wish you never heard that bastard's name.
I will take you in every manner possible, batter you with

my manhood in orifices you would never have dreamed of, force you to perform unspeakable acts on me, humiliate you, demean you, beat you, make you beg for death. But you will not be able to escape me. I will keep you chained to our bed."

Seeing the horrified expression on Isabel's face, Diego realized he had gone too far in the heat of his anger and revealed more than he had planned. But he was so sure of himself, he didn't think she would dare to back out of their agreement. "Do you wish to change your mind?" he taunted. "If so, I can arrange for the prisoner train going to Mexico to be stopped, and your savage hanged on the spot."

Despite her shock at learning just how depraved Diego really was, Isabel's mind latched onto one word. "Mexico? I thought you were sending him to the Jemez mines here in New Mexico?"

Too late, Diego realized his mistake. "What difference does it make where he goes, he's alive, isn't he?" he blustered.

"No! I said the Jemez mines, and you agreed. To be sent to the silver mines in Mexico is a punishment worse than death." Seeing the closed expression coming over Diego's face, Isabel jerked free and stepped back, saying angrily, "You deliberately lied to me, didn't you? From the very beginning, you planned to deceive me. You never intended to keep our agreement."

Diego thought Isabel looked magnificent in her fury with her color up, her eyes flashing, and her beautiful breasts heaving. His lust came surging to the surface. He stepped towards her, saying thickly, "You are particularly enticing when you are angry. I think for that reason I shall keep you enraged. And I will no longer wait. I will take what is mine, now!"

Isabel backed up, saying, "No! You will never have

my body! You sent Stands Alone to a hell on earth. The agreement is off. I would die before I would marry you!''

Isabel's defiance brought forth another lust within Diego, the craving to break her spirit, to have her begging for mercy. Furious, he stalked her around the kitchen, his eyes glittering, saying, "That can be arranged, also. After I have finished with you.''

He lunged, but Isabel's reflexes had been sharpened by her Indian ball playing, and she anticipated his move and jumped away. Then catching the glitter of something lying on the table, she reached for it. Diego reached, too, but Isabel was faster. Brandishing the butcher knife, she said, "Get back, Diego! Now! Let me assure you, I know how to use one of these. If I can butcher a buffalo, I can gut you. I've been told it's a terrible way to die, slow, yet sure, with your guts spilling out all over the floor.''

Diego didn't doubt Isabel's claim. She was much too at ease with the wicked-looking weapon. "Bitch!" he threw out, then reluctantly stepped back.

At that moment, the door to the kitchen opened, and Maria stepped into the room. Seeing Isabel had a knife pointed at Diego, she immediately drew her own conclusions and said to Diego, "Leave my house at once, Captain. This instant!''

It would have been hard to say who seemed the most threatening, Isabel with her knife, or the fierce duenna who looked as if she could tear him apart with her bare hands. But being bested by two lowly women was almost more than Diego could bear. He stomped to the door, opened it, then turned, and said in a haughty voice, "We will discuss this further tomorrow.''

"We will discuss nothing, tomorrow, or ever,'' Isabel replied. "Now, get out!''

So furious his eyes were bulging and his face was beet red, Diego whirled around, then slammed the door behind him so hard the little adobe building shook.

As Maria rushed to the door to bolt it firmly, Isabel dropped the knife on the table with a loud clatter. Maria turned from the door and saw her shaking all over.

"There is nothing to be afraid of. He's gone," Maria assured Isabel, hurrying to the younger woman.

"I'm not afraid! I'm furious! He lied to me. He sent Stands Alone to one of those horrible silver mines in Mexico. He would have been better off dead. In trying to save his life, I've only condemned him to a horrible existence of pain and misery."

The last was an anguished sob, and Maria took Isabel in her arms and said, "Sssh. You meant well. You couldn't have known."

"No! I should have known. I knew Diego was a liar. I should have never trusted him." Then remembering all the terrible things he had said he would do to her, Isabel said, "Oh, Maria! You should have heard the terrible things he had planned for me. I knew he was cruel and corrupt, but I never dreamed he was a sadist, too. He's evil to the core."

"Yes, I know. But what are you going to do now?"

"I'm not going to marry him! I'd die first!"

"I don't mean that. What are you going to do about Stands Alone? Try to rescue him?"

Isabel had been so enraged she hadn't even stopped to consider what she might be able to do to help Stands Alone. And that was an option that was open to her now. She pushed away from Maria, sat down on a chair beside the table, and said, "I've got to think."

But Maria was way ahead of her. "It's obvious you can't do anything by yourself. Those prison trains are well guarded. You said his father and brother would try to rescue him if they knew what was going on."

"If he was sent to the Jemez mines, yes. But he's been sent to Mexico."

"That's never stopped the Comanches before," Maria replied dryly. "They raid down there as much, or more, as here. Why, they probably know the lay of the land better than our people."

"But there are hundreds of silver mines in Mexico, and we don't know which he's being taken to. And two weeks have already passed. The trail might be too cold to follow."

"Those are problems Stands Alone's father and brother will have to deal with. Your problem is to get word to them about what's happened."

Suddenly it was all very clear to Isabel what she had to do. "No, not word. I'll go myself."

"Then you know how to find their camp?" Maria asked in surprise.

"No, not really. I didn't pay all that much attention on the trip down from the mountains. But I've got to try. It's Stands Alone's only chance."

Maria turned and hurried to the door, saying over her shoulder, "I'll wake up Ramon, so he can summon Pedro."

Isabel came to her feet. "Pedro? What for?"

"You can't go alone. You need a man for protection. Besides, Pedro is a good woodsman and fairly adept at tracking himself. It's something he picked up from those Indian friends of his. Perhaps he can find the camp if you can't."

"Pedro has a wife. He can't just go running off to help me."

"Pedro considers Stands Alone one of his truest friends. He will insist upon helping. As for his wife, she will not mind. He is already away so much with all the hunting he does." Maria smiled. "Ramon says Pedro should have been a conquistador or an explorer. He's much too adventuresome for the pastoral life."

"Then wait until morning, at least. He and his wife might be . . ." Isabel blushed, ". . . occupied."

"No, I think you should leave tonight, before Diego realizes you might escape. I wouldn't put it past him to put a guard on the house."

"My God, I forgot about him. What if he tries to follow me?"

"First he will have to realize you are gone. When he comes to visit, Ramon and I will say you are too distraught to talk to him. But we will make hints that you might be reconciled to the marriage, after all, if he will but give you a little time. Then, when we eventually have to admit you are gone, we will say Pedro took you to your family in Mexico. Even if he does not believe us, it will give you and Pedro a few days' head start. By then, hopefully you will have disappeared into the Sangre de Cristo Mountains. If Diego does follow, remember that he never found the Comanches' camp before. There is no reason to think he would now."

Isabel smiled and said, "You missed your calling, Maria. I never dreamed how adept you were at intrigue."

Maria grinned and answered, "You might be surprised at my hidden talents."

Indeed, Isabel thought. Ever since they had left Mexico, Maria had been surprising her.

Twenty-six

Isabel and Pedro left Rosario several hours later in the dead of the night, slipping past even the dozing shepherds on the hillsides. The only living thing that took note of their leaving was a sheep dog who lifted his head, then seeing it was Pedro, lowered it once more to rest on its paws, its eyes alertly scanning the countryside for wolves and other predators.

Because time was so critical, the two traveled all day and way into the next night. Then, after a few hours sleep, they continued. Isabel found she didn't feel at all awkward at being alone with a man other than her husband. The bond of friendship that she and Pedro had forged during their childhood stood them in good stead. She felt as comfortable with him as she would have felt with a brother, had she had one.

Because they traveled longer hours and were not being held back by a rickety *carreta*, they made the trip to Taos in two days, instead of three. As they approached the Spanish town, Isabel said to Pedro, "I would like to return to the merchant whose home Diego quartered me in. If possible, I would like to get back my Indian clothing and saddle." She repositioned herself for the hundredth time on the sidesaddle that now felt so awkward to her.

"I had thought to go into town anyway," Pedro answered. "I'm curious to know if Stands Alone's kinsmen have inquired about him. It's been several weeks now. Surely they are concerned about his safety."

It turned out the merchant still had Isabel's clothing, simply because there wasn't much demand for Indian dresses and moccasins, no matter how finely crafted. Indian men did not buy for their wives what the women could make for themselves. But the trader was a thrifty man, and had put the things up for sale, anyway, and Isabel had to buy them back. The saddle, finely crafted according to Stands Alone's specifications, however, had been sold. If the merchant was curious to know how she had managed to escape Diego, he showed no sign of it, and never even mentioned their previous dealings. For all practical purposes, he could have never laid eyes on her, and by silent, mutual agreement, Isabel made no mention either. When Pedro questioned the man about Stands Alone's kinsmen, he drew a complete blank. The man fervently claimed he knew nothing, as did everyone else in Taos.

As they rode from the town, Pedro said angrily, "They're all lying. I know it! I can feel it in my bones."

"I should have known it would be that way," Isabel replied with a sigh. "It's the only way these people can survive, taking no sides, revealing nothing they see or hear. If it's any consolation, I doubt if anyone else would have learned anything either."

"Are you suggesting they would have lied to the Comanches, also?"

"Now that I think about it, I strongly suspect just that. Stop and use their logic, Pedro. What if the Comanches took offense at their not aiding Stands Alone when he was captured and decided to punish them? These settlers are walking a fine line between the Indians and their own people, even between the different tribes.

The more prudent policy is to see nothing, hear nothing, reveal nothing."

Pedro got his first really good look at Isabel. Before, he had been too angry to notice. He thought she looked very natural in her Indian finery, with her long black single braid hanging down her back, and very pretty. "That dress becomes you," he remarked. "I don't think I've ever seen anything so beautifully beaded."

Isabel was especially pleased. She had labored all winter over the intricate beading. "Thank you. I made it myself."

"You mean, sewed the skins and everything?" Pedro asked in surprise.

"And tanned them," Isabel answered, proud of her accomplishment.

Pedro studied Isabel quietly for a moment, then said, "I expected you to have changed. After all, you weren't much more than a child when you left Rosario. I expected to find a beautiful, spirited woman, or at least, hoped that was what I would find. Some women do not survive Indian life well. It destroys them, leaves them but a shell of what they once were. But you seem to have thrived on it. Besides being more beautiful than ever, you've matured. You seem more thoughtful than the women I know, more sensitive to everything around you, yet that beautiful spirit that made you so special is still there. I always liked you, but I like the person you've become even better."

Isabel smiled. She knew what Pedro had observed was true. She was a better person today than she had been a year ago and had the Indians to thank for it. Her experiences had tempered her, just as fire did the fine Toledo steel the Spanish so valued, and the Indians' influence had changed her way of thinking and feeling. No longer did she think just of herself, but of the needs of her Indian family, and, yes, she was even beginning to think in terms of what was good for the entire band. Only when she achieved that high measure of growth would she be a true *Nema*. And that was her ultimate goal, God willing, to truly become one of "The People."

"Thank you, Pedro," she replied simply.

That night, in their camp, Pedro noticed Isabel fingering the cross that hung from her neck. He had observed she always wore it and always stroked it when she was preoccupied with her thoughts. "That is a beautiful crucifix, very highly crafted," he remarked. "I don't remember you wearing it as a child."

Isabel's hand stilled. She looked down at the cross lovingly and replied, "It was a gift from Stands Alone."

"He gave you a crucifix?" Pedro asked in surprise. "Don't tell me you have converted him to Christianity."

"No, he doesn't know its meaning. He just thought it was pretty. He said the stones reminded him of my eyes."

Pedro glanced at Isabel's beautiful eyes. "Yes, except yours are an even prettier blue. I'm surprised Diego let you keep it, in view of the fact that he took everything else that was Indian away from you."

"He didn't know it was a gift from Stands Alone, or I'm sure he would have taken it from me. Like you, he assumed it was a gift from my family. He was terribly jealous of Stands Alone."

Pedro smiled sheepishly and admitted, "As a child, I was, too, at first. Then when it became obvious that you two were meant for one another, I got over it and decided to settle for just being your best friend."

"Thank God, Pedro. I need a friend, desperately, not another admirer."

"I am your friend, Isabel," Pedro answered solemnly,

"and Stands Alone's, although I am sure he has forgotten me. I could never understand why he stopped coming to visit Rosario with the others. I missed him terribly."

"So did I, and I, too, thought it peculiar. I asked my father about it once, and he got very agitated. Now, I think it must have had something to do with his and Yellow Sky's agreement." Isabel paused thoughtfully, then said, "I'm worried, Pedro. What if Stands Alone's father and brother think I betrayed him? What if they don't believe my story that Diego deceived me? Or even if they do believe, maybe they will be angry that I didn't try to escape and come to them immediately. Looking back on it, that does seem the wiser thing. Knowing Diego as I did, I was foolish to trust him. My delay in going to them might well cost Stands Alone his life. And if they are angry, will they punish me? And what about you? Oh, Pedro, what have I gotten you into?" Isabel ended on an anguished note.

"Stop torturing yourself!" Pedro answered in an emphatic, but soft voice. "Hindsight is always better than foresight. What is done is done. As for their reaction?" He shrugged his shoulders. "Well, I have always found the Indians fair. Harsh, perhaps, but fair." He paused, then said, "Either way, it's pointless to get yourself upset over what may or may not happen. We can't turn back. We've got to alert them. It's Stands Alone's only chance."

"But I don't have to involve you."

"Don't think you're going to get rid of me," Pedro answered firmly. "I'm as committed to this as you are. I told you. Stands Alone is my friend."

Isabel was touched by Pedro's sincerity. "And a good friend you are. I only hope Stands Alone comes to realize that."

"That would be all the reward I would ask for."

* * *

The next morning, Isabel woke up retching, just as she had been doing for the past two weeks. Pedro rushed to her side to support her head, until the vomiting ceased. "I'm sorry," Isabel muttered, wiping her mouth with the cloth he offered her. "This is so embarrassing. At least yesterday, I managed to get out of camp before it happened. I don't know what's wrong with me. This has been going on for two weeks now. I thought dread over my marriage to Diego was causing it. I guess I still haven't got my nerves under control."

"Two weeks, you say? Do you have any other symptoms?"

"Symptoms?" Isabel asked in alarm. "Do you think I'm ill?"

"No, I suspect you're pregnant. My wife did the same thing the first three months."

"Pregnant?" Isabel blurted in astonishment.

"Yes. I can't believe you didn't realize."

"How would I know? My mother never had any other children, and you know how prudish our people are about sharing information about things like that."

"That's true. Teresa only knew because she had an older sister. But you've lived with the Indians. They're much more open about things like that."

"But I still wasn't around anyone who was pregnant." Then, she remembered something Tekwitchi had told her, that women ceased having their monthly flow when they were pregnant. She hadn't even realized her time had come and gone. She was suddenly filled with happiness; a glow came to her face. "Oh, Pedro, I do hope so. I've been wanting a baby so badly."

Pedro frowned, then said, "That may be so, but the timing couldn't be worse. I think you should reconsider

looking for the Comanches' camp. All that horseback
riding may be bad for you. Let me go on alone."

"Absolutely not!"

"Isabel, you do not want to lose this baby," Pedro
cautioned her firmly.

"I don't want to lose its father, either."

"Are you making a choice?"

Isabel felt torn, then said. "No. I leave it in God's
hands." Seeing the doubt still written all over Pedro's
face, she placed her hand on his and said, "I will be
careful, but I *must* do this."

Pedro saw the fierce determination in Isabel's eyes and
knew he could sooner move a mountain than change
her mind. Grim-lipped, he nodded in acceptance.

"Did you say your wife was expecting?" Isabel asked.

The grim expression on Pedro's face was replaced
with one of pride. "Yes, in four months."

Isabel gazed off thoughtfully, then said, "Wouldn't it
be nice if our children could be playmates and friends
like we were?"

"Nice, yes, but not very likely," Pedro answered sadly.
"Even if Stands Alone is rescued, he will still be considered a criminal by the Spanish government. It would
be very dangerous for him or any in his band to show
their faces at Rosario, now. I'm afraid what you and I
and Stands Alone shared is a thing of the past. Each
day the Comanches and Spanish become more at odds
with one another. Someday it will be all-out war between
the two."

Isabel knew what Pedro said was true. Eventually one
or the other would have to give, and neither had a particularly compromising nature. But Isabel didn't think
that would necessarily eliminate the possibility of their
children being playmates. She had never revealed to
Pedro, or anyone, her deepest fear—that Stands Alone

would never believe she hadn't betrayed him, and would no longer want her. She knew how firmly convinced of her guilt he was. She had seen the hate and the pain in his eyes. Now, if she did have to face a lifetime without him, she would at least have a part of him, his child. And no one, she vowed fervently, no one short of God, Himself, would take that away from her.

For the next several days, Pedro and Isabel wandered around the mountains, looking for the trail that led to the Comanche camp, climbing steadily higher and higher. Even Pedro, with all of his tracking expertise, was at a loss. He could well understand why Diego and his patrols could never find the camp. There was simply nothing to follow.

Pedro's and Isabel's frustration was compounded by the daily violent thunderstorms, for summer had arrived in full force. Not wanting to relinquish even one minute of valuable time, they continued to search in the driving rain, braving the dangerous lightning. Then every evening, they would sit beside their campfire, soaked to the skin, miserable, and discouraged.

Eventually, it was the Comanches who found them. Suddenly, as if they had materialized out of nowhere, they were surrounded by the Indian hunting party, giving both Isabel and Pedro quite a fright. Then recognizing one of the warriors, Isabel quickly related in Comanche that they were lost and had urgent news for Chief Yellow Sky.

"Where is Stands Alone?" the warrior replied. "We have been very concerned for his safety. And why are you not with him?"

"That's what we need to talk to Chief Yellow Sky about."

"Tell me."

"No. If Chief Yellow Sky wishes you to know, he will tell you."

His curiosity left unsatisfied, the warrior looked at Pedro and asked suspiciously, "Who is the man with you?"

Pedro understood just enough Comanche to guess what the question was. "I am an old friend of Stands Alone's," he answered in Spanish.

"I recognize him now," one of the warriors said excitedly. "He is from Rosario!"

A look of fury came over the warriors' faces. "No, he is not an enemy," Isabel quickly assured the hunters. "He is a friend. And we bear most important news. Please, just take us to Chief Yellow Sky. Let him be the judge."

The hunting party complied, but just to play it safe, bound Pedro to his saddle and tied a blindfold around his head. Pedro accepted their treatment calmly, knowing resistance might only increase their suspicion. In what seemed a ridiculously short span of time to Isabel, they crested the mountain pass that overlooked the village, making her realize she and Pedro had been practically right on top of the camp and not seen it, so well was it hidden.

Isabel had been apprehensive all along about how the news of what had happened to Stands Alone would be received. As she rode through camp, that apprehension only grew. She knew she was recognized, but not one person gave a smile or even a nod. They might as well have been stone statues she was passing. And the camp was so quiet you could hear a pin drop. Not even the camp dogs let out a whimper, making the unnatural silence seem all the more ominous. By the time they reined in before Chief Yellow Sky's tepee, Isabel's stomach was tied in knots.

Having been told of their approach, Chief Yellow Sky was waiting for them. Isabel was shocked when she first saw him. He seemed to have aged ten years. "Where is my son?" he demanded of Isabel.

"He is being held by Spanish soldiers."

"Then he is alive?" he asked, the years seemingly being lifted from him.

"The last time I saw him, he was."

Chief Yellow Sky glanced at Pedro, then said, "This is the shepherd's son, is it not? The boy my son used to play with?"

"Yes, this is Pedro, his friend."

"No one from Rosario is our friend," Chief Yellow Sky growled, his eyes glittering with a fury that would have made even the most courageous of his warriors cringe.

"No, you are wrong," Isabel answered bravely. "Pedro knew nothing of the betrayal. My father kept that a secret from the entire village, just as he kept it from me. Only Ramon, Pedro's father knew. The other witness died years ago."

"Then how did you learn the truth? This Ramon is dead. Greyfoot killed him last year."

"He did not die. He was gravely wounded, but he did not die. Our Sure Enough Father must have willed it, so the truth could be known."

Isabel was relieved to see Chief Yellow Sky accepted this reasoning and that she had not put Ramon's life at further risk. "Does Stands Alone's being held have anything to do with what happened last year?" Chief Yellow Sky asked.

"Yes, it does. It has everything to do with it."

Chief Yellow Sky glanced around at the others, who

were curiously listening in. "Come into the tepee," he told Isabel brusquely, then motioned to Pedro and commanded the hunters, "Him, too, after you have untied him and removed his blindfold."

"When Isabel entered the tepee, she saw Greyfoot sitting on a pallet at the back of the tepee, a stony expression on his face. Then she saw Beaver Woman, Corn Woman, and Tekwitchi sitting to the side, the two younger women staring straight ahead. But Beaver Woman couldn't conceal her apprehension, and Isabel's heart went out to the woman. Despite Comanche protocol, she said to her mother-in-law, "He is alive."

There was no thank you, but Isabel saw the fleeting look of relief in the woman's dark eyes. Then Chief Yellow Sky brushed past her, saying gruffly, "Sit!

Isabel sank to her knees and sat back on her heels. Chief Yellow Sky sat on his pallet, then motioned for Pedro to sit also. A long moment passed before the chief said to Isabel, "I would ask you to smoke the pipe if you were a man, to know you tell the truth."

"And if I were a man, I would smoke it," Isabel replied.

Yes, she was brave and bold, Chief Yellow Sky thought with secret admiration. Now, if only she is truthful. "Tell us what happened."

Isabel related the entire story, from the moment of Stands Alone's capture to the moment she realized Diego had deceived her. To her credit, she didn't try to make herself look any better than she was, even openly admitting that Stands Alone thought she had betrayed him, and why she had lied to her husband in Taos—something she knew both Yellow Sky and Greyfoot thought disgraceful—and that she had been foolish to believe Diego. To the Comanches' credit, they didn't interrupt. She finished with, "I thought if I could get to you, you could rescue him, and Pedro would not let me travel alone."

Greyfoot slammed to his feet and said angrily, "I do not believe her! How do we know she did not betray him? How do we know she is not setting a trap for us?"

"I did not betray him!" Isabel responded fervently. "I love him!"

"You did not love him when you first came here," Chief Yellow Sky pointed out.

"No, you are wrong. I loved him, but I hid it from him and everyone. I even tried to hide it from myself. I thought to love him would be to betray my father, but I've always loved Stands Alone. Now more than ever." Isabel paused. Greyfoot's and Chief Yellow Sky's dark eyes bore into her, angry and accusing. "Please, you must believe me," she implored. "Stands Alone's life depends upon it!"

"She speaks the truth."

The soft, calmly spoken words took everyone by surprise. All eyes flew to Beaver Woman, who had said the words. Then, choosing to overlook his wife's shocking breach of conduct, Chief Yellow Sky asked, "And how do you know this?"

"Because she speaks from the heart."

Beaver Woman had told Yellow Sky who her guardian spirit was, just as he had revealed his to her years ago. He knew she had deer power, and could see into people's hearts, as well as aid them in matters of the heart. The girl spoke the truth! He turned to Greyfoot and said, "I assume you wish to lead the rescue party."

Greyfoot glanced from his father to Beaver Woman and back again, his look incredulous. "You both believe her?"

"Yes, we do, and you must trust our wisdom. Do you wish to lead the rescue party? As you know, I injured my back last week. I fear I would slow the party down. When I have recovered in a few days, I will take another party and seek vengeance on this Diego. You need not watch your back. The Spaniard will no longer be a threat to anyone, I promise you."

"Yes, I wish to lead the rescue party," Greyfoot answered fervently. "I am his brother! It is only fitting."

"I will leave the preparations up to you, but you must move quickly," Yellow Sky responded. "We have already lost much precious time."

"We will leave as soon as I have picked my men and we have gathered our horses and supplies," Greyfoot responded.

As Greyfoot started for the door, Isabel jumped to her feet and called out, "Wait!" She turned to Chief Yellow Sky and said, "I wish to go along."

"That's impossible!" Greyfoot blurted.

Isabel whirled around to face him. "No, it is not! I know *Nema* women sometimes go on war parties. Stands Alone told me so."

"Strong women! Warrior women!" Greyfoot responded.

"I cannot use a bow, but I can shoot a musket, and I can ride as well as any of you. You have seen me race. I will not slow you down."

"I do not think you realize what this trip will entail, Isabel," Yellow Sky interjected. "It will be grueling, even for the toughest warriors. They will be traveling almost day and night, through some of the most hostile country on this earth. Rugged mountains, searing deserts, almost impenetrable brush. And it will be dangerous. They're going into Apache territory, where they will be heavily outnumbered. Each warrior is prepared to die, by his own hand, if necessary. Capture is unthinkable. The Apaches have the most unimaginable, heinous torture methods. They are masters at it. You will be killed by one of our men, if you cannot perform the act yourself."

A shudder ran through Isabel. Then she replied, "I understand. I still want to go."

"Then you will have to ask Greyfoot's permission. As leader, he is in complete charge."

Isabel turned back to Greyfoot, her eyes imploring.

"No!" Greyfoot told her firmly.

"Isabel, I don't think—" Pedro began.

"No!" Isabel interrupted him in mid-sentence. "You keep out of this!"

Isabel faced Greyfoot squarely. "I know we have not been on the best of terms. Since I could not hate Stands Alone, I took my hatred out on you and Yellow Sky. I was wrong, but please don't hold it against me. This isn't just a silly whim. I must go. I must be a part of his rescue. It may be the only way I can redeem myself in his eyes. Telling him of my innocence may not be enough. I might have to prove how much I love him, and what better way than to risk my life to save his? You're doing it. Why can't I?"

Isabel knew Greyfoot's resistance was wavering when he glanced at Yellow Sky. She pushed her advantage, saying, "I promise I will not slow you down. Nor will I expect any special consideration. If I prove a burden to you in any way, you can leave me behind, just as you do the old people who cannot keep up and endanger the group."

While Greyfoot still hesitated in his decision, Pedro said, "I would like to go, also. If Isabel has to be left behind, I could take her to safety."

"No!"

"Don't decide too hastily," Pedro cautioned Greyfoot. "I could be a valuable asset to you. I could go ahead into Spanish villages and make inquiries. They will tell me things they would never tell you. Nor might they divulge those things to Isabel. They would wonder why she is traveling alone."

"You would go ahead and set up a trap, you mean!" Greyfoot answered angrily. "You are the enemy!"

Pedro came to his feet and faced the furious warrior. "I am not the enemy," he answered calmly. "I am Stands Alone's friend. I, too, wish to have a part in his rescue. But you must look into my heart and decide if you trust me."

Pedro met Greyfoot's piercing gaze levelly. The warrior remembered Stands Alone's telling him about his Spanish friend. He had said Pedro was unlike the others, that he respected the Indian way, that he had a kindred spirit. It was too short a time for Greyfoot to judge for himself. He decided he would have to trust Stands Alone's judgment. "You may come," he answered somewhat reluctantly.

"And me?" Isabel asked anxiously.

Greyfoot looked at Yellow Sky, seeking his counsel.

"She is strong," the older man replied with solemn dignity, as if he were a judge handing down a decision. "She has proven that by how well she has adjusted to our difficult way of life. She is brave, or else she would not have come back to face our fury." He glanced at Beaver Woman. "She is pure in heart. I am convinced she truly loves my son. She is a fighter." His serious demeanor cracked, and he grinned. "Does she not win every contest she enters? What more could you ask of a warrior woman? Let her go."

Greyfoot turned to Isabel and nodded his head curtly.

"Thank you," Isabel said fervently, then turned to Yellow Sky and repeated the words.

Greyfoot said to Pedro, "Come with me. You can pick a string of riding horses for yourself from my herd. Each man will take three. Isabel has her own string to pick from." Then he turned to Beaver Woman and said, "Help Isabel prepare supplies for herself and this man." Then Greyfoot turned to his father and said, "I would like your assistance in picking my men."

Chief Yellow Sky was proud of his son. As capable as he was, he was deferring to his elders, a commendable *Nema* trait. He nodded gravely and followed the two younger men from the tent.

As soon as the men disappeared, Corn Woman and Tekwitchi became suddenly animated, jumping to their feet, rushing to Isabel, and hugging her so tightly she feared for her ribs, telling her over and over how worried they had been and how much they had missed her. Finally Beaver Woman interrupted the joyous reunion, saying quietly, "I, too, would like to welcome Isabel."

Isabel turned to Beaver Woman and said, "But first, let me thank you for helping me. I don't think I would have ever convinced Greyfoot and Yellow Sky on my own."

"I only told them what I saw in your heart."

Isabel looked at the woman she had thought so severe, the woman she had resented so highly, and realized there was a genuine warmth beneath her reserved exterior, and untold wisdom, for hadn't she counseled Isabel from the very beginning to accept her lot? Isabel hadn't realized she had done that and, in accepting, had found happiness with what she had. Of all the lessons Beaver Woman had taught her, that was the most valuable. "Still, I would like to thank you, for that and everything." She paused just a moment, then added meaningfully, "mother."

Isabel's calling her *"pia"* brought tears to Beaver Woman's eyes. Perhaps she was so touched because she had had to work so hard to get the respected title from

Isabel, or perhaps it was that Isabel was so much like the daughter she had lost, spirited and full of life. Either way, Beaver Woman was unable to retain her usual composure. She did something her two daughters-in-law had never dreamed they would see her do. She took Isabel into her arms and hugged her tightly.

Twenty-seven

As soon as Beaver Woman had regained her composure and set Isabel back from her, and Corn Woman and Tekwitchi had recovered from their astonishment, Corn Woman said to Isabel, "I wish Tekwitchi and I could stay longer to visit a little before you leave again, but we have to go and prepare for Greyfoot's departure." She shot her younger sister a pointed look, then said, "But before we go, I'm sure Tekwitchi wishes to tell you her exciting news."

Isabel turned to Tekwitchi and asked, "What news?"

Tekwitchi beamed with happiness. "I am with child," she told Isabel proudly.

"Oh, Tekwitchi, I'm so happy for you!" Isabel cried out, then embraced the Indian girl.

When Isabel stepped back, Tekwitchi said, "As soon as I stopped worrying about it, it happened. Isn't that strange?"

Could just nervousness keep it from happening, Isabel wondered, then asked, "What about Elk Woman? Are you going to keep her?"

"Of course we are going to keep her!" Corn Woman answered fervently before Tekwitchi could even respond. "We love her. She is our daughter. We would never dream of giving her back."

"No, Elk Woman is very much a member of our family," Beaver Woman said, entering the conversation. "That was the first thing both Yellow Sky and Greyfoot said when they learned of the pregnancy. Elk Woman would not go back."

"I'm glad," Isabel answered. "I've grown attached to her myself."

"We must go, now," Corn woman announced, gently nudging her younger sister towards the door. "We will see you before you leave."

But the chubby younger woman resisted and said to Isabel, "Do you think you should go with the rescue party? I think you are brave, and feel very honored that Yellow Sky called you a warrior woman, but it could be very dangerous. I would not like to lose you again."

Isabel was touched. "Thank you for your concern, but you heard what I said. I must go. But I will be very careful, I promise you."

"And you will be in very capable hands," Corn Woman added, her faith in Greyfoot's ability unshakable.

"Yes, I will," Isabel agreed. "After Stands Alone, there is no other man I would rather trust my life to."

It was the first time Isabel had shown Greyfoot any respect, and both of his wives thought it long overdue, although they had kept their silence because of their friendship with Isabel. It had been hard on them, being torn between two people they loved. Hearing Isabel praise Greyfoot and knowing she was sincere, they both beamed with pride. Then, perfectly attuned to one another after so many years of living and working together and feeling there was nothing else to say, they turned and left the tepee.

After they had gone, Beaver Woman said to Isabel, "There is something I wish to ask you before we begin our preparations. You said you had bought a fertility potion from a healer in Taos. Did you use it?"

Isabel flushed. "I wasn't doubting Stands Alone's fertility. I was doubting mine."

"I understood that. But did you use it?"

"No. Stands Alone was captured, and I was going to have to marry Diego. I certainly didn't want his child."

"Good. Those potions can be dangerous, particularly if you're already pregnant."

Isabel had not planned on telling anyone of her pregnancy, for fear they would object to her taking the arduous and dangerous trip. That's why she had warned Pedro away when he had started to object. Stunned by Beaver Woman's words, she asked, "How did you know I'm pregnant?"

"I saw it in your heart. This child was conceived in love, and is very much wanted."

"Are you going to tell Greyfoot? I'm sure he won't allow me to go if he knows."

"No, I'm sure he wouldn't. Nor would Yellow Sky, if he knew. But I do not intend to reveal it to anyone. I know how important this is to you. That, too, I saw in your heart."

"Then you must know how terrified I am that Stands Alone will not believe me and will no longer want me."

"Yes, I saw your fear. But I think you will be successful in your quest. I have used my powers for too long to find a wife worthy of my son's love. Now that he has found her, I will do everything in my power to see he does not lose her."

Isabel knew Beaver Woman had given her the ultimate compliment. "Thank you," she answered, fresh tears brimming in her eyes.

Seeing them and fearing she might break down emotionally once again, Beaver Woman turned away, saying brusquely, "Now we will start collecting your provisions."

They filled two small sacks with jerky and dried fruits. Then Beaver Woman gave Isabel a smaller sack filled with the usual medicinal herbs in case she needed them. As she handed the sack to her, Isabel asked, "Do you know of anything that will help with the nausea in the morning?"

"Is it bad?"

"It's terrible. I wake up every morning vomiting."

"Good."

"Good?" Isabel gasped in disbelief.

"Yes. The baby has a firm hold in the womb, or at least, that is my opinion. With my daughter and Stands Alone, I had terrible morning sickness, but with the others, almost none. I eventually lost those."

"How many were there?"

"Three."

"I'm sorry," Isabel muttered, for lack of a better response.

Beaver Woman nodded her head solemnly, then said, "I will not give you away to the others, but I feel I must warn you. You might be jeopardizing this baby's life with this trip."

"Pedro has already pointed that out to me, but I still must do this. I'll be as careful as I can."

"He knows then?"

"Yes, he saw me vomiting. I didn't even know that was a symptom."

"Will he tell the others?"

"No, I don't think so. He had his opportunity, but I warned him off. When he said he could take me to safety if Greyfoot had to leave me behind, I think that's what he was thinking of, that I might develop problems along those lines."

"You said you did not know vomiting was a symptom of pregnancy. Do you know the symptoms of threatened miscarriage?"

"No."

"If you have any spotting of blood or cramping in your lower abdomen, you must stop riding and rest for several days. I have known women who did this and kept the child."

Isabel didn't know what she would do if that happened. She could only pray it wouldn't. She nodded her head, not so much in assent, as understanding.

"If you are considering going on despite this, do not forget what women's blood does to the warrior's medicine. That in itself could doom the rescue attempt to failure."

Isabel hadn't even considered that, and still wasn't convinced there was any truth to it. "I won't do anything to jeopardize the raid. I promise."

Beaver Woman was much too astute not to realize Isabel had given her an ambiguous answer, but she accepted her promise. "You said you can shoot a musket?"

"Yes, I learned as a child. Everyone in Rosario had to, even though there weren't that many around. I haven't shot one in years, but there was a time when I was fairly good at it."

"You will take Stands Alone's musket and his lead and powder. I will collect them from your tepee while you are selecting your horses. That way we will save time. You don't want the war party waiting for you."

Indeed not, Isabel thought. Greyfoot might change his mind.

"Is there anything else you need from your tepee?" Beaver Woman asked.

"No, I already have my clothes and the blanket I brought with me from Rosario, but I do have need of an Indian saddle. Diego took mine from me and the merchant at Taos sold it."

"You can borrow mine. It's lying outside beside the tepee. Anything else you need?"

"No."

"Then I will meet you back here shortly."

Ten minutes later, Isabel was back with the two horses she had chosen for alternate mounts. She stripped the hated sidesaddle from Golden Heart's back and placed the Indian saddle on it, then tied her spare horses' lead reins to the saddle. After loading the sack of food and the sack of medicinal herbs, she mounted and waited.

Pedro and Greyfoot rode up, followed by their string of horses. When they came to a stop beside her, Isabel leaned across and handed Pedro his sack of food. As she did, he asked in a low voice, "Are you sure you know what you're doing?"

"I'm sure," she answered in a determined voice.

Corn Woman and Tekwitchi walked up, both carrying babies strapped to their backs. Corn Woman handed Greyfoot his provisions and solemnly bid him farewell. Tekwitchi stepped forward and gave her farewell. Isabel was astonished at the total lack of emotion on the women's faces. Their husband was going on a dangerous mission, could possibly never return. Surely they must be frightened. But to look at them, you would never know it. They were the very picture of Comanche stoicism.

Beaver Woman shouldered her way through the crowd of well-wishers that had circled the group. She walked up to Isabel and handed her Stands Alone's musket, powder horn, and pouch of lead balls. Then, to Isabel's surprise, Yellow Sky emerged from the tepee, carrying a war shield. "I didn't think he was going," Isabel remarked to Beaver Woman.

"He isn't," Beaver Woman answered. "That is Stands Alone's shield. We have decided that you should carry it. Wives may do this, you know. Carry their husbands' shields. Perhaps some of his power will be transferred to you."

Isabel sincerely doubted that the shield held any of Stands Alone's power, if Beaver Woman was referring to his medicine. There was nothing from an elk on it. Rather, the buffalo hide oval was surrounded with horses' tails, symbolizing its bearer's superb horsemanship.

As Yellow Sky lifted the war shield, Isabel thought he was handing it to her and asked in dismay, "How am I supposed to carry the musket and that heavy thing?"

Yellow Sky chuckled and answered, "You will not carry it. I will tie it to your horse's side. Even the warriors do not bear it until the moment of battle arrives."

After Yellow Sky had tied the shield to Isabel's saddle, he stepped away to confer with Greyfoot, who leaned down from his saddle to better hear. Beaver Woman took advantage of their preoccupation, handing Isabel a small sack and saying in a low, confidential tone of voice, "This is an herb that will help with your nausea. Just suck on one of the dried leaves when you feel the need. Do not worry about taking too much. It is harmless." She glanced around to make sure no one else might be watching, then handed Isabel a small amulet, saying, "Wear this next to your heart and keep it out of sight of the others, or they might badger me to make them one. Some women with my powers sell amulets to help with matters of the heart, but I think that a misuse of our power. I only use them in very special cases."

"Thank you," Isabel answered, surreptitiously slipping the amulet around her neck, then dropping it beneath her dress.

When Beaver Woman stepped back from Isabel, Tekwitchi and Corn Woman stepped forward. "Goodbye, Isabel," Corn Woman said solemnly. "Be careful," Tekwitchi added anxiously.

Isabel smiled reassuringly and answered, "I will, and by the way, thank you for taking such good care of my horses while I was away."

"You are welcome, and don't worry about them while you are gone this time. We will care for them," Corn Woman answered.

"And when we gather roots and fruits, we get extra for you," Tekwitchi informed her.

They were true sisters, Isabel thought, taking over her present chores and tending her future needs.

"We go now," Greyfoot announced.

With grave dignity, Greyfoot moved his mount away, and Pedro and Isabel fell in behind him. As they rode through camp, the other warriors joined them, leading their string of horses behind them, until Isabel counted fifteen in all, fifteen of what she knew had to be the bravest, fiercest fighters of the band, all whipcord lean and sober-faced, armed with bows and arrows, lances, war clubs, and only an occasional French musket.

The band came out to wish the party well, but there was no shouting, no singing, no drums and rattles, no rousing stories of previous coups to stir the warriors to gain new war honors. Had there been time, that would have been done at the war dance the night before. Now the crowd lent its support by sharing the same somber tone of the raid itself. This was serious business.

As they turned to ascend the trail that led up the mountainside, Isabel realized fully the enormity of what she was doing and felt a moment of doubt. She looked back. Her eyes fell on Beaver Woman, standing beside Yellow Sky. The older woman's steadfast gaze seemed to close the distance between them, infusing Isabel with her calmness, her stamina, her utter belief in Isabel's purpose. Feeling reassured, Isabel glanced at Yellow Sky. What she saw in his eyes was an immense pride. Surely, that look was for Greyfoot, she thought, glancing at the party leader. But to her surprise, she realized Yellow Sky's eyes were resting squarely on her, not his son. And then she realized why he was looking at her that way. She was finally fulfilling his expectations of her, and deep down Isabel was glad she was meeting his measure of worth.

Then Isabel looked at Tekwitchi and Corn Woman, standing a few feet away from their in-laws, with Red Feather at their side. Knowing them so well, Isabel saw what she hadn't seen before, what the two women had bravely hid from their husband. Their fear.

Isabel turned her head and rode up the narrow path, a heavy feeling pressing down on her. She prayed to her God, to Stands Alone's God, to their mutual God, that this mission would be successful. The future happiness of so many depended on it.

Twenty-eight

The Comanche rescue party moved swiftly and surely over the next few days, riding straight down the Sangre de Cristo mountain range and giving Santa Fe a wide berth. They moved rapidly because Greyfoot didn't waste time trying to find the prison train's trail outside the capital. He knew the Spanish had only one way out of New Mexico, *El Camino Real*, which followed the west bank of the Rio Grande until the desert, so he followed an old Apache trail that ran parallel to the rutted road on the east side of the mighty river, far enough removed from the "royal highway" not to be discovered by any Spanish patrols.

Scouts were put out a half-day ahead to watch for possible Indian parties, a necessity since most of the tribes in that region were the Comanches' enemies. Switching off horses at regular intervals assured the group of fresh mounts, so despite the rugged terrain, they covered almost fifty miles a day, something that would have been unheard of for the Spanish cavalry, which would never realize the wisdom of bringing a remuda of fresh horses with them on patrol. The Comanches traveled twenty hours a day, through the summer heat and through violent thunderstorms, taking a brief break at night for some much needed sleep, but not until after the warriors had smoked the ceremonial pipe Greyfoot brought along with him and sang several sacred songs. Needless to say, conversation was at a minimum. No one was foolish enough to exert energy on something so unnecessary.

Isabel found the pace grueling. Compared to it, the search for buffalo the year before had been a picnic. She was exhausted after two days, barely able to keep her eyes open long enough that second night to ask Greyfoot a question that had been puzzling her. "Why wasn't Ramon scalped?" she asked in Spanish, when she and Pedro were alone with the leader.

Greyfoot was taken aback by the direct, unexpected question. Then recovering, he gave Pedro a sharp glance and answered in like tongue, "I saw no need to. Only one scalp is required for a vengeance raid to be successful. We had that."

"The Pueblos I know say it counts highly to scalp any living man," Pedro commented.

"Yes," Greyfoot answered, "but I did not think it would be a particularly honorable thing. He was an old man, and dying, or so I thought. Somehow he did not seem so much the enemy."

"Ramon is my father," Pedro said.

"I know," Greyfoot answered warily, half-expecting an attack of some kind.

"I thank you for being an honorable man," Pedro returned softly.

After he recovered from his surprise, Greyfoot looked embarrassed and averted his eyes, and Isabel gained an insight into the man that she had never suspected. He had been a reluctant executioner, performing something that was necessary, but distasteful, grimly following the dictates of his people's rigid code of justice. She had told Tekwitchi and Corn Woman there was no man she would rather trust her life to, other than Stands Alone, and had been sincere. Greyfoot was a capable man who took his responsibilities very seriously. But while she respected his strengths, it had not meant she liked him. Now, knowing how he had felt about the attack, she found him much more appealing as a relative. But she could still never accept him as a husband, no matter how practical it might be. That position belonged exclusively to Stands Alone, even after death.

On the fourth day of their travel, Isabel saw the desert ahead of her and was filled with dread. Called *Jornada del Muerto,* the Day's Journey of the Dead Man, the desert had been named by some beleaguered Spanish colonist following the first governor of New Mexico through the Apache-infested territory. It was ninety miles of the most arid, desolate, unrelenting land in the entire world, a wilderness of erosion, lifeless canyons and arroyos, and waterless gullies where only scrubby mesquite, creosote, yuccas, and cactus grew, the hills short, steep, barren, the cracked ground burnt orange, yellow, and black with lava. Isabel had been through the waterless desert twice already and knew what rigors were ahead of her. The *Jornada* was the only place the *El Camino Real* left the Rio Grande, and only because the Fray Cristobal Mountains pushed the river into a broad sweep to the west and the mountains came right up to the water's edge in steep, unpassable cliffs. But her earlier trips had been in the winter and in the spring, and this was summer. She knew she would be riding into an inferno and was filled with dread. The color drained from her face.

Seeing her expression and her pale face, Pedro said softly, "You don't have to do this, Isabel. No one will think any the less of you if you bow out now."

Isabel was tempted, particularly in view of her condition. Her stomach stayed uneasy, despite her sucking the dried leaves Beaver Woman had given her almost continuously, the queasiness intensified by the rocking movement of riding. And she felt so unbelievably tired. Several times she had fallen asleep on her horse, and would have tumbled from the saddle, had Pedro not caught her. But Isabel couldn't back out. "No, I've got to go on," she answered with grim determination.

Pedro could only shake his head, a part of him thinking her a fool, while yet another part of him paid tribute to her grit and bravery.

Instead of going to Fray Cristobal, where the Spanish trains stocked up on water before making the long trek across the desert, the Comanches went to *Ojo del Muerto,* Dead Man's Springs, six miles to the west. A watering hole favored by the Apaches, the Spanish trains did not venture there. Thankfully, none of their enemies were present, and the group filled their water bags almost to the bursting point. Then grim-lipped, they headed south into the *Jornada.*

It was even more horrible than Isabel had imagined, for the Spanish trains had always traveled at night. The afternoon temperature hovered near 130 degrees, so hot her perspiration evaporated as soon as it cleared her pores, totally defeating its cooling purpose. The choking dust was so thick she could hardly breathe, the air so hot, her lips were cracked and bleeding within hours. The glaring light of the sun made her eyeballs hurt, and her thirst was unbearable, despite the stone Greyfoot had given her to suck on. Heat waves shimmered off the baked ground, creating mirages of cool pools of water, a cruel trick of nature that only added to her misery.

The sun went down in a blazing ball of fire, followed by a lingering dusk where the heat from the ground still surrounded them as if they were loaves of bread baking in an oven. As night progressed and they traveled under a sky that was velvety black and filled with millions of glittering stars, the temperature dropped drastically, making Isabel shiver with cold. When the usual time for their stopping came and went and the Comanches kept going, Isabel said to Pedro, "Surely we're not going through this desert non-stop. I know we're in a hurry, but it will serve no purpose to kill ourselves."

"I was beginning to get concerned about that myself," Pedro answered, "and asked. Greyfoot said we will travel until mid-morning, then rest until darkness and travel the rest of the desert at night. By doing this, we'll be picking up one day."

It seemed an eternity until mid-morning to Isabel. Then to her dismay, she discovered she couldn't sleep when they did stop. Despite the blanket that Pedro had strung over her to shade her from the blistering sun, it was too hot. She felt as if she were being roasted alive. She sat up and glanced at the warriors lying all around her, impervious to the unmerciful sun beating down on them. They, at least, were not encumbered with clothing as she was, she thought, longing to strip the oppressive buckskin dress from her. Even Pedro had slipped off his shirt in deference to the heat. For a moment, she listlessly watched a blister bug crawling up the stem on a nearby creosote bush. "This has got to be the hottest, driest, most miserable place on earth," she muttered, thinking out loud.

"Believe it or not, it isn't."

Isabel jumped, then turned to see Greyfoot standing a few feet away. "Is it too hot for you to sleep, too?" she asked.

"No, I am standing guard. I have been up on that

boulder," he explained, motioning to the big rock. "I
only came down for a drink of water. It is hot up there."

"It's hot everywhere out here, surely too hot for anyone to attack us."

"Not the Apaches. The heat does not seem to bother
them."

It hadn't seemed to bother the Comanches, either,
Isabel thought, then asked, "Is there really a place that's
worse than this?"

"Yes, to the east of here, a desert covered entirely
with white sand as fine as dust, where nothing grows.
Only insects and reptiles live there, as pale as the sand
itself. It is so barren, so lifeless, the *Nema* have let the
Apaches keep it."

Isabel didn't think Greyfoot's claim arrogant. She
knew if the Comanches had wanted that desert, they
would have taken it, just as they had taken so much of
the other Apache territory. "Well, this place isn't much
better. That bug over there is the only living thing I've
seen."

"Then you must have been sleeping in your saddle
last night. There was life all around us. Tonight, when
you are not so weary, watch."

That night, Isabel did watch. She saw things she had
never even noticed on her other trips across the *Jornada*.
The desert was teeming with life. Coyotes crept through
the creosote, stalking their quarry. Grey foxes pursued
tiny desert deer through scrubby mesquite thickets.
Birds flitted from bush to bush, feeding on the insects
there, prey themselves of owls and nighthawks that
swooped down out of nowhere. Roadrunners chased
swift little lizards in hopes of a tasty meal, while jack
rabbits bounded through beds of prickly pear cactus.
Everything came out to hunt, or be hunted, even the
sluggish beaded gila monsters. When morning came,

they all disappeared, the only signs of the night activity, a bone picked clean, a feather, a tuft of fur.

The next morning, they left the *Jornada* behind, as well as the splintered peaks of the San Cristobal Mountains. Here, the Rio Grande still flowed through desert, looking like a slithering, copper-colored snake, but there were water holes and the going was much easier. Then, past San Miguel, before the mighty river made its eastward turn towards the Gulf of Mexico, Greyfoot started looking for the trail of the prison train. All of northern Mexico stretched out before them, a vast sparsely populated land dominated by huge unfenced haciendas on the central plateau, while the mountain ranges on both sides were pitted with silver mines, any one of which Stands Alone could have been sent to. Suddenly, Isabel came face-to-face with the enormity of their quest.

But Greyfoot was undaunted. He sent Pedro to inquire at a small Spanish village on the main Chihuahua trail while the others waited in camp. Isabel was picking the small purplish fruits on a prickly pear cactus when she saw the Spaniard returning. She dropped what she was doing and hurried back, but knew even before Pedro dismounted the news must be good. A wide grin was spread across his face.

"The prison train passed through ten days ago," Pedro told Greyfoot, without even bothering with greetings. "There were about twenty prisoners, mostly Apaches, shackled together, and eight mounted guards."

Greyfoot nodded, then asked, "Did they have guns?"

"Yes. They also had a train of four mules to carry their supplies, which I assume include some powder and shot."

"Did the villagers know where the train was going?"

"No. The man I talked to said it could be anywhere. South of here, a dozen or more trails leave the main road."

Seeing Greyfoot scowl, Isabel asked anxiously, "Do you think you can find the trail they took?"

"Yes, by the marks the chains leave," Greyfoot answered. "But if they are traveling to a mine nearby, we might be too late. That was ten days ago. Once they have the prisoners down in those mines, a rescue would be impossible. They are too well guarded."

"Then we have to find that train before it reaches its destination?" Isabel asked.

"Exactly. From now on, we will move as fast as our scouts can take us."

The scouting party did not have to search long to find the trail. They found the chain marks on the main Chihuahua road. Over the next two days, other trails veered off, but not the one they were following, leading them to assume Stands Alone was being taken to a mine in the interior of the country.

Isabel knew the further they were taking Stands Alone, the better their chances of rescuing him, but the ride was almost as arduous as the trek across the *Jornada*. It was a land of vast grasslands dotted with cactus, mesquite, and scrub oak thickets surrounded by deserts with dry, cracked lake beds. During the day, it was blistering hot; at night, freezing cold.

One day, Isabel thought the heat particularly bad. A dozen dust devils danced around them. Then on the broad plain before them, coming through the shimmering heat waves, she thought she saw an army, silks and velvets fluttering in the air, metal helmets and armor glittering in the sunlight, long lances flashing. She could have sworn she heard the jingle of silver bridle ornaments, the squeak of leather, the soft snorting of horses. She squinted her eyes to see better. Beside the armored horsemen, walked the footmen, carrying crossbows and harquebusses, swords and shields, and behind the fighting men, thousands of servants leading spare horses and pack mules and driving cattle and sheep. Then her eyes zeroed in on the man at the head of the column. With the blazing sun on his gold-plated armor and his blond hair gleaming, he looked as if he had been gilded and rode a stallion of pure Arabian stock. A shout seemed to come from a far distance, "Glory, God, and Gold!" Then everything was gone, the sights and the sounds, leaving Isabel feeling stunned.

Isabel knew it had to have been a mirage, but it had seemed so very real. She questioned everyone around her, but no one else had seen anything, much less heard. But still the feeling that it had been more than just her eyes and imagination playing tricks on her persisted. She knew Coronado had come this way on his search for the Seven Cities of Cibola and had read that he was blond and blue-eyed. Had it been a mirage, or the ghosts of that army of conquest, still searching in vain for the riches that didn't exist?

About fifty miles outside the city of Chihuahua, the trail they were following left the main road. Then that night, a violent thunderstorm swept through the area, obliterating the chain marks they had been following. Any hopes that the road might continue straight and singular until they could catch up with the prison train were lost that afternoon, when the road forked into three smaller trails. Greyfoot sent his scouts up ahead on all three trails, but they returned, reporting they had found nothing, not even hoof marks.

Hearing the bad news, Isabel sank to her lowest point of despair. It seemed a cruel twist of fate to lose the trail when they were so close. Tears welled in her eyes as she stared glumly at the fork. Then, on the twisted trail to the right, she saw an elk. He stood perfectly still, looking directly at her as if to gain her attention. Thinking it was yet another mirage that had been plaguing her, Isabel blinked her eyes. But the elk was still there. Then he turned and ran down the trail, surprisingly fleet and graceful for what she had always considered a big, cumbersome animal.

"Did you see that?" Isabel asked Pedro.

"What?"

"That elk over there."

"There are no elk down here," Pedro answered, wondering if she was becoming ill with all the strange things she was seeing.

Frustrated, Isabel glanced around, then saw Greyfoot standing as still as stone and staring at her intently. She remembered Tekwitchi's telling her that brothers told one another everything, even revealing their guardian spirits. Suddenly, she realized the significance of her vision. She jumped to her feet, ran to Greyfoot, and said urgently, "The elk was there, in that fork of the road. Then it turned and ran down it. It was a sign. I know it was a sign. That's the direction they went!"

Greyfoot quickly ordered the group to mount, and if anyone thought it strange that they were acting on a vision the woman had seen, they did not comment. Even Pedro held his tongue. An advance scout was sent out. He didn't return until the next morning, but everyone knew he bore good news. He was shouting, "We've found them! We've found them!" as he came tearing over the hill they had camped beneath.

It was the only time Isabel saw the war party lose their usual solemn demeanor. The warriors began yelling and dancing about. As soon as the scout came to a skidding halt and jumped to the ground, Greyfoot asked, "Did you see Stands Alone?"

"Yes. He didn't appear to be as weak as the others, or as thin. Some of the prisoners are down to skin and bone. The soldiers looked weary also. Nor were they alert. I was close enough to one to almost touch him, yet he did not see me."

"Did you scout ahead for a likely spot to attack?"

"Yes. The road winds around a hill rather sharply. If we were waiting there. . . ."

As the scout's voice trailed off, Greyfoot turned and said to the party, "As soon as we have made our preparations, we go."

The preparations consisted of applying their war paint. Then the Comanches flew into the saddle, holding lances or bows in one hand, war shields in the other. Almost to the man, they scorned their muskets, leaving them tied to the side of their mounts.

As Greyfoot mounted, Isabel did also. Seeing her, he said sternly, "You cannot go with us."

"You can't deny me this, not after what I've gone through. I've earned the right to be there," Isabel answered fiercely.

"It is too dangerous. I will not gain Stands Alone's life, to lose yours."

"Then let her at least watch," Pedro interjected, having painted his face, also. "Didn't the scout say there was a hill? She should be safe at the top."

Because Greyfoot knew Isabel had earned the right, he relented. She rode with the group as they made a wide circle around the road the prison train was traveling on. Then while Greyfoot was positioning his warriors for the attack, Pedro took Isabel behind the hill and helped her up the steep incline, leaving her behind a large boulder on the top, where she could see below, but not be seen.

When the attack came, there was no contest, it was so sudden and swift and well-executed. The Comanches swept down on the train from every direction, yelling blood-curdling war cries. Only two soldiers managed even to fire their muskets, before the entire guard was riddled with arrows and lances. Isabel's eyes were on Stands Alone at the moment of attack. Seeing his brother and friends rushing in, he whipped his arms over the head of the guard standing with his back to him, and caught the poor man's neck with his wrist chains, choking him to death before he could even raise his musket. A split second later, a half-dozen arrows pierced the soldier's body. Then Greyfoot was there, jumping from his horse and embracing his brother, while the others let out a victorious cry that seemed to shake the hills.

Isabel ignored the gory business of the Comanches' scalping their victims, her full attention on Stands Alone and Greyfoot. She saw Greyfoot pointing at the hill she was on and knew he was telling Stands Alone she had come with the war party, but she was much too far away to see the reaction on Stands Alone's face. Then Pedro, who had been rifling the guards' pockets for the key to the manacles, stepped up and began unlocking Stands Alone's.

Once Stands Alone had been freed from his hand and feet irons, Pedro offered the key to Greyfoot, knowing it was his right to decide the fate of the other prisoners. They were, after all, Apaches and enemies. Greyfoot declined and motioned to Stands Alone, who took the key and unlocked every manacle. The released Apaches huddled together and waited, not knowing what terrible fate the Comanche might have in mind for them. Then Stands Alone pointed to the hills and said, "Go! You are free."

After they recovered from their surprise, the Apaches scattered and ran, a few limping badly. Within minutes, they had disappeared among the hills, already beginning their long trek home.

Isabel made her way down the hill. As she walked up to Stands Alone, she was filled with trepidation, not knowing how she would be greeted. As he had done so often in the past when they were around others, he ignored her, seeming to look right through her. Isabel was besieged with a mixture of emotions. She wanted to scream at him, she wanted to shake him, she wanted to hug him, she wanted to cry with relief. She did none, but simply stood and drank in the sight of him.

Stands Alone had dropped a good twenty pounds; his hair was matted; his wrists and ankles were rubbed raw and oozing blood; his back was crisscrossed with angry welts where he had been beaten; he smelled to high heaven, but he stood proud and erect. Isabel thought he was the most magnificent creature she had ever seen, and her heart almost burst with love. Then Greyfoot was urging her to mount, saying they must leave, in case someone heard the musket shots and came to investigate.

When they left, Stands Alone and his brother rode side-by-side, while Isabel rode behind them next to Pedro. The rest of the war party followed them, bringing the Spanish mules and horses behind them, to be split up later as war bounty. They rode until late afternoon, stopping only to pick up the extra horses they had left behind, and Isabel wondered bleakly if her husband intended to ignore her the entire trip back to New Mexico. He hadn't even so much as glanced back at her.

Finally, Greyfoot called a halt and said to Stands Alone,

"We will leave you now, so you and Isabel may have some time alone. We will make camp over that rise."

Greyfoot and the rescue party rode off, leaving Stands Alone and Isabel sitting in a flurry of dust. Only Pedro looked back, shooting a look of pity at Isabel, a look that did nothing to quell her rapidly rising apprehension now that she was finally alone with Stands Alone.

Stands Alone dismounted. So did Isabel. They stood and looked at one another for a long moment. Then Isabel gathered her courage and said, "I did not betray you, and I did not help Diego plan your capture. I had no idea he was anywhere around until he suddenly appeared that day. The reason you couldn't find me in Taos was because I had gone to a healer for a fertility potion. I was afraid to tell the truth for fear you would think I had doubts about your ability to father a child, which wasn't so. I could never question your virility in any manner. I feared there was something wrong with me."

Isabel thought she saw just a hint of surprise in Stands Alone's eyes, but when he made no comment, she continued. "Diego told me if I cooperated with him and let you think I had betrayed you, he would spare your life. That's why I agreed to marry him. Then I found out he had lied to me, that he had sent you to a heinous mine down here, instead of to one of the turquoise mines, as I thought we had agreed."

Isabel waited for a response, but there was none. A mask seemed to have fallen over Stands Alone's face. She had absolutely no idea what was going on in his mind. "Ramon survived the attack last year," she told him when he maintained his nerve-racking silence. "That's how I found out the truth about my father's betrayal. I'm sorry I didn't believe you." She hesitated, feeling terribly vulnerable, terribly exposed, then blurted, "I love you. I've always loved you."

A smile spread across Stands Alone's face, the most beautiful smile Isabel had ever seen. "I love you, too," he responded softly, "and I am so very, very proud of you, my beautiful, brave warrior woman."

Isabel's heart beat like a tom-tom, so loud she feared Stands Alone could hear it. "Does that mean I'm forgiven? That you still want me?"

"There is nothing to forgive. As for wanting you, I have always wanted you, even when I was so angry with you. But this time I will not simply take. I will ask." He held out his hand. "Will you come with me and be my wife?"

Isabel knew exactly what was ahead of her. It would not be an easy life. But it would not be without pleasures, either. And no matter what trials she might encounter, she would always have the support of her Comanche family. But even if that hadn't been true, her decision would have been the same. She would rather live in hell with this remarkable man by her side, than in heaven with any other. She put her small hand in Stands Alone's large, capable one and answered, "I will be proud to be your wife."

He drew her nearer and said quietly, "I know you do not like me dictating to you, but you must not take that fertility potion. It could be dangerous. What is meant to be, will be."

Isabel wondered if she should tell him her wonderful news, then decided against it. This was their special time together. The other could wait. But she did know one thing. She had no intention of going years without making love after the birth of their child. What she and Stands Alone did in the privacy of their tepee was their business. She smiled, then answered, "Don't worry. I won't take the potion."

Stands Alone wondered at the smile. It had an almost

secretive quality about it. Then, dismissing its strangeness, he glanced at a nearby stream and said, "Now, I think I would like to bathe. The smell is so bad, I can't stand my own stench."

"I'll help you."

Isabel helped him bathe, then applied a poultice of creosote leaves to the festering wounds on his back and bound his raw wrists, taking immense pleasure in performing her wifely duties and basking in his warm look of love. Then they sat beneath a gnarled mesquite and watched the sun go down, his long, slender fingers entwined with hers. They felt no passion. They both knew they had a lifetime of making love ahead of them. What they felt was sublime happiness, their emotions having reached almost spiritual planes. By the simple act of joining hands, they were one, man and wife, for eternity, and each knew that nothing or no one could ever separate them again.

Author's Notes

When I began working on this book, the story was vague in my mind. All I knew for certain was that I wanted it to take place in New Mexico, a new locality for my writing. During the course of my research, I came upon the story of Tome, "the village of the broken promise" as the Indians called it. Here, in 1768, Don Ignacio Baca negotiated a treaty with the chief of a Comanche band and sealed the bargain with the betrothal of his young daughter to the chief's young son, an agreement the sly Spaniard had no intention of keeping from the very beginning. When the time for the marriage drew near, Don Ignacio sent his daughter to relatives in a nearby village, then showed an empty grave to the Comanches when they came to claim the bride. Learning of the deception, the Comanches took vengeance on the village, killing Don Ignacio, the village priest, and eighteen other men, and kidnapped the bride, who later became reconciled to her savage husband. Hidden in a history book, I had found the potential for a better romance than my original story, and what you have just read is my variation of the story of Tome, with considerable embellishments on my part.

Since history gave me the backbone of my story, I thought a few later historical events might be of interest to my readers. In 1763, Great Britain triumphed over the French at the end of the Seven Years' War. In an effort to keep their American holdings out of their hated enemy's hands, the French ceded the Louisiana Territory to Spain. This had a direct effect on the Comanches, since the French trade with the Wichitas was severed. Unable to attain French guns, and being badly decimated by the Osages who had access to English guns, the Comanches in New Mexico found it prudent to make peace with the Spanish government. Despite the bands' being characteristically independent of one another, the western Comanches united under the leadership of a much respected chief named Leather Jacket. The Spanish government was also ready for peace. They needed the Comanches to fight the Apaches, who had become particularly bothersome. So the Treaty of 1786 came into being, a treaty that granted general amnesty to all western Comanche bands, a treaty that was unprecedented as agreements between the Indians and white men went, for it lasted fifty years.

The Comanches, however, did not believe the treaty made with the Spanish in New Mexico included the Spanish in Texas and Mexico. These places, they continued to raid with impunity, taking their plunder back to New Mexico to trade with the New Mexican traders, who became known as the *Comancheros*. The New Mexican practice in dealing with stolen goods persisted during the Mexican era, and even long after New Mexico had become a possession of the United States. The "turning a blind eye" custom particularly thrived after the Civil War, when both Indian and anglo rustlers brought stolen Texas cattle to sell, dirt cheap, to New Mexican traders and ranchers.

But the New Mexicans weren't the only ones reluctant to give up old customs. Long after the Comanches had been placed on reservations in the Indian Territory, they still slipped away to raid Texas. When one army officer, weary of chasing down the renegades and bringing them back, complained to a chief about this unacceptable practice, the chief suggested if the government did not want the Comanches to raid Texas, they should move it far away where the young warriors could not find it.

Old habits die hard.

SAVAGE ROMANCE
FROM CASSIE EDWARDS!

#1: SAVAGE OBSESSION   (0-8217-5554-4, $5.99)

#2: SAVAGE INNOCENCE   (0-8217-5578-1, $5.99)

#3: SAVAGE TORMENT   (0-8217-5581-1, $5.99)

#4: SAVAGE HEART   (0-8217-5635-4, $5.99)

#5: SAVAGE PARADISE   (0-8217-5637-0, $5.99)

FROM ROSANNE BITTNER:
ZEBRA SAVAGE DESTINY ROMANCE!